The Night Visitor

By

Patrick Redmond

MANATEE BOOKS

Manatee Books

First published in 2018.

This book is primarily a work of fiction. Other names, characters, businesses, organisations, places and events are the product of the authors imagination or are used fictitiously. Any resemblance to actual persons, living or dead, events or locales is entirely coincidental.

Published by Manatee Books

Paperback ISBN: 978-1-912347-24-7
Kindle ISBN: 978-1-912347-25-4

Cover design by Aimee Coveney of Bookollective
Images used under licence from Shutterstock.com

To David Webb

(1930 – 2018)

With love always

Prologue: Suffolk, August 1991

Meg was tired. She had spent all afternoon in Ipswich with her mother, shopping for a uniform and all the countless other things she would need for her first day at school. Now they were back in Wickenham with rumbling stomachs and a car boot full of bags, and as a reward for being a good girl her mother had brought her to Pritchard's Café for a cake and a bottle of coca cola with a straw.

Her favourite table was empty. It was by the window. As her mother waited at the counter she sat down and stared out at the village green. It was full of people walking dogs, passing the time of day or just sitting on benches, enjoying the glorious weather. She recognised her neighbour; Mr Clark, throwing a ball for his terrier, Skipper, and wished for the umpteenth time that she had a dog of her own. She had asked her parents, but her father had said that dogs were a bloody nuisance who did nothing but eat, bark and make a mess, though her mother, who also loved dogs, had promised to try and make him change his mind.

Wickenham Primary School was on the other side of the green. It was a small, red brick building with a yard at the front. It was quiet now but soon, when the new term started, it would be full of children and Meg would be one of them. The prospect excited her. Though she loved playing with her sister, Grace was only two and it would be fun to have friends her own age. She wondered what their names would be. Grace didn't want her to go to school but she had explained to her sister that she was only going so she could learn new games for them to play together and that Grace would always be her best friend.

Her mother was still at the counter. As she looked about her she began to feel a tingling sensation. It started in her fingers then passed through her whole body, making it tremble. Her senses began to heighten; the sounds around her growing louder, the smells more intense and the colours brighter. Energy surged through her as if an electric current was powering her from within.

A boy stood beside the next table. He was a little older than her and had unruly red hair that covered his head like a bird's nest.

Her mother had told her that some people considered red hair a sign of good luck, but it didn't seem to be lucky for the boy. He looked terribly sad. Meg felt sorry for him and wished that she could be his friend.

The boy sensed her gaze, turned towards her and gave her a smile so big it threatened to split his face in two. The sight made Meg giggle. The boy stuck out his tongue. Still giggling she did the same. By now he was giggling too. He came to stand beside her. 'What's your name?' he asked.

'It's Meg,' she told him. 'What's yours?'

As Edith Harris sipped her tea and listened to her daughter, Alice, complain that her sons could not be in the same room for more than a minute without fighting she pondered her future. Alice had moved with her family to Ipswich two years ago and though Edith visited regularly it wasn't the same as having them live close by as they once had. Now that Edith was a widow there was little to keep her in Reading, and Suffolk seemed a nice county. Perhaps she would move here. Alice had already suggested as much. The two of them had always been close and enjoyed the time they spent together.

As she lifted her cup she felt someone tug at her sleeve. A pretty dark-haired girl of about five stood by the table staring solemnly at her with deep blue eyes. The sight made her anxious. Was the child lost?

'Are you alright, dear?' she asked. 'Can't you find your mother?'

'Don't be sad,' said the girl.

'I'm not sad.'

'Yes, you are.'

She smiled. 'Why do you think that?'

'That's what Edward says.'

'And who is Edward?'

'He's my friend and he's your friend too.'

'That's nice, dear. Why is he my friend?'

'Because he's your brother.'

For a moment Edith's heart stopped. From somewhere that sounded very far away she heard Alice gasp.

'People call him Teddy,' the girl continued. 'And they call you Edie. But you don't like those names. You think they're silly.'

Edith's hand started to shake; the cup she was holding suddenly feeling like a lead weight.

'You have better names,' the girl told her, then stopped; half turning her head as if listening, before nodding and smiling. 'His name is Doug and yours is Pearl. Those are your secret names. You use them when you play in the wood.'

Edith dropped the cup. Steaming hot liquid spread across the surface of the table and down onto her skin. The heat was intense, but it didn't matter. Suddenly nothing mattered but the child who stood beside her.

She opened her mouth, trying to speak but at first no sound would come.

'I like those names,' the girl said. 'I think they're nice.'

'You can see him?' It came out as a whisper.

'Yes.'

'Stop this!' Alice exclaimed. 'Stop this right now! Mum, don't listen to her.'

Edith ignored her. 'Why is he here?'

'You're always sad when you think about him. It makes him sad too.'

Alice rose to her feet. 'That's enough!' she shouted at the girl. 'What are you? Some sort of con artist?'

The girl shook her head, now looking upset. A woman appeared behind her; aged about thirty with the same pretty dark looks. 'Don't shout at my daughter!' she said fiercely. 'She's only a baby.'

'She's a trickster and so are you! What are you after? Money? How could you upset an old lady like this? Shame on you!'

By now everyone in the café was looking. People began to call out; some for Alice to leave the girl alone; others for the girl to leave Edith alone. The girl was in tears, looking utterly bewildered. Her mother put her arms around her, preparing to pull her away.

But Edith couldn't allow it. Not yet.

Not until she knew.

Reaching out she grabbed the girl's arm.

'Tell me!' she cried. 'Please tell me. Does he still…does he still…'

The girl wiped her eyes. While her mother argued with Alice she again turned her head as if listening to someone. Then, through her tears she managed a smile.

'He doesn't blame you. He never did. It wasn't your fault. It was just a game. He wanted to climb to the top. He would have done it anyway. He was having fun. He was always happy when he was with you. You were his best friend. He loved you best in the whole world. That's what he wants you to know. That he still loves you best and he always will.'

A furious Alice was still shouting but Edith didn't listen. Once again, her daughter and everything else seemed far away. In her head she was a child; back in the wood that lay behind her house in Shropshire, playing with her twin brother Edward.

The wood had been their domain. They had known every inch of it; every path, every tree and every stream. A host of smells came rushing back to fill her nostrils; the earth damp after rain; the rich scent of oak and the delicate fragrance of wild flowers. For hour after glorious hour she and Edward had played there; making dens, climbing trees and carving their special mark into the branches; two Es facing each other to form the number 8. It had been their secret world and they had had secret identities too; special names they had never told another living soul. He had been Doug after Douglas Fairbanks and she had been Pearl after Pearl White. Their parents had thought the movies frivolous, but they had both loved them and when alone would pretend to be their idols; acting out all their stunts and adventures, the two of them always laughing; just happy to be together with no one to disapprove and tell them no.

Until that dreadful day when everything changed.

They had been nine years old and sitting together three quarters of the way up the tallest tree in the wood. It was as high as they had ever dared go. But this time she had dared him to go higher. She had sat and watched as he pulled himself upwards through the slender branches towards the summit, cheering and telling him that even Douglas Fairbanks himself couldn't have climbed as fast.

And then she had heard a branch crack.

For a moment he had seemed to hang in the air. Their eyes had locked and his had been wide and fearful and full of what looked like reproach. And then he was gone; lying far below her, motionless on the ground.

She had remained where she was, clinging to the tree trunk, too afraid to move; just screaming his name over and over again. She had still been there that evening when people came looking for her; a terrified child, frozen to the spot, staring down at the body of her dead twin.

Her parents had told her it wasn't her fault. That it was an accident. Eventually she had said that she believed them, but she had lied. In her heart she knew she was to blame and that in the moment of his death he had known it too. And when at last the guilt was too much to bear she had locked all her memories of him in a cave down in the deepest corner of her mind. As the years passed she had thought the key lost and had been glad of it. Images that had once been beautiful would now be decayed and rotten and all they could ever cause was more pain.

But she remembered them now. They danced before her eyes like pictures made of sunshine and light. Time had not dulled them. They were still as vivid as if they had happened yesterday; just as bright and just as clear.

And just as beautiful.

She couldn't help it. She burst into tears.

Alice was now sitting beside her, trying to give comfort, while a waitress was wiping the spilled tea from the table. As Edith moved her hand she saw that heat and sweat had left a palm print. As it faded she saw a mark at its centre.

Only it wasn't a mark. It was a symbol.

Two Es, facing each other to form the letter 8.

While something brushed her left cheek; as soft and as tender as a child's kiss.

'Ignore them, Mum,' Alice was saying. 'They're just crooks.'

She shook her head. 'No…'

'Yes! They feed on others grief. You know that. You do, don't you? Tell me that you do?'

She turned. Her daughter was staring at her with wide, anxious eyes. She longed to tell Alice the truth but knew she would not be believed. No one would believe her. They would all think it was a trick too.

But she believed. She believed with all her heart.

And that was all that mattered.

'Yes,' she said softly. 'I know.'

Alice hugged her. As she hugged back she looked over her daughter's shoulder. The other mother and daughter were now leaving the café. The little girl was still in tears, but the mother was looking at her.

Wiping her eyes, Edith mouthed the word 'Thank you.'

The mother nodded; her lips turning upwards in the faintest of smiles.

And then they were gone.

Part 1

THE NIGHT VISITOR

Suffolk: July 1992

Chapter 1

The summer holidays were less than a week away. In the most junior class of Wickenham Primary School, children who were supposed to be colouring maps of Europe instead whispered to each other; sharing their plans for the long weeks of leisure that lay ahead. In the collective excitement old animosities and feuds were forgotten as all of them miraculously became the best of friends.

All except one.

'Murderer!' hissed a voice.

Meg did not react. In her desk near the front of the class she remained perfectly still, staring down at her map, trying to decide what colour Portugal should be.

'You killed him,' hissed the same voice. 'We know you did.'

'And we all hate you,' hissed another.

Meg swallowed. Glancing up she watched her teacher, Mrs Fisher, marking homework. Clearly Mrs Fisher hadn't heard what was being said. Or had she? Sometimes she wondered if Mrs Fisher simply pretended not to hear. Sometimes she wondered if Mrs Fisher thought she was a murderer too.

School had never been easy for her. By the time she had arrived for her first day the whole village had heard about what had happened at Pritchard's Café. Some believed that she had indeed seen the dead boy, but most considered her a wicked liar. They had passed their beliefs onto their children and from the start she had been viewed as someone who was strange and different and existed simply to be mocked or shunned. Yes, it had never been easy, but it had never been as bad as this.

It was because her classmates had loved Baskerville. Mr Thomas was the school janitor and Baskerville had been a Cairn terrier who followed his master everywhere except during playtime when he would run around, barking, licking faces and trying to join in every game going. Mr Thomas said that the only thing Baskerville loved more than playing with the children was chasing people on bicycles.

That was why, when he was doing maintenance work in the playground, Baskerville was kept tied to the school gates to stop him charging off after passing cyclists.

One lunchtime two weeks ago, while watching Baskerville push a football around with his nose, Meg had felt an ache at the back of her head. Momentarily she had felt dizzy, her vision had blurred and suddenly, somewhere far behind her eyes, she had seen Baskerville lying on the road outside the school. The image was so real that had she reached out her hand she could have touched his broken body. When her vision cleared she had burst into tears and Mr Thomas, who had always been kind to her, had come to find out what was wrong. She had told Mr Thomas that something bad was going to happen to Baskerville if his lead wasn't tied securely. But Mr Thomas had just smiled, patted her on the head and told her that Baskerville was a little imp who was more than capable of looking after himself and by the time the final school bell rang Baskerville had been killed by a car and now everyone said that she had made it happen.

'You're horrible,' one girl shouted at her. 'You like making people cry. You made Mr Thomas cry just like you made Peter cry and you made that woman in the café cry too. You're wicked and you're a thief. The only reason you knew where to find Mrs Fisher's purse was because you stole it and thought you were going to get caught. You killed Baskerville and we all wish you were dead instead.'

The name calling continued. She tried to look like she was enjoying her colouring but inside she just wanted to lay her head on the desk and sob. It wasn't fair. She had loved Baskerville too. She would never have hurt him. She was only trying to protect him. She had tried to tell the other children that, but they had refused to listen.

Mrs Fisher put down her pen. 'That's enough noise, children.'

Instantly the room fell silent. Meg gave Mrs Fisher a grateful smile. Mrs Fisher gave her one back only it wasn't real. It was like the smiles the waitresses gave her when her mother took her into Pritchard's Café; big, broad gestures that somehow fell short of the eyes. She had told her mother about the false smiles, but her mother had said that the people in the café were just silly and that she wasn't to take any notice of them.

And she tried. She really did.

But it wasn't that easy.

Five minutes passed. The giggling and whispering started up again. This time Mrs Fisher ignored it. Staring down at her partially coloured map, Meg tried to do the same.

At the end of the day she stood in the school yard, staring at the sea of waiting faces, searching for those of her mother and Grace. As a group of boys pushed past her someone punched her arm. Peter Price was in the group. Peter's grandmother had died a month ago. Peter and his family had always eaten their Sunday roast dinner at his grandmother's house and Peter was always telling everyone that his grandmother's food tasted like poo and that she smelled and that kissing her was like kissing poo. One day he had told his grandmother the same thing and she had cried and told him he was wicked. As punishment his parents had not let him watch television for a week and by the time the week was over his grandmother had died in her sleep.

Two days after the funeral Meg had been standing in the playground, watching Peter and his friends play chase and wishing, as she always did, that they would ask her to join in. The sun was bright and as she squinted into the light she felt the familiar tingling sensation start in her fingers and saw that she was not the only one observing the game. Peter's grandmother stood nearby wearing the same floral dress she had always worn on the days when she had come to collect Peter from school. She had waved to Meg who had turned, walked to the furthest corner of the playground and shut her eyes as tightly as she could. But when she opened them again Peter's grandmother was standing beside her, asking her to tell Peter that she didn't think he was wicked, that she loved him very much and that she knew that he had not meant the horrible things he had said to her.

'If I do,' Meg had whispered, 'will you leave me alone?'

'Yes. Just tell him. Please.'

So, she had told Peter, only for him to become upset and for the other children to say that she was mean for making him cry. In the days that followed Peter had hit her every chance he got and when finally, she had had enough and punched him in the face Mrs Fisher had labelled her a bully and made her spend the next three playtimes in the classroom, doing sums. On the final day Mrs Fisher, who had been sitting with her, had been called away. Meg had stared down at her piece of paper, chewing her pencil and on looking up again had seen Peter's grandmother sitting in Mrs Fisher's chair.

'Why are you here?' she had demanded. 'I did what you asked. Why won't you leave me alone?'

'I wanted to thank you, and to say that I'm sorry. I know Peter is being unkind to you.'

'He thinks I'm a liar.'

'He's still upset. He doesn't want to remember what he said. But he does. He always will. And one day when he's older he'll realise that you were telling the truth and when that day comes he'll be more grateful than you can possibly imagine.'

'I don't want him to be grateful,' she had shouted. 'I just want you to go away and leave me alone!'

She had heard laughter. A group of girls from her class were staring at her through the window. One of them had shouted 'Freak!' and then, still laughing, they had all run away. As she watched them go, Meg remembered how much she had looked forward to starting school but now every morning she woke up wishing she didn't have to go at all. Still angry she had turned back to Peter's grandmother but saw nothing except an empty chair.

Her arm was stinging. As she rubbed it she saw her mother waving to her. Grace was waving too. Not wanting them to see she was upset she put on her best smile and waved back.

That evening as she lay in the bedroom she shared with Grace she heard her parents arguing downstairs. After checking that her sister was asleep she went to listen on the stairs.

'It's your fault,' her father was saying. 'You're the one encouraging her to tell these bloody stories!'

'They're not stories,' her mother insisted.

'Of course, they are. What else can they be?'

'You know what.'

'It's all in her head, and what's worse is that you put it there. All that nonsense about your mother.'

'Don't talk about my mother! You never knew her.'

'Thank God! One nut case in the family is more than enough!'

Meg heard her mother gasp. 'Ken, that's a terrible thing to say!'

'I know. I know. I didn't mean it. I just...' Her father exhaled. 'I just don't want people to treat her like she's different.'

'She's not different. She's special.'

'Is she, Becky? Or do you just want her to be?'

'No. All I want is for her to be proud of who she is. She has a gift, Ken, and that gift *is* special. Think of what she's done. Remember the woman in the café...'

Her father snorted. 'Not this again.'

'How could she have known what she did?'

'She probably heard the woman talking about her brother and let her imagination run riot. It's what kids do.'

'Not Meg. She *knew* things, Ken; things she couldn't possibly have known and yet she did. The old lady said as much.'

'The old lady said she was a liar.'

'Only because it was easier than having to deal with a world full of people as cynical as you. You didn't see the look she gave me when we left. She wanted me to thank Meg. You didn't see it, just like you don't see anything.'

'Oh, but I do. Shall I tell you what I see? I see a daughter who some people think is a liar and some people think is sinister and everyone thinks is odd. And that's down to you, Becky. This whole bloody mess is down to you...'

Later her mother came to check on her and Grace.

She sat up in bed. 'Mum.'

'Why are you still awake? It's late.'

'I heard you and Dad arguing.'

'You didn't hear anything, darling. It was just a dream.'

'No, it wasn't. Dad was angry. He was shouting and then he went out. I heard the door slam.'

Her mother sat down on the bed. 'It was just a silly row.'

'Dad hates me.'

'No, he doesn't.'

'Yes, he does. Like at school. They all hate me there. When Grace goes to school she's going to hate me too.'

'No, she won't. Grace adores you. She told me today that you're the best big sister in the whole world.' Her mother stroked her hair. 'You're not going to sleep, are you? Why not come downstairs and I'll make you a nice drink.'

Ten minutes later she sat on her mother's lap sipping hot chocolate. The chair was next to the fireplace where every day in winter a fire burned. Meg wished it was winter now. She loved watching the flames dance in the air.

'I don't want to be different,' she said.

'You're not different, Meg. You're special.'

'I don't want to be special either.'

'Neither did your grandmother. Not when she was your age. It was only when she was older that she was glad.'

'Why was she glad?'

Her mother smiled at her. 'You know why.'

'Tell me again.'

'When your grandmother was a young woman she was working as a secretary in London. One day she was having lunch in a restaurant with a friend. On the next table were a married couple and their son. He was only a little boy; no older than you. They looked like such a happy family. They were laughing and joking all the time. It made your grandmother happy to watch them and as she did so, she felt the same ache in her head that you sometimes get and when she shut her eyes she saw the mother and little boy still wearing the same clothes lying dead on the street.

'By the time she could see properly again the family were leaving the restaurant. Your grandmother rushed after them. The father was saying goodbye to the mother and little boy who were about to climb into a taxi. Your grandmother told them not to get in; that if they did something terrible was going to happen. They told her she was mad but in the delay the taxi driver grew impatient and drove away. As he reached the corner of the road a lorry raced out of a side street and drove straight into the side of the taxi. The driver wasn't hurt except for some cuts and bruises. But the back of the taxi was destroyed. If they'd been in it the mother and boy would have been killed.

'But they weren't. Your grandmother saved them. The little boy's name was Robert and when he grew up he became a doctor and the last thing your grandmother heard he was working in Africa, saving lives himself. In his last letter to your grandmother he told her that it was because of her that he was doing it. That she had shown him just how precious life was and that he wanted to do everything he could to help preserve it. Your grandmother told me that when she read that letter she wished she could go back in time and talk to the child she had been and tell her that even though she hated her gift it was in fact the most wonderful present she could ever have been given and that one day she would thank God for it with all her heart.'

Meg rested her head against her mother's shoulder. 'I haven't saved anyone.'

'Yes, you have. You saved that old lady in the café from years of pain. And you saved that boy in your class too. The one called Peter. His grandmother was right, Meg. One day he will be grateful. One day he'll thank you with all his heart.'

'I didn't save Baskerville.'

'But you tried. You did everything you could.' Her mother took her chin in her hand and gazed into her eyes. 'And Meg, that is all you *can* do. A lot of people won't want to listen. You just have to make them. And as you get older it *will* get easier.'

The two of them stared at each other. Her mother smiled. Meg tried to smile back but couldn't. There was a secret she needed to share; one that had been eating away at her for days.

'Dad goes to London, doesn't he?'

'Yes. He goes there sometimes for work.'

'I saw him going there.'

'When? Were you…' Her mother paused, looking thoughtful. 'Do you mean that you saw him in your head?'

'Yes.'

'What did you see?'

'I saw Dad with a suitcase. He was going to London and he wasn't coming back.'

She saw her mother swallow.

'I'm sorry, Mum. He's going to leave us and it's my fault.'

Her mother covered her mouth with her hand. 'Meg, listen to me. Your father is not going to leave us. He loves us.'

'But…'

'But even if he did leave it wouldn't be because of you. I promise you that.'

'Cross your heart and hope to die?'

'Cross my heart and hope to die. Now will you promise *me* something?'

'What?'

'Promise me you will never feel ashamed of who you are. You are a wonderful person, Meg Parker, and I am proud that you are my daughter. If ever people try and make you feel ashamed I want you to remember what your grandmother did and I want you to remember what *you* did in the café and what you tried to do for Baskerville and all the glorious things you are *going* to do. Because they *will* be glorious, Meg; more so than you can possibly imagine. And one day, when you're older you'll remember this conversation and wish that you could talk to your younger self and tell her that, just like your grandmother wished she could have done. Will you promise?'

She didn't answer. Her mother was staring anxiously at her. As Meg stared back into the face she loved best in the world she raised a silent prayer to the God she still believed in, even when most of her classmates told her that when she died she was going straight to Hell.

Please God, don't ever let me ever see anything bad about my Mum.

'Will you?'

'Yes. I promise.'

'I love you, Meggie.'

'I love you, Mum.'

They hugged each other. Meg snuggled against her mother's chest, slowly allowing her eyes to shut. And when, an hour later her father returned home from the pub he found the two of them sleeping peacefully together in the chair.

The following day Mrs Fisher read the class a story. As Meg looked about her she saw Peter's grandmother standing outside the window. This time she didn't feel angry or upset. Instead she felt pleased.

'I'm glad I told him,' she said loudly. 'And one day he will be glad too.'

Mrs Fisher put down the book and frowned. 'Be quiet, Meg Parker.'

'Freak!' hissed one of the boys in the back row. The others began to snigger.

Meg turned around and looked them straight in the eye. 'I don't care what you think,' she told them. 'You can think what you want.'

'That's enough!' snapped Mrs Fisher.

Meg turned back to her teacher. 'And so can you, Mrs Fisher.'

'That's enough! If you make another sound, you'll go and stand in the corridor and miss the rest of the story.'

'I don't care about that either. I know the story already. My Mum read it to me and she read it much better than you.'

'Get out!'

Meg rose to her feet, blew a loud raspberry at the boys in the back row then headed towards the door. As she did so she saw Peter's grandmother smile at her and mouth the word goodbye. Smiling back, she did the same.

Then, with her head held high she went to stand in the corridor.

Chapter 2

October 1995. Three years later.

It was breakfast time. As her mother buttered toast and Grace recited her three times table, Meg heard the post arrive. Leaving the kitchen table, she went into the hall, picked up the letters that lay on the doormat and checked the postmarks. None were from London. Not that she was surprised. But old habits die hard.

It had been three years since her father had left. One day during the summer holidays her mother had taken Grace and herself to Southwold for an afternoon on the beach. Her father had waved them off in the morning and by the time they had returned he was gone, leaving nothing but a note that said that it was better this way. Both Meg and Grace had cried themselves to sleep for nights afterwards but by the end of the school holidays Grace had all but forgotten him and returned to her usual cheerful self. Meg had tried to do likewise but it was hard when in her heart she knew his leaving was her fault. Her mother had told her again and again that it wasn't; that sometimes mummies and daddies just stopped loving each other but they never ever stopped loving their children. Meg wanted to believe it, but that was hard too when after a year the trickle of letters and cards from London had dried up completely.

But she could forgive him that. She could forgive him anything except hurting her mother.

She could still remember the night when she had woken to hear her mother sobbing in the living room. She had risen from her bed and gone downstairs where her mother had wiped her eyes and tried unsuccessfully to look happy. 'You should be in bed. You've got school tomorrow.'

'I'm sorry, Mum.'

'Why?'

'Because it's my fault you're crying.'

'I've told you, darling. It wasn't your fault. Daddy and I just stopped loving each other. That's all.'

'No, it isn't. You still love Dad. That's why you're crying. You want him to come home.'

Her mother shook her head.

'Yes, you do. If I wasn't here he'd come back.' She stopped, struggling for words. 'If I…'

'Your dad will never come back. He loves another lady now. He loved her even before he left. He's going to marry her. He wrote today to tell me. So, you see it really was nothing to do with you.'

Again, her mother tried to look happy. Again, she failed. Meg went and hugged her, squeezing as tight as she could and feeling suddenly much older than her years. 'Don't cry, Mum. I'll look after you. You *and* Grace. Always. We don't need Dad. If he loves another lady better than you then he's stupid and I hate him.'

'You mustn't say that, Meg. He's your dad and he always will be, and you mustn't hate him…'

A photograph of her father still stood on the hall table. She stared at it, wondering what he looked like now. Not that she cared. And not that he cared what she looked like either. They didn't even know where he lived anymore; he and his new wife who she hoped was a horrid old witch who burned his breakfast and spent every evening watching the TV soap operas he detested.

Because she did hate him. She did, and she always would.

She re-entered the kitchen, handing the post to her mother who glanced at the envelopes and grimaced. 'More bills. What a lovely way to start the day. Look at the time. You two should be finished by now. Go and brush your teeth and then I'll walk you to school.'

'You don't need to walk us,' Meg told her. 'I'm a big girl now.'

Her mother looked amused. 'You're nine.'

'Exactly. Don't worry about us, Mum. I'll make sure we get there on time.'

Ten minutes later she and Grace started up the lane towards the road that led to the village green. Their next-door neighbour Mr Clark was in his garden, tending to his flowerbeds. His terrier, Skipper, ran towards the gate, barking excitedly and trying to jump over it.

'He wants you to play with him,' Mr Clark called out.

'We'll play with him when we come home,' Meg called back

while holding her sister's hand and trying to hurry her along. Grace kept reciting her three times table. 'We've got a test,' she told Meg. 'Mrs Abbott gets cross if we do badly.'

'You don't want to take any notice of Mrs Abbott. She's a right cow. Next year you'll be in Mrs Roper's class and she's lovely.'

'Will you test me now?'

'What's four times three?'

'Twelve.'

'What's eight times three?'

'It's...um...' Grace began to look upset. 'I don't know.'

'Yes, you do. Remember, if you don't know the answer then count threes on your fingers like I showed you.'

Grace did, mouthing the numbers and then smiling. 'It's twenty-four.'

'Well done! You'll do great and if Mrs Abbott gets cross with you then I'll get cross with her and I can get much crosser than she can.'

Grace laughed. She was wearing the pretty red brooch that their mother had given her for her sixth birthday two weeks earlier. Meg frowned. 'I thought you weren't going to wear that to school.'

'But I like it. Are you going to tell Mum?'

'No but be careful not to lose it.'

'I won't. I love it. It's my favourite thing in the whole world.'

'I thought your teddy bear was.'

'No. Teddies are for babies. I'm a big girl now like you.'

Meg gave her sister an affectionate look. 'Of course, you are.'

They reached the school gates. Grace gave Meg a hug. 'Thanks for testing me,' she said, then ran off to join some children from her class. Meg remained where she was. A group of boys were performing tricks on skateboards. Stuart Scott stood watching them. Stuart was in her class. He was a quiet, thoughtful boy who loved reading, history and going on long walks just like she did. The previous year the two of them had been friends. Stuart had come to play at her house a few times and once she had been invited to his. It was a lovely house; much grander than the small cottage she lived in. They had built a den in his back garden and his mother had brought them sandwiches and cakes. Both his parents had been very welcoming. It was only when she had come inside to use the bathroom and overheard them talking that she discovered the truth.

'I feel bad about this,' Stuart's mother was saying. 'She seems like a lovely girl, but you know what people say about her.'

'It's just gossip,' Stuart's father told her.

'But what if it's not? What if she really does see things? What if she sees the future? What if she actually makes these things happen? What if she sees something bad about Stuart? What if her seeing it makes it come true?'

'She likes Stuart and he likes her. You're always worrying about him being bullied for being too quiet. Well he won't if he's friends with her. She can stick up for herself and she'll stick up for him too.'

'I know that. I know. I just…I'm sorry. I like Meg and I want Stuart to have a friend. I'd just feel safer if it wasn't her.'

Forgetting about the bathroom she had gone back outside and told Stuart that her mother would be expecting her at home. And when, the next day at school, he had kept his distance she had not blamed him. It wasn't his fault. He was just doing what his parents had told him to do. He loved his parents just as she loved her mother. If her mother had made the same request she would have acted in the same way.

But she still liked him and would always stick up for him. When a gang of older boys had started picking on him she had given the leader a black eye and then chased the rest of them around the playground with a cricket bat, landing herself yet another week of detention. Not that she had cared. They were the bullies and she despised them for it, and when the week was over Stuart had thanked her and given her a kiss on the cheek and that had made it all worthwhile.

She walked towards her classroom. Peter Price and two of his friends were standing nearby. 'Watch out,' cried Peter. 'I see a witch.'

She stopped, folded her arms and stared levelly at them. 'I don't,' she retorted. 'All I see is an idiot and a pair of sheep.'

'Shut your mouth!' one of the friends shouted.

'Don't you mean baaaaa,' she shouted back.

The gang began to look embarrassed while from behind her she heard laughter. The boys on skateboards all looked amused while Stuart gave her a furtive thumbs up.

Grace was waving at her. After holding up a hand with fingers crossed she entered her classroom.

At the end of the day she stood by the school gates, waiting for Grace. Other children filed past. Stuart was one of them. He gave her a shy smile. 'You were funny this morning,' he said.

'Thanks.'

'I wish I was funny like you.'

'You are. You're the funniest person I know.'

Stuart's smile widened. 'Baaaaa!'

'Baaaaa!' she replied.

They both started to laugh. In the distance she saw Stuart's mother approaching. Stuart did too. 'I have to go,' he told her.

'I know. Bye, Stu.'

'Bye, Meg.'

He headed off towards his mother. Grace emerged from the main school building. Normally she came hurtling towards her big sister but today she walked slowly, looking upset. Meg was worried. 'What's the matter? Did Mrs Abbott shout at you?'

'No.'

'She'd better not have done! If she did…' Meg stopped, noticing something. 'Where's your brooch?'

Grace stared at the ground. 'I lost it.'

'Where did you lose it?'

'I don't know.'

'Well where did you have it last? Try and remember. We'll go and look for it. I'm sure I'll find it.'

'No, you won't.'

Grace was still staring at the ground. Suddenly Meg understood. 'Someone took it, didn't they?'

'No.'

'Yes, they did. Who was it?'

Grace swallowed. 'It was Jessie.'

Meg scanned the playground. Jessie Bishop was tall and powerful for her eight years and had picked on Grace more than once before. She was standing by the hopscotch squares with some friends. Their eyes locked. Jessie gave Meg a challenging smirk. By now Meg's blood was boiling. She clenched her fists, preparing for battle.

And then unclenched them again.

She had a better idea.

'Have you got your crayons?' she asked Grace.

'Yes. They're in my satchel.'

'Give me the red one.'

Grace handed it to her. 'What are you going to do?'

'I'm going to get your brooch back *and* make sure Jessie never picks on you again. Wait here. I won't be long.'

Then she began to make her way towards Jessie.

'I don't have it,' Jessie called out. 'She's a liar, just like you.'

Meg carried on walking.

'I don't have it and if she says I do then I'll smash her face in and then…'

Meg stopped quite suddenly; staring levelly at Jessie.

Then, slowly, raised her left hand and pointed at her.

'Hora sinistra hora. Magnificat Gloriana hora. Sinistra.'

Jessie's smirk faded. 'What are you doing?'

'Hora! Magnificat diabolo. Diabolo hora!'

'What are you doing?'

'You stole from my sister. I'm putting a curse on you.'

'No, you're not. You don't scare me.' Jessie swallowed. 'Stop it.'

Still staring directly at her and with her left hand still raised, Meg knelt down, pulled the red crayon from her pocket and began to draw symbols on the ground. They were nothing but a random collection of circles, triangles and stars, just as the chant was nothing but a random collection of exciting sounding words she had heard in church and on TV.

But Jessie didn't know that. And by now she looked terrified.

'Hora diabolo. Diabolo! Equinox solarium aqua marine. Diabolo!'

Bursting into tears, Jessie pulled the brooch from her own pocket and threw it at Meg. 'Here it is! Now leave me alone.' Then she ran off towards the school gates.

Feeling triumphant Meg returned to Grace and handed her the brooch. 'Told you I'd get it back. Come on. Let's go home.'

'Wait!'

She turned. Jessie's mother was striding towards her. 'What did you do to my daughter?'

'Nothing.'

'Yes, you did! I saw you. She's scared to death!'

'Good! Now she knows how my sister feels.'

'What did you do?'

'I didn't do anything. It was just a joke.'

Jessie's mother's eyes widened. 'You think this is *funny?*'

'Yes. I wish it did mean something. I wish I could put a curse on her because your daughter's a horrible bully and she deserves it.'

Jessie's mother raised her arm as if to strike her. Crying out, another mother grabbed her before the blow could land. 'Annie! No! She's just a child.'

'She's a monster! We've all heard the stories. We all know what she can do.' Jessie's mother pointed at Meg. 'You're a wicked girl, Meg Parker, and mark my words, one day you will be punished for it!'

By now Meg was also scared. But she was not going to let anyone see it. Jutting out her chin she stared Jessie's mother straight in the eye. 'I'm not wicked. If you think I am then you're as stupid as your daughter. You don't scare me any more than she does so take your threats and stick them up your bum!'

Then, seizing Grace by the hand she turned and marched away.

They walked in silence until they turned into their lane. Only then did she burst into tears.

She stood for a couple of minutes, fighting to bring her emotions under control. An anxious looking Grace tugged at her sleeve. 'Meg…'

'I'm sorry. I'll be OK in a bit.'

'Don't cry. Here, you can have this.' Grace handed her the brooch.

'Gracie…'

'No, you can have it. Just please don't cry.'

She wiped her eyes, feeling ashamed. She had never cried in front of her sister; not since their father left. Taking a deep breath, she made a silent vow that she would never do so again.

'I'm fine, Gracie. Don't tell Mum, like I won't tell her about the brooch.'

Grace stared solemnly at her. 'Meg?'

'What?'

'You're not bad, are you? You're not…wicked?'

'Of course, I'm not. I only did that to scare Jessie. And she did deserve it. You know she did.'

'Yes.' Grace sighed. 'But…well, sometimes people in my class say…'

'That I'm a witch? Well, I'm not. Mum doesn't think I am. Who are you going to believe? Mum or the people in your class?'

Slowly Grace's face broke into a smile. 'Mum.'

'Good.' She managed to smile too. 'Besides, even if I was a witch, who's the last person in the world I'd put a spell on?'

'Who?'

'You, silly! And if I ever did put a spell on you then it would only be a good one like making sure you got full marks on your test.'

'I did get full marks! I was the only one in the class who did!'

She clapped her hands. Grace did the same.

'You keep the brooch, Gracie. Come on. Let's go home. Mum will be making tea and when we've eaten it we'll ask Mr Clark if we can take Skipper onto the common and play Robinson Crusoe.'

'I want to be Robinson Crusoe!'

'No, I'm going to be him. You can be Man Friday.'

'But I was Man Friday last time.'

'No, you weren't.'

'Yes, I was.'

'Liar liar, pants on fire!'

'You're the one with pants on fire.'

'Which is better than Jessie. I bet she wet her pants. If ever she says anything mean to you then you just call her wet pants Jess and she'll probably wet them again!'

By now they were both laughing. In the distance they could hear Skipper barking. Quickly they ran down the lane to greet him.

That evening she sat by the fire with Grace; the two of them listening to the story their mother was reading. It was one she had written and illustrated herself. Meg had almost a dozen similar stories on her bedroom shelf and counted them amongst her most treasured possessions.

By the time it was finished, Grace had fallen asleep. Meg stared at the flames, watching them dance; so absorbed that at first she didn't realise her mother was talking to her.

'What happened today, Meg?'

'Nothing. Just school.'

'Something did. When you came home I could see you'd been crying. Did one of the other children say something? Did they upset you?'

'No. None of them can upset me anymore.'

'But someone did.'

'It doesn't matter.'

'Yes, it does. Please tell me.'

'You know that girl, Jessie. Her mother's one of the helpers at church.'

'What about her?'

She told her mother what happened, prompting a sigh and a shake of the head. 'Oh, Meg…'

'I don't care. She deserved it.'

'Even so…'

'She won't pick on Gracie again. Not if she knows what's good for her. She probably did wet her pants. Stupid baby!'

'You still shouldn't have done it.'

'Why not? Grace is my sister. I won't let anyone be mean to her. You should be thanking me, not getting cross.'

'I'm not cross...'

'Yes, you are.'

Again, her mother sighed. Her face was drawn and there were bags under her eyes. She spent her days cleaning houses for wealthy families in Ipswich and four evenings a week working as a waitress in a restaurant there. On the evenings she was away, Meg and Grace stayed with the Clarks next door. Meg had heard Mr Clark telling her mother that she worked too hard and that she should write to her ex-husband to ask for money, but her mother had replied that she didn't know where he lived anymore and even if she did she would rather work all the hours God sent than bother him for funds he didn't want to give.

Meg began to feel bad. 'Sorry, Mum.'

Her mother put an arm around her. 'No. I'm sorry. You were right to stick up for your sister. You just mustn't do it like that. I know it was only a joke, but it wasn't funny to Mrs Bishop. She takes church very seriously.'

'We do too. We go every Sunday.'

'I know, but...' Her mother stopped, looking thoughtful.

'What?' she prompted.

'Your gift is special, Meg, just like your grandmother's was. I believe in God and I believe that your gift comes from him. I believe it with all my heart. But not everyone feels that way. To people like Mrs Bishop, your gift has nothing to do with God. To them it's the opposite. To see the dead; to know the future the way you sometimes do...to them that's wrong. Only God can know the future. Only he should have that power. Not a little girl like you.'

The flames were dwindling now; the logs nearly burned to ashes. Picking up the poker Meg prodded them, trying to stir them back into life.

'Do I make the future?'

'Make it?'

'That's what Stuart's mother said. That time I went to his house. I heard her say to his father that she was scared. That maybe my seeing things *made* them come true.'

'But they do come true.'

'No, but...' She struggled for the right words. 'What if they wouldn't happen if I didn't see them? Like with Katie Bates's father.'

'Is that the window cleaner's daughter?'

'Yes. What about that? I saw her father falling off his ladder. I told her, and she just laughed and said that her dad had never had an accident in his whole life and then two days later he had a fall and broke his leg.'

'But you didn't make that happen. You tried to warn her, and him.'

'But I hated Katie. Of all the people that picked on me when I first started school she was the worst. I remember one day she was so mean that when I went to the toilet I cried and then I got angry and vowed that one day I'd make her cry. She did cry when her dad had his fall. She was scared he'd never walk again.'

'But he can walk. And he still cleans windows.'

'But what if my hating her made it happen?'

Her mother stared anxiously at her. 'Meg...'

'But what if I did? Like with Dad. Before he left you and he argued all the time. Sometimes, the next morning I could see you'd been crying. I used to get so angry with him for that. What if me being cross with him made him leave?'

'And what of Baskerville? What did he ever do to you? Nothing. You loved him, and you tried to save him and if Mr Thomas had listened to you then Baskerville would still be alive today playing games with all of you in the school yard. You don't *make* these things happen, Meg. You try to stop them happening. That's your gift, and it should make you feel proud, not ashamed.'

'Are you proud?'

'You know I am.'

They hugged each other. On the table in the corner of the room was a vase full of roses. Her mother adored roses and always tried to have some in the house. Meg loved the smell. It was her mother's smell; warm and safe and everything that was precious and good.

Her mother released her. 'Did you really tell Mrs Bishop to stick her threats up her bum?'

'Yes.'

Her mother's lip started to twitch. 'Meghan Parker!'

'Well, she deserved it too.'

'You're not scared of anyone, are you?'

'I *was* scared. Inside.'

'But you didn't let her see it; just like your grandmother didn't. I wish you could have known her. You two are so alike.'

'You miss her, don't you?'

'How could I when I have your sister and you?'

'Do you miss Dad?'

'No. Not anymore. We don't need him, do we? We're OK as we are?'

'Yes. And we always will be. I'll make sure of it.'

Again, they hugged each other. Grace lay curled up on the rug nearby. Reaching out her hand, Meg stroked her sister's hair; her anxiety gone; just happy to be with the two people she loved best.

The following morning she stood in the bathroom, watching Grace brush her teeth. 'Hurry up, slowcoach. I've still got to brush mine.'

'Mwah mwah mwah,' replied Grace; her mouth full of toothpaste.

She laughed, opening her mouth to make the same noises back.

And felt an ache in the back of her head.

It crept across her brain until it was right behind her eyes. She began to feel dizzy; her vision blurred and in the darkness she saw…

Herself.

She was walking with Grace; the two of them were holding hands and following a dark-haired man she didn't recognise up a path towards an ugly modern house. As he reached the door the man turned towards them and she saw that she did know him after all.

He was her father.

And in his hands he was holding two small suitcases.

As he opened his mouth to speak the image faded; her vision cleared, and she was back in the bathroom where Grace was still brushing her teeth. Turning on her heel she ran downstairs to the kitchen where her mother stood at the sink washing the breakfast dishes. 'That was quick,' her mother observed. 'Are you sure you brushed them properly?'

By way of answer she flung her arms around her mother and burst into tears.

'Meg, darling. What is it?'

'I saw Dad. I saw him in my head!'

Her mother crouched down, cupping Meg's face in hands that were covered in soap suds. 'What did you see, Meg? Is he alright? Is something going to happen…'?

'He's going to take us away!'

'Away?'

'Me and Grace. He had suitcases and we were with him. He's going to take us away from you, Mum. Don't let him take us away.'

'He won't. Meg, listen…'

'But I saw it!'

'What did you see? Tell me exactly.'

She did. Her mother wiped away her tears and smiled. 'Meg, that doesn't mean he's going to take you away.'

'Yes, it does!'

'Now listen to me. I have something I need to tell you. You know Mr Addison from the garage. Well last week Mr Addison went to London to look at a new car and while he was there he bumped into Dad.'

She swallowed. 'He saw Dad?'

'Yes. And he said that Dad wanted to know all about you and Grace. How you were? How you were doing at school? Mr Addison phoned me last night to tell me. And do you know what I think? I think Dad is going to ask you and Grace to go and visit him and his new wife and daughter.'

'Yes, but…' She stopped, focusing on what her mother had said. 'What daughter?'

'Your father has a new daughter. You and Gracie have a little sister.'

'Oh.'

'Isn't that exciting?'

'Um…'

'That's what you saw, Meg. That's all it was. It wasn't anything frightening or bad, honestly it wasn't.'

'But I don't want to see Dad. I hate him.'

'I told you before that you must never hate him.'

'I don't care. He made you cry. I hate him and I always will.'

Her mother looked angry. 'I won't have you talking like this. He's the only father you've got and whatever he's done to me he still loves you and your sister.'

'No, he doesn't. If he did then why doesn't he ever write, or come and see us?'

'Perhaps because his new wife doesn't want him to. Perhaps she's changed her mind now. Perhaps she wants the two of you to meet your new sister.'

'Well his new wife can piss off.'

'Meg!'

'I'm not going. You can't make me.'

There were footsteps on the stairs. 'That's enough,' her mother told her. 'I don't want you upsetting your sister. We'll talk about this later.'

'How? You're working this evening.'

'Then we'll talk about it when I'm back and Grace has gone to bed. OK?'

'There's nothing to talk about.'

'*OK?*'

'OK.'

'Good. Have you brushed your teeth?'

She nodded, refusing to feel guilty. Though she would never normally lie to her mother, today was not a normal day.

Grace appeared, beaming from ear to ear. 'I've got the cleanest teeth ever!'

Her mother smiled. Not wanting to worry her sister, Meg did the same.

As they left the cottage Meg saw mist rolling down the lane to greet them. It made her skin feel damp. She quickened her pace, forcing Grace to break into a trot.

'Meg, wait for me!'

'Sorry.' Slowing, she gave her sister her hand. For the next five minutes she said nothing, listening to Grace chatter away about the day ahead.

'Gracie,' she said eventually. 'Do you remember Dad?'

'No.'

'So, you don't miss him then?'

'No.'

'You did when he first went away. You cried and cried.'

Grace looked surprised. 'Did I?'

'Yes. We both did.'

'Oh.'

'So, you don't ever...want to...'

'What?'

She didn't answer; remembering the image of the two of them following their father into a strange house. When she saw things in her head they always came true. She had seen it, so it would come true.

But would it? If Mr Thompson had only listened, then Baskerville would still be alive. If Katie Bates had only told her father to be careful then he would not have broken his leg.

And as long as she kept working on her mother they would not have to visit their father. They didn't need him. They were just fine on their own.

'What?' Grace asked again.

'So...um...do you know what games you want to play at the Clarks tonight?'

As Grace began to list every board game known to man Meg led her through the mist to school.

That afternoon her class had a maths test. Their teacher, Mrs Morton, had written ten sums on the blackboard and given them twenty minutes to solve them. She also told them that they could not use calculators; prompting a chorus of groans to echo around the room.

With five minutes to go Meg had already finished. Others were not faring as well. Pens scratched on papers while hands scratched on heads. From the other side of the room Stuart gave her a beseeching look.

'Which one can't you do?' she mouthed at him.

'All of them.'

Using her fingers, she began to signal the answers. Before she had finished Mrs Morton rose to her feet and began to walk between the rows of desks. Knowing her teacher had eyes in the back of her head Meg turned away and tried her best to look innocent.

Her desk was by the window. Through it she could see the playground. The mist was heavy now; stopping only feet away. She found the sight eerie. It was as if the outside world had been swallowed whole, leaving her and her classmates as the only people left alive.

But she was wrong. They were not the only ones.

Someone was walking towards her.

And the tingling in her hands had begun.

At first, they were no more than an outline; as indistinct as a shadow. But as they grew closer and stepped out of the mist she saw that it was a boy of about her own age. She watched his approach, wondering who he was. There was something familiar about him.

He stopped a few feet away from the window. His hair was red; as thick and unruly as a bird's nest.

Just as it had been one fateful August afternoon in Pritchard's Café.

Shock made her gasp. She began to breathe heavily; the warm air from her lungs turning to condensation on the glass.

For a time they just stared at each other. His expression was sad. He looked as if he had been crying. Her alarm faded, replaced by concern. Why was he upset? And what did he want?

He opened his mouth to speak.

'Right! Time's up. Pens down. Meg Parker, why are you staring out of the window?'

She jumped. Mrs Morton was standing right beside her.

'Well?'

'Um…I've already finished.'

'And checked your answers?'

'Yes, Mrs Morton.'

'Then go and collect everyone else's.'

She hesitated, turning back towards the window.

'Now!'

Quickly she did as she was told. Peter Price made a face at her. Normally she would have made one back. This time she ignored him; eager to complete her task and return to her desk.

But when she did the playground was empty.

She sat down again. The glass was almost free of condensation now. Almost. There was only one tiny patch remaining.

And in it was written a single word.

Die.

She gasped; involuntarily blinking as she did so. But when her eyes opened again the word was gone.

Eight o'clock that evening. She sat at the table in Mr and Mrs Clark's kitchen, staring at a monopoly board.

'Rent,' said Mr Clark.

She continued to stare at the board.

'Rent, Meg. I've landed on Old Kent Road. I owe you rent.'

'Oh.'

'Well, don't look too pleased, will you? Mind you, it's only a couple of pounds so it's hardly going to break the bank. Thank God it wasn't Mayfair, eh?'

'I suppose.'

Mr Clark frowned. 'Are you alright? Usually you wipe the floor with me when we play this game and talk my ear off in the process. Would you rather play something else?'

She shook her head. Mr Clark was staring at her. He was a

small, stocky man with a face like that of a garden gnome. His wife, who looked like the female equivalent, sat at the other end of the table watching Grace draw a picture of horses while on the floor beneath their feet, Skipper chewed on the remnants of a bone.

'No. I'm enjoying the game. I'm just a bit tired. That's all.'

Mr Clark smiled. Meg felt relieved. The Clarks had always been like substitute grandparents. She had heard Mrs Clark tell her mother that an evening with Grace and herself was better than any tonic.

Only she wasn't being much of a tonic that night.

The doorbell rang. 'That'll be the milkman,' Mr Clark told her. 'I was supposed to pay him this morning but forgot.' Taking his wallet from his pocket he headed into the hall.

Grace held up her picture. 'Do you like it?'

'Yes. It's very good.'

'Isn't it,' agreed Mrs Clark. 'I'm sure your father will be impressed with how well you can draw.' Meg's mother had told the Clarks about Mr Addison's meeting with their father and Mrs Clark had talked about it over supper. Grace had become very excited at the prospect of having a little sister and Meg had secretly become very cross with Mrs Clark for not keeping her mouth shut.

Not that it mattered. They weren't going. She would make sure of it.

Grace began to prattle on about school. She pretended to listen but in her head she was far away; thinking as she had been for hours about her visitor that afternoon. At last she thought she knew what the word on the window meant. Edward's sister had died. The woman in the Café had been elderly and why else would he be upset? Yes, it all made perfect sense. It really did.

Except for one thing.

If his sister was dead, then the two of them would be together again.

And why would he be upset about that?

From the hallway she could hear voices. Mr Clark was talking to someone. It didn't sound like the milkman. She wondered who it was.

Staring at the board she tried to remember which pieces of property she now owned.

Footsteps echoed down the hall. Mr Clark reappeared in the kitchen. His face was white and his lip was trembling.

'The police are here,' he said.

Two o'clock in the morning. The mist that had blanketed the area all day was finally lifting; slinking away across the car park as if ashamed of what it had done.

Doctor Nigel Wilkes stubbed out his cigarette, took a deep breath and re-entered the hospital.

The waiting room was at the end of the corridor. As he approached it the door opened and an old man with a face like a garden gnome hurried towards him. Nigel's heart sank. Though he had performed this particular duty more times than he cared to remember it never got any easier.

'Is there any news?' the man asked; his face alive with hope.

'She didn't make it. I'm so sorry.'

The hope died. The man put a hand over his mouth.

'I really am sorry. We did all that we could.'

'I'm sure you did. Thank you.'

'You don't have to thank me. It's my job.' As soon as the words were spoken Nigel regretted them. They sounded so unfeeling. But one thing he had learned long ago was that to survive in his chosen profession he could never allow himself to care too much.

'She shouldn't have been driving,' the old man told him. 'Not in that mist. My wife and I tried to tell her, but she said that she needed the money. She said she'd be alright.'

'Is the little girl still here?'

'Yes.' The old man gestured towards the waiting room. 'She's sleeping now. I tried to tell her not to come but she wasn't having any of it. She's a strong-willed girl, is Meg. Just like her…' The man swallowed. 'Oh God…'

'Do you want me to…?'

'Tell her? No. It should be someone she knows.'

‘Well, if you’re sure.’

‘I am. Thank you, Doctor. I know you did your best.’

The man re-entered the waiting room. Nigel walked up the corridor; approaching the reception and the rows of people waiting for A&E. The air was full of the usual sounds: muttered complaints, drunken arguments and the occasional snore.

Until suddenly, cutting through them all like a knife, a child began to scream.

Chapter 3

St Alfred's Church in Wickenham had stood for eight hundred years. For century after century it had played host to all the key events in the lives of the villagers; the weddings, the christenings, and on this particular October afternoon, the funerals.

Meg sat in the front row holding Grace's hand. Mr and Mrs Clark sat on either side of them. Mrs Clark was holding Grace's other hand. Both were crying. Meg wanted to cry too but would not allow herself to do so. If she started she would never stop and now, more than ever, Grace needed her to be strong. The Clarks were kind, but they were not real family. Who else did Grace have now but her?

The Vicar was talking about their mother; discussing her fine qualities and bemoaning her tragic death. His words made Meg angry. The woman he was describing could have been any mother; any woman, any person. He had not known her the way her daughter had. He could never truly understand just how wonderful she had been or how catastrophic her loss really was.

At the front of the Church was a stained-glass window. A smiling Jesus gave food to the starving, while angels floated overhead singing praises to God. Once, years ago, Meg had prayed to that same God to never let her see anything bad about her mother. Now that prayer had been answered. Foreknowledge of her mother's death had been denied her. She should have been grateful but how could she when it felt like the cruellest trick in the world?

Because if I'd known I could have saved her.

God was love. That was what she had been taught. He was kind and compassionate and could save people from pain. But her pain was like a dagger, jabbing away at her heart until it was nothing but raw shreds of bleeding flesh. How could God have done this to her? Why, if he loved her, did he want her to suffer like this?

Is God angry with me? Is that why he's taken my mother?

Her gift came from God. That was what her mother had said. She wanted to believe it, but it was hard with all the dark thoughts that buzzed inside her brain like locusts and made her want to scream.

The Jesus in the window had a beard. Katie Bates's father had a beard too. She had hated Katie. She had hated her so much and then Katie's father had fallen from his ladder. She had hated her own father for hurting her mother and then her father had left. Had she made Katie's father fall? Had she driven her father away?

Was she wicked, just like Jessie's mother had said?

Is that why God is punishing me?

Her grandmother had been a good person who had used her gift to save people from suffering. But more often than not when Meg tried to save them no one listened, and they suffered anyway. Why did that happen? Had her mother been wrong? Was it possible that her gift didn't come from God at all? Was it from the Devil? Did it come from the Hell that she had been told so many times that she was destined for?

The thoughts buzzed ever louder; filling her head until there was only room for one terrible possibility.

Did I kill my own mother?

She didn't know. She couldn't bear to know. All she knew was that whatever her gift was she didn't want it. Not anymore. She would renounce it the way people renounced sin. No matter how hard it was she would do it. She *had* to do it. She didn't want to hurt people. She didn't want to be wicked. At that moment in time the only thing in the world that she wanted was a hug from the one person who would never be able to give her one again.

A lump came into her throat. Tears were moments away. Not wanting Grace to see her upset she turned her head, looking for distraction.

And found it.

A man had entered the Church. He was tall and thin and wearing a dark suit. As he made his way to a seat at the back she recognized her father.

He noticed her gaze and gave her a sad smile. Refusing to return the gesture she turned back to face the front.

Later, when the burial was over, he approached them. It was raining. They all stood sheltering under umbrellas. Crouching down he held out his arms to Grace and herself. 'I'm so sorry,' he said softly. 'More than you can ever know.'

Grace backed away, pressing her face into Meg's coat. 'Don't be frightened, Gracie,' Mrs Clark told her. 'This is your father.'

'Don't you remember me?' her father asked.

Grace shook her head.

'Are you surprised?' Meg asked him.

He lowered his eyes. 'No.'

'Why are you here?'

'For you and your sister.'

'We don't need you.'

'Yes, you do.'

'Mum didn't need you either. None of us did.'

She saw him flinch. Mr Clark gave her a reproachful look. 'Meg…'

'It's true.'

'You need him now,' said Mrs Clark gently. 'You need a home.'

'We have a home.'

'Yes, you do,' her father told her. 'Your home is with me. It's a nice home. You'll like it. You'll have a new mother and a new little sister too. I've got a picture of your sister. Her name is Susan. Would you like to see it?'

He held out a photograph. Slowly Grace reached out her hand and took it. As she stared at it her tear stained face broke into a smile. Grace had always loved babies; even when she was little more than one herself.

'You see,' her father said softly. 'It will be alright. I promise it will.' As he spoke he looked at Meg and again gave her a smile. She turned away, seeing nothing but her mother and feeling her heart die.

Three days later.

Their father lived on the outskirts of London in a town no different to dozens surrounding it, with a small shopping centre and rows and rows of semi-detached houses, all just different enough to be identical.

As their father led them up the drive towards a house just as ugly as the one she had seen in her head their stepmother came out to greet them. She was younger than their father; a tall, slim, blonde with perfectly styled hair and flawless make up.

'This is Alison,' their father told them. Alison smiled at them; a dazzling gesture that, like those of the women in Pritchard's Café, somehow fell short of her eyes. Bending down she offered them her cheek to kiss. Her skin tasted of powder and smelled of scent. Grace's attempt to hug her was politely rebuffed.

'Come inside,' she told them. 'Susan is waiting to meet you.'

Their half-sister was a chubby toddler with a sulky expression and a mass of her mother's blonde hair who sat on a carpet surrounded by enough toys to stock a small shop. Grace tried to hug her but was pushed away. 'Don't be scared, Susie,' she said cheerfully. 'I'm your sister.'

'Her name is Susan,' Alison said firmly. 'We don't call her Susie, and neither should you.'

Their father showed them their new bedroom. It had two single beds, a wardrobe, a cupboard and bare white walls. He helped them unpack. 'You must keep your toys in the cupboard,' he told them. 'Don't leave them lying around on the floor. Alison likes things to be tidy.'

Meg opened her suitcase, pulled out a photograph of her mother and put it on her bedside table.

'Perhaps that should go in the cupboard too?' their father suggested.

'No. I want to see it. We both do.'

'Well, I'm sure that'll be alright. Let's go downstairs. Alison is making tea.' He held out a hand. Grace took it eagerly. He held out the other to Meg. She stared into his face and thought, *you hurt my mother. You made her cry. Now you want to pretend that none of that happened, but it did and I am not going to forget.*

She walked out of the room, leaving him and Grace to follow. Tea was fish fingers and chips. It was Grace's favourite meal.

'Alison has made it especially for you,' their father told her.

Susan sat in a high chair, banging on her tray and screaming when she didn't have her mother's undivided attention. Not that she needed to do it often. Alison fussed over her like a little princess. Meg had no appetite and left her food untouched. 'You should eat it,' her father told her. 'Alison will be disappointed if you don't.'

'I'm not hungry,' she told him firmly. He looked saddened while a seemingly unconcerned Alison began to clear the plates away. Grace, suddenly tired and emotional, began to cry. Their father gave her a hug then began to pull faces to make her smile. Alison stopped in the kitchen door, watching them both; her expression inscrutable. Sensing Meg's gaze, she turned towards her, raising an eyebrow as if issuing a challenge. Meg stared back thinking, *you hurt my mother too. You stole my father away from her and I hate you for it just as much as I hate him.*

For a time their eyes remained locked. It was Alison who finally looked away.

That night, as she lay awake in a strange bed in an ugly house that would never be her home she smelled roses. Suddenly it was as if the room was full of them; the scent so powerful that it was as if her mother was right beside her. For one glorious moment she felt safe and loved. Then the feeling was gone, replaced by the terrible knowledge of what she had done.

I killed you. I didn't mean to, but I did.

And you hate me for it.

Hiding under the sheets she sought refuge in her own head; reciting the capital cities of Europe and then the twelve times table and anything else that required enough concentration to keep her mother and all her anger and reproach at bay. For a time, the smell was overpowering while the sheets seemed to sag as if touched by a hand.

Then it faded; leaving her alone to the dark, her tears and her guilt.

In the days that followed the battle lines were drawn. Her father continued trying to befriend her. She continued to keep him at a distance. Every night, when she went to bed, she would discover that

Alison had taken her mother's picture and stored it in the cupboard. Each time she would return it to its rightful place until one day she found it lying on the floor with its frame smashed.

'It was an accident,' Alison told her. 'It fell when I was dusting.'

She had nodded meekly then gone to the corner of the living room where Alison kept her collection of china figurines, picked up the most delicate and hurled it to the floor. 'It was an accident too,' she said when challenged. 'I was just looking at it. I didn't mean it to fall.' As punishment she was sent to bed early, but from that day on her mother's picture was never moved again. And after that her father gave up his attempts to win her friendship. Alison, who had never tried, spoke to her as little as possible. Not that she cared. After what they had done to her mother she would never want, let alone need, their good opinion.

But Grace did. Within a week she was calling their father 'Dad,' and would bounce around the house with excitement when he came home from work, wanting nothing more than to climb upon his knee and tell him all about her day. As Susan was so very much her mother's child, her father was pleased. He would hold her tight, tickle her chin and call her his angel. Sometimes Alison would stop and watch them; an exasperated expression on her face. 'Don't get her worked up, Ken,' she would tell him. 'She won't eat her supper if you do.'

'We're just playing,' he told her.

'Why not play with Susan? She hasn't seen you all day either.' Alison exhaled. 'I'm going to lay the table.'

Grace jumped off her father's knee. 'I'll help,' she cried, running after Alison, grabbing her around the waist and giving her a hug. It was the same way she had acted back in Suffolk when the table needed to be laid. The sight made Meg angry. For a moment she felt as if she hated her sister too.

That night, as they undressed for bed, Grace asked, 'Are you cross with me?'

'Yes.'

'Why?'

'Because you like them.'

Grace looked confused. 'But they're nice.'

'No, they're not. They hurt Mum. I hate them and so should you.'

'I don't want to hate them.'

'So, you think it's OK to hurt Mum? Then I hate you too.'

Grace swallowed, looking close to tears. Momentarily Meg felt ashamed. She knew she wasn't being fair. Grace was scared and lonely and just wanted affection. But as she looked into her sister's face it was her mother she saw staring back at her and with the realisation came a wave of pain so great that she couldn't stand it.

'Go to sleep,' she said. 'I don't want to talk to you anymore.'

That night as she lay in bed she heard Grace crying. She tuned it out, just as she was learning to tune out so much else; retreating into her own head and keeping the outside world at bay.

For the next few months she did little more than exist. She started at a new school that was big and loud and very different from her village school in Suffolk. The other children made fun of her accent. 'You mustn't do that,' their Headmistress told them. 'Poor Meg has just lost her mother. You must all be kind to her.' Her classmates all nodded obediently then continued with their teasing.

One day, while her class sat reading, she heard someone call her name. An old man stood by the window, staring in at her, just as Peter Price's grandmother had done back in Suffolk. She knew what he wanted. It was what they all wanted; to trick her and make her cause pain. But she wouldn't listen. She was not that person. Not anymore. She was not wicked. She was good.

Or at least she wanted to be.

The man kept calling her name. She tried to tune him out but couldn't and eventually could stand it no more.

'I won't listen!' she shouted at him. 'I hate you. I hate you all!' Her teacher jumped while around her the other children started to laugh. The man went away but by then the damage was done. In the days that followed the label 'freak' was attached to her, just as it had been in Suffolk. The taunts hurt. Sometimes she wanted to cry only she never could. There was no point when her mother would not be waiting to offer comfort when she went home.

Often, she would stand in the playground watching Grace play with the younger children. Back in Suffolk the two of them had often spent playtime together but now Grace, who had accepted and appeared to belong in this new world, didn't seem like her little sister anymore. It made her angry. It made her sad. But most of all it made her feel alone.

Back at home she would sit in her room, doing her homework, staring out of her window at the ugly houses that surrounded them and feeling as if she was suffocating. She wanted to be back in Suffolk; to see green fields and a big sky.

From downstairs came the sound of Alison laughing. Grace was downstairs too. The two of them now spent a lot of time together. They would play with Susan and then, when Susan had her nap the two of them would prepare supper together, whiling away the time until their father came home from work.

Once, as she sat reading the book they were studying in English class she thought she heard Grace scream. Startled, she strained her ears and heard Alison chuckle and call out the name 'butterfingers'. For a moment there was silence. Then, more softly, Grace laughed too.

Putting it from her mind she continued with her reading.

It was not for some time that she realised something was wrong. Grace started having nightmares. She would wake up screaming. Sometimes she wet the bed. Meg, shocked out of her own sleep, would watch as their father and Alison rushed in. Their father tried to ask Grace what had upset her, but Alison would always shoo him out of the room. 'I'll deal with this,' she would tell him. 'It's my job.' After changing the sheets, she would take Grace to the bathroom and help her change her nightdress. Meg would sit up in bed, waiting for the two of them to return. 'What did you dream, Gracie?' she would ask. 'What scared you so much?'

'It was nothing,' Alison would snap. 'Why are you asking her questions? Are you trying to upset her?'

'No!'

Alison snorted. Meg tried to catch Grace's gaze, but Grace just turned away, lying back down in bed and shutting her eyes. 'Don't be scared,' Alison would whisper. 'There's nothing to be scared of. The dream is over now and it won't come back.' Her tone was soothing but her words misleading; the nightmares becoming ever more frequent as the weeks progressed. Often Meg wanted to ask her sister about them, but she never had the chance. Alison now helped Grace get dressed in the morning and undressed at night. She would always take Grace to the bathroom to do so. Sometimes their father would offer to do it himself, but Grace never wanted him. She didn't seem to like him as much anymore. Not as much as she liked Alison. She wanted to be with her all the time. Whatever the emergency, only Alison would do.

One day at school Meg stood in the playground watching Grace sitting alone on a bench in the corner. Her friends who were nearby called for her to join them, but Grace refused. Shrugging their shoulders, the friends went to play elsewhere.

Concerned, Meg made her way over.

'Why don't you want to play with them?' she asked.

'I just don't.'

'But they're your friends.'

'No, they're not. They hate me.'

'Did they say that?'

'No.'

'Then who did?'

Grace didn't answer. Meg sat down beside her. It was April now and the weather was growing warmer. A spider crawled up onto the sleeve of Grace's shirt. Knowing her sister was frightened of spiders Meg brushed it away. As she did so she touched her sister's arm and felt her flinch as if in pain.

'What's the matter? Are you hurt?'

Grace tried to pull her arm away. Meg gripped it, pulling up the sleeve to see the skin beneath. There was a mark on it; raw and angry. At first she thought it was a bruise. Then she realised it was a burn.

'Who did this to you?'

'No one.' Again, Grace tried to pull her arm away; this time successfully.

'Tell me! Was it one of them?' She gestured to Grace's friends who were playing hopscotch nearby.

'Leave me alone!'

'But Gracie…'

'You hate me too! You said you did.'

'I didn't mean it.'

'Yes, you did. It's true. That's what…'

Grace fell silent; her eyes wide and fearful.

'Who said I hated you?' Meg demanded.

'Go away! I wish you were dead like Mum.' Grace ran off towards the other side of the playground. Hurt and anxious, Meg watched her go. Some of her classmates did the same. 'She thinks you're a freak too,' one boy shouted. 'Everyone does.' They gathered around her, chanting 'Crazy Meg,' over and over again. The boy's face was inches from her own; his spit hitting her face like drops of rain.

And suddenly she was on top of him, pounding his face with her fists, screaming out her rage while he howled beneath her, the other children cried for her to stop and adult arms tried to pull her away.

The boy suffered a broken nose. His parents wanted her expelled, but the Headmistress stuck up for her. The boy had a history of bullying. In the past he had come close to expulsion himself. Instead she was punished with two weeks of detention; spending a couple of hours each afternoon after school sitting alone in a classroom with extra work to do and a bad-tempered teacher to supervise her.

One afternoon towards the end of the first week it was the Headmistress herself who supervised. Her name was Mrs Windsor; a plump middle-aged woman with a no-nonsense manner but kind eyes.

She sat at the front of the room, working her way through a pile of marking while Meg worked her way through a pile of long division. They had only just studied them in class and she was finding them hard. As she chewed on her pen she looked up to discover Mrs Windsor now sitting in the next desk.

'I know how you're feeling, Meg,' she said softly. 'I really do.'

'How do you know?'

'My mother died when I was ten. She fell down a flight of stairs. The last time I saw her she was waving my brother and I off to school and when we came home that afternoon we were met by a neighbour who told us she was dead.'

She stopped chewing her pen. 'What happened to you?'

'Our father was already dead. He'd been killed in the war. My brother and I had to go and live with an uncle and aunt. They lived a hundred miles away. We barely knew them. My brother was only six. Within a few weeks he was calling them Mummy and Daddy. But I wasn't. I didn't want anything to do with them. All I wanted was to have my real mother back.'

A lump came into her throat. She swallowed it down.

'They tried to be my friends, but I wouldn't let them. I hated them. For a long time I hated everyone, including my own brother. Then, one day I woke up and just didn't have the energy to hate anymore. And when I stopped I realised that life wasn't so bad. My uncle and aunt were stricter than my mother. They had different rules. But they were good people. They wanted to do their best for my brother and me and they did. They realised I was clever and encouraged me to work hard at school. Thanks to them I became the first person in our family to go to University.' Mrs Windsor smiled. 'They were so proud of me. I remember my aunt telling me that I'd done my mother proud too. And that's what you have to remember, Meg. Your mother isn't gone. Not really. She's still inside you and whatever you achieve will be a reflection on the person she played her part in helping you become.'

She shook her head.

'It's true. You're a clever girl; one of the brightest I've ever taught and far brighter than I ever was. You can do anything you want with your life. You could be a doctor. You could be a politician. Maybe you could even become Prime Minister. You'll always be your mother's daughter, Meg. Why not show the world just what her daughter can achieve?'

The lump was back. This time she couldn't swallow it. 'My sister hates me.'

'No, she doesn't. She loves you, just like you love her.'

'My mum hates me too.'

'Why would you think that?'

'Because it's true. It's my fault she's dead. It's all my fault…'

'No!' Mrs Windsor took Meg's chin in her hand and stared into her eyes. 'Meg, listen to me. What you're feeling is natural, but it isn't the truth. With death there is *always* guilt. When we lose someone we love as much as you loved your mother we always feel that we could have done something to save them. But we couldn't.'

'I made it happen. God was angry with me because I'm bad…'

'But you're not bad. There is *nothing* bad about you. Do you think I couldn't see it if there was? I've taught so many children. I can look into their faces and see what sort of people they are and when I look into yours all I see is good. And if I can see it then God can too, far more clearly than I. God isn't angry with you, Meg. What happened to your mother was terrible, but it was no one's fault, least of all yours.'

She stared into her teacher's face, wanting to believe.

'It's true, Meg. If your mother were here now she'd tell you the same thing. Why not honour her memory by making something wonderful of your life? And why not do it for your father and stepmother too? They're good people, just like my uncle and aunt were. If you just give them a chance I'm sure you'll see that I'm right.'

The floodgates burst. She shed her first tears since that dreadful night in the hospital back in Suffolk. Mrs Windsor held her, stroking her hair and whispering words of comfort as she released all the pain that had been building up inside.

Eventually, when she was calm, Mrs Windsor looked at her watch. 'I know you're supposed to stay here for another half hour but why not go home early?'

'I haven't finished my sums.'

'It doesn't matter. And tomorrow I'll be sitting with you again so if you want to have another cry you can.'

She kissed Mrs Windsor's cheek. 'Thank you.'

Her father's house was only half a mile from school. Alison, who took them there and back every day, had refused to do so a third time so Meg walked home alone. As she wandered along the streets she looked at the ugly houses and realised they weren't so ugly anymore. It wasn't as pretty as Suffolk, but Suffolk was still there. Maybe when she was grown up she would live there again. Maybe she would be an artist. She had always enjoyed drawing and was good at it. Maybe she would paint pictures of the Suffolk countryside and people would buy them. Her mother would have liked that. Perhaps Grace would too.

She reached the house. The drive was empty. Her father was still at work. He was hoping to earn a promotion and for the last couple of months had rarely been home before mid-evening. She walked around to the back of the house. Alison always left the conservatory door open. She assumed Alison and Grace would be in the kitchen. They would be surprised to see her, but she would explain that Mrs Windsor had let her leave early. If they were making supper she would offer to help. Back in Suffolk she had enjoyed helping her mother cook. Perhaps she could learn to enjoy it here too.

The conservatory was adjacent to the kitchen. The kitchen door was slightly open. As she walked towards it she heard Grace say, 'I don't want to.'

'But I'm telling you to,' Alison replied.

'But I don't want to. Please don't make me.'

Peering through the crack in the door Meg saw Grace with her back to the oven and Alison standing over her. One of the gas rings was lit. The flame spluttered and danced in the air.

'But I'm your friend,' Alison said softly. 'What other friend do you have? Not the children at school. They all hate you. They all laugh at your stupid accent. They call you a silly cry baby. You know they do. I've told you often enough.'

Grace swallowed. ‘But Dad…’

‘You can’t listen to your father. I’ve told you that too. He never wanted you here. He doesn’t want you here now. He hates the way you cling to him. You make him sick. If it was down to him, you and Meg would be in an orphanage and you know what happens to cry babies there? They beat them with sticks and lock them in cellars. You’re frightened of the dark. You’d be all alone with no one to help you, least of all Meg. She hates you too, remember? Everyone hates you but me.’

Grace started to cry.

‘Stop that,’ Alison hissed. ‘Stop that now.’ Reaching out she grabbed Grace’s arm and bent it back, digging her nails into the skin near the elbow. ‘If you don’t stop crying you know what will happen. You do, don’t you?’

Grace’s eyes darted towards the flame. Meg’s stomach turned over. In her head a voice was screaming for her to act. It sounded like her mother.

A knife lay on the kitchen table; its blade catching the sunlight. She stared at it, willing herself to move but shock had frozen her to the spot.

‘I’m going to count to five,’ Alison continued. ‘One…two…three…’

Grace managed to bring her tears under control.

Alison released her arm. ‘Did I hurt you?’

Grace nodded.

‘Well, that’s good. I hurt you, but you managed to stop crying. You see, I’m teaching you to be brave. I’m teaching you to be a better person. I’m doing that because I’m your friend.’

Grace gave another nod.

‘And what do you say?’

‘Thank you, Alison.’

Alison bent down, offering her cheek. Slowly Grace leaned forward and kissed it. Meg felt as if she was going to be sick. From somewhere far away she heard a clicking sound as if a lock was turning.

‘And now I want you to say it.’

Grace hesitated.

'Say it! Do it or I'll hurt you again and if you cry…' For a moment Alison's face was black with hate. Then a tenderness came into it that was far more chilling. Reaching out she stroked Grace's cheek. 'Come on,' she whispered. 'Do it for me.'

The knife blade kept catching the light. Meg stared at it, fighting against her paralysis.

And as she did so she saw that she was no longer the only one watching. Her father stood half hidden behind the door that led out into the hallway. His face was white. He looked as if he were going to be sick too.

Then Grace opened her mouth and said 'My mother was a dirty whore. I'm not Dad's real child. I'm a bastard because of my whore mother. I hate my whore mother and I hope she burns in hell.'

A gasp burst out of Meg's throat. Alison's head turned in her direction; her eyes widening with fear. It only lasted a second, but it was enough to break the spell that Meg was under. Again, she heard her mother's voice screaming for her to act and this time she was ready.

'You didn't see anything,' Alison hissed at her, 'because if you say you did…'

She ran for the knife. By the time Alison realised what she was doing it was in her hand. As she lunged she felt her father grab her. The blow fell wide, just missing Alison's shoulder. Her father cried out for her to stop. She fought him like a wildcat, dropping the knife in the process. Alison grabbed her too; pulling at her hair so hard that it felt as if her scalp was being removed. She turned, sinking her teeth into Alison's hand as deep and as hard as she could; her mouth filling with the harsh metallic taste of blood.

Finally, her father pulled her away. A whimpering Alison clutched her injured hand.

'My meeting was cancelled,' he whispered. 'I was coming home early to surprise you. Oh, Alison, what the hell have you done?'

Alison didn't answer; just stared at him.

'Jesus Christ, woman, how could you do this?'

'Don't look at me like that. You're no better than me.'

'But she's just a child. She's my child.'

'She's the child you abandoned; the child you didn't want. You didn't want either of them. I didn't force you to leave their mother. You chose to. You walked away and never looked back. You think you love her, but you don't. All you feel is guilt.'

'That's not true!'

'Of course, it's true!' Alison almost spat the words at him. 'If people find out about this do you really think they won't blame you too? They'll say you knew what was happening to her and didn't care, just like you didn't care what happened to her before we were forced to take her in. The stench of it will follow you just as much as it will follow me. How long do you think you'll keep your job? How long do you think you'll keep Susan once social services start sniffing around?' Alison paused, wiping her mouth, 'And the one thing I don't need at the moment is stress. Not in my condition.'

'What condition?'

'I'm three months pregnant. If you hadn't been so preoccupied with your job you might have noticed. I had a scan today. I was going to surprise you. I've had the scan and they're sure it's a boy. You're going to have a son, just like you've always wanted.' She gestured towards Meg. 'Do you remember what you said to me the week before their mother died? You said you'd never been so happy. You said the only thing that could make our life even more perfect would be to have a son. Now you're going to have one. It's so easy, Ken. It really is. No one has to know about this. We just tell social services we can't cope with the girls. We can send them away and go back to how things were. Things were wonderful then. They'll be even better now. They'll be perfect. How can you say no to that?'

Meg felt her father's grip weaken. She turned, staring up into his face, searching for anger but instead seeing confusion.

And, buried deep beneath all the shock and horror, a tiny shred of delight.

That was when she knew it didn't matter what he decided. It was Grace and her against the world. That was how it had to be because even if he did take her part his indecision meant that she could never feel safe with him.

So, she made his choice easy.

Grace was crouched in the corner, sobbing. Meg ran towards her, wrapping her arms around her. 'Don't you come near her!' she screamed. 'I'll kill you if you do! We don't want to stay here. We don't want to see either of you ever again…'

Midnight. Two weeks later.

The Milton Children's Home was a large Victorian house on the outskirts of London. Meg sat in her bed, staring down at her sister. The curtains were open; allowing the moon to bathe the room in pale white light. Grace's cheeks were blotched and her eyelids swollen. She had cried herself to sleep. Meg bent down and kissed her softly on the forehead. 'No more nightmares, Gracie,' she whispered. 'It's all over now.'

Her own bed was on the other side of the room. Her mother's photograph stood on a table next to it. The walls were bare. Karen Matthews; one of the helpers at the Home had told her that she could put posters on them if she wanted to. Karen seemed nice. Perhaps she really was. But after what had happened Meg would never allow herself to trust anyone ever again.

Time passed. She waited for sleep, but it refused to come. Eventually, after checking that Grace was still peaceful, she rose from the bed and went to sit on the window ledge. In front of her lay a sea of buildings. Countless lighted windows made the night seem like day. The night had never been so bright in Suffolk. From her bedroom window in the cottage all she could see was trees.

She wished she could see them now.

From far below floorboards creaked; the weary sighs of an old building. They sounded like footsteps. Perhaps they were. She wondered who they belonged to; which other occupant of the house? Whoever it was they were made of flesh and blood just as she was. The dead couldn't reach her. Not anymore. Her barriers were too firmly in place and none of them would ever break through and trick her again.

None but one.

The air in the room was heavy, stale and full of dust; but dancing over all of it, as delicate as a sigh, was the scent of roses.

She wished she could have believed Mrs Windsor. But her father and stepmother had not been good people. And if Mrs Windsor was wrong about that then she was wrong about God too. God was all powerful. He could see things that Mrs Windsor never could. He knew what she had done and how wicked she had been. God hated her, just as her mother did.

Almost as much as she hated herself.

But she would make it right. She would show that she was good. She would be the person she needed to be to keep her sister safe.

Shutting her eyes and tuning out all sound she whispered into the air:

'I'm sorry. I know it's my fault that you're dead. It's my fault that they hurt Grace too. I should have protected her. But I'll protect her now. I always will. I'll do it for you because I love you and I swear that one day I will make you proud of me again.'

Behind her the air seemed to move. Something brushed the back of her neck. Though she knew it couldn't be, it felt like a kiss.

She remained where she was; her eyes still closed, reciting her vows like a litany while the scent faded into nothingness, never to return.

Part 2

THE NIGHT VISITOR

Cornwall: February 2017

Chapter 1

For places, as for people, life can be hard. Saltran stood on the west coast of Cornwall. Though it still called itself a town it was really little more than a village. A population of less than two thousand lived in homes built of granite; that sturdy, resilient stone so ideal for providing shelter from winds that roared in from the sea like devils, intent on tearing all man-made structures to pieces. And with the winds came mists so thick that those who ventured into them could believe their friends and neighbours had been swallowed whole and that it was only a matter of time before they too were devoured.

Once it had been much larger. In the nineteenth century it had been at the centre of the Cornish Tin industry but by the 1880s the industry had died, taking much of the town's life with it. Hundreds had been forced to emigrate to avoid starvation and most of those who remained now earned their living elsewhere.

The centre of the town was the Square. It was home to the few local businesses that still remained including a supermarket, an art gallery and two pubs; The Corsair and The Kings Arms. The first boasted a pool table and weekly quizzes; the second darts and accommodation to the intrepid hikers who came even in the most inclement weather to explore the coast.

To the east of the Square were a church and a close. To the west was a car park and rows of cottages, most of which had housed miners back when the industry still flourished. Beyond the cottages were fields; all enclosed with crumbling stone walls. This was the route the hikers took; continuing on to where the land was wild, and a single footpath weaved its way through a maze of gorse and bracken until finally reaching the sea.

They would stand at the edge of the cliffs, tasting the salt in the air, watching the coastline roll away as the waves pounded the rocks and sea gulls danced on the wind; their cries as mournful as a lament for the countless sailors lost to elements as old and unforgiving as time itself. And as they gazed about them they would see the countryside was dotted with stone chimneys and derelict engine houses; remnants of the mines that had once dominated the landscape. From a distance they looked like the ruins of a lost civilization built by a Cornish Ozymandias who had never dreamed that all he had so proudly created would one day crumble and be lost.

But nothing is ever truly lost. Walls are like sponges; soaking up the energies of those who live within them; their joys and sorrows, triumphs and tragedies. They act as custodians to countless unspoken prayers and dark desires; keeping them safe and whole, waiting patiently for the arrival of that one special person with the power to set them free.

Thursday afternoon. As she stood in the kitchen at the back of her house waiting for the kettle to boil, Meg listened to the roar of the wind as it drove raindrops against her window like pebbles. Through the glass she could see fields and the occasional farmhouse; the light from their windows the only illumination against the dark that was already descending. It was a very different view to the one she enjoyed from her flat in Central London. There, even at midnight, the sky was so full of light that it was as if the day had never ended. But here in her new home the night was like a living thing; descending like a blanket to hide her and the town from sight.

Her house was called 'Redlands': a name she assumed was ironic as it was built of grey granite like everything else. It was a pretty place though, with two good sized bedrooms; one of which she had already converted into a study. The door and windows were painted white and the furnishings all had the simple, rustic quality that screamed vast financial outlay.

It stood in the close. From one of her bedroom windows she had a clear view of the church. It dated back to the fourteenth century and judging by their decrepit state most of the grave stones did too. Its bell rang at all times of the day and night. At first the sound had often disturbed her sleep but already she was so used to it that she rarely noticed it at all.

A month earlier she had never heard of Saltran. It was her

boss, Henry Flynn who had mentioned it as she sat in his office telling him that she had changed her mind and was now willing to take a sabbatical.

'It's in the west of Cornwall; only a mile from the coast and about ten miles from Penzance. A friend of mine owns a house there. The tenant has just moved out.'

'And you thought of me as a replacement?'

'It's a lovely place, Meg. The people are friendly and the scenery is magnificent. The house is lovely too. It dates back to the 1850s. It was very run down when my friend bought it, but he's spent a fortune doing it up.'

She had nodded, feeling little enthusiasm but knowing she had to get away.

'You're interested?'

'Is there wi-fi or will I need to arrange it myself?'

'Why would you want that?'

'So I can still work.'

He had sighed. 'Meg, we've talked about this. After all you've been through you need a proper break.'

'I won't be doing much, Henry. Just keeping my hand in…'

And it was true. That was all she was doing.

Or so she told herself.

The kettle boiled and the coffee made, she made her way upstairs to her study and the pile of work that awaited her.

She rose each day at seven. After making coffee she checked her e-mails. As far as her clients were concerned she was still the youngest and most dynamic Partner in the Corporate Department of one of the largest law firms in the City and they were unwilling to trust their business to anyone else. Some Japanese clients were buying an electronics business in Birmingham and usually sent her a long list of questions overnight.

At half past nine she phoned the office to give her secretary, Debbie, instructions for the morning and, more often than not, to receive a comprehensive summary of all the latest office gossip:

'Have you heard about Geoff Brooker? He's having an affair with a woman in the Property Department. One of the cleaners caught them at it in a meeting room.'

'Christ! Does his wife know?'

'I don't think so. Everyone else does though…'

Debbie prattled on, caught up in the intrigue. Meg listened eagerly, surprised at her uncharacteristic prurience.

Only it wasn't prurience; just nostalgia for the life she had left behind.

But six months wasn't long. Soon she would be living it again.

At half past ten she drove to her gym in Penzance where she split her time between weights and the running machine. Exercise had always been an important part of her routine. It raised her energy level and increased her productivity.

Her workout completed, she sat in a café on the waterfront, drinking a latte and checking her phone for messages. From her table by the window she could see the harbour. Intrepid windsurfers braved the wind and rain; dancing over the waves in front of the tree covered island of St Michaels Mount with its castle at the top. 'From the end of March they open the Island to the public,' one of the waiters told her. 'It's well worth the trip, believe me.' She said that it sounded like a fun outing while knowing she would never have the time to make it.

At one o'clock she drove home again. Parking space in the close was limited and she often had to manoeuvre around her neighbour Dan's white van. There were only three houses in the close. She and Dan lived next door to each other; sharing a common wall and facing the home of an accountant called Andrew, who worked in Truro and seemed to spend most of his time there too. Dan was an artist and craftsman who made his living selling paintings and furniture in local galleries and doing odd jobs for the neighbours. Whenever he saw her he would give her a cheery grin while she fought the urge to tell him to go back to driving school and learn how to parallel park.

After eating a sandwich, she phoned Debbie again, giving instructions for the afternoon and checking when her conference calls were scheduled. She was still running acquisitions for two UK clients, both of which were at a delicate stage.

Often Henry would come on the line, urging her to take a step back. 'You're supposed to be relaxing,' he would remind her.

'I am.'

'Not from where I'm standing.'

'Well, you're not standing here, are you?'

'Meg...'

'Anyway, the clients asked for me specifically. It wouldn't reflect well on the department if I said I wasn't available.'

'I just think...'

'Look, I know you care and I'm grateful. But I'm fine, Henry. Trust me. This break is doing me a power of good.'

Later in the afternoon she spent an hour cleaning the house. Though the previous tenant had left contact details for a local cleaner she had yet to make use of them. There didn't seem any point when it was easy enough to find a window in her schedule to take care of it herself.

When evening came she made herself available to her American clients. All were based on the west coast and seemed unaware that England was eight hours ahead. Not that she minded. She knew they depended on her and besides, it wasn't as if she had anything else to do.

And when, finally, she had answered all their questions and solved their latest set of problems she would relax in front of the television. She could usually find an episode of CSI or Law & Order she hadn't already seen. During the commercial breaks she would flick to the business channel, checking recent developments that might affect her work and making notes on a pad of all the things she would need to do the following day.

Occasionally her concentration was broken by the sound of Dan returning from the pub, followed by the soft thud of the rock music he seemed to play constantly when he was home. Though others might have complained she had always found the sound soothing. It reminded her of the noise of London and helped her imagine, just for a moment, that she was back where she belonged.

And when there was no work to be done she would walk. She would make her way to the coast, past the cottages and through the fields, wearing her walking boots and waterproof jacket even if the sun was shining. The weather could turn in minutes and having spent a wretched afternoon battling her way home through rain that came down in sheets she knew to always be prepared.

Once at the coast she would follow the path north. Already she knew the area well; the beaches you could access and the ones you couldn't though somehow she managed anyway. Her favourite was little more than a cove, covered in boulders that looked like dinosaur eggs waiting to hatch. The path led her down through black granite rocks dotted with green shrub and yellow gorse flowers and into a valley that led to the sea. Gulls perched on the boulders, calling greetings to each other like inhabitants of a village gathering in the local pub to pass the time of day. 'Had a good morning?' 'Not bad. Took a battering from a sou' westerly but caught a big fish.' Occasionally one would swoop down and barge another from its perch like the pub bully outraged that someone should dare occupy his chosen seat. A stream flowed through the valley, bubbling over the boulders to mix with the waves that broke ever closer as the tide rushed in. She would sit very still, breathing in the scent of wet earth, salt and seaweed while marvelling that a place so full of noise could be so restful.

A mile further up the coast a ruined engine house stood on an outcrop of rock. It was next to a chasm where the waves slammed into the cliffs and sent plumes of white spray high into the air while overhead huge rocks in which the elements had carved caricatures of faces stared down at her like the statues of Easter Island. If the hour was late and the weather tranquil, she would sit and watch the sun sink towards the sea; turning from yellow to orange and finally red, while dragging its light across the water and down beyond the horizon, leaving her to make her way home in the dark.

THE NIGHT VISITOR

Friday. It was late afternoon. Jed Anstey stood at the counter of Saltran Supermarket waiting patiently for his next customer. He heard a bus pull up in the Square outside, depositing children returning from the school in nearby St Just. A small boy entered to buy a can of coke while two teenage girls poured over the magazine rack, giggling and gossiping with each other; both radiating the excited energy that marked the start of the weekend and the promise of freedom.

Eventually they made their way over. 'Can I have this, please?' asked one, handing him a magazine.

'Of course, you can, Lorna.'

'And can I have twenty Benson & Hedges too?'

'Yes.' Jed folded his arms and stared levelly at her. 'In two years time, when you're eighteen.'

Lorna rolled her eyes. Her friend, Aishling, just giggled.

'And how was your day?' Jed asked.

'Well, it was going great until now…'

'No, it wasn't,' Aishling corrected her. 'You said Mark was going to ask you out and he didn't.'

'I don't care.'

'Yes, you do.'

'I don't want him to ask me out!'

'Yes, you do!'

Jed watched them with wry amusement. It seemed no time since both had been little girls, begging their mothers to buy them sweets and thinking that boys were the most revolting creatures on Earth. The startling thing was that he could remember standing at the same counter years ago listening to their mothers having all the same conversations. It was at moments like this that he really felt his age.

As the girls continued to squabble he saw another customer enter the shop; a tall, slender woman who moved silently between the aisles, placing purchases in a basket. Lorna noticed her too and nudged Aishling. 'Talk to her.'

'No. You talk to her.'

The woman approached the counter. Again, Lorna nudged Aishling. Again, Aishling nudged her back.

'I like your jacket,' Lorna told the woman. 'It's really stylish.'

'Thank you. I like your uniform.'

Lorna's eyes widened. 'Really?'

'Yes. The colour suits you both.'

'Thanks.' Lorna flushed slightly, looking pleased.

'You're from London, aren't you?' asked Aishling.

The woman nodded.

'It must be great living there.'

'Yes. But living here is great too.'

Aishling laughed. 'Well, sometimes.'

'I've never been to London,' said Lorna wistfully.

'I'm sure you will one day,' the woman told her.

'I hope so.'

Silence. Lorna half opened her mouth as if preparing to say something before deciding against.

'Besides,' said the woman kindly, 'you have plenty of time. It's not going anywhere.'

It was Lorna's turn to laugh. 'No. I suppose not. Well, bye. Have a nice weekend.'

'You too.'

Lorna and Aishling left the shop. Jed began to bag the woman's groceries. 'You mustn't mind the girls,' he said. 'They're just curious. You seem very glamorous to them.'

'There's nothing glamorous about me.'

'You come from the big city. For most of the kids round here that's glamour enough.'

'London's just a place. It may be bigger than here but it's still just a place.'

Jed continued to bag the groceries. The woman stood, waiting patiently for him to finish just as she always did. For the last three weeks she had come into the supermarket almost every day to buy something. With most of his customers that was more than enough time to learn their life story but hers remained as mysterious as it was on the first day she had approached his counter.

Her name was Meg Parker. He knew that much. And she was from London. He knew that too. He believed she was a lawyer. That was what her neighbour, Dan, had told him. She looked to be about thirty and was undeniably beautiful. 'A real stunner,' Brian, the landlord of the Corsair had announced, one evening the previous week, prompting a disapproving look from his wife. 'If she'd only put on a couple of pounds she'd be perfect.'

'Maybe so,' Jed had told him, 'but she'd still be a good twenty years too young for you.'

Everyone had laughed. 'So, what's she doing here, then?' Brian had asked Dan.

'Beats me.' Dan ran a hand through his untidy dark hair and gave his characteristic grin. 'But if any of you find out she's an art collector let me know so I can make some sales!'

Perhaps she did collect art. There was no harm in asking. Only Jed held back. There was something unapproachable about her. It was not that she was unfriendly. Her manner was always warm. Yet it was also guarded; as if she was wary of the world and wanted to keep it at bay. But he was sociable by nature and so persevered.

'How long will you be staying with us?' he asked.

'Six months. Well, five now.'

'So, you'll catch some of the summer. It's lovely here then. We'll be overrun by tourists, though coming from London you must be used to that.'

'I am. And at least here you have the space to escape them.'

'That's very true.'

Another silence. He smiled at her. She smiled back; a quick gesture that fell just short of the eyes. In some such behaviour might appear dismissive, but not in her. She did not intend to be rude. It was just that her eyes were full already. There was a world of sadness in them. He didn't know if others saw it, but he did, as clear as day. He wondered what the cause was and wished, in his kind-hearted way, that he could help make it better.

Just as he wished that someone could do the same for him.

He handed over her change. Outside the wind was howling. 'I bet you don't get wind like that in London,' he observed.

'No. It doesn't even come close.'

'Some people find it eerie. They say it sounds like the cries of the dead.'

'Not me. I don't believe in ghosts.'

It was a simple answer yet delivered just a fraction too quickly. His curiosity about her increased, though he knew that on this particular occasion it would not be satisfied.

'See you soon,' he told her.

'Yes. Good bye.'

She left the shop. He remained where he was, listening to the wind and musing on a multitude of unanswered questions.

For Meg weekends were the hardest. There was never enough work to do. She often thought of returning to London but her flat had been rented out and it seemed rather sad to drive all that way just to stay in a hotel. Besides, it wasn't important where she was. The only thing that mattered was remaining so active that she never had time to stop and think.

She kept up her gym visits: burning off hundreds of calories as she pushed her body to breaking point. And when she returned home she would walk the coast for hours, often ending up so exhausted that no matter how bad the weather she would be forced to sit and wait for her energy to return.

On one particular Sunday she climbed out onto an exposed crag and stared down at the sea. The wind was fierce. Clouds raced across the sky, obscuring the sun and then revealing it; allowing its rays to hit the water, turning it from grey to turquoise while its surface flickered with drops of brilliant white light as if lit underneath by hundreds of candles.

An elderly couple carrying rucksacks stopped and stared at her. 'Be careful,' the woman cried out. 'That's a dangerous place to be.'

'I'm fine,' she told them.

'Do you have a death wish?' cried the man.

She didn't answer.

'You should come down from there,' the woman told her.

'Leave me alone, please. All I want is to be left alone.'

Shaking their heads, they walked inland. She continued

watching the water while the wind grew ever stronger, threatening to tear her from her perch and smash her to pieces on the rocks below.

That evening Dan sat in his study, staring at the half-completed canvas before him. It was a landscape, just as most of his paintings were. His friends in the pub were always telling him to try something more avant garde in the hope that it might get him noticed; that he was thirty-five after all, and it was time to start making his mark. They were probably right but when the scenery around him was so magnificent he found it hard to be inspired by anything else.

The room was stuffy. Leaving his stool, he went to open a window, lit a cigarette and stared down at the close. In the distance he could hear the church bell ringing the hour. Glancing at his watch he was surprised to see that it was already eight o'clock. But that was always the way when he painted. The act of creation took over and in the process he lost all track of time.

He had promised to have a drink with Brian at the Corsair. He was running late but it wouldn't be a problem. Brian would understand and besides, as the pub landlord it wasn't as if he had anywhere else to be.

As Dan prepared to shut his window he heard footsteps. Meg Parker walked into the close. Her pace was brisk; her arms wrapped around herself as if seeking protection against the cold. Had she been walking all this time? Where did she find the energy? If he tried to keep her schedule he would collapse with exhaustion within a week.

He called down a greeting. She didn't respond; clearly lost in thought. He called again. This time she heard him and looked up.

'It's a chilly night for a walk,' he told her.

'I don't mind the cold.'

'You probably don't feel it; the speed you walk. Where did you end up today? Scotland?'

She gave a quick laugh. 'No. I just followed the coast.'

'Well, it's worth following.'

'Yes, it certainly is.'

She took her front door keys from her pocket. He remained

where he was, studying her. Brian was right. She was beautiful. But too skinny. He liked his women with more meat on them. No, she was not his type at all.

But that didn't stop him being curious about her.

On a whim he said, 'Do you want to come to the pub for a drink?'

She shook her head. 'I have some work to do.'

'Can't it wait?'

'Not tonight. I'm sorry.'

'Never mind. Another time, perhaps.'

'Of course. Good night, Dan.'

'Good night, Meg.'

She entered her house, closing the door behind her. He remained where he was, finishing his cigarette and feeling disappointed even though there was no reason to be.

THE NIGHT VISITOR

Chapter 2

March.
It was late Saturday afternoon. As she vacuumed her hallway Meg switched on the overhead light. The bulb blew. Instantly all the other lights went out too.

'Damn!'

She rummaged through the hallway cupboard, searching for the fuse box while wishing she had paid closer attention when her landlord had told her its whereabouts. It wasn't there, and she couldn't find it in the kitchen either. Outside it was growing dark. Soon she wouldn't be able to see. The landlord's number was on her mobile. She dialled it, only to get his answering service. As she left a message there was a knock on the front door. She opened it to find Dan holding a letter.

'This is for you,' he announced cheerfully. 'It was put through my door by mistake.'

'Thanks.' She took it from him.

'You never struck me as an environmentalist.' He gestured to the dark interior. 'Saving our planet's resources.'

'A blub blew. It took out the other lights.'

'Shall I show you where the fuse box is?'

Her spirits lifted. 'Do you know?'

'It's in the kitchen. Bottom left hand drawer next to the cooker.'

'But I've already looked there.'

He grinned. 'Bet you didn't look behind the panel though.'

'What panel?'

'The panel at the back is actually a door. Press the right side and it'll open. I should know. I helped install it. Now, do you have a torch?'

'No.'

'Hang on a second. I'll get mine…'

Five minutes later she knelt beside him as he showed her how to operate the trip switch. 'Hey presto,' he said and suddenly the lights were back on.

'Thanks.'

'No problem.' He rose to his feet and stretched. 'Milk and two sugars, please.'

'Sorry?'

'I take my tea with milk and two sugars.'

His presumption made her indignant. But her gratitude outweighed it, so she put the kettle on and made them both a cup.

They drank them in the living room. He looked about him, taking in the décor. 'When does the Queen arrive?' he asked.

'What do you mean?'

'Your house is spotless.'

'Well, it's tidy.'

He shook his head. 'My mother's house is tidy. This place could make the front cover of an interior design mag.'

'I just like keeping things neat.'

'You put me to shame. In my place you can barely get to the dining table. Here I'd happily eat my dinner off the floor.'

She nodded.

'So, what are you cooking this evening?'

'Steak.'

He rubbed his stomach.

'I've only enough for one.'

'Never mind. We can go to the pub instead. They do great food.'

Again, she felt indignant. 'Who says I want to go to the pub with you?'

He raised his hands in a supplicating gesture. 'Relax. I'm not hitting on you. There wouldn't be much point what with you batting for the other side.'

'You think I'm a lesbian?'

'Well, you're not exactly sociable, are you?'

'We're socialising now, aren't we?'

'No. We're making polite conversation. There's a difference.'

'And what's wrong with being polite?'

'Not a thing. It's very…um…stimulating.'

'I'm glad to hear it.'

He started to laugh.

'Besides,' she continued, 'what does sociability have to do with being a lesbian?'

'Nothing. I was joking.'

'Very droll. Maybe you should go on Britain's Got Talent. You'd slay them at the audition.'

His laughter increased.

'I'm not a lesbian, Dan.'

'It's alright. I believe you. Millions wouldn't.'

'I'm not! I like men.'

'Great. So, I'll knock for you at eight o'clock.'

She opened her mouth then closed it again, realising she had been played.

'It'll be fun,' he told her. 'There's a rock band tonight. Then again, that's probably not your thing. Don't lesbians prefer jazz?'

'Don't you have a home to go to?'

Still laughing, he headed for the door. After closing it behind him she exhaled. The last thing she felt like was an evening in a crowded pub; an evening of people and their curiosity and questions.

But she had agreed, and it would be rude to cancel. Sighing to herself she resumed her hoovering.

Half past eight. She sat at a table in The Corsair, waiting for Dan who was placing their food order at the bar.

Like almost every building in Saltran The Corsair was made of stone. It had a low ceiling and white walls covered in photographs showing the town's mining past. Their table was in the corner, next to an open fire. A log slid to the front of the hearth, sending sparks shooting up the chimney. Dan was talking to the landlord; a middle-aged man with a bald head who kept looking curiously at her.

Does he think I'm a lesbian too?

Not that it mattered. People could think what they wanted.

Though she still found herself giving him a friendly smile.

Dan returned, carrying drinks; stopping en route to say hello to the band as they set up their equipment. She hoped they didn't start playing until she had finished her meal. Lip reading had never been one of her strengths.

He handed her a glass of wine then downed a mouthful of beer. 'Brian, the landlord has been asking about you.'

'Let me guess. The subject of my sexual orientation just happened to come up.'

Grinning, he wiped froth from his top lip.

'I'm not a lesbian, Dan.'

The grin widened.

'I spent years trying but every girlfriend I had knew I was faking it.'

His jaw dropped.

'Got you.'

He laughed. Smiling, she studied his appearance. He was about thirty-five and the same height as her, with a stocky build, thick dark hair, twinkling brown eyes and enough stubble to count as a trainee beard.

'What is it?' he asked.

'I was just thinking. All you need is an ear ring, an eye patch and a parrot on your shoulder and you'd make a good pirate.'

'I was just thinking too.'

'About what?'

'You've got a lovely smile. You should use it more often.'

Their food arrived. She tucked into her lasagne. 'You're not too hot, are you?' Dan asked.

'No.'

'I love this table. I always try and sit here when they've lit the fire. You can't beat the smell of burning logs.'

Unbidden, a memory came to her; so vivid it was as if she was actually there. She was sitting with Grace by their fireplace in Suffolk, drinking hot chocolate and listening to their mother's fairy tales. Meg wished she still had copies of them but they, like so much else, had been lost in the aftermath of her mothers' death.

Suddenly she could taste the hot chocolate in her mouth, feel the heat of the fire against her cheek and see the flames dancing like the fairies her mother described. For a moment the memory enfolded her like a blanket, making her feel warm and safe.

Dan was saying something. Quickly she snapped back to the present. 'Do you light your fire?' he asked.

'No.'

'Would you like to? I can show you how. I've also got a spare fire guard if you need one.'

'I know how to already,' she told him. 'But thanks.'

'No problem. We Penalunas aim to please.'

'Is Penaluna your surname? It sounds Spanish.'

'Actually, it's a Cornish name, though I do have a bit of Spanish blood in me. According to my mother, one of her ancestors came over with the Armada and was shipwrecked off the Cornish coast on the way home.'

'Did you grow up in this area?'

'No. In Bodmin…'

He began to tell her about his life. About his parents who had run a small bed and breakfast before retiring to Spain, and his elder brother who was now a sheep farmer in New Zealand. About his year working in a bank before realising that the monotony of office routine would drive him crazy if he stayed. About how his dream was to make enough from his paintings and woodwork to eventually be able to do it full time.

She was struck by how open he was. It was like listening to her secretary, Debbie. Neither kept anything back. The only difference was in their accents. Debbie had the clipped tone of the Home Counties while Dan's speech had the soft burr of the West Country and the twang that turned 'tiny' into 'toiny.'

As she listened, she ate her food. Though she wasn't very hungry the landlord kept glancing over and in her new mood of affable heterosexuality she wanted to leave a clean plate. The band continued to tune. She began to wish they would start playing. The louder the background noise the easier to avoid the questions she knew Dan was about to ask.

Only it wasn't that simple.

'So, what brings you to this neck of the woods?' he asked

eventually.

'Do I need a reason?'

'It's hardly London, is it?'

'I just fancied a change of scene.'

'Don't your bosses mind?'

'No.'

'You must get lonely though.'

'Why?'

'You haven't had any visitors yet.'

'How do you know?'

'We're neighbours. You notice these things.'

'I go back to London sometimes for meetings. I see people when I'm there.'

He finished his beer. 'Is your sister going to come? I'm assuming the girl in the photograph in your living room is your sister. You look really alike.'

She didn't answer. Suddenly what little appetite she had was gone.

'Will she?'

'No.'

'Why not? Aren't you close?

'Not anymore.'

'Have you had a falling out?' Again, he laughed. 'My mother and my aunt are always having them. They vow they'll never speak again and then a month later they're drinking tea together and gossiping about their neighbours like nothing ever happened.'

'My sister died four months ago.'

The blood drained from his face. She downed the rest of her wine, wishing it was something stronger.

'Christ, Meg, I'm sorry. I never would have said anything if I'd known.'

'Well now you do.'

'Is that why you're here? To…I don't know. Deal with it.'

'Something like that.'

'How are your parents coping?'

She gave a hollow laugh.

He looked confused.

'My mother died when I was nine. My father might as well have done.'

The confusion gave way to mortification. 'Me and my big mouth. If they gave medals for putting your foot in it, I'd win gold every time.'

'You said it.'

She saw him swallow. Instantly she felt guilty.

'I'm sorry, Dan. I didn't mean that. Please don't feel bad. There's no need.'

Silence. In the background a band member announced they'd be starting their set in a couple of minutes.

'Can I ask you something?' he said eventually.

'Yes.'

'You're always busy. From the sound of it you have a heavy work load and when you're not working you're going for long walks or to the gym. You never seem to stop. Not even for a minute.'

'So, what's your question?'

'How is that dealing with anything?'

Another silence. He was staring at her. His face had the sympathetic look that in the months since Grace's death she had come to hate. What did people want her to do? Break down in front of their eyes? Why couldn't they see that she was fine? That she didn't need help or support from anyone. That all she needed was to be left alone to deal with things in her own way.

Wanting to avoid his gaze she stared at the fire.

And once again she was back in Suffolk, leaning against her mother, feeling the warmth of her body and listening to the softness of her voice. Her mother had had a beautiful speaking voice. She remembered people commenting on it.

Grace had had a beautiful voice too. She had inherited it from their mother, just as she had inherited her smile and her warmth.

Oh, Gracie, I am sorry. I am so very sorry...

'I'm tired, Dan. I need to go.'

'Please don't. I didn't mean to upset you.'

'You haven't. Thanks for the meal. I enjoyed it. I really did.'

She left the pub, her food unfinished, while finally the band began to play.

Dan remained where he was, staring at his empty pint glass and giving himself a metaphorical yet no less painful kicking.

Brian wandered over, carrying another drink. 'This one's on the house. Someone made a quick exit. Don't tell me the Penaluna charm fell short.'

He didn't answer.

'Forget her, mate. There are plenty more fish in the sea.'

'It's not like that. I told you. She's not my type.'

Brian laughed.

'It's true.'

'You're well rid if you ask me. Being gorgeous doesn't make up for being stuck up. Not in my book.'

'She's not stuck up.'

'Hmmm…'

'She's not, ok? She's anything but. Stop being so bloody judgmental. You'd really like her if you just gave her a chance.'

Brian held up his hand in a gesture of supplication. 'OK. I'm sorry. I take it back.'

'Good.'

'No, honestly I do. If you say she's a nice person then that's enough for me.'

Brian remained where he was, looking anxious. The sight made Dan feel bad. 'Forget it, mate. I shouldn't have snapped. And thanks for the pint. I appreciate it.'

'No worries. If I don't give you the occasional freebie you might not let me kick your arse at pool.'

They both laughed; the earlier tension forgotten.

Brian returned to the bar. Dan remained where he was, thinking about Meg. Her smile really was lovely. He wished he saw it more often; for her sake more than his.

And then he thought of something that just might, for a moment, make it return.

THE NIGHT VISITOR

That night, unable to sleep, Meg went to stare out of her bedroom window. A full moon bathed the Square in eerie light. The sky was cloudless and full of stars. She gazed up at them, trying to identify the constellations. Once she had known them all. Her mother had taught them to her over countless nights when an excess of childish energy had rendered sleep elusive. But she couldn't remember them now. The realisation made her feel ashamed, while in her head she heard Grace's voice raised in anger:

I remember when we were kids how you used to bleat on about how Mum's death was your fault. About how you could have stopped it, like you were God or something.

It was true. Once she had believed that. Now she knew better. You were born, you lived and eventually you died. There was nothing else. No heaven. No hell. No punishment or second chances. When you lost someone they stayed lost and you had to learn to live without them.

Like the sister she would willingly have given her own life to save.

Like the mother who had taught her to never be afraid of where her gift might lead...

She went to her study and switched on the light. Documents from one of her acquisitions lay spread across the desk. Though she had checked them a dozen times she began to read through them again; pouring every drop of concentration onto the pages and keeping all other thoughts at bay.

It was dawn when she returned to bed, and noon when she rose again. While dressing she heard a knock at the door. By the time she reached it the caller had gone, leaving a fire guard and an envelope containing a drawing of Long John Silver receiving a 'Man of the Year' award at the Annual Foot in Mouth Oscars. He was making a speech, saying he owed it all to the parrot that was perched on his shoulder, wearing dark glasses and smoking a cigar. At the bottom was a single word;

'Sorry'.

It made her laugh. She thought about going to tell Dan he had nothing to be sorry for, but his van was gone.

After attaching the drawing to her fridge with a magnet she fetched her sports bag and drove to Penzance.

Her gym was half empty: just the hard-core regulars she had come to recognise. As she stepped onto the running machine she saw a staff member staring at her, only to look away quickly when she returned his gaze.

Later, as she rested between sets on the shoulder press he approached her. 'I'm sorry,' he began. 'I know this is none of my business, but don't you think you might be overdoing it?'

She wiped sweat from her face. 'What do you mean?'

'Well…' He looked hesitant. 'You've lost an awful lot of weight.'

'Isn't that the point of coming to the gym?'

'Yes, I suppose…'

'There we are then.'

He remained where he was.

'Was there anything else?'

'No.'

'Then do you mind if I continue my workout?'

He moved away. After finishing her final set, she stretched out her muscles while deciding which piece of equipment to use next.

And caught her reflection in one of the mirrors.

She was tall and slim with short brown hair and an excellent figure. Her face, which people considered beautiful, had always been lean: her cheekbones high and strong. But they had never appeared jagged. Not like they did now. And her cheeks had never looked hollow.

Her face was still sticky with sweat. As she reached for her towel she noticed how thin her arm appeared. She turned in profile, running her hand over her stomach. It had always been flat and smooth. Though her ribs did not normally feel so prominent.

Yet again the man was watching her. She could see his face in the glass.

Does he think I'm anorexic?

She turned. Instantly he resumed what he was doing. His furtiveness made her angry. This was her place. She came here to feel good. Why couldn't he see that? Why was he trying to spoil it?

There was a vending machine in the corner. After finding some change in her pocket she purchased a bar of chocolate and began eating.

Why am I doing this? I don't have anything to prove.

But she kept going until the bar was gone and her stomach felt so full it threatened to burst.

An hour later she arrived home. As she climbed out of her car she saw Brian from The Corsair standing on the corner of the Close, talking to Jed from the supermarket. Both gave her a wave. Putting on her best smile she waved back.

'I enjoyed my meal last night,' she called out to Brian.

'I'm glad,' he called back. 'Come again soon.'

'I certainly will.' She took her sports bag from the boot of the car. Brian continued to talk to Jed; his voice too low for her to make out what was being said.

But she could guess.

He's talking about me. He's saying I didn't finish my food.

He thinks I'm anorexic too.

Suddenly she felt exposed. Exposed and angry; just as she had in the gym. It was her life. It had nothing to do with them. Nothing at all.

In her kitchen, while waiting for the kettle to boil, she stared at Dan's drawing. Once it had made her smile. Now it made her angrier still. She pictured Dan in the pub after she had left, discussing her with Brian. Telling him about her loss. Sharing his fears that she wasn't dealing with it the way she should.

Fears that Brian was now passing onto Jed.

Because that was what people did in small communities. They

gossiped about each other; pouring over every nugget of information as if it was made of gold.

Just as they had done in Wickenham.

The air in the kitchen seemed stale. She needed to be outside; to feel the wind in her face. To have it drive all the thoughts from out of her head.

Without bothering to fetch her waterproofs she left the house. Jed was gone. Brian stood outside The Corsair smoking a cigarette. 'There's going to be a storm,' he told her. Better not stay out too long. You might get drowned.'

Pretending not to hear him she headed for the coast.

For a while the storm held off. She strode along the coast path and down to her favourite beach. It was already dusk and dark clouds raced across the sky. Every instinct told her to hurry home and avoid a soaking but nervous energy drove her on. As she approached the outcrop of rock next to the chasm she heard the first rumble of thunder. The air became electric. For a moment she could almost see it spark before her eyes.

And then came the storm.

It was like being trapped in a car wash. Rain pounded her face and body, soaking through her clothes as if they were made of rice paper and turning her skin to ice. In need of shelter she entered the engine house.

It was just a shell. The roof was long gone. But a ledge ran along the east side; about four feet high. She huddled beneath it, wrapping her arms around herself in a vain attempt to keep warm.

There was a window in the west wall. Through it she could see the sea. Bolts of lightning danced across its surface as if following the rhythm set by the thunder. Though tired and cold she could still appreciate its beauty.

As a small child she had been frightened of storms. It was her mother who had taught her to make them into a game. 'Isn't it glorious, Meg? It's like nature giving us a special firework display. Who can guess when the next flash of lightning will be? Five seconds? Ten?

Let's count together.' In time her fear had vanished, and it *had* become a game. The three of them would stand by a window; she and Grace competing while their mother kept score. Not that she had ever cared about winning. It was enough that she was with the only two people in the world who truly loved her.

More than enough.

Much more.

And she wanted it back. That feeling. Just for a moment to escape the sense of being so utterly alone that she wanted to curl up and die.

But it was gone. There was nothing left.

Except grief.

Finally, the tears came. She lowered her head and wept; huddled under a ledge in a ruined building while the thunder continued to roar, the lightning to flash and the wind to hurl rain drops at her like a bully throwing stones.

Time passed. She didn't know how long. It was only when she was all cried out that she realised the storm was over.

Wiping eyes that felt raw she again looked out to sea. The lightning had stopped, and the surface of the water was turning dark as the cloud obscured sun sank beneath the horizon, dragging what little light there was after it. All that was left was the wind.

Until suddenly it dropped.

And in the silence she heard a child crying.

Startled, she sat and listened.

What are they doing here? Are they lost?

'Hello?'

No answer. The crying continued. The sound tore at her heart. This was no place for a child to be alone.

Emerging from her hiding place on legs that were stiff from lack of use she raised her voice.

'Hello? Are you OK? Do you need help?'

The wind rose again, drowning out the sound. Leaving the engine house, she stood on the crag. Though the light was almost gone she could still make out the landscape around her: the cliffs, the bushes of gorse and in the distance a ruined chimney from another abandoned mine.

But there was no one there.

'My name is Meg. Please don't be scared. I just want to help.'

There was movement behind her. She turned, expecting to see the child but it was just a gull landing on a nearby rock and letting out a squawk as it did so. The wind caught the sound: distorting it so that for a moment it was almost human.

Like the cry of a child.

Only now it was more like a laugh; mocking her for her gullibility.

She stood, shivering with cold while realising she had a long walk home.

Better hurry, while I can still see where I'm going.

She moved away while the gull remained on the rock: its squawks echoing after her like taunts.

Twenty minutes later she was back at the beach. The stream trickled through the valley. She crossed the bridge and started up the cliff towards the coastal path; her already exhausted legs screaming in protest.

As she approached the top she slipped and fell, landing on her ankle. A bolt of pain shot through her and she let out a cry of frustration. At that moment in time she needed a sprained ankle like a hole in the head.

Standing up again she put pressure on it, prepared for more pain but feeling only a dull ache. Thanking her lucky stars she prepared to proceed.

And realised there was someone behind her.

Startled, she turned to face them.

But the valley was deserted, just as the crag had been.

It was tiredness. Her mind was playing tricks. The sooner she was soaking in a hot bath the better.

She finished scaling the cliff and continued along the path. The sky over the sea had a bluish tinge. In spite of her exhaustion she stopped to admire the sight.

And felt someone at her back; so close that if she stretched out her hand she would be able to touch them.

Again, she turned. Again no one was there.

Of course there isn't. You'd hear them if there was. You'd see them.

Unless they were hiding. Unless they didn't want to be seen.

Unless they couldn't be seen.

But that wasn't possible. They were all in the past, and none of them could ever find her now.

She reached the end of the path and turned inland. The sky became darker. That was something she had noticed on her previous evening walks. The further from the coast the blacker the night became. It had never bothered her before.

But it did now.

Even though she knew she was alone.

She started down the narrow path that led to the fields. Sprigs of gorse and bracken caught on her clothes, just as they always did.

But never before had they felt like fingers.

Instinctively she quickened her pace.

She entered the fields. In the distance she could see the lights of the town. Relief consumed her. She gave a quick whoop of delight.

And felt someone touch the back of her neck.

She froze; momentarily too frightened to move.

It's nothing. It's all in your head. There's no need to look back.

But still she did.

The field was empty. She stood knee deep in wet grass with the wind now as weak as a sigh brushing her face. Though the night was cold it felt warm. Hot even.

Like someone breathing on her cheek.

'No! I don't want this. Leave me alone. Leave me alone!'

She began to run, almost vaulting the stile that led into the final field.

And collided with someone.

She let out a yell.

So did he.

A hefty middle-aged man was staring at her with a concerned expression. 'Are you alright? Is someone chasing you?'

'Yes. They…I…'

She stopped, suddenly realising how ridiculous it would sound. How ridiculous it was. It was as if the collision had knocked some sense into her. A seagull had spooked her, and she had allowed her imagination to run riot.

'No one is chasing me. I was shouting at myself for being stupid. I went for a walk and got caught in the storm.'

'You're wet through, you poor girl. Do you want my coat?'

'No. I'm fine, thank you. I'm sorry. Did I hurt you?'

The man smiled. 'It would take more than a slip of a thing like you to injure me.'

In the distance a dog was barking. 'Samson!' shouted the man. 'Get over here.'

'Is that your dog? What breed is he?'

'God knows. We got him from a dog shelter. Samson, come here and say hello.'

Samson trotted towards her. She held out her hand to pet him.

He stopped, growled and backed away.

'That's odd,' said the man. 'He's usually very friendly.'

'I probably scared him with my screaming. I'll let you get on. Goodnight.'

'Goodnight.'

The man walked away, Samson hurrying after him. She watched them go, feeling embarrassed at her own stupidity.

She entered the town. A couple of teenagers stood on a street corner. Both noticed her bedraggled appearance and laughed. Normally she would have felt indignant. On this occasion she laughed too.

Chapter 3

It was long past midnight. She sat in bed reading a book, stretching out her legs beneath the sheets and feeling more relaxed than she had in months.

On returning home she had spent an hour soaking in a deep bath. After emerging from the water, her skin as wrinkled as a prune, she had found herself ravenous. Heading for the kitchen she had cooked a mound of pasta; convinced that she would never eat it all but managing to nonetheless.

Later she had sat in her living room, watching a black and white film. It was a romance; the sort Grace had always loved. Though not normally sentimental she had found herself crying at the end. As she wiped her eyes she remembered all the times she had teased her sister for her sentimentality. Again, she felt loss. Again, she felt alone. Only this time the pain was bearable; allowing her to believe for the first time that she really was starting to heal.

The room had a fireplace. Dan's fireguard stood in front of it. The next day she would buy some logs and enjoy the warmth of a proper fire.

In the corner of the room was a bookcase. On the top shelf was a collection of paperbacks the previous tenants had left. Among them was a history of smuggling in Cornwall. She had taken it up to bed, intending to read only a few pages but quickly becoming gripped by tales of ships being lured to their doom on the rocks. She wondered how many had been wrecked along her own stretch of coast and felt grateful to be living in a safer age.

Time passed. She began to yawn. Putting the book aside she turned off her bedside light, plunging the room into darkness. As sleep approached she realised she had left the window open. She knew she should fasten it but couldn't summon the energy. There was barely any wind; just enough to make the curtains sway. The storm had passed, and she told herself there would not be another. Slowly she allowed her eyes to close.

When she opened them again the church bell was ringing.

Was it signalling the hour? What time was it? How long had she been asleep?

The curtains were still swaying; sending beams of moonlight racing across the room. She found the sight hypnotic. Most barely made it half way across the floor before vanishing. Lying in her bed she made a game of it, trying to guess how far each would travel.

Then one came that was stronger than the rest. It surged across the room, hitting the far wall and her dressing table mirror. She turned her head, staring into the glass; watching the reflection of the curtains as the wind blew them open.

And saw something slide through the window.

It happened so quickly she barely had time to register it before the curtains closed and the room was yet again plunged into darkness.

She opened her mouth to scream but no sound came out. Terror paralysed her vocal chords. She was too frightened to move.

For what seemed like an eternity nothing happened. There was no movement. No sound. The room was perfectly still. Perhaps she had imagined it. Perhaps, as before, it was all in her head.

Two hands crept over the foot board. The fingers were long and thin. They moved like snakes, sliding along the wood before gripping it tightly. Still paralysed she watched as her intruder rose into view.

It was a woman; tall and slim with hair that fell over her face. Though her arms were bare she was wearing a long dress.

But it wasn't a dress. It looked more like a shroud.

Wind kept driving light into the room. The woman pulled the hair back from her face. She was young; no more than twenty. Her skin was pale; her features delicate and pretty. Except for the eyes which were huge and unblinking; two dark pools of energy that held Meg more securely than any chains. She stared into them, feeling their hunger as they sized up their prey.

The girl lent over the footboard, reaching out towards her. At last Meg managed to move; jerking backwards, cracking her skull on the headboard.

And waking up.

It was still night. The curtains were still swaying. But she was alone.

She sat up in bed, rubbing her sore head and trying to remember when she had last had so vivid a nightmare. After shutting the window, she lay back down and closed her eyes. As before sleep came quickly.

Only this time it was dreamless.

The next morning, she knocked on Dan's door. His head emerged from an upstairs window. 'Is everything OK?' he asked. 'You should have left for the gym twenty minutes ago.'

'How do you know when I go the gym?'

'You always leave at half past ten. I could set my watch by you.'

'What are you? Saltran's answer to Sherlock Holmes?'

'Hardly. I don't wear a deerstalker and I'm not hooked on crack.'

'Actually, it was morphine. Crack wasn't around then and even if it was Sherlock Holmes would have been too posh to smoke it.'

He laughed. 'You sound like Whitney Houston.'

'What?'

'Did you ever see that Whitney interview when she announced that she made too much money to ever smoke crack? I just had a vision of Sherlock Holmes sitting in his rooms at Baker Street, saying 'It's elementary, my dear Watson. Crack is whack.'

The image flashed in her mind. It made her smile.

'I wanted to thank you for the fireguard,' she told him. 'And for the drawing. I love it.'

'I'm glad. Come in and have a cup of tea.'

'I can't stop. I…'

'Let me guess. You're too posh for PG Tips.'

'No, it's not that…'

'Great. The door's open. Let yourself in and I'll put the kettle on…'

Ten minutes later she sat on a sagging sofa in his living room. Piles of papers and books lay on the floor; all in need of good dusting. She battled an urge to start tidying.

Dan appeared from the kitchen. 'Sorry about the mess.'

'It's not that bad.'

'Liar! You'll be telling me to get the hoover out soon.'

'You mean you actually own one?'

'Touché.' He handed her a mug then sat down beside her. 'So why aren't you at the gym?'

'I overdid it yesterday. I decided to give myself a day off.'

'So, what are your plans?'

'It's not really a day off. I've still got to work.'

He nodded.

'I can't take a break,' she told him. 'We're at a crucial stage on a deal.'

'It must be frightening for your firm. What if you got sick? The deal would collapse, wouldn't it?'

'Not necessarily.'

'You said no one could do the work but you.'

'I never said that.'

He grinned. 'So, in other words you could take a break if you really wanted.'

She sipped her tea, again feeling as if she had been played.

'How much of Cornwall have you seen?' he asked.

'Quite a lot.'

'Let me guess. Here, the surrounding coast and the inside of your gym. Wow. You should write a guide book.'

'I've been busy.'

'And you don't want the ruination of your firm on your conscience.'

'Very funny.'

'You'd like Truro. I'm going there tomorrow to deliver some furniture. Why not come with me?'

She shook her head.

'Go on. You might actually enjoy it.'

'Another time, maybe.'

He nodded. She sensed he was disappointed.

'I mean it,' she said. 'Another time it would be fun.'

His face lit up. The sight bothered her. She didn't want to give off the wrong signals. He was just a neighbour, after all. In London she had always kept them at a distance, but here in Saltran it wasn't so easy.

Seeking distraction, she looked about her. Paintings of the Cornish coast covered the walls. 'Did you do those?'

'Yes.'

'They're very good.'

'Try telling gallery owners that.'

'I will if you think it'll help. I know a couple in London. I could talk to them.'

Looking embarrassed he shook his head.

'Why not? It couldn't hurt. My firm buys a lot of art too and your paintings would look great in one of our conference rooms.'

Again, he shook his head.

'We'd pay well.'

'No.'

'Why not?'

'Because I slaved over them. That's why not.' Suddenly his tone was sharp. 'I want them to be appreciated, not just act as wallpaper.'

'They *would* be appreciated.'

'Yeah, right.'

'I'm sorry. I didn't mean to offend you.'

Silence. She finished her tea, wishing she had kept her mouth shut.

'I'm the one who should apologise,' he said eventually. 'I appreciate your offer. It's just…you know…'

'I envy you,' she said.

'Why?'

'Because you have talent.'

'So do you.'

'No, I don't. Anyone can do what I do. All it takes is attention to detail and a refusal to tolerate bullshit. What you do is special. It's unique. And it'll last.'

Again, his face lit up. This time the sight pleased her.

'My sister was an artist,' she told him. 'She illustrated children's books. She was really good. She got it from my mother. When we were little Mum used to write stories for us and illustrate them herself. She'd spend hours on them, just like you do on your paintings.'

'And what about you?' he asked.

'Sadly that's one talent that passed me by.'

He was staring. She sensed he didn't believe her.

She gestured to one of the paintings. 'That's my favourite beach. I go there all the time.'

'Do you like the painting?'

'I love it.'

He rose from the sofa and took it down from the wall. 'Then it's yours.'

She was taken aback. 'Dan, I can't accept this.'

'Yes, you can.'

'But you could sell it.'

'And have it hang in some conference room as wallpaper? No thanks. I'd rather it go somewhere where it'll be enjoyed.'

'You'll never get rich that way.'

'You think I do it to get rich? Maybe that's why you do your job but it's not why I do mine.'

'Then I'll take it. Thank you.' She was on the point of leaving but then stopped; realising there was something else she needed to say.

'And thank you for Saturday night. I'm sorry for my rudeness in leaving the way I did but for what it's worth it did me good to get out of the house.'

'What rudeness? I don't remember any.'

'Honestly?'

'Yes.'

'Wow. Just how drunk were you?'

He burst out laughing. She laughed too.

Then, his gift in her arms, she made for the door.

Five minutes later she stood in her hallway, staring at the painting. It showed the beach at dusk. The tide was drawing in; creeping over the boulders and displacing the gulls that looked indignant at losing their resting place. He had captured the scene perfectly. He really had. Smiling to herself she entered the living room.

Someone's been here

The thought came from nowhere. As startling as a scream. She stood quite still, looking about her, though uncertain as to what she was looking for.

The phone rang. It made her jump. She picked up the receiver to hear Debbie announce that all the documents on one of her deals needed to be redrafted by close of play. Her mind began to race. She had other deadlines. How could she juggle her time to meet them all?

And by the time the call was over the feeling was forgotten.

Eleven o'clock that night. Stifling a yawn she made her way upstairs. She was carrying a mug of coffee; her fourth of the evening. A final deadline had still to be met. Once that was done she would call it a night.

A moth fluttered about the landing, hovering over a wooden chair that stood in the corner, just to the right of her bedroom door. She stopped for a moment, watching it and wishing for the umpteenth time that she had a garage where she could store the chair. It was a heavy, ugly piece and her attempt to prettify it with a shiny new cushion had been a complete failure. Sighing to herself she entered her study.

Half an hour later she sat in front of her computer screen, typing an e-mail to her American clients. The coffee stood on her desk, next to an empty plate that had once been covered in biscuits. Her appetite was back with a vengeance. She wiped crumbs from her mouth, vowing that tomorrow her gym regime would resume.

From behind the far wall came the soft thud of rock music. Clearly Dan was working too. She had hung his painting above the fireplace in her living room. It looked good there. She would tell him so the next time they met.

After sending the e-mail she remained at her desk, sipping her coffee and making an action list for the following morning. When she had finished she switched off her computer and walked out onto the landing. The moth was now darting around inside the lampshade. She brushed at it with her hand, blinking at the brightness of the bulb. Eventually it flew out and headed back towards the chair. She followed it, hoping to drive it into her bedroom and out of a window.

And saw that the cushion on the chair was sagging.

She stood perfectly still, staring at it.

And felt a tingling start in her fingers.

It spread through her like an electric current, causing her body to shake. Her senses heightened. Smells she had never before registered suddenly overwhelmed her; the wood of the chair, the paint on her bedroom door and even the tiny specs of dust on the banister rail while the flapping of the moth's wings grew as loud as those of an eagle. Everything seemed more vivid. More real.

As if a long dormant part of her brain was starting to wake.

The moth continued to dance in front of her. Eventually it brushed against her face. Instinctively she closed her eyes.

And when she opened them again the cushion was full and round.

It had all been an illusion; brought on by stress and overwork. That was all she would allow it to be.

Because she was not that person anymore. She had killed that other self years ago and there was no force on earth that could ever bring her back to life.

But still she felt afraid.

Turning, she entered the bathroom. Inside its cabinet was a bottle of sleeping pills her doctor had prescribed in the aftermath of Grace's death. She had only used them for a few nights. They had always left her feeling groggy from sleep that had been too long and too deep, but always dreamless.

She tapped the bottle. A pill fell into her hand. She swallowed it down with a handful of water. After brushing her teeth, she marched across the landing and into her bedroom, shutting the door behind her and leaving the moth to dance alone.

The next morning she did indeed feel groggy. Groggy but better. In the cold light of day her fears of the previous night seemed laughable. Caffeine was a stimulant and she had simply drunk too much coffee. In future she would stick to tea.

After phoning Debbie to give her instructions for the morning and to hear the latest on Geoff Brooker's affair she collected her gym kit and made for her car. Dan's van was nowhere to be seen. Presumably he was already on his way to Truro.

All the regulars were at the gym; the male instructor too. He watched her as she made her way towards the running machine. Ignoring him, she focused all her energy on getting her routine back on track.

Late that afternoon she went to the supermarket in the Square to restock her supplies of tea and biscuits.

There were bags of logs by the door. After adding a box of firelighters to her basket she went to look at the paper rack. The girl, Lorna, was already there, flicking through a magazine.

'How was school today?' Meg asked her.

Lorna groaned.

Meg smiled. 'I remember that feeling.'

'No. It was OK, really. It's just…well, you know…'

'Sitting in the same classroom, day after day, staring at the same faces; most of which you've known for years and some of which you can't stand?'

Lorna laughed. 'Exactly.'

'University is more fun. You meet people from all sorts of backgrounds. There's just so much variety.'

'Which University did you go to?'

'Oxford.'

'Wow!' Lorna looked impressed. 'I want to go there, only

I'm probably not clever enough.'

'Of course, you are. People used to tell me I wasn't clever enough, but I stuck at it and showed them all.' Again, Meg smiled. 'Just like you will.'

'You're a lawyer, aren't you?'

'Yes.'

'I want to be a lawyer.'

'What sort?'

'What sorts are there?' Lorna asked then looked embarrassed. 'That's a stupid question.'

'No, it isn't. When I was your age I didn't know any of this stuff.'

Lorna began to pick her brains. She answered the questions as best she could; remembering her own lack of guidance as a teenager and feeling pleased to be of help.

Jed stood at the counter, watching Meg talk to Lorna. The sight made him happy. Word was already spreading through the town that its newest inhabitant was not the ice queen she appeared to be. Not that Jed had ever needed convincing, but he was glad that others were realising it too.

Eventually Lorna left the shop and Meg made her way over with her basket.

'So, you've been playing the careers adviser,' he observed.

'For what it's worth.'

'It's worth a lot. Lorna's a bright girl. She could do a lot with her life.'

'I'm sure she will; just as long as she doesn't smoke her way to lung cancer in the meantime.'

'She didn't ask you to buy cigarettes for her, did she?'

'No. And even if she had I would have refused; just like all the people who I asked to buy them for me when I was her age.'

He chuckled. 'So how goes your day?'

'Very well. I'll take a bag of logs too, please.'

'Are you going to light your fire?'

'It seems a shame not to. You can't beat an open fire.'

'That's what Dan always says.' He kept his expression neutral while studying her face. To his amusement he saw the faintest trace of a blush.

'Is it?' she asked casually.

'Yes. He's a nice bloke, Dan.'

'Well, he's a nice neighbour.' She reached for her purse. 'How much do I owe you?'

He told her. 'I gather you met Tom Mercer,' he said as he counted out her change.

'Who?'

'He was walking his dog in the fields on Sunday night.'

'Oh, I remember.' She gave a quick laugh. 'I think I spooked his dog.'

'He said you seemed pretty spooked yourself. He said you were running like you had the Devil behind you.'

'I was walking on the cliffs and got caught in the rain. I just wanted to get home.'

Jed didn't answer; just watched and waited.

'That's all it was,' she added quickly.

'It's a wild place. It can be dangerous out there at night.'

'Not if you're careful.'

'It's hard to be careful in the dark. There are things you can't see.'

'There's enough light. Besides, I have good eyesight.'

'I'm sure you do,' he said softly. 'I imagine it's very good indeed.'

He handed over her change. She left the shop, collecting the logs on the way. He watched her go; wondering just what it was that had spooked her so much.

Ten o'clock. After finishing work and having a bath Meg lit the fire. It took three attempts before the logs began to burn. Her mother had always made it look so easy. But practice made perfect and she would improve with time.

After switching off the overhead light she sat in the darkened room watching the flames grow higher. Outside the wind sent rain pounding against the window like dozens of tiny hands. She listened to the sound, feeling happy to be safe indoors, far away from the cliffs and all the things that couldn't be seen.

She stretched out on the carpet; warmth enveloping her like an embrace.

When she opened her eyes the fire was dying. She stared up at the ceiling, feeling too lazy to move. Briefly she considered staying put, but the floor was hard, and the room was growing cold.

After returning the fire guard to its proper place she made her way upstairs.The landing was in darkness. She reached out to turn on the light.

And heard a rocking sound coming from inside her study.

She froze; her hand suspended in mid-air. Dread slid up her spine like a finger. From behind the study door the rocking continued; its rhythm slow and deliberate. The sound was like a challenge; taunting her for her fear.

No! This is my home and I will not be intimidated.

She pushed open the door. The curtains had not been drawn. Moonlight flooded the room, illuminating the figure sitting at her desk; their long hair hanging over the back of the chair like a cloak.

This time there was no pushing the fear away. It burrowed through her skin like a tic.

The rocking stopped. Her visitor turned. The face was just as she remembered; as pale as chalk with eyes that turned her blood to ice.

For a moment they just stared at each other.

The girl began to rise...

Chapter 4

The ruins of Trevaron Mine stood on an outcrop of rock with a spectacular backdrop of chasm and cliffs. In the six months since he had discovered them, Dan had made countless attempts to capture their stark beauty.

Now, as he sat in his studio, smoking a cigarette and staring at the newly completed painting on his easel he realised that yet again he had failed.

His iPod was playing Guns n' Roses. He wondered if a different genre of music might stimulate his creativity. Not that it was an option. All he owned was heavy rock. He checked his watch. It was long past midnight. He rubbed his eyes, deciding it was time for bed.

And heard a scream.

Shock nearly made him jump out of his chair. The sound came from the other side of the wall, where Meg had her study.

What's happening? Is she being attacked?

As if by way of answer he heard her cry, 'Keep away from me!' Then, the sound of running, followed by a crash.

There was no point calling the police. Urgent action was needed. Jumping to his feet he began rifling through a drawer, searching for a set of keys to her house. Moments later he was through her front door, only to find her sprawled in a heap at the bottom of the stairs.

'Jesus Christ! Meg, are you OK? What happened? Where are they?'

She didn't answer; just stared up the stairs with a look of terror on her face. Reaching out he touched her shoulder. Screaming, she began to pummel at him with her fists.

'You don't exist! You don't exist!'

'Meg, it's me. Of course, I exist!'

Her eyes seemed to focus. 'Dan?'

'What's going on? I heard you scream. Is there someone here? Have they threatened you?'

Her eyes darted back up the stairs.

'Where are they?' he demanded.

She reached out and touched his cheek as if proving to herself that he was real.

'What's going on, Meg? I heard you scream. I thought you were being chased.'

'I'm awake.'

He saw relief flood her face. At last he understood.

'Were you having a nightmare? Is that what it was?'

She burst into tears. He put his arms around her and she rested her head against his chest. Her whole body was shaking. She seemed more like a frightened child than the confident woman he had come to know. For the first time in their brief acquaintance he felt needed. To his shame he enjoyed the sensation.

'It's OK,' he said gently. 'It's over now.'

She wiped her eyes. Putting his arm around her he helped her to her feet. 'Are you hurt?'

'No. Just a bit bruised.'

'Can you walk OK?'

She nodded. Gently he guided her into the living room and they sat together on the sofa. 'You were lucky,' he told her. 'A fall like that could have done some real damage.'

'I kept telling myself she wasn't there. I closed my eyes to make her go away but when I opened them again she was moving towards me and I couldn't let her touch me. I just couldn't…'

'Her?'

'The girl from Sunday night...'

He was confused. 'You know her?'

'She came through my window. I was…'

'What window? What are you talking about?'

He felt her stiffen. Suddenly she pushed him away.

'Who is she, Meg?'

'She's no one.' Her tone was business-like. 'I just had a bad dream.'

He gave a hollow laugh. 'It was a bit more than that.'

'No, it wasn't.'

'Meg, you were sleepwalking. You fell down the bloody stairs!'

'So, what if I was sleepwalking? Lots of people do it. I did it all the time as a child. My mother was always finding me wandering around the house.'

'But your mother's not here now. You live alone. Imagine if I hadn't come in when I did. Just think what you could have done to yourself.'

Her eyes narrowed. 'What *are* you doing here? How did you get in?'

'I've got a set of keys. I had them from when I helped refurbish this place.'

'The refurbishment's done. Why do you still have them now?'

'I don't know. I just forgot to give them back.'

'Well, that's one explanation.'

'You think I'm planning to rob you?' Fury consumed him. 'Let me tell you something Miss Superior City Bitch. I may be hard up, but I would *never* rob anyone, let alone someone I was starting to think of as a friend, and if you believe I would then you're bloody crazy.'

'I am not crazy!'

The words came out as a scream. He jumped. 'Whoa!'

'I'm not crazy! I'm not seeing things. There is nothing wrong with me. I just had a bad dream. Why are you trying to make out that it's more than that?'

His anger faded. 'I don't think you're crazy, Meg. I'm just worried about you. What happens if you have another dream like this one? You could end up in hospital or worse.'

'I won't.'

'How do you know?'

'I just do.'

'But, Meg…'

Her tone softened. 'Look, Dan, I'm sorry for what I said. I know you're no thief and I'm grateful for your help. But it was *just* a nightmare. The sort people have all the time. Please don't try and make it more than that.'

They stared at each other. Her eyes were guarded. He knew she was hiding something.

'I meant what I said, Meg. I think of you as a friend.'

'I think of you as one too.'

'Friends confide in each other.'

'Only when there's something to tell.'

'You can trust me.'

'Does that mean you won't tell anyone about tonight?'

He sighed.

'Does it?'

'If that's what you want.'

'It is.' She held out her hand. 'Now could I have the keys back please?'

'No. I'm keeping them. That's another thing about friends, Meg. They watch out for each other and for all I know I might need them again.'

He waited for the protest, but it never came.

'It's late,' she said eventually. 'You should go.'

'I can stay if you want.'

'No. It's over. All I want is my bed.'

He let himself out. The wind blasted his face. He stood in the close, feeling a mass of emotions sweep over him; anger, worry, hurt.

Knowing he would not be able to sleep he headed into the square, making for the cliffs, determined to walk all his energy away.

Meg remained where she was, listening to his footsteps fade into nothing while anxiety pricked at her like needles.

What if he's lying? What if he does tell someone?

Only there was nothing to tell. She had simply been lost in a world of dreams that had vanished on waking like dew dissolved by the morning sun.

She rubbed her arm. It felt sore but not broken. Just some bruises that would fade. As she thought of how lucky she had been a shiver ran through her and with it a wave of memories she had spent over twenty years trying to forget. In London it had been easy to keep them at bay. Her life had been so hectic there had never been room in her head for more than the events of the day.

But here in this place where there was space and time and the elements seemed to have a will of their own…

It's this place that's doing it to me.

It's this place I need to escape.

And she would.

But first she had to sleep.

And that meant going upstairs.

Hours passed. It was not until light began to creep through the curtains that she made her way to the bathroom and swallowed the pill that would keep her dreams at bay.

She was woken by her mobile. The clock on her bedside table read 10.39. She assumed it was Debbie calling for her morning instructions. Normally she would have answered it. This time she let it go to message.

She sat up in bed, thinking over the decision she had made the previous night; looking for reasons to change it but finding none. This place was bad for her. It was messing with her head. What she needed was the buzz and the certainty of her life in London.

Her leaving would not be without complications. She had committed to a six-month lease and would be liable for outstanding rent. Her flat had been rented out, so she would need to find somewhere else to live. Her boss, Henry would disapprove of her decision and try and talk her out of it. Yes, there would be complications, but none of them insurmountable.

When should I go?

She weighed up the practicalities. It would take hours to pack everything and arrange for those possessions that wouldn't fit in her car to be sent on afterwards. She would need to contact her firm and make sure they were ready for her return. She would need to find a serviced flat with private parking in a suitable location available immediately. Yes, there was a lot to do, but if she made a start now she could have everything sorted by the evening. That way she could be back in London by midnight and at her desk the following morning. The prospect made her feel warm inside.

An hour later, after showering and grabbing a slice of toast she was back in her bedroom, loading clothes into a suitcase while talking to Debbie on her mobile.

'So, I'll be in at my usual time,' she said.

'Are you sure about this? You're supposed to be resting.'

'I *am* rested. I feel great.' She rifled through her wardrobe, trying to decide which clothes to take.

'What's Henry going to say?'

'Nothing. You're not going to tell him.'

'But, Meg…'

'Please, Debbie. He'll only make a fuss.'

'But he needs to know. Claire Maddox is using your office.'

'*What?* Since when?'

'Last week. She says yours is bigger and she needs the space.'

'Why didn't you tell me?'

'There didn't seem any point.'

She swallowed down her irritation. It wasn't Debbie's fault and beside she needed her secretary onside. Outside the wind was strong. It pounded the windows, making them rattle. She sensed another storm on the way and hoped it would have passed by the time she set off on her night time drive.

'Look, Debbie, don't worry about that. I'll sort it out once I'm back. All I need you to do is reschedule my conference calls. Will you do that for me?'

'Yes, of course.'

'Thanks. You're a star. And rest assured I'm no longer the stressed-out bitch I was when I left.'

'You weren't that bad.'

She laughed. 'Pull the other one. It's got bells on.'

'I'm serious. Even at your worst you weren't a patch on Claire. Her secretary's quit so I'm working for her and she's vile!'

'Well, I'll sort that out too. The only person in our department allowed to be vile to you is me.'

Debbie giggled. 'I'm glad you're coming back.'

'So am I. Call me if there are any problems with the rescheduling, OK?'

'OK.'

She put another work suit into her case. Already it was so full she doubted she could close it. Her other cases were in a cupboard on the landing. She went to fetch one, smiling as she did so; excited at the prospect of returning to office life and all the arguments and power struggles that went with it.

And heard a chair rocking.

The sound was coming from her study; just as it had in her dream.

Fear began to close in. Angrily she tried to push it away. She was still overwrought from the previous night.

She crossed the upstairs hall and entered the study. Her chair was empty and still, just as she had known it would be.

But a sense of unease remained.

Fifteen minutes later all the clothes she would need were packed. Feeling thirsty she made her way downstairs for a cup of tea. Her study door was closed. Though she knew there was nothing to fear she still quickened her pace as she passed.

She stood in her kitchen, waiting for the kettle to boil and listening to the wind. It was really blowing now. The back door was rattling so hard it threatened to burst open. The lock was flimsy. She kept meaning to tell the landlord to have it changed. Now there was no need.

Dan's drawing was still on the fridge door. She stared at it, wondering whether she should tell him of her plans before deciding against. He would only start asking questions she didn't want to answer.

Briefly she felt guilty. It was no way to treat a friend. But their acquaintance had been so short could it really be classed a friendship? It was not as if they had anything in common. Hopefully the new tenants when they arrived would be more to his taste.

But she would take his painting. If she left it behind he might be hurt, and she didn't want that. He was a good man. Perhaps, if things had been different they really could have been friends. Good friends, even.

But it wasn't going to happen now.

Once the water was boiled she filled her mug then reached for a carton of milk. The wind continued to pound at the door, each gust like a foot trying to kick it in. Until suddenly the lock gave and the door flew open, accompanied by a blast of cold air. Shock made her drop the carton. Dollops of milk covered the floor like an archipelago of islands.

'Damn it!'

After securing the door she rummaged through a cupboard, searching for a cloth. When she had found one she prepared to wipe the floor clean.

Then she froze.

The archipelago had fused. Now there were only four islands; each shaped like a letter of the alphabet that spelled out a single word.

STAY

Her stomach turned over. She felt as if she was going to be sick. Rushing from the room she charged upstairs to the bathroom, only for the feeling to have passed by the time she had reached it. She stood with her back against the door, breathing slowly, listening to her heart pounding like a drum inside her chest.

It's this place. It's this bloody place!

For a moment she wanted to flee. Just grab her car keys and go.

Only she wouldn't. Pride would not allow it. She was an adult, not a child. She was not going to give into fear.

She walked onto the landing. The chair she had always hated was in front of her. The chair she had tried to brighten up with a cushion.

A cushion that was now sagging with an unseen weight.

No! It's not real. It's not real!

She shut her eyes, telling herself that when she opened them everything would appear normal. It had worked the previous time. It would work again now.

But the sag was still there, only not as deep. As if the weight had shifted. She reached out her hand to touch it.

The chair in her study resumed its rocking.

Panic overwhelmed her. No longer caring about her possessions she ran down the stairs, grabbed her handbag from the table in the hall and rushed outside.

She climbed into her car. Dan's van was blocking her exit route. She began to manoeuvre around it; scratching the paintwork in her desperation to get away while in her windscreen mirror she saw him emerge from his house and hurry towards her.

'Meg! What's the matter with you? Wait! I'll move the van.'

She ignored him. He hammered on her window, calling for her to stop. But at last she had room. Gunning the accelerator she drove away, leaving him standing there, calling for her to return.

Half past six. She sat in a service station cafeteria, drinking a cup of coffee.

She was tired. Her journey had been a difficult one. An accident just east of Exeter had resulted in two hours of immobility on the motorway. Now, as she approached the outskirts of London the rush hour was upon her and she didn't have the energy to keep fighting the traffic. Better to have a break and wait until the flow of vehicles had eased.

The cafeteria was filling fast. On a nearby table a couple stared wearily at each other while their two small children screamed alternately for ice cream and at each other. The mother noticed her gaze and mouthed an apology. She responded with a smile. They could have set off a dozen rockets and she wouldn't have minded. All that mattered was that she was nearly home.

Her mobile was in her pocket. She called a hotel in the West End. As she made a reservation she watched the mass of people come and go. Now all the tables were occupied, and it was only a matter of time before someone asked to share hers. As her stomach had started to rumble she found the prospect pleasing. Whoever joined her could guard her seat while she went to buy some food.

There were other things she had to buy. Toiletries were top

of the list. Fortunately the West End was full of late night chemists. If she delayed her return to the office until the following afternoon she could spend the morning buying a couple of changes of clothes, finding a temporary flat and arranging for her possessions to be sent on after her. After weighing up her options she realised the only person she could ask to do it was Dan. He had a set of keys after all. She remembered his refusing to hand them back and thanked God for small mercies.

She would need to have a story to tell him. Something about a friend in crisis who needed her help. Yes, that would do. She would call him tomorrow and work out all the details in the meantime.

People kept passing by; all looking for seats yet missing the three empty ones on her table. She hoped someone joined her soon. Her stomach was beginning to think that her throat had been cut.

Pulling out a pad from her bag she began to make an action list.

Jennifer Metcalfe was tired. She had been visiting a cousin in Kent and was now half way through the long drive back to her Oxfordshire home. As she walked along the service station buffet, selecting items for her evening meal, she wished for the umpteenth time that she didn't have to make the journey alone.

She caught her reflection in a pane of glass. A small, plump woman with neat white hair and owl-like glasses stared back at her with a weary expression that made her look every one of her seventy years. Had her husband, Giles, been with her, he would have told her that she didn't look any older than she had on their wedding day, but Giles had died three years earlier and though Jennifer still sensed his presence, it would never be as comforting as having the real person standing beside her.

But theirs had been a long and happy marriage and she could still take comfort from that.

As she stood in line in the cafeteria she listened to the conversation of the young couple in front. The two of them were trying to plan a holiday; the woman wanting to go somewhere that involved sightseeing while the man was firmly in favour of a relaxing fortnight by the beach.

Only it wasn't their spoken conversation that had grabbed her attention.

'...didn't mean anything. Just a one-night stand. That's all she...'

'...someone else. I'm sure there's someone else....'

'...so why can't I stop thinking about her...'

'...but he wouldn't cheat. He loves me. I know he does. He tells me often enough...'

'...I'm going to call her. It'll just be a drink. I don't want anything else...'

'...and I love him too. I have to believe in him. I have to...'

'...not unless she does...'

The waitress took their money and handed them their change. 'You win,' the man told the woman. 'We'll go on a cultural odyssey.'

'Are you sure?'

'Of course.'

'So, I guess you love me after all.'

'Sure I do. I tell you often enough, don't I?'

They took their trays and moved away. Jennifer paid for her own meal, feeling a mixture of concern and guilt. She hadn't wanted to eavesdrop, but sometimes thoughts could resonate more loudly than screams.

They were walking through the cafeteria, searching for seats, yet somehow missing two perfectly good ones that lay right before their eyes. And as she watched them Jennifer realised why.

Once she had her change she made her way towards the table herself. 'Do you mind if I sit here?' she asked the young woman who was making notes on a pad.

'No. Please do.'

She sat down. The woman gestured to her tray. 'That's smells good.'

'Doesn't it? Though after the journey I've had, stale bread and cheese would seem like manna from Heaven.'

The woman laughed. 'Tell me about it! My journey's been

terrible too.'

'Sorry to hear that. I'm Jennifer by the way.'

'And I'm Meg. Would you mind keeping my seat while I get some food?'

'Of course, we will.'

Meg made as if to rise. Then stopped. 'Why did you say that?'

'Say what?'

'You said 'we'.'

'Yes.'

'*We?*'

'You and your companion.'

'What companion?'

'The one sitting beside you.'

'What are you talking about? There's no one here except me.'

Jennifer didn't answer; just waited.

'She can't be here! I left her back in Cornwall.'

It came out as a wail. The surrounding tables fell silent as people turned to stare. Meg blushed, stared down at the table and quickly enough the sound of conversation resumed.

'So, you know her,' said Jennifer.

'Can you really see her?'

'Not in the way I see you. She's more like…' Jennifer paused, searching for the right word. 'Like an aura. Something made of light rather than flesh and blood.'

'What are you? Some kind of spiritualist?'

'Not anymore. I used to be, but I gave it up. I couldn't do it. Not like the others. Many of the ones I knew were fakes; just perceptive people with a talent for guessing what would make their clients happy. It's easier that way. When you really do have a gift it's harder because you can see the truth and often that's the last thing in the world people want to hear.' Jennifer paused. 'But I'm sure I don't need to tell you that.'

She saw Meg shiver. 'How did you know?'

'About you? Call it spiritual gaydar if you like. You just get a vibration from certain people. Sometimes it's as faint as a whisper.

And sometimes, as in your case, it's as loud as a bass drum.'

'Why is this happening to me?'

'Why do *you* think?'

'I don't know! I don't want it to. I don't want any of this.' Meg ran a hand through her hair. 'I'm not that person anymore. I killed her years ago.'

'You can't kill who you really are. You can try but it never works.' Jennifer sighed. 'I speak from personal experience.'

'But why would *you* want to do that? You seem…'

'Happy? No. But I've learned to live with it. It was the only thing I could do. It's like being tuned into a frequency that others can't hear and no matter how hard you try you can never truly switch it off.'

'I did. I managed it for twenty years. Eventually it seemed so unconnected with me that it was like a story I'd read about someone else. Only now…' Meg swallowed. 'And I just can't go through this again.'

'What happened to your mother?'

Meg's eyes widened. 'Why are you asking about her?'

'Because she's the reason you're so afraid. You think that if you surrender to your gift you'll hurt someone like you believe you hurt her.'

'I did hurt her. It's my fault she's dead.'

'How could it be? How could anyone hurt someone they love as much as you loved her?'

Meg seemed to crumble before her eyes. A look of utter helplessness flooded her face while her shoulders sagged as if the whole weight of the world was resting upon them. Lowering her head, she began to cry.

Her hand was on the table. Reaching out, Jennifer took it and gave it a squeeze. As she did so a bolt of energy surged through her; like an electric current so strong it made her whole body vibrate. Up to that moment she had believed she was dealing with an equal. Now she realised that the troubled young woman who faced her had a gift that was infinitely more powerful than her own.

Thoughts bombarded her. She tried to make sense of them, but their sheer number was overwhelming. All she could really register was fear and guilt.

And that Meg's mother was the key to it all.

'What happened to your mother?' she asked softly.

'I can't talk about it. I'm sorry. I just can't.'

'It's alright. You don't need to if you don't want to. I just hate seeing you in so much pain. You don't deserve it.'

'How do you know what I deserve?'

'Because there's real good in you. I can feel it.'

'Yes, I'm a good person; just like my father and stepmother. That's what my Headmistress told me.' Meg gave a hollow laugh. 'She didn't know me any better than you do.'

'But your mother did. She knew you better than anyone. Did she think your gift was bad? Did she think it was just a tool to hurt people?'

Again, Meg swallowed. 'Don't...'

'She didn't, did she? She saw you for what you are and was proud of you for it. Or are you telling me that your mother was such a stupid woman that she didn't even know her own daughter?'

Meg's eyes began to flash. 'Don't talk about her like that.'

'Why not? I'm only telling you what you already believe.'

'Who the hell do you think you are? You didn't know my mother. You didn't have that privilege. There was nothing stupid about her and she was worth ten of you.'

Jennifer smiled. 'Exactly.'

Silence. The two of them stared at each other

'If she was proud of you, Meg, then it was because she had good reason. And if she was proud of you then why can't you be proud of yourself?'

'Because...' Meg stopped, shaking her head. 'You wouldn't understand.'

'But I do. I know how frightening it can be to have a gift that you haven't asked for; that most people don't understand and that more often than not you don't even understand yourself. Nobody wants to feel different, especially not a child.'

Meg's eyes softened. 'I feel like a freak.'

'You're not a freak. That's the last thing you are. Everyone has a little of it. Why do you think your table remained empty so long? People sense there's someone with you even though they don't realise they're doing it. I doubt there's a single person in this room who hasn't at some point had an experience they couldn't rationally explain. You and I just have more of it than most. That's all.'

'I'm going back to London. That's where I'm from. I thought…'

'That you could leave the girl behind?' Jennifer shook her head. 'The dead are faster than the living. When they choose us it's useless to run. She'll find you wherever you go.'

'Why has she chosen me?'

'Because you can hear her. Who knows how many years she's been searching for someone who can?'

'I used to hear my mother after she died. Only I wouldn't listen. I couldn't bring myself to. And now I never hear her at all. I don't hear either of them.'

'Them?'

Meg didn't answer.

'Perhaps they don't want you to hear them. Perhaps they think it would upset you too much if you did. Or perhaps they realise that you're not yet ready to listen.'

'I'm not ready to listen to this girl either. I never will be. Why doesn't *she* realise that?'

'Perhaps because her need for you to do so is just too great.'

'What does she want?'

'I don't know.'

'She scares me.'

'That's because you don't know her.'

'I don't want to know her.'

'But she wants to know you.'

'So, what should I do?'

'Stop running. Listen to what it is she's trying to communicate. I can't tell you what that is but one thing I can tell you is I don't think she means you any harm.'

'It doesn't seem that way.'

'Of course, it doesn't. The unknown is always frightening.

Only by facing it can you hope to conquer that fear.'

'I can't.'

'Then keep running.'

'I just want my life back.'

'Then you have to listen. It's the only way. Open yourself up to her. Give of yourself. That's what she wants. And that's what your mother would want too.'

Again, Meg shook her head.

'It is, Meg. In your heart you know I'm right.'

'But what if I get it wrong? When I was a child it seemed that when I tried to help people I usually made things worse, not better.'

'But you're not a child now. For years you've been trying to escape from who you really are. Maybe it's time to just accept it. Embrace it even. Perhaps, by doing that, you can finally start to forgive yourself. Maybe you may even come to realise what I know already.'

'And what is that?'

'That you have nothing to forgive yourself for.'

Another silence. Meg stared down at the table. Beside her the aura seemed to lose its shape; expanding to envelop Meg like a transparent cloud.

What is it you need? What is it you think Meg can give you? If I could help you I would but I can't. My gift doesn't work like that. It isn't strong enough. Only hers is.

'I must go,' said Meg eventually.

'Where?'

'Back to Cornwall. What other choice do I have?'

Jennifer reached inside her purse, pulled out a piece of paper and wrote down her contact details. 'Call me whenever you need to talk; anytime, day or night. I want to help you, Meg. I really do.'

Meg put the paper in her pocket, made as if to rise and then stopped. 'Do you really think…you know…?'

'Yes. I really do think that you have nothing to forgive yourself for. I know you don't believe me. But one day you will.'

'Thank you.'

Meg left the café, the aura drifting after her like a mischievous shadow. Jennifer remained where she was, praying that she would be proved right.

It was after midnight when Dan heard an engine revving in the Close. Looking out of his window he saw Meg's BMW. Relief swept over him. He made his way outside. She was climbing out of the car, her face grey with tiredness.

'I'm sorry,' she said. 'Did I disturb you?'

'No.'

She gestured to the scratches on his van. 'I'm sorry about that too. I'll pay for the repairs. Just let me know how much.'

'Who cares about that? I was worried. You seemed in such a state.'

She gave a weak smile. 'You could say that.'

'Do you want to talk about it? I'm not trying to pry. I know it's none of my business.' He hesitated. 'It's just that…'

'I look like I could use a friend?'

'Yes.'

'I could.' It was her turn to hesitate. 'Assuming I can call you one?'

'What do you think?'

'That it's late.'

'I've always been a night owl. There's a bottle of wine in the fridge just begging to be opened.'

She locked the car door and followed him inside.

Chapter 5

They sat together on his sofa. He sipped his wine, waiting patiently for her to speak. Eventually she did.

'Do you remember how angry I became last night when you said I was crazy?'

'I didn't mean it. I don't think…'

'I know you don't. I'm talking about my anger. When I was at school the other kids used to call me crazy. I hated it. You saying that brought it all back.'

'Why did they call you that?'

'Because of the things I said.'

'Like what? That England will one day win another World Cup? That would be pretty crazy. They'd probably lock you up for that.'

'Why do you make light of everything?'

He felt embarrassed. 'I'm sorry. I wasn't being flippant…'

'I didn't mean it as a criticism. I just wondered who you got the habit from. Was it one of your parents?'

'No. It was my maternal grandfather. He could never resist cracking a joke, even at the most serious of moments. My mother used to get furious at him.'

'So, your grandfather was a comedian?'

He nodded, smiling at the memory.

'My grandmother was psychic.'

She fell silent; rolling the wine around in her glass. He held his questions back, wanting to take things at her pace.

'She was my mother's mother. I never knew her. She died before I was born. But I always felt like I did. My mother talked about her all the time; at first because she missed her but later because she saw just how like her I was.'

He remembered the things she had said the previous night that had made no sensc. Now, suddenly they did.

She was studying his face; presumably searching for any trace of scorn.

'Go on,' he said gently.

She told him about the evening when she had gone walking on the cliffs and been caught in a storm; the sense of being followed on the way home and everything that had happened since. She also told him about her childhood in Wickenham; about the woman in the café and the boy with unruly red hair who only she could see. She told him about her schooldays; about the taunts and accusations. About the times she had tried to warn people, only for her words to be ignored. She told him about her mother's death and her belief that it was a punishment. 'That's why I had to shut it down. I had to stop it before I hurt anyone else. That's what I believed.'

'And you still believe it?'

She didn't answer. There was no need.

'It wasn't your fault, Meg. How could it be? You were only a kid. You just misinterpreted what your gift was telling you.'

'So, it *was* my fault.'

'No! You didn't *make* it happen.'

'But I didn't stop it either.'

'How could you? I'm no expert on the paranormal but one thing I do know is that it's not an exact science. A gift like yours doesn't come with instructions. You just get what you're given. The important thing is how you use it.'

'And I messed up.'

He realised what he'd said and gave himself a metaphorical slap. 'You did nothing wrong, Meg. That's what you need to realise. Think of the old woman who lost her twin. You showed compassion for her. Isn't it time you showed some for yourself?'

Again, she didn't answer.

'If your mother was here she'd tell you the same.'

'How do you know? Are you psychic too?'

'I don't need to be psychic to know that.'

'Do you think I'm crazy?'

'No. There are more things in heaven and earth, Horatio, than are dreamed of in our philosophy.'

She looked thoughtful. 'That's Hamlet, isn't it?'

'Yes. We studied it in school. It's about the only thing from school I still remember. That quote just struck a chord with me. I believe it and I believe you too.'

'Thanks.'

'You don't need to thank me.'

'Yes, I do.'

Her glass was empty. He refilled it. 'What happened?' he asked. 'When you went to live with your father?'

'We only stayed six months. It didn't work out. After that we had a year in a children's home before being fostered by a middle-aged couple called Davis who lived in Pinner.'

'What sort of people were they?'

'My sister liked them.'

'Didn't you?'

She stared down at her hands.

'What was wrong with them?'

'Nothing. They were decent people. It's just that after what happened…' She hesitated. 'I had Grace to look after. However nice people seemed it was safer to keep them at a distance. That way they could never take me by surprise.'

'You really loved Grace, didn't you?'

'Of course. She was my little sister. After Mum died I was all she had.'

'And she was all you had.'

'Yes.'

'So why don't you talk about her? You never do. Not really. I understand how much her loss must hurt. But sometimes it seems that the only way you know how to deal with it is by pretending she never existed. And that never works.'

'Don't…' she began.

'But it's true. It didn't work with your gift. It won't work with Grace either. You can talk to me about her. You can talk as much as you want. It may help you start to feel better. If you…'

He saw her swallow. 'Please…'

'I'm sorry. I won't mention it again. I'm just…' He stopped, reaching for the right words.

'Trying to be a friend,' she said, finishing the sentence for him.

'Yes.'

'Thank you, Dan. I'm lucky to have a friend like you.'

'Ditto.'

'Liar.'

'I mean it. You may be a control freak but at least you're not teetotal.'

Slowly her face broke into a smile. He smiled too; happy she was there. Happy they were friends. Happy to feel needed.

And she *did* need him. In his head he her saw sprawled at the bottom of her stairs. What if he hadn't been there? What if the woman in the service station was wrong? What if this spirit did mean her harm? What if he couldn't protect her?

'It'll be OK,' he told her. 'We'll work this thing out together.' As he spoke he realised he was not so much trying to convince her as himself.

It was dawn by the time Meg entered her house.

'You've got what you wanted,' she whispered. 'I'm back.'

She stood in the hallway, waiting to hear something; to sense something. But there was nothing except a sour, rank odour coming from the kitchen. The milk was still splattered across the floor. The shapes no longer spelled out a word. Perhaps they never had. Perhaps, in spite of everything, it really was all in her head.

Perhaps the earth was flat, and the moon was made of cheese.

As she wiped it away she remembered what Jennifer had said about the dead being faster than the living. 'If you really are faster,' she said aloud, 'you might have cleaned this up before I got back.'

Again, she waited to sense something, but time passed and there was only tiredness and the longing for the comfort of a warm bed.

She went upstairs to the bathroom and took her pill, despising herself for her cowardice but knowing that more than anything she needed undisturbed rest.

But before she escaped into it there was one thing she wanted to do.

In the bottom drawer of her study desk, buried under a pile of papers, was an old biscuit tin. She opened it and took out a framed photograph of a young woman sitting on a wall; a pretty woman with thick, dark hair and a smile that could light up a room. A woman she had never known but who had influenced her life from the day she was born.

Her grandmother.

For years she had hidden it away. Often she had planned to throw it out yet never could. This woman had once been the centre of her mother's world, just as her mother had once been the centre of hers.

And now as she looked at the smiling face she was glad she had it still.

'If you were any sort of Grandma you'd get off that wall and help me,' she told the woman in the photograph. 'This is your fault after all. The next time you give me a gift, why not make it something simple like a handbag?'

Her limbs ached. She crossed the landing to her bedroom. Suitcases covered the bed. She moved them away, then, still in her clothes, climbed between the sheets and fell instantly asleep.

As on the previous day she was woken by her mobile buzzing on the bedside table. It was Debbie, wanting to know what time she would arrive at the Office.

'I'm not coming in.' She struggled to sound clear headed. 'I was about to call you. I've decided to stay in Cornwall. I'm…um…not as rested as I thought.'

'Oh.'

It was only a word, but Meg could hear the disappointment behind it and was touched. 'I'm sorry to mess you about, Debbie, but I haven't forgotten what you said about Claire Maddox. I'll get Henry to assign her a new secretary. And don't worry. Claire won't know you've been complaining about her.'

'Thanks, Meg. I appreciate that.'

'It's the least I can do. And remember, if anyone else gives you grief I'm only a phone call away.' As she spoke she went to draw the curtains, almost falling over a suitcase in the process. Outside the sun was shining. It promised to be a lovely day, though as she knew from experience here one could never take the elements for granted.

She found paper and pen. 'Can you give me a list of my calls?'

Debbie did so. As she noted them down her eyes kept wandering towards the door that led onto the landing.

'Meg, are you still there?'

'Yes.' She focused on the task in hand.

When the call was over she walked onto the landing and stood at the top of the stairs. The previous day she had fled down them from whomever it was that had invaded her home. Now she was back and ready to face them.

'Come on,' she whispered. 'What are you waiting for?'

Still there was nothing. The house was silent.

Was it over? Could it be over?

Or was her visitor just sleeping?

Do spirits sleep? Is that what she's doing? Whoever she is. Whatever she is.

'I'm here! I'm ready! What is it you want from me?'

The silence persisted; as heavy as lead.

Early that afternoon Dan knocked on her door. 'I would have come earlier, he said, 'but I didn't want to risk disturbing you. You looked like you needed your rest.'

'I did. God bless the tablets. No dreams at all.'

'Has anything happened?'

'Not yet which is a blessing. I've got so much work to do.'

His eyes widened. 'You're *still* working?'

'I have to. It's not going to do itself.'

'Don't you think that in the circumstances work should take a back seat?'

'No. Apart from your lousy jokes it's the only thing keeping me sane.'

'My jokes are not lousy.'

'And rain isn't wet.'

He laughed. She did too.

'Do you want to come in for a coffee?' she asked. 'I could use a break.'

'I can't. I came to tell you I'm off to Truro. A friend of mine is doing up a house and needs help with the wiring.'

She nodded.

'He wants me to stay over but I don't like to leave you. What if…'

'Don't worry. I'll be fine.'

'You've got my number. Call if you need me. Call even if you don't just to let me know you're OK.'

'I will.'

He didn't look convinced. Reaching out her hand she gave his arm an affectionate rub. 'That's a promise.'

'Good.'

Five minutes later she was back in her study, staring at a document on her computer screen and sipping a glass of wine.

As she scrolled through the pages she found herself remembering a former boss who had always frowned on afternoon drinking as the sign of an undisciplined mind. She had agreed with him then. She still agreed with him now.

But she needed something to steady her nerves.

She wondered what his reaction would have been to the story she had told Dan. Would he have understood the way Dan had?

She wanted to believe it but knew in her heart that he wouldn't.

Not that she could blame him. The Meg Parker he had known would never have admitted that such things were possible, not even to herself.

She missed that girl; hoped she wasn't lost for ever.

Time passed. She continued to work.

And wait.

'Still nothing?' Dan asked.

'Still nothing.'

It was ten o'clock at night. She sat in her living room, talking to him on the phone. 'How goes the wiring?' she asked. 'Electrocuted anyone yet?'

'Only three people and they won't sue.'

'Did you get that in writing?'

'Sadly, no. The force of the explosion blew their hands off.'

She burst out laughing. 'That's bad!'

'Well I know how much you depend on my lousy jokes. How goes your oh so important work?'

'It *is* important.'

'You don't have to convince me. If it wasn't for you our nation's economy would collapse.'

'Oh, bugger off!'

'Charming! I don't mind you being crazy but one thing I won't tolerate is a potty mouth.'

'I'm very bloody sorry.'

'I'm very bloody glad to hear it.'

'Work is going well,' she told him. 'I've got a lot done.'

She heard him sigh.

'I can't make it happen, Dan. I'm here. I'm ready. What else can I do?'

He began to describe his day. As she listened she thought of the mountain of unfinished work on her desk. All of it was urgent. If only she could concentrate. But tomorrow would be different. She would tackle it then.

The conversation over, she turned on the television. A weather report warned that Yorkshire would have a night of storms. In Saltran there was no wind at all. Hours earlier she had walked to the supermarket through air so still it felt like a cloud. Perhaps, like her visitor, the elements themselves were sleeping.

She flicked through the channels, eventually selecting a crime drama. But her mind kept wandering and when the final credits rolled she could remember nothing of what she had watched.

The following afternoon she was back in her study. The window was open. She heard a lorry drive into the square and Brian from The Corsair call out a greeting. The pubs always received their deliveries at this time of day. Soon she would hear the bus bringing Lorna and the other local children home from school, followed by the trickle of commuter traffic from Penzance and other towns in the area. In Saltran the routine was as predictable as the setting of the sun.

It was her own routine that was falling apart.

The pile of work was as high as it had been the previous night. Hours of effort had yielded no progress. How could it when her attention was always elsewhere?

An e-mail arrived from a client, describing a problem that threatened to scupper one of her deals. It was the sort of crisis she had always thrived on; adrenaline flooding her veins as she prepared for battle. She waited for the feeling now, but it never came.

And in its absence came the realisation of what she had to do.

She phoned Henry and told him he had been correct all along. Work was too much for her. What she needed was a complete break. He was delighted, just as she had known he would be. 'You're doing the right thing, Meg. You really are.'

'I'm sorry to be leaving you in the lurch.'

'Actually, it's a blessing. Half the department is twiddling its thumbs. Your case load will keep them busy until things pick up....'

Later, after she had phoned Debbie to explain the situation and repeat her assurance that she was still available to put the likes of Claire Maddox in their place, she began to brief those of her colleagues who were taking over her deals. Claire was one of them. 'You mustn't worry about a thing,' Claire informed her in a sugared tone. 'I'll do everything I can to keep the clients happy in your absence.'

Yeah, right. You'll try and poach them every chance you get. Not that you'll succeed. Once I'm back in London I'll reclaim all that's mine.

And she would. She knew she would.

Whenever that might be.

She continued making the necessary arrangements, reflecting on the irony that her mind was clear, and she felt herself again just at the moment she relinquished the one activity that had always defined her.

By the time she had finished it was early evening. Dan, now returned from Truro, stood in her study, watching her send a last e-mail.

'I can't believe you're doing this,' he told her.

'Neither can I.'

'How do you feel?'

'Bereft.'

He rolled his eyes.

'It's not just a job, Dan. For me it's a way of life.'

'It's your way of avoiding life if you ask me.'

'Actually, I didn't, but I'm grateful for your insight on my damaged psyche.'

'The only damage you're suffering is an excess of sobriety, but a trip to the pub will sort that out.'

She opened her mouth to tell him she was tired and he should go without her. But if he left then she would be alone and suddenly that was the last thing in the world she wanted.

So, she agreed.

They sat at the table by the fire. She picked up a menu. 'Are we eating?'

'That depends. Are you paying?'

'I'm glad to see chivalry's not dead.'

'No. It's just having a bit of a nap.' He paused. 'I'm joking by the way.'

'I know, but I will pay. You did last time and besides, I'm glad you're here.'

His face lit up. She remembered the first time they had sat

together beside the fire. Then he had been nothing but her bumptious next-door neighbour. Now he was someone she had come to value; a true friend.

The pub was nearly empty. The only other occupants were a couple of tourists who sat with their arms around each other, studying guidebooks. She watched them for a moment then noticed Dan doing the same.

'Why don't you have a girlfriend?' she asked. 'It seems a waste, you being single.'

'Is that a compliment?'

'I guess so. You're quite endearing in an irritating sort of way.'

'I'm touched.'

'And I'm serious. Why don't you?'

'I could ask you the same question.'

'Why would I want a girlfriend? I thought we'd established I'm not a lesbian.'

He laughed.

'Anyway,' she continued, 'I asked first.'

He downed a mouthful of beer. 'At first all my girlfriends love my bohemian lifestyle. They find it romantic. But then I start getting lectures on the importance of a steady income and career prospects. If someone wants to change you then it isn't really love or at least that's what I think.'

His words struck a chord. 'I know what that's like. All the guys I've ever dated have wanted to change me. They couldn't accept me for who I was.'

'Do you mean they wanted you to work less?'

She nodded.

'I'm sorry for what I said about your job. I didn't mean to sound flippant. I know how important it is to you.'

She shook her head. 'It isn't the job itself that's important. It's the fact that it keeps me busy. When you have clients screaming at you and dozens of deadlines to meet you don't have time to think of anything else.'

'And now you do.'

Again, she nodded.

'Are you scared?'

'Yes. And not just for the reason you think. All my adult life I've been Meg Parker the high-powered lawyer. I don't know how to be anyone else.'

'But you'll figure it out. Who knows; you might even like the new you better.'

'I doubt it.'

'How can you say that? You don't know her yet.'

'You sound like Jennifer. She said I'm only scared of the girl because I don't know her. And that's the irony. It's the prospect of getting to know her that scares me most of all.'

'People wanted to know you as a child. People like her. You weren't scared then.'

'Only because I was too dumb not to be.'

Remember,' he told her, 'you're not alone.'

She smiled, grateful for his words but finding no comfort in them. He was not the one who had been chosen. He still had the option of escape.

Picking up a menu she scanned its contents, focusing all her attention on it just as if it were one of her legal documents so that just for a moment there was no room in her head for anything else.

Old habits die hard.

After eating they played pool. As she was a novice he taught her the rules then spent the whole game laughing as she missed every pot. The pub became busier and an elderly couple came to watch. Their names were Ron and Moira Drake. Ron had worked at the nearby Geevor Tin mine until it had closed twenty years earlier. 'It was the last active mine in this area,' he said wistfully. Now it was a tourist attraction and Ron led tours of the underground tunnels. 'You should come and see them,' he suggested. 'Unless you're claustrophobic, that is.'

She shook her head. It wasn't small spaces she feared.

When the game was finished Ron told her about the history of mining in the area. 'You wouldn't believe how deep some of the tunnels go. It wasn't a problem in my day. We had lifts but back in the nineteenth century it could take a miner two hours climbing ladders to reach the surface. Some of the tunnels go right out under the sea and on stormy days you can hear the boulders rolling on the sea bed overhead.'

She sat and listened, asking questions; enjoying the conversation yet aware that she was also delaying the moment when she would have to go home.

It was closing time when they finally left. She walked with Dan across the Square towards the Close. The wind was back; sweeping in from the sea. She breathed it in, tasting the faintest trace of salt; imagining it racing across the cliffs towards her and wondering what it brought in its wake.

They reached her door. 'I could stay,' Dan suggested. 'I could sleep on the couch. That way I'll be on hand if you need me.'

She longed to agree, but instinct told her that whatever the night might bring she had to face it alone. 'I'll be OK,' she told him. 'Besides, you're only next door.' It sounded more like a continent than a few feet separated by a wall.

She entered the house and stood in the hall. For a moment she felt nothing. For a moment she dared to believe that it had not started up again.

And then it began; the tingling in her fingers that spread rapidly through her whole body. Her senses heightened. Suddenly the light in the hall bulb was blinding. A multitude of smells assaulted her nostrils while the beating of her heart within her chest became as loud as a drum. Her eyes drifted up towards the landing and the door to her study. There was no rocking sound. There was nothing except the dreadful certainty that she was not alone.

Where are you? Are you behind me? Why can't I see you? Is it because I'm older? Is it because I'm frightened? Is it because I've spent so long blocking my gift that the only way you can truly reach me is in my dreams?

Slowly, on legs that felt as weak as matchsticks she made her way upstairs. As she reached the landing she looked at the chair and saw the cushion plump and full.

She entered the bathroom and turned on the tap. Hot water sent clouds of steam to cover the surface of the mirror. She watched it flow, wanting to run but knowing it was futile. Wherever she went the girl would find her, just as her mother had done all those years ago.

But she had blocked her mother. She had kept on and on doing it until eventually her mother had visited her no more.

And if I could do it then, I can do it now.

Because I cannot do this! I cannot be that person again. She only ever made things worse and so will I.

'I'm sorry,' she whispered to the air, 'but it really is better this way.'

She took her sleeping tablets from the bathroom cabinet and opened the bottle, preparing to shake a tablet out into her hand. As she did so she glanced at the mirror.

And saw a word written in the condensation.

NO

Shock made her drop the bottle. It smashed on the sink. Water seized the pills and dragged them down the drain. She tried to grab them but failed to save a single one. Suddenly her fear was gone, replaced by anger.

'Why does it have to be me? I don't want to know you. All I've ever wanted is for you and your kind to leave me alone.'

Again, she looked in the mirror. The word had vanished; covered by fresh steam.

She went to her study. Her grandmother's photograph stood on the desk. She carried it into her bedroom and put in on the bedside table. Once she had climbed into bed and turned off the light she picked it up again, wrapping her arms around it, pressing it against her chest as if it were a charm to ward off evil.

The wind was still high. She lay in the darkness of the empty room, listening to its roar, holding the photograph ever tighter as her eyes began to close...

When she opened them again the room was no longer empty. Her visitor stood motionless at the foot of her bed.

She sat up, the photograph still pressed against her chest. 'You've won,' she said. 'I'm here and I'm listening.'

The visitor leaned across the bed, holding out her hand. The eyes were just as hungry as she remembered. She stared into them. 'You're making a mistake,' she whispered. 'Whatever it is you want I'm not the one to tell it to. I'll only hurt you like I hurt my mother and the others. If you're in pain already then do you really want me to make it worse?'

No answer. The hand remained outstretched. Knowing she had no choice she reached out and took it.

Chapter 6

There was a light in her eyes so bright she couldn't see. At first, she thought it was a torch. Then, as her vision cleared, she saw it was the sun.

She was standing on a cliff overlooking the sea. The water was calm, the sky perfect blue and the sun a brilliant yellow orb at its centre.

Two girls stood beside her. Each was about nine and wearing blue cotton dresses. The one nearest to her was jumping up and down and waving to a ship on the water.

'Look, Kat!' she shouted to her companion.

'Look at what, Ellie?' asked the other.

'Look at the ship.'

'Who are you?' Meg asked the girl called Ellie.

Ellie ignored her. Meg reached out to touch her shoulder, only for her hand to pass straight through it and out the other side. It was like trying to grasp warm air.

She screamed. Both girls appeared oblivious. 'We'll be on a ship soon,' Ellie told Kat. 'You, me, Pa and Uncle Matt. We're going to America and we're going to be rich.'

'Rich?'

'Yes. Like Uncle John and Aunty Clara. We're going to have a big house like them. Bigger even. That's what Pa says.'

Meg studied the girls. They were the same height and had the same thick blonde hair, pale green eyes, delicate features and noses that turned up just a little at the end.

They're twins. Identical twins.

But as she looked more closely she saw they were not quite identical. The girl called Ellie had a face alive with character and eyes that sparkled with energy. Kat's eyes were dull and her expression blank. She reminded Meg of a boy who had spent a term in her class before leaving for a special school: a boy the other children had christened 'retard.'

'Will Ma be in America?' Kat asked.

'No.' Ellie put her arm around her sister. 'Ma's in Heaven.'

Kat sighed. 'I miss Ma.'

Ellie kissed her cheek. 'I know you do but remember what I told you. You've got me, and you always will. I'll look after you, just like she did.'

Meg felt something in her hand. Looking down she saw it was her grandmother's photograph. She also saw that she was still in her pyjamas. For a moment she felt exposed. Then she realised it didn't matter. Neither girl could see her.

Her feet were bare. The ground on which she stood was rough and covered in stones, but she could not feel them, just as she could not feel the heat of the sun or the breeze that blew around her. It was like being a ghost; trapped in a world that appeared real but in which she had no place.

She looked about her, searching for bearings. To her left was a path that led down into a valley. A stream ran through it towards a beach covered in boulders that looked like dinosaur eggs, many with gulls perched upon them.

It's my beach!

Turning, she stared over the fields, looking for Saltran. It was there, only it couldn't be. Hills she knew to be bare were now covered in houses. It looked twice the size. A different place completely.

And it was not the only thing that was different.

To her right, the stretch of coast she knew as an empty place dotted with ruins was now full of life. On an outcrop of rock, next to a chasm topped with stones that looked like the statues on Easter Island, was a working mine. The chimneys of engine houses pumped smoke into the air. Tracks ran between them, each with trolleys full of rubble, pulled by horses spurred on by men, all wearing clothes that were stained a bright orange colour. The sea around the mine was stained too. It had a reddish tinge as if the water itself was bleeding.

There were voices behind her. Men of all ages made their way through the valley. As they reached the path some called out greetings to the girls. Ellie waved to them, pulling Kat clear of their route. Meg tried to stay clear too only it wasn't so easy when no one could see where she stood. She shut her eyes, feeling brief rushes of warm air as they passed through her. None sensed her presence except a man of about sixty with a weather-beaten face who stopped and looked about him.

'Alright, Stan?' asked one of his companions.

He shook his head. 'Som'at just walked on my grave.'

His companions laughed. 'What grave, you daft bugger? You'll outlive us all.'

Laughing too he resumed his journey.

The men kept coming. Some were barely in their teens. One made a face at Kat as he passed. 'Hey, Kat,' he cried, 'ain't they put you in the asylum yet?'

'You shut your mouth!' Ellie shouted. 'She ain't never goin' there, and if she does you'll be in Hell long before.'

He raised his fist to her. She threw a stone at him, hitting him square on the nose. Crying out in pain he made a move towards her, but an older man grabbed his shoulder, told him he'd got what he deserved and pulled him away.

The men continued on towards the mine, stopping to exchange words with others who were leaving it. From somewhere far away a whistle sounded. Clearly it was the end of a shift.

'Can you see 'im?' Ellie asked Kat. 'Can you see Pa?'

Kat shook her head.

'There he is! He's waving at us. Look!'

Kat looked. Meg did too and saw a tall, thickset man was indeed waving. So that was their father. But *whose* father was he? Who were these girls? And what had they to do with her dreams?

The man quickened his pace. Ellie and Kat raced towards him. He picked one up in each arm and spun them round while they screamed with excitement. Ellie's eyes were wide and shining. She looked intensely alive.

And in that moment Meg knew who she was.

You're her! You're my visitor. You're her as a child.

Another man had followed the father. He was younger but bore a strong resemblance to him. Meg assumed they were brothers. As if to confirm it Ellie cried 'Uncle Matt!' He picked her up and marched towards the edge of the cliff. 'Shall I throw 'er over, Will?'

he asked the father.

Will laughed. 'Aye. Less baggage on the ship.'

Matt pretended to do so. Kat screamed in alarm and ran towards him. Laughing he put Ellie down and stroked Kat's hair. 'I'm only teasin', little one. I'd never hurt your sister. You know that.'

'I wish we was on the ship,' Ellie cried. 'I want to go now!'

Will tugged her nose. 'Why'd you want that then? You'll be sick soon as we're out of the harbour.'

'No, I won't.'

'Yes, you will.'

'No! No! No! No! No!'

Kat joined in, also shouting the word. Again, Will picked them both up, twirling them through the air, kissing each in turn. Other men were now filling the area, all watching and cheering. Meg tried to avoid them, backing away until she was on the very edge of the cliff. Ellie's feet were inches from her face. Though there was no risk of contact instinct still made her back away.

And lose her footing.

She fell, plunging through the air as her grandmother's photograph slipped from her hand and the rocks below rushed up to greet her. She closed her eyes, bracing herself for the impact…

And woke up.

She was lying on her stomach, hanging over the edge of her bed. One arm brushed the floor where the photograph lay face down.

Slowly she sat up. Light was creeping under the curtains. Dawn was breaking; banishing the night.

She picked up the photograph. To her relief the glass was unbroken. Her grandmother smiled out of the frame. Impulsively she smiled back. 'We survived,' she whispered.

And it was true. They had.

But survived what exactly?

She pictured the happy child she had seen, comparing her to the young woman whose ravenous eyes had turned her to stone.

What happened to you in America? How did you become what

you've become?

And why are you back here now?

The air in the room was stale. She went to open a window. The square was silent as the grave. She remembered the old man who had sensed her presence. To him she had been a ghost; an unwelcome guest in his world, just as Ellie was in hers.

Her throat was dry. She went downstairs to make a cup of tea. The house, like the square, was silent. Empty too. Though her senses were alert she could not detect another presence. Perhaps it was Ellie's turn to sleep.

The kettle boiled she sat in her living room, staring at the painting of the beach that hung over her fireplace. Though it had only been painted a few weeks ago it looked just as it had in her dream. Even the gulls looked the same; the same beak shapes and wing spans passed down over the generations.

But how many generations? What year had she stepped into?

Had Ellie and Kat played on that beach? Had they imagined the boulders were dinosaur eggs and invented conversations between the gulls just as she had?

Why do I care? I don't want to know. All I want is for this to be over.

But the questions kept coming; as relentless as an incoming tide.

'You don't know what year it was?' Dan asked.

Meg shook her head.

He felt frustrated. 'You must have some idea.'

'Why? This wasn't some documentary on the History channel that started with the caption 'Cornwall 1780' while women in crinolines climbed into carriages.'

It was nine o'clock. She had knocked on his door half an hour ago. Now they sat together in his kitchen, eating breakfast. He swallowed a piece of toast. 'And you don't know Ellie's surname?'

'No.'

'That's a shame. We could have tried googling her.'

She laughed. 'Maybe she's on Facebook.'

'I'm being serious!'

'I'm sorry. I'm being frivolous. I just feel…' She hesitated. 'Jennifer was right. The unknown is always frightening. Now I've faced it I don't feel so afraid. Whatever Ellie is now, back then she was just a kid and a nice one too, excited about moving to America.'

'So, her Dad was a Cousin Jack.'

'Jack?' She looked confused. 'His name was Will.'

'It's an expression. Back in the latter half of the nineteenth century thousands of Cornish miners emigrated to work in mines in America, Australia and loads of other places. They were known as Cousin Jacks because more often than not another relative who'd already emigrated badgered his boss into giving a job to his cousin Jack back home.'

'How do you know this?'

'I saw a documentary about it on the History Channel. It was full of women in crinolines climbing in and out of carriages.'

Again, she laughed. She looked more relaxed than she had in ages. The sight made him glad.

'So, what are you doing today?' he asked. 'Now you don't have deals to broker.'

'I don't know.'

'I do. We're having a day out. I'm going to show you there's more to Cornwall than this place and your gym.'

She rolled her eyes.

'Is that a yes?'

'I guess it is.'

Three o'clock. Meg sat on a bench in Bodmin, listening to Dan describe their surroundings.

It had been a busy day. They had spent the first part of the morning in Truro, exploring the city. She had particularly admired Lemon Street with its elegant Georgian architecture. One of the buildings was now a solicitor's office. She had watched a group of lawyers emerge from the building, talking animatedly about their work and felt a pang for the life she had temporarily left behind.

'You're done with all that,' said Dan as if reading her mind.

'Only until I've sorted things out with Ellie.'

He had exhaled. 'You don't change, do you?'

'What do you mean?'

'You talk about her like she's a client. Why not open a file? You could keep a record of how many hours you spend on the case and submit a bill at the end.'

'Great idea, Dan. What's she going to pay me in? Ectoplasm?'

'Better make it plasma. You could build a new TV screen.'

She had punched his arm, prompting exaggerated cries of pain. An old woman walking past had given them a wry look.

'Do you like it here?' he had asked.

'Yes. It's lovely.'

'A bit quiet compared to London though.'

'That's not a bad thing.'

His eyes had widened. 'Wonders will never cease. We'll make a country girl out of you yet.'

'No way, matey. I'll be an Urbanite till I die.'

'Want to visit the Cathedral?'

'Yes, but if it's not as big as St Pauls I'm walking straight out again.'

It wasn't but she had stayed anyway, listening to a choir rehearse for a forthcoming concert. She had stared at the images on the stained-glass windows around her and wondered if Ellie had ever seen and admired them as she was doing now.

How would she have travelled here? On foot? By horse or carriage? How did people travel in those days and what days were they anyway?

After leaving Truro they had headed east towards Bodmin Moor. As a child she had read Du Maurier's 'Jamaica Inn' and wanted to see the lodging house that had inspired the novel. The reality had proved a disappointment: just a refurbished hotel on a side road off a busy highway. A drive through the villages that hugged the edge of the Moor had proved more rewarding. Many had the picturesque quality of the Cotswolds but were surrounded by dank marshland over which clouds hung so low that it seemed as if the sky was being sucked down into the earth.

'We came here all the time when I was growing up,' Dan had told her. 'Dad was a great believer in the importance of long walks on a Sunday afternoon. He, Mum, my brother and me would spend hours burning off the calories from the Sunday roast and then spend the evening in a local pub putting them back on again.'

'That sounds like fun.'

'Oh yeah, it was *great* fun. Dad always managed to get us lost just when the heavens opened. It's a miracle we didn't all die of pneumonia.'

She had thought back to her own childhood Sundays; countless hours spent with her head buried in school books, focused on her goal of University, a good career and the prospect of Grace and herself never having to depend on anyone else's charity ever again. It was a goal she had achieved; only it didn't seem like much of an achievement. Not now Grace was gone.

'Meg?'

Dan was watching her; his expression anxious. 'I'm sorry. I know I had it good compared to you. I didn't mean to sound like I was gloating.'

'You didn't. Your family sound nice. You must miss them.'

'Not like you must miss yours.'

She remembered Ellie telling Kat that their mother was in Heaven. Both must have missed her but at least they had still had their father, their uncle and most importantly each other. She was glad of that. She really was.

Even though she didn't want to be.

They had eaten lunch in a place called Blissland. Of all the villages they had seen she had thought it the prettiest. A group of stone houses surrounded a village green. 'This was Mum's favourite place,' Dan had told her. 'More often than not we'd end up here after our walks.'

The pub was small and friendly. The landlord had recognised Dan and greeted him like an old friend. She had sat at a table watching him exchange jokes with the locals, many of whom recognised him too. All seemed pleased to see him. Not that she was surprised. He had a warm manner that invited conversation; a genial everyman to her hard-nosed career woman. They made a strange pair indeed.

Now they were in his home town of Bodmin. He had shown her his childhood home, his school, the youth club where he and a band comprised of school friends had played their one and only gig and the field behind it where he had lost his virginity a couple of hours later.

'Her name was Sinead,' he told her. 'Sinead Barry.'

'And how drunk was she?'

'Very. In spite of the fact I could only play two chords she kept telling me I was going to be the next Jimi Hendrix!'

'Wow! Drunk and deaf. You lady killer, you.'

'It gets worse. Three months later she came out as a lesbian!'

She burst out laughing. 'No way!'

'Seriously. It took me years to live it down. Every time I spoke to a girl after that one of my friends would ask whether she'd ever read Virginia Woolf and if her favourite film was The Killing of Sister George. It's a miracle I ever got laid again.' He sighed. 'What a waste. Sinead was gorgeous. Pity I don't have her number. I could put the two of you in touch.'

'Stitch me up, I've split my sides.'

'So, tell me about the guy who deflowered you.'

'I'm not telling you that!'

'Go on. Or can't you remember his name?'

'It was Ian and last I heard he was married with four children so it's fair to say my first time was considerably more successful than yours.'

'Did you schedule it around business meetings?'

'No.'

'Did you give him an appraisal afterwards?'

'No!'

'I bet you did. Mind you, with him being a lawyer he was probably glad of one.'

'Who says he was a lawyer?'

'All you do is work. Where else are you going to meet someone?'

'Actually, Ian and I were at school together. It happened just after we left. We'd been dating, he kept pushing it and eventually I decided it was probably a good idea to get it out of the way before I went to University.'

He gave her a despairing look. 'Oh, Meg. You even manage to make losing your virginity sound like part of a career plan.'

'I do not!' She felt herself blushing. 'It wasn't like that.'

'Not much it wasn't!'

'Why are you always taking the piss out of me?'

'Because you take yourself too seriously. Anyway, you give as good as you get. Five minutes with you and my fragile ego is in pieces.'

'Fragile? Listen, matey, the only thing fragile about you is your grip on the concepts of sensitivity and tact!'

He laughed. She noticed an elderly man giving them the same wry look the woman had given them in Truro. 'So what other sights are there?' she asked Dan.

He thought for a moment. 'There's one you have to see. It's probably Bodmin's most famous landmark and definitely worth a visit...'

Bodmin Jail was on the outskirts of the town. It was a huge, square structure of grey granite with slit like windows that made it look like a giant toad.

There was a public bar on the ground floor. They bought tickets there and were told they could explore at their leisure. The barmaid gestured to a man sitting at a table drinking a pint of beer. 'He's a local historian. If you have any questions once you've had a look around I'm sure he'll be pleased to answer them.' As if to confirm it the man gave them a friendly wave.

The jail covered five floors; all accessed by a steep staircase. They followed a middle aged American couple up to the top. The man, who was overweight and wearing a garish Hawaiian shirt, complained about the lack of an elevator. Dan made a face at Meg. Biting down on her lip she made one back.

They reached the top floor. Much of it was closed to the public. There was just a small walkway and a single cell. The windows had bars rather than glass, allowing the air to whistle in. Though the sun was shining it still felt cold.

'Not much to see here,' grumbled the American man.

'The floors below are much bigger,' Dan told him.

'Pity you didn't tell us that before we hiked all the way up here.'

'Well I would have done but I thought you could use the exercise.'

The man glared at Dan. 'Do you think you're a comedian?'

'Not half as much as your tailor does.'

The man's face darkened. 'Don't be angry with him,' said Meg quickly. 'It's not his fault. He's only just left the secure unit and we're still trying to get his meds right.'

Dan looked horrified. 'You promised you wouldn't tell anyone.'

'You haven't given me much choice. What happens if you start stripping like you did in the restaurant? God, I hope you're wearing clean underwear.'

Now looking alarmed the man turned and headed back down the stairs, pulling his wife after him.

Dan turned to face her. '*Stripping?*'

She started to laugh. He did too; both of them covering their mouths so the sound wouldn't travel. Soon she was bent double, rocking back and forth feeling like a teenager celebrating a successful prank.

The wall was at her back. She put out her hands to steady herself. Its surface was damp. It felt cold and slippery; like a dead fish.

Yet something pulsed within it.

A chill ran through her.

Instantly the need to laugh was gone, replaced by a sense of unease.

Dan struggled to compose himself. She stood and watched him, wiping her hands on her jeans as if trying to brush the feeling away.

'Let's go to the next floor,' he suggested.

She wanted to refuse. Suddenly she wanted to leave.

Only she didn't want to spoil his day.

'OK,' she said.

Half an hour later they explored a lower floor.

It was much bigger than the one at the top. Rows of cells surrounded them. Inside were wax figurines depicting the criminals who had once been kept there, together with plaques describing their crimes. The lighting was dim, leaving whole areas in virtual darkness. The air was heavy and moist.

The American tourists were nowhere to be seen. Dan struck up a conversation with a British couple who were on a camping holiday. As he and the man discussed the best ways to light a fire the woman smiled at Meg. 'This place reminds me of the Chamber of Horrors in Madame Tussauds. Have you been there?'

'Yes.'

'That's creepy too.'

'Not like this. Tussauds is just an exhibition. This place is…' She hesitated, searching for the right word. 'Real. All of what we see actually happened here.'

'The Tussauds waxworks are better though.' The woman gestured to a figure of a man sitting on a bench staring down at the floor. 'These are a bit amateurish. Don't you think?'

She nodded. Dan and the man had moved away. The woman went to join them. Meg remained where she was; staring into the cell at the figure who skulked there; wondering what his crime had been and what price he had paid for it. There was a plaque giving all the information she required. Though it would have been the easiest thing in the world to go and read it still she held back.

She didn't want to risk touching the walls.

They were the heart of this place. They had witnessed it all;

the fear, the hate and the suffering. Like sponges they had absorbed everything; centuries of human misery stored in stone, packed in so tight that all it needed was a gentle jolt to set it free.

Behind her she heard laughter. Two boys darted in and out of the darkest areas, whooping at each other while their mother called for them to behave. The sight of them made her feel ashamed. They were not afraid. Why should she be?

So, she went to read the plaque.

The man had been a murderer. In the early nineteenth century, he had killed a girl on Bodmin Moor; cutting her throat and throwing her body down a well. A huge crowd had been expected at his hanging, only it had never taken place. On the night before his execution he had slit his own throat in this very cell.

The wall was damp. She could see drops of moisture on it. They gleamed like sweat on skin.

But it was just a wall.

She reached out her hand to stroke its surface. It wasn't as cold as the wall upstairs. Not so cold at all.

Something was gleaming in the cell. The figure held a razor blade in its hand. It was a nice touch. Authentic. She wondered why she hadn't noticed it before.

The wall felt warm. Pleasantly so. It was like pressing against a radiator on a cold winter's day. How could she have thought this place sinister? There was nothing frightening here. The two boys had the right idea; treating it like a playground. She watched them for a moment, smiling as she did so, before turning back to the figure staring down at the ground.

Only it wasn't staring at the ground anymore.

It was looking right at her.

And it was no longer a figure.

It was a man.

He had dank, greasy hair, pock marked skin and wide, manic eyes. As she stared into them they began to shine as his face broke into a smile.

And he rose to his feet.

The fear was back; far greater than before. She tried to move but felt paralysed. All she could do was stand and watch.

He reached the bars. The grin was so wide that it threatened to split his face in two. She could smell him now; a rank combination of sweat, dirt and excrement that made her want to retch. He raised his hand; the razor catching what little light there was, making it sparkle. Opening his mouth, he began to scream.

While slashing the blade across his throat.

Warm liquid splashed her face. Instinctively she closed her eyes, moving away from the wall and screaming herself. But when she opened them again all she saw was a badly made figurine staring down at the ground; its poorly defined fingers grasping nothing but air.

She touched her face. Her skin was dry.

Dan appeared beside her. 'Are you OK? What happened?'

She opened her mouth to tell him but then closed it again. Everyone else was staring at her too. If she told them the truth they would think her crazy. And she knew how that felt. She knew all too well.

'I…um…I thought I saw a mouse. I'm scared to death of them.'

His face relaxed; as did those of the others. The boys began to laugh. 'What a baby!' one of them jeered.

'Nathan!' the mother snapped. 'Don't be so rude.'

'It's alright,' Meg told her. 'I deserved it.'

Dan stroked her arm. 'You poor thing. Come on, we're done here. Let's go and have a drink.'

They made their way towards the stairs while behind them the boys continued to laugh; the sound following her across the floor just as so many years ago it had followed her across the playground.

The historian was still in the bar. 'I've got some questions I want to ask him,' Dan told her. 'What do you want to drink?'

'Actually, I could use some fresh air. You stay here. I'll be back soon.'

She walked outside. A group of people were gathered by the

entrance; the British couple amongst them. The woman gave her a wave. 'That's where they used to hang people,' she said, gesturing to a cage like construction by the far wall. 'They're about to give us a demonstration. Are you going to stay and watch?'

After what had happened on the lower floor it was the last thing in the world Meg wanted to see. Quickly she reached for an excuse. 'I'm interested in architecture. I'm going to explore the outside of the building.'

The woman nodded. Meg walked along the side of the jail. In front of her was what appeared to be a courtyard. It looked too confined for her liking. What she wanted was space.

To its left was a path. At its end she could see houses and hear the faint hum of traffic. Eager for the sights and sounds of normality she headed towards them.

The path ran alongside a building that was run down and in need of repair. As she walked past it she heard birdsong. Looking up she saw groups of them flying in and out of the building itself. There was an entrance at the rear. Curious to see if they had built nests she walked inside.

It was a long, rectangular building; built of granite like everything else in the Jail. There was no roof. In its place were roots growing out of cracks in the stone; spraying out like branches of a tree. Birds flitted between them, calling out greetings to each other just like the seagulls at her favourite beach. Their song was lovely. She walked the length of the building, staring up at them as they danced in beams of sunlight like mischievous fairies.

It was only when she reached the end that she realised she was in another cell block.

There were rows of them; three stories high. None had doors. They were just gaping holes; as if the building itself had a hundred mouths all emitting silent screams.

The birds were still singing, only the sound was now shrill. It was no longer lovely. Instead it sounded like a warning.

Get out! Get out now before it's too late.

She prepared to do so but found herself dizzy. All the air seemed to have gone, sucked in by the open mouths, leaving her trapped in a vacuum.

Move! Just turn and walk out. That's all you have to do.

But it wasn't that simple. The dizziness was increasing; playing tricks on her vision. The makeshift roof drifted away into the sky while the walls were drawing closer; eager to suck her in through the cracks and trap her for ever.

Something moved behind her. She could hear it darting across the floor. In her head she saw the man in the cell with the razor. Was that him now? Was it her throat he was planning to cut?

She tried to move but once again felt paralyzed. The walls held her like magnets. It was worse than the lower floor. A thousand times worse. This was no museum. This was a prison from which she was never going to escape.

The sound was right behind her. Only inches away. She opened her mouth, willing herself to scream.

A mouse ran over her foot, darting across the ground and into one of the cells.

The scream came, and with it the ability to move.

Turning, she ran towards the entrance and out into the light.

She was standing on a patch of rough ground. Twenty feet away was the thick stone wall that ran around the prison. There was a gap right in front of her. Through it she could see a small hill with rows of houses upon it. Someone stood in the upstairs window of one of them, wiping at it with a cloth. Another window was open; emitting the faint sound of rock music. It was a perfectly ordinary sight. The sort she had seen a thousand times before.

As she stared at it a voice that was not her own screamed inside her head.

You're going to die! You're going to die right now!

Terror turned her muscles to jelly. Her legs collapsed beneath her.

There were footsteps. She heard Dan calling her name. He ran towards her, putting his hand on her shoulder. Pushing him away she vomited onto the ground.

Half an hour later she sat in his van as he drove them back to Saltran.

'How do you feel now?' he asked.

'Better,' she told him. To some extent it was true. Her nausea had gone while her terror had faded into a dull sense of dread.

'This is my fault. I never should have taken you there. Not with its history.'

'I thought I was going to die. I really did.' She shook her head. 'And it doesn't make sense. It was just a view. There was nothing special about it but just looking at it made me more afraid than I've ever been in my life.'

'I'm so sorry, Meg. I'm supposed to be taking your mind off things. Some friend I am.'

'You are a friend, and for what it's worth up until we got to the prison I'd really enjoyed my day.' She touched his arm. 'Don't beat yourself up. I don't want you to.'

He reached out and squeezed her hand. She squeezed back.

They were past Penzance now and on the road towards the coast. She stared out of the window at the fields that surrounded them, watching the light fade as night began its unstoppable descent.

That evening she sat in his living room listening to him move around in his kitchen. The sound was comforting. After what had happened that afternoon she did not want to be alone.

The room was still a mess. Piles of papers surrounded her. 'Do you have a duster?' she called out.

'Why do you ask?'

'Why do you think?'

He entered the room carrying two mugs of hot chocolate. 'I don't need you to tidy up.'

'Yes, you do. You're a slob.'

'Aren't you late for your CFA meeting?'

She sipped her drink. 'What's CFA?'

'Clean Freaks Anonymous.'

'I am. You should come too. HA meets in the next room.'

'What's HA?'

'Hygiene Allergic.'

He laughed. His mobile began to ring. 'That'll be my mother,' he told her. 'She phones from Spain same time every week. I'll take it upstairs.'

He left the room. She remained where she was. The chocolate was rich and creamy. It sat heavily on her stomach, making her drowsy. Before she knew it, sleep was almost upon her. Briefly she tried to fight against it. She didn't have the energy to deal with her dreams.

But she didn't have the energy to fight either.

So, her eyes closed.

And she did dream.

She was back on the lower floor of the jail. The local historian they had met in the bar was leading a tour. People surrounded her; all jostling for the best view. She wanted to leave but they were like a wall through which she could not pass.

The historian walked towards a cell in the far corner. 'This is our most celebrated display,' he announced. 'We call it; The One Who Got Away.' The group moved forward. Curious, Meg moved with them, pushing her way to the front and a clear view of the cell where a waxwork of a young woman sat on a bed, staring through the bars at those who had come to gawp. It was a crude a piece of work; the face as devoid of expression as a shop mannequin.

Yet still she could recognise herself.

Again, she wanted to leave. Again, the crowd barred her way.

'She killed her mother,' the historian told them.

'Didn't she kill her sister too?' someone asked.

The historian nodded. 'And her sister's unborn child. Not that it could ever be proved. She got away scot free; legally anyway. As for her conscience, well that's another story.'

People began to mutter. The mood was turning ugly. Knowing it was only a matter of time before they recognised her but with nowhere to hide she shut her eyes as if seeking refuge in the darkness behind them.

And heard a door slam shut.

When she opened them again she was sitting on the bed in the cell; staring through the bars at the appalled yet fascinated faces that peered through them. She tried to turn away but couldn't move. She was now a waxwork; just a cheap exhibit like all the rest.

The historian finished talking. The group moved away. She remained where she was; encased in wax for eternity with only her conscience for company…

When she woke she was still on Dan's sofa. A blanket covered her. Dan was sitting in the corner of the room, staring at his laptop screen.

She sat up. 'What time is it?'

'After midnight.'

'You should have woken me.'

'I thought you could use the rest.' He hesitated. 'I would have done if…well, you know…'

'Thanks.' She sat up. 'How was your mother?'

'Fine. I spoke to someone else too.'

'Who?'

'The historian. He gave me his card in the bar. He said I could call if I had any more questions.'

She felt alarmed. 'You didn't tell him about me?'

'Of course, I didn't. What do you take me for?' Something beeped in the kitchen. 'That'll be the microwave. Let me get my jacket potato. Are you hungry?'

'No.' She gestured to the laptop. 'What are you doing?'

'I'm reading about the history of the jail. It's fascinating.'

She thought of the man who had cut his own throat in a cell. 'That's one way of putting it.'

He headed towards the kitchen. 'You'll never guess what the historian told me,' he called over his shoulder.

'What?'

'You know the building with the birds in it?'

Her legs felt stiff. In order to stretch them she walked over to the computer. 'That's where they used to keep the women prisoners,'

Dan continued.

She glanced at the computer screen. On it was what appeared to be the lower half of an article.

'...and before they moved the executions inside the Jail grounds...'

The words 'monstrous,' 'bestial' and 'deranged' jumped out at her.

'...they used to hang people over the wall...'

Her curiosity peaked she scrolled up the page. At its top was a photograph.

'...at the very part where the gap is now.'

It was a grainy black and white image of a girl no older than twenty with delicate features and ravenous eyes. Beneath it were two brief lines that finally revealed the identity of the girl who was haunting her sleep.

Ellen Foley: Murderess (PR – can we centre these two sentences?)
Hanged at Bodmin Jail; 16th September 1881

Chapter 7

Six o'clock in the morning. She paced up and down Dan's living room, ignoring his pleas for her to stop while his jacket potato, still untouched and now stone cold sat on a plate in front of him.

'You need to calm down,' he told her.

'Stop telling me what I need!' She ran a hand through her hair. 'Don't you get it? I was feeling what Ellen felt. The claustrophobia of being locked up in a cell and the blind terror of knowing you're about to have the life choked out of you. She was in my head, Dan. That psycho was in my head!'

'You don't know she's a psycho.'

She stopped pacing and stared at him. 'You read the article. You read what she did. There was blood everywhere. The Judge at her trial said that in forty years it was the most gruesome murder he'd ever encountered. Dozens of stab wounds, the eyes cut out and the genitals hacked off. When the police found the body one of them actually threw up. That's how bad it was.'

'Even so…'

'And what about when she was arrested? What were her words? ''I did it and I'm glad of it.'' She never expressed any remorse; not then and not at her trial. When the victim's brother cried out that she was a monster who deserved to hang she actually looked pleased. Even Myra Hindley had the grace to look ashamed at the end. But not her. Not once. The brother was right. She was a monster.' A shudder ran through her. 'And yesterday afternoon I had that monster in my head.'

She waited for Dan to respond. Instead he remained silent; his expression thoughtful.

'Well?' she demanded.

'You said she was a monster.'

'Not just me. Everyone at the time said it too.'

He shook his head. 'That's not my point.'

'Then what is?'

'What made her one?'

'Who cares?'

'You should. Think about it, Meg. The girl you saw on the cliff was no monster. She was a nice kid. You said so yourself.'

She gave a snort. 'Appearances can be deceiving.'

'I don't buy that.'

'Then I bow to your wisdom. After all Hitler loved his mother and was kind to animals. Yes, he killed six million people and tried to wipe the Jews from the face of the earth but deep down he was a good person, just like Ellen.'

Looking angry he rose to his feet. 'You're not listening to me!'

'That's because you're not saying anything worth hearing. She was in my bloody head! Can you imagine what that feels like? I feel dirty. I feel sick!'

The anger faded. 'I'm not making light of what happened, Meg. I just think…'

'What? That we should give her the benefit of the doubt? Imagine if it was your brother, Dan. Imagine if he visited from New Zealand and met me. Imagine if he and I started a relationship. Imagine he told you that he loved me and wanted us to get married and then a few days later I stabbed him to death, hacked his privates off and stuffed them in his mouth. Do you really think you'd be telling people that in spite of what I'd done I was still basically a good person?' She shook her head. 'No way, Dan. You'd be right at the front of the lynch mob.'

He looked as if he were preparing to speak. Not wanting to hear it she turned away. Through the window she could see the dawn breaking. The light was crisp and clear; promising, temporarily at least, fine weather.

'I can't breathe in here,' she told him. 'I'm going for a walk.'

'Then I'm coming with you.'

'Do what you want.' Without bothering to wait she headed for the door.

An hour later she marched through clumps of gorse and bracken; not caring where she was heading; knowing only that she had to outpace her fear. Dan was close behind. She kept increasing her stride, trying unsuccessfully to leave him behind.

The undergrowth ended. She emerged onto the cliff path. Dan, still following, kept calling for her to slow down. The sound was like a drill in her ear. It was driving her mad. She spun round, shouting for him to shut up, caught her foot in a hole in the ground, fell over and gave her knee a hefty whack.

As she rose to her feet a bolt of pain shot up her leg, causing her to wince.

Dan hurried towards her. 'Are you OK?'

'No thanks to you.'

'I suppose you think this is my fault.'

'If you hadn't insisted on following me…'

'I'm worried about you!'

She sat down on the ground. 'No one asked you to be.'

'So, you want me to just leave you here?'

'Yes! At last he sees sense. Hallelujah!'

His face darkened. 'Fine! I'm off. Have fun limping home on your own.'

'I will.'

He remained where he was.

She waved her hand at him. 'Bye then.'

'Oh, grow up you silly bitch!'

'Piss off you asshole!'

'Up yours you ball breaker!'

'Drop dead you wanker!'

'Kiss my arse you uptight clean freak.'

'See you in hell you useless slob.'

'Not if I see you first you frigid power dresser.'

She opened her mouth then closed it again.

'Come on,' he told her. 'It's your turn to hurl an insult.'

'I can't think of one.'

'Then I win. Back of the net and one nil final score.' He pumped his fist in a gesture of triumph. She stared up at him from the ground, telling herself that she had never hated anyone so much in her life.

And felt her lips start to twitch.

He noticed. The fist pumping increased, now accompanied by whooping sounds.

The smile spread across her face.

He sat down on the ground beside her. 'How's the knee?' he asked.

'Painful.'

'I'm sure you'll live.' He gave it a gentle squeeze. 'I can't feel any swelling. It's probably just bruised. Rest it for a bit and it'll be right as rain.'

'Thanks for the diagnosis, Doctor.'

He laughed. She did too. In front of them the sea stretched out towards the horizon. Its surface was calm. The air was still yet she heard the faint rumbling of thunder.

'There's a storm coming,' she announced.

'Don't be an idiot. That was my stomach!' As if in confirmation it rumbled again.

'You never got to eat your jacket potato, did you?'

'No. And it was smothered in cheese and pickle.' He gave a wistful sigh.

'Your diet is so unhealthy.'

'It's not *that* bad.'

'How many portions of fruit and veg do you eat?'

'I don't know. Three or four.'

'We're talking a day, Dan, not a year.'

He looked sheepish. 'What is it with you? Whenever we're together I end up feeling like a naughty schoolboy.'

'That's because you still are one.'

'Whereas you were born middle aged.'

'I was not!'

He rolled his eyes.

'I just…'

'Need to feel in control,' he said; his expression suddenly serious. 'That's why you lashed out at me. In this situation with Ellen you feel powerless and it terrifies you. If I'm being honest I actually think it frightens you even more than Ellen does.'

A twig lay on the ground beside her. Picking it up she began to scratch at the earth.

'I'm right, aren't I?' he asked.

'Yes. I feel weak and I hate it. Ever since my mother died I've had to be strong. Not just for me but for my sister. She needed me. I was all she had and what with all the stuff with my father...' She swallowed. 'At first it was an act. I was still a kid. I was terrified half the time. And then I wasn't. Suddenly it was natural. I'd become the person I needed to be. I liked being her too. And now every day I feel her slipping further and further away.'

He put his arm around her. 'That's not true. You're still you. You're going through something massive and you wouldn't be human if you weren't frightened. But you'll work out what it is you have to do.'

'Do you really think so?'

'Yes.'

'Thanks.'

'Don't mention it. What are friends for?'

She turned and stared at him. He was wearing his trademark grin. A wave of affection washed over her. She was glad he was here; glad that he understood. Glad that she could let down her guard without him despising her for it.

'I meant what I said in the pub the other night,' she told him. 'It *is* a waste you being single.'

'Are you hitting on me?'

She was taken aback. 'No! I just meant...'

He wiped his forehead. 'Phew!'

'Oh charming! Get over yourself, Brad Pitt.'

'It's not that. You're great looking. You're just too bloody bossy.'

'And you've got facial hair.'

'A lot of women like it.'

'Yes, and a lot of women like guys who can belch the tune of every Nirvana song ever written but I'm not one of them.'

'Actually, it's Guns' n' Roses.'

'Well that makes *all* the difference.'

'It does. Their track November Rain is beautiful.'

She raised her eyes to heaven.

'Want to hear it?'

'I'm not even going to answer that.'

'So, how's your leg feeling?'

'Strong enough to kick you senseless if you even try.'

He rose to his feet then helped her do the same. She put weight on her knee, feeling nothing but a dull ache. Relieved, she looked about her, focusing on her surrounding for the first time since leaving town.

A shudder ran through her as she saw where they had ended up.

'Do you see that?' she said, gesturing to a stretch of cliff. 'That's where I was standing in my dream. That's where I saw Ellen and her sister.' Turning, she pointed to the ruined engine house on the outcrop of rock. 'And that was the mine where her father and uncle worked.'

'*That* was the mine?'

She nodded.

'So that's the engine house where you sheltered from the rain? That's the place where you heard a child crying?'

'Yes. Why?'

'When you described it, I thought it was somewhere else.'

She was confused. 'What does it matter what place it was?'

'Because that's Trevaron Mine.'

'It's just a mine. There are loads of them here.'

'Are you OK to walk?'

'Yes.'

'Then come with me. There's something you need to see.'

She opened her mouth to protest.

'No arguments! I'd kill my own mother for a fried breakfast but this is more important.'

He continued on his way. Reluctantly she followed.

They reached the engine house. He began to hunt through the gorse that grew around it. She stared up at the sky. It was cloudless.

If only it had been cloudless that night she would not have had to take shelter and none of this would have happened.

'Here it is,' he exclaimed, pushing aside the undergrowth to reveal a weather-beaten plaque. From the distance it appeared to be a list of names. As she grew closer she saw there was a heading at the top. Bending down she read the words.

In Memory of the Brave Men of Saltran who lost their lives at
Trevaron Mine
23rd July 1872

'A tunnel collapsed,' Dan told her. 'It was right out under the sea.'

'What happened?'

'The tunnel flooded. All the men inside were drowned.'

He continued to talk only she was no longer listening; her attention now fixed on the names of those who had lost their lives.

Two names in particular.

Matthew Foley
William Foley

Foley. The same surname as Ellen.

Ellen who had had a father called Will and an uncle called Matt.

Ellen who had been hanged in 1881 at the age of eighteen.

Ellen who, in her dream had been about nine.

Oh God, when did it happen? Was it a month after I saw her? A week?

Was it the next day?

She thought of a child waving to a ship out at sea. A child who was full of excitement at the prospect of a new life in America with no clue as to the vicious trick fate was about to play.

Her emotions were churning. She took a deep breath; trying to calm herself. For a moment she could taste the salt in the air. Then it was gone; replaced by the smell of polish and antiseptic. The smell of a hospital waiting room in Suffolk where her elderly neighbour had told her that her mother was dead.

Suddenly she was back there; watching his face, hearing his words and feeling as if a hand had reached into her chest and ripped out her heart. Like Ellen she too had been nine. The memory was as visceral as a knife wound; the pain just as intense as it had been all those years ago, just as raw and just as unbearable.

She started to cry.

Dan moved towards her. She held up her hand, keeping him at a distance as she struggled to bring herself under control.

Five minutes passed. She pointed to the plaque. 'It's Ellen's father and uncle. They died here. That's why she was crying. This is where she came to be close to them. She came at night when no one could see and when there were no more tears left she'd go back and pretend to the world that she was fine.'

'How do you know that?' he asked.

I don't know, she was about to say, but didn't. Because she *did* know. She knew because she had done the same. She had never cried in front of anyone because Grace might find out and feel afraid. Grace had depended on her, just as Ellen's twin, Kat, had been dependant. She could never let Grace think that she couldn't cope, just as Ellen couldn't let Kat think it. No matter how bad they felt each had understood that protecting their sister came before everything else.

'I just do,' she said softly.

'It all makes sense now,' Dan told her. 'So, does that stuff in the article about her mother's sister…'

'What about her mother's sister?'

'It said that at the time of the murder she was living with her aunt and uncle, and that her aunt was her mother's sister.'

She didn't remember. She had not focused on such details. At the time all she could take in was the horrific nature of the crime.

'Clara,' she said. 'That was the aunt's name. Uncle John and Aunty Clara. They were rich. They had a big house. Ellen told Kat that they would have one too when they went to America. Ellen was so excited about the voyage; so happy and so alive.' She swallowed.

'At least they had people to take them in. That's something, I suppose. It doesn't take the pain away, but it is something.'

'And that's why you have to find out what happened,' Dan told her. 'Whatever she became she wasn't a monster then. You know she wasn't.'

'How do I know?'

'Because you feel for her, Meg. You feel for the child she was. I can see it in your face. Deny it all you like but I know it's true.'

She didn't answer. There was no point.

Then she remembered the crime. She thought of a young man stabbed to death with his genitals hacked off and thrust into his open mouth.

'No! I don't care. Whatever happened to her afterwards it doesn't excuse what she did. His name was Samuel. He was only twenty-five and he loved her. He wanted to marry her. He wanted them to be together and she did that to him and was proud of it. How am I supposed to care about someone who's capable of that, Dan? Tell me how.'

He didn't answer.

'You see. You can't.'

'When I was at school there was a boy in my class called Alan Dunne. Have I ever told you about him?'

She felt exasperated. 'What does he have to do with this?'

'Alan and I were friends. He was always up for a laugh. He was a real tearaway but there was no malice in him. He was a good kid. He really was.'

'So?'

'In his garden he had a tree house. A group of us formed a gang and held our meetings there. One day, early in the summer holidays before we started Secondary school we were mucking about in there and Alan fell out. He was knocked unconscious and had to be rushed to hospital. His mother was hysterical. She was convinced he was going to die. It was frightening. I'd never seen a grown up so upset before.'

Her curiosity was roused. 'What happened to him?'

'He regained consciousness a couple of hours later. Apart

from a broken ankle there was no permanent damage, or so we thought.

'But he was never the same person after that. He was moody all the time. He began picking fights for no reason. Within six months of us starting secondary school he didn't want to be in our gang anymore. He formed a new gang with the so called bad crowd. By the time he was thirteen he had cautions for shoplifting and criminal damage. By the time he was sixteen he was robbing houses to feed his drug habit. He even stole from his parents and when his mother challenged him over it he punched her in the face and broke her jaw. Everyone told her to press charges, but she refused. He was her son. She loved him. How can you press charges against someone you love?

'Then, when he was eighteen, he beat up his pregnant girlfriend so badly she lost the baby. This time he was charged and went to prison. Three months into his sentence they found him stabbed to death in the shower. They couldn't prove it, but they were sure it was some dispute over drugs. He was still using. That's what the authorities told his mother. She phoned our house to tell us. I was the one who took the call. She was crying and as I listened to her I remembered how she'd cried when he fell out of the tree house and how euphoric she'd been when he woke up and could move and knew his name and that two and two made four. And it broke my heart because back then she'd had no idea that her nightmare wasn't over. It was only just beginning.'

Silence. They stared at each other. She waited for him to speak while sensing he was doing the same.

'Do you think I'm a nice guy?' he asked eventually.

'Yes, of course.'

'Imagine if I'd been the one who'd fallen out of the tree house. It could so easily have been. We were always having play fights in there. When he was a kid Alan liked drawing. He and I used to make comic books together. He wanted to be an artist just like I did. Imagine if I'd been the one who'd fallen out and it was Alan standing here telling you about his friend Dan Penaluna who'd been a lovely kid before getting stabbed to death in a prison toilet over ten quid's worth of smack.' He exhaled. 'I hate what Alan did. He deserved to go to prison. But he didn't deserve what happened to him that summer day when we were eleven. He was a good kid, just like I was and just like Ellen was.' He gestured to the engine house. 'And that's what this is all about.'

'What do you mean?'

'What do you *think* I mean, Meg? Even if Ellen died a monster she wasn't born one. Something changed her in the same way something changed Alan and it's your job to find out what that was and stop it from happening.'

'Whatever it was it happened over a hundred years ago. I'm not God, Dan. I can't turn back the clock. How do I stop it?'

'You use your gift. Why do you think your mother called it that? Because that's what it is. You can change lives, Meg. You really can. Remember the woman in the tea shop whose twin brother had died. You wiped away decades of guilt in a matter of seconds. You were five years old. You were little more than a baby and that's the power you had. And if you could do that then, just think what you can do now.'

She shook her head. 'My gift doesn't work like that. Sometimes I can see the dead. Sometimes I can see the future. But I can't change the past.'

'How do you know? Think about it. Think about what happened when you were a child. You saw the boy in the café. You saw the grandmother in the playground. You saw them because they wanted you to change something in *your* world. With the boy it was about stopping his sister feeling guilty. With the grandmother it was about making her grandson feel the same. That's why you could see them. They wanted you to change the present. But you can't see Ellen. Not here in our world. You only see her when you sleep and then she takes you into her world. Don't you get it? She wants your help, just like the boy and the grandmother did; only the help she needs is in her world, not ours.'

She didn't answer. Her brain was whirring.

'You know I'm right,' he told her.

'And what if I can't?'

'There's no such word as can't. Not for you. If you run Ellen will follow, just like she did last time. She's going to keep on and on following until you give her what she wants.'

A sense of utter helplessness swept over Meg. Turning she walked towards the edge of the rock, staring down at the chasm below.

'If not for Ellen then do it for Samuel,' Dan called after her. 'He didn't deserve to die. You have the chance to save him. How can you turn your back on that?'

The waves raced across the chasm, slamming into the rocks and sending spray up into the air. Once, a few weeks earlier, she had sat on another cliff, staring down at the sea while the wind had threatened to tear her from her perch and send her hurtling down to her death. A pair of hikers had been frightened and cried out for her to take care. If they had not appeared perhaps she would have let it happen. It would only have taken a second. A sudden drop down onto the rocks and all the life would have been crushed out of her.

And then maybe, just maybe, she would see her mother and sister again.

Oh God, I miss them so much. I'd sell my soul just to be able to hug them and tell them I love them and have them hug me back and tell me the same.

Time passed. She continued to watch the waves. Their motion was hypnotic. So absorbed did she become that at first she didn't realise she was being embraced.

It was a soft gesture like a caress: a warm pressure at her back and a pair of arms around her waist.

Small, childlike arms.

It's you, isn't it? You're in my head again. You know what I'm feeling. You know because you felt it too. That's why I heard you crying that night. You let me hear you because you knew I'd understand, just like you understand me.

The arms tightened around her. For a moment she enjoyed the sensation. Then she felt ashamed. She was an adult. She should not be accepting comfort from a child.

Not when it should be the other way around.

What made you change? That day on the cliff you were no monster. Why did you become one?

And how do I stop it from happening?

Dan appeared beside her. He was speaking but she wasn't listening; aware only that the arms were gone.

'Alright,' she said softly. 'I'll do it.'

'Do you mean it?'

'Yes. How else am I going to shut you up?'

He pulled an imaginary zip across his lips.

'You're an idiot,' she told him.

'Are you insulting me?'

'What do you think?'

'That you should quit while you're ahead. When it comes to slanging matches you know I'll always win.' Again, he punched his fist in the air, making a whooping noise. It made him look like an impish schoolboy. Perhaps his friend Alan had looked the same way on that summer day before everything changed.

Impulsively she reached out and hugged him. 'Promise me something?' she whispered.

'What?' he whispered back.

'That you'll keep away from tree houses until this is over.'

'And what about afterwards?'

'Afterwards I don't care. Bubonic plague will kill you long before your diet does.'

He kissed her cheek. 'It's a deal.'

She heard voices. A group of walkers approached. 'Come on,' she said. 'Let's go home and get you some breakfast before you start eating your own arm.'

They left the rock. The walkers smiled at them as they passed. 'It's wonderful here, isn't it?' said one of them. 'You can see history everywhere you look.'

'That's right,' she replied. 'This is the place where history comes to life.'

She and Dan continued on their way while the walkers took photographs of the engine house and speculated as to what its history might be.

Chapter 8

Nine o'clock that evening. She sat in her living room, staring at a piece of paper she had been given in a service station on the outskirts of London.

Picking up her mobile she dialled the number. It rang five times and then was answered. 'Hello?'

'Hello, Jennifer. This is Meg Parker.'

'Meg! I'm so pleased to hear from you.'

She felt relieved. 'So, you remember me.'

'Of course, I do! I've been thinking about you all day. I had a feeling you might call. How is it going down in Cornwall? You are back in Cornwall, aren't you?'

'Yes, and things are…' She struggled for the right word. 'Eventful.'

'Tell me.'

She did; ending with the discovery at the engine house and the discussion that had followed. 'Dan thinks I have to find out what changed Ellen and stop it from happening.'

'And what do you think?'

'That it's easy for him to say when he's not the one playing psychic Miss Marple.' She laughed. 'Men, eh?'

'He sounds like a good one though.'

Again, she imagined him as a schoolboy, play fighting with his friends in a tree house, before picturing herself back on the outcrop of rock, talking to a man called Alan about his childhood friend Dan. By the sound of it she would have liked that Alan. Perhaps they could have been friends. But still she found herself raising a silent prayer of thanks that she had never had to find out.

'He is,' she said. 'I don't know what I'd have done without him. It's just…'

'That when you dream you dream alone.'

Her fire was lit. She stared at the flames. 'Yes.'

'Are there any clues in the article as to what made her change?

Her laptop was on the coffee table in front of her. The article about Ellen was displayed on its screen. She had tried to read it in detail but couldn't. The facts of the crime still unnerved her too much.

But she did remember something.

'The night before her execution the guards heard Ellen in her cell cursing her mother. She seemed to blame her for all that had gone wrong in her life.'

'Perhaps that's something else you have in common.'

She was confused. 'I don't blame my mother.'

'I mean perhaps she was psychic too.'

'Or perhaps she was just crazy. What normal person does what she did, let alone feels proud about it?'

'But she *was* normal once, just like Dan's friend. I'm sure Dan wishes he could go back to that day and change the outcome, but he can't. He doesn't have your gift.'

'You sound like him. You make it sound easy too.'

'I don't mean to. But I do think he's right about Ellen. Whatever she needs you to do, it has to take place in her world, not ours. That's why she's taking you there.'

'But taking me there isn't enough. In my dream when I was on the cliff with her I couldn't feel anything or touch anyone. It was as if I was made of air and viewing her world through a pane of glass. How can I change anything if I can't even communicate?'

'Do you remember,' Jennifer asked, 'what I said to you in the service station about spiritual gaydar? I sense vibrations in others. Sometimes it's as faint as a whisper and sometimes, with people like you it's as loud as a bass drum.'

'Yes. I remember.'

'There's one thing I didn't tell you. In all my life I have never sensed a vibration as strong as yours. No other has even come close. I don't know how you communicate with Ellen, Meg, but one thing I do know is that you have the most extraordinary gift I have ever encountered and if anyone can find a way to reach her then it's you.'

She didn't answer. She knew the words were meant to encourage, yet all they did was make her task seem more impossible.

'Meg? Did you hear what I said?'

'Yes.'

'Does it help?'

'Yes.' She tried to sound convincing.

'No, it doesn't. But it should. Your problem is that you're still viewing this situation like a puzzle you have to solve. I guess the lawyer in you dies hard. With a gift like yours it's not about being analytical. It's about allowing yourself to feel; to really connect with Ellen and her world. Give of yourself, Meg. Do that and you'll find all the answers you need.'

'Thanks.'

'That didn't help either, did it?'

'No.' Again, she laughed. 'But what does help is talking to you. Dan's been brilliant. He really has. But he'll never understand what I'm experiencing in quite the same way as you. It means a lot to me to know that you're there.'

'I am. All you have to do is pick up a phone. I can even come down to Cornwall if you want.'

They continued to talk; Meg pouring out her anxieties while Jennifer listened patiently, offering reassurances when needed. Outside it was raining hard. As she listened to the drops hit the window Meg felt snug, only it wasn't the fire that was responsible. Jennifer's voice was as soothing as a hug. It made her feel like a child confiding in a parent, safe in the knowledge of not being judged.

The conversation over, she remained on the sofa, staring at the flames. The air in the room seemed static. She knew she was alone.

Her body ached. Lack of sleep from the previous night was catching up with her. She needed rest, though how much she would get was anyone's guess.

She switched off the laptop then went to put out the fire. As she watched the flames shrivel and die a tingling in her fingers told her she was alone no longer.

The fire extinguished, she made her way upstairs.

In the stillness of her darkened bedroom she stared up at the ceiling, counting cracks in the plaster, listening to the roar of the wind and struggling against the weight of eyelids that felt as if they were made of lead. Each time they closed she forced them back open. It grew ever harder; like fighting against the rush of an incoming tide.

Until suddenly it was easy and she knew the battle was lost.

She sat up. Ellen stood at the foot of the bed with arm outstretched. She stared into the unblinking eyes and told herself that the monster before her had once been a frightened child crying alone on the cliffs at night for those she had lost.

'I'm sorry they died,' she whispered. 'I'm sorry you had to feel that pain. I know what it's like. I really do.'

She waited for an answer, but none came. The arm remained outstretched...

This time there was no blinding light. She remained in virtual darkness; the only illumination coming through a crack in the curtains. For a moment she believed herself still in her own bedroom. Then, as her eyes adjusted, she saw that she was not.

The room she now stood in was longer and thinner; the ceiling was lower, and the door was against the left side wall. There was little furniture; just a chest of drawers with two single beds on either side of it.

Where am I? What house is this?

She walked towards the window, reaching instinctively for the curtain but grasping only air. The floor beneath her had no carpet and her feet were bare. She should have felt cold but didn't. She felt nothing, just as she could touch nothing. Yet again she was a ghost; unseen in a world that was not her own.

She peered through the gap in the fabric, searching for anything that would give her some bearings. A full moon sent its light to shine on the row of buildings opposite. One of them was tall and thin and had a sign above the door. Squinting to see better she read the words 'The Kings Arms.'

It's the square! I'm in Saltran Square.

She tried to picture the square as she knew it. All the buildings were now shops. Which one was she in?

It's not The Corsair. The angle is all wrong. Is it the

butcher's? The art gallery?

There was no road running through it or a War Memorial at its centre. Its surface was rough earth through which a lone dog pawed as if searching for food.

She heard a sigh. The occupant of the bed to her right had turned in their sleep, shifting the blanket from off their face. She approached; instinct making her tiptoe even though there was no chance of disturbing the sleeper. In spite of the poor light she could see that it was a girl with long fair hair spread around her head like a halo.

It's Ellen. I've come to her as she dreams just as she comes to me.

She bent down; studying the features of the face, trying to determine age. Ellen was older than she had been on the cliff. That much was clear. But how much older? What year was it now? And why had Ellen brought her to it?

From far away a floorboard creaked. Ellen's eyes sprung open. A startled, Meg backed away. The creaks grew closer. They sounded like footsteps; soft, hesitant footsteps as if someone else was on tiptoe. Ellen looked towards the door, her hand tightening on the blanket that covered her. As she followed her gaze Meg saw a faint trace of light appear under its frame.

'Kat,' Ellen whispered. 'Are you awake?'

No answer came from the other bed. Ellen sighed with what sounded like relief.

The light grew brighter and the footsteps louder until they stopped on the other side of the door. Still unable to fight instinct Meg retreated to the darkest corner of the room then watched as the handle turned, the door opened and the visitor was revealed.

It was a man of about forty-five; tall and heavy set with thinning hair and soft, fleshy features. He was barefoot, dressed in a nightgown and carrying a gas lamp that sent shadows scuttling across the floor. From her corner Meg saw Ellen had pulled the blanket up over her head.

The man put the lamp on the chest of drawers then stared down at Ellen. He whispered her name just as she had whispered

Kat's. She didn't answer; just lay motionless as he sat down on the bed and pulled the blanket from her face. At last Meg could see her properly. She was no more than twelve; still a child except for her eyes which had a watchfulness that had not been there before.

The man stroked Ellen's cheek then slid his finger down towards her chest. She sat up, trying to push his hand away. He grabbed her wrist and squeezed it. 'Hush, now,' he whispered. 'There's no need for that.'

'I'm tired, Uncle John. I want to sleep.'

'You will sleep, sweetheart. You'll sleep afterwards. You'll sleep well, I promise, once you've made me happy.'

'No. I don't want to. Not tonight. Please, not tonight.'

'Yes, you do. How could you not when it's so easy?'

'Please, Uncle John. I'll make you happy tomorrow. I promise I will.'

'Tomorrow's no good. It has to be tonight. You want to make me happy, don't you? You know how important it is.' John gestured to where Kat lay curled into a ball. 'Look at your sister. Look how soundly she sleeps. Do you think she'd sleep so well in the asylum?'

Ellen's eyes widened with fear. 'You wouldn't send her there.'

'But that's where she belongs. Everyone says so. Everyone but me. I say they're wrong. I say she belongs with us. We're her family and families belong together. Families take care of each other.' Again, his finger caressed Ellen's cheek. 'Families make each other happy.'

'You won't send her away? You promise?'

'No. I'll never do that. Not as long as you're a good girl and make me happy. You want to make me happy, don't you? Tell me that you do.'

Meg saw Ellen swallow. 'Yes.'

'Now lie back. That's all you have to do. Just lie back and relax…' The voice was soft as silk but at its centre was a core of steel. The sound of it made Meg's skin crawl. It was just like the tone her stepmother had used to Grace in the kitchen.

She felt sickened. She felt dirty and ashamed.

But most of all she felt rage.

Her hands clenched into fists. She wanted to run across the room, pull John from Ellen and beat him to a pulp. But she couldn't. She couldn't stop him. She couldn't even touch him. She was as useless as Kat whose eyes now kept opening and shutting while the ball in which she was curled grew tighter as if she were trying to take refuge within her own body.

She's awake! Oh God she's awake and she can see it all.

But I don't have to. I can wake up. I can escape.

Meg shut her eyes, trying to will herself back to the safety of her own bed. She slapped her own face, pulled her hair and scratched her arms. The pain was intense but still she remained trapped in her dream.

But was she trapped in the room?

John had not closed the door properly. It stood open a crack. Was there enough space for her to pass through, and if not, could she walk through the wall itself? She didn't know but had to try. She hurried towards the door. The gap was bigger than she had thought. She peered through it, bracing herself to make the effort.

Then she screamed.

Someone stood in the hallway, blocking her path.

It was a woman; tall and slim, wearing a white gown and with long, fair hair that hung loose around her shoulders. Even in the poor light Meg could see the resemblance to Ellen. The woman was like an older, plainer version.

It's Clara. It's her aunt.

'Do something! Stop him! She's your niece! She's your sister's child! How can you let this happen?'

Clara's head was resting on the wood of the door. Her body was shaking while tears rolled down her cheeks. Suddenly Meg's anger was gone, replaced by pity.

She wants to help. She wants to stop it. Only she's too afraid. She's…

From behind her she heard movement. Turning, she saw that John had risen to his feet and was reaching for the lamp. When she looked back Clara had vanished.

John made his way to the door. 'You bastard,' Meg hissed as he passed. 'You'll burn in hell for what you've done.' He continued on his way, as oblivious to her presence as he had been to that of his wife, closing the door behind him and plunging the room back into darkness. Silence too. Just for a moment.

Then Meg heard someone sobbing.

At first she thought it was Ellen. Then, as her ears followed the sound to its source she realised it was Kat. As her eyes adjusted to the dark she saw Ellen leave her own bed and hurry towards that of her sister. 'Shush, Kat. I'm here and everything is alright.'

Kat gave a gulping sound. 'But I saw…'

'No.' Ellen's voice was firm. 'You didn't see anything. You were dreaming. That's all it was, Kat; a bad dream.'

'Uncle John…'

'He's asleep in bed. He's been there all night.' Ellen kissed her sister. 'You should be asleep too. You'll be tired in the morning if you don't sleep now.'

'I'm scared, Ellie.'

'Why? There's nothing to be scared of. I'm here and I love you. Don't you remember what I told you when Pa and Uncle Matt died? I told you that you're not alone. I'll always look after you. You believe me, don't you?'

Kat didn't answer; just hugged her sister as if her life depended on it.

They remained like that for some time; two sisters clinging to each other in the stillness of their room. As Meg watched them she remembered two other sisters doing the same on their first night in a Children's Home on the outskirts of London. The younger had been crying for a dead mother and an absent father while the elder had tried to offer comfort; pushing her own fears to one side while promising that that there was nothing to be scared of as she would always keep her safe.

But I failed. I failed her, just like Ellen will fail Kat.

She couldn't bear it. A sob burst out of her throat.

Ellen's back stiffened. Her head turned.

'You heard that?' cried Meg. 'You can hear me? Tell me you

can hear me!'

Ellen stared vaguely in her direction then turned back to her sister.

'What is it?' Kat whispered.

'It was nothing. Move up, Kat. I'll lie beside you until you fall asleep.'

The two of them lay down in the bed. Kat pressed herself against Ellen who began to stroke her hair and hum a lullaby. Meg moved across the room; staring down at them. Kat's eyes closed, and her breathing deepened while Ellen continued to hum.

'You did hear me,' Meg told her. 'You sensed me. You sensed something. I know you did.'

From out in the square the dog began to howl. Ellen turned towards the window, still humming and stroking her sister's hair.

'What is it you sense? Is it my pain? Is it my tears?'

No answer came; just the mournful lilt of the lullaby. A wave of frustration swept over Meg, followed by dizziness as her vision seemed to blur…

When it cleared she was back in her own bed.

It was still dark. Her alarm clock read 3.47. Dawn was hours away but there would be no more sleep for her that night; not after what she had seen.

Her eyes were wet. She rubbed at them with her hand. Her skin felt dirty. She felt dirty all over.

Twenty minutes later she sat in a hot bath, trying to scrub the feeling away. Her arms were covered in scratches while strands of newly washed hair floated in the soapy water. In her desperation to wake she had done herself more harm than she had realised. Not that it had done any good.

But it could have been worse.

She could have been Ellen.

Her mind kept playing the scene over and over again. It was as if there was a projector in her head that she couldn't turn off. She lay down in the bath, submerging her head in the hope that the water would act as a barrier to the unwanted image. But in its place came another: Ellen's father and uncle standing in a dimly lit tunnel, staring up at the ceiling, listening to the sound of boulders rolling across the sea bed, joking with each other just as they had on the cliff with no awareness that in seconds the ceiling would collapse and the sea would rush in and devour them whole.

She sat up again, gasping for breath. The air in the bathroom tasted stale. The air in her father's house had tasted the same way. Alison had had a phobia about air born germs. Even on the hottest of days the windows had remained shut and as she had paced from room to room she had felt as if she was walled up alive.

But it could have been worse.

She could have been Grace.

The projector in her head clicked back on, only now the film was different. There were new players, there were new scenes, and yet again she could not switch it off.

Time passed. The water grew cold. It made her shiver. Still she remained there, rubbing soap into her skin.

Only now it was guilt she was trying to wash away.

Ten o'clock in the morning. Dan knocked on Meg's door.

There was no answer. He peered through her living room window and saw her pacing up and down the room, wrapped in a dressing gown and with a phone pressed to her ear. He tapped on the glass. She nodded then vanished into the hallway. The door opened. As he entered he saw her return to the living room, still talking into the phone.

'So, you've definitely got it in stock.'

A muffled hiss came from the other end of the line.

'I'll pick it up later today. Thanks again for your help. I really appreciate it.'

He followed her into the room. Her laptop was on the coffee table. The screen displayed the cover of a book called 'Crimes of Cornwall.' As he scrolled up the page he saw it was from a website for a second-hand bookshop in Truro.

The call ended. ‘Is this who you were talking to?’ he asked.

‘Yes. The book’s got a whole chapter on Ellen’s case. It’s bound to be more use than the other stuff I’ve found.’

‘What other stuff?’

She gestured to a pile of papers on the table. He flicked through them. Judging from their contents she had visited every site on the web that mentioned Ellen’s name. Most had little information; barely a paragraph. The most comprehensive coverage still came from the article on the Bodmin jail website. She had printed that out too and covered its contents in hand written notations. One in particular caught his eye; the word ‘Wrong,’ followed by a row of exclamation marks.

He held up the page. ‘What’s wrong?’

‘The address in Bamber.’

‘Bamber?’

‘That’s where the murder actually happened. Not here in Saltran. Ellen’s family must have moved there but I don’t know when. Hopefully the book will tell me more.’

He tried to recall the article. At the time of reading it her distress and his own shock had caused him to forget much of the contents. ‘How do you know it’s the wrong address?’

‘I’ve been reading up on Bamber. The article says the murder happened in a house on Ellis Street, only I’ve checked with tourist information and there’s no road with that name. There’s one called Ellis Avenue but it’s in completely the wrong place. Their house was by the harbour. There’s a place called Easton Street. I’m guessing that’s it.’

He opened his mouth to speak.

‘And before you ask, I’ve checked the layout of the place back in the 1880s and my theory holds good.’

He put down the papers. ‘Someone’s been busy,’ he remarked.

‘I have to find out everything. The dreams are just random scenes. I need to know the whole story.’ As she spoke she ran a hand through her hair. The sleeve of her dressing gown dropped revealing deep scratches on her arm.

'Jesus! What happened to you?'

Looking uncomfortable, she pulled the sleeve back into position.

'Meg?'

'Can you stay for a while?'

'Yes; for as long as you want.'

'Then why don't you put the kettle on. There's another book shop I need to phone. Once I've done that I'll tell you all about it...'

Half an hour later he sat on her sofa listening as she described the events of the previous night.

'I tried to wake up,' she told him, 'but I couldn't. I couldn't stop her uncle either. I couldn't do anything.'

'That's not your fault,' he told her gently. 'Don't beat yourself up.'

'There's no need. I've done that already.'

'I'm sorry. That was a dumb thing to say.'

'No, it wasn't.' She sighed. 'I just feel so helpless. I don't know how to reach her. I nearly did at one point. She seemed to sense my presence, but when I called out to her she couldn't hear me.'

'But you *will* reach her. I'm sure of it.'

'At least I know one thing. The Ellen I saw last night was no monster. She was still the same person I saw on the cliff. Whatever changed her happened later. I just have to find out when.'

'Maybe you won't need to. Maybe she'll show you. Do you know what I think? I think the dreams are her way of gaining your trust and proving to you that she's someone worth saving.'

'She's done that already. Her only goal is to protect her sister. She knows she's the stronger of the two and that Kat needs her protection. No matter what happens she never loses sight of it and that makes her a much better person than me.'

'That's not true.'

'Yes, it is. I lost sight of it when our mother died. That's why our stepmother was able to...' She stopped; exhaled. 'It was my fault. If I'd been looking after Grace properly it never would have happened.'

'What wouldn't?'

She didn't answer.

'You don't have to tell me. But I wish you would. You have to talk about Grace sometime. You can't go on trying to block out the past. You'll only hurt yourself if you do.' Reaching out he stroked her arm. 'And I'd say you're hurting more than enough already.'

'I don't mind hurting. It's Grace being hurt that I can't deal with. When my mother was alive I promised her I'd always take care of Grace. But I didn't. Not when we were kids. And not when we were adults either.'

'But you tried your best. Isn't that what your mother always told you? That all anyone could ask of you was that you tried your best?'

Again, she didn't answer. This time he didn't push her; sensing that she was finally ready to open up.

'When my mother died, my father was living in London. He had a new wife, a new daughter and a whole new life. I'd thought he'd forgotten about us, but he hadn't. He came to the funeral, and when it was over he took us home with him again…'

So, she told him about those months with her father; of what her stepmother had done to Grace and how she had always felt responsible for letting it happen. 'After Mum died I just shut off from everyone. Even Grace. That's why she didn't tell me what Alison was doing. If I hadn't been so self-absorbed none of it would have happened.'

'No! It wasn't your fault. You were a kid, just like your sister. She wasn't your responsibility. You had adults to be responsible for you. You didn't fail her. Your father and stepmother failed you both.'

She didn't answer.

'You know I'm right.'

'Maybe you are. But I did fail her. I failed her at the end.'

'What do you mean?'

'Grace was pregnant when she died. Did I tell you that? She was four months pregnant with her first child. She and her husband were living in Kent, but she came into London for a check-up. I went with her. She told me I didn't need to but I insisted.' She stopped. Again, she sighed. 'Just like I always did…'

It was a Thursday lunchtime. Meg walked with Grace down Fleet Street towards Ludgate Circus. Their progress was slow. The pavement was full of people, just as the road was full of traffic. Everyone seemed to be in a rush. It started to rain. Grace reached into her bag.

'You don't need a brolly,' Meg told her. 'We're nearly at the restaurant.'

'I'm sorry. What was I thinking?' Grace shut her bag again.

'Well, get one if you want.'

'Do I have your permission?'

'You don't need my permission.'

'That makes a change.'

'What's that supposed to mean?'

'Nothing.'

They continued down the street. The rain grew heavier and more and more people were opening umbrellas: one of which nearly poked Grace in the stomach. 'Watch what you're doing!' Meg snapped at its owner. 'This woman is pregnant.'

Looking embarrassed the man scuttled away.

'How kind of you to remember,' said Grace archly.

They reached a set of traffic lights. 'What's the matter?' Meg demanded. 'You've been in a foul mood since we left the doctor's.'

Grace didn't answer. Just exhaled.

'Well?'

'Come on. We've got the green man.' Grace crossed the road.

A confused Meg hurried after her. 'What have I done?'

Grace turned to face her. 'I'm pregnant, Meg. Me. Not you.'

'I know that.'

'Well you could have fooled me. It was my doctor's appointment, but I barely got to open my mouth. You did all the talking. You asked all the questions. I might as well not have been there.'

'Don't be silly. It wasn't like that.'

'Yes, it was. It was like being with my mother, not my sister. I'm not a child, Meg. I'm a grown woman.'

'I know you are...'

'But you don't know it. In your eyes I'm still six years old.'

'I'm just watching out for you.'

'Well I don't need you to so back off, OK?'

The words hurt. Meg's defences rose. 'This is Pete talking, isn't it?'

'No. He's got nothing to do with it.'

Meg snorted.

'He doesn't!'

'I'm not stupid. He didn't want me to come with you today, did he? Well maybe if he'd come himself I wouldn't have had to.'

'He had meetings.'

'So did I, but I cancelled them because you and your baby are more important.'

'Oh, for heaven's sake...'

'I'm right, aren't I? He should have been here today only he couldn't bear to change his precious schedule.'

Grace shook her head. 'You never stop, do you?'

'Stop what?'

'Trying to make trouble between Pete and me. Every time I see you you're taking shots at him.'

'Me? He's the troublemaker. He's always been jealous of me.'

'You're the one who's jealous, Meg. Not him.'

'Rubbish...'

'You are! And it's getting worse and worse. When Pete and I first got together you really liked him. You two got on famously.'

Meg didn't answer.

'You did,' Grace told her.

'I know.'

'So...'

'But that was before.'

'Before what?'

'Before I started losing you.'

Grace's expression softened. 'Oh, Meg...'

'We used to be a team.'

'We still are.'

'Not like we were. Now I feel shut out.'

'I'm not shutting you out.' Grace sighed. 'It's just...'

'What?'

'Things change, Meg. I'm married. I'm going to have a baby. You're still my sister. I love you and you'll always be an important part of my life. But it can't be like it was when we were growing up. I've got a family of my own and they have to come first now. Don't you see that?'

They stared at each other as people pushed past them. Rain was dripping down Grace's face. Meg battled an urge to wipe it away.

'Don't you?' Grace asked again.

She didn't answer. A voice in her head screamed for her to agree.

But she felt rejected. And it hurt.

So she lashed out.

'You selfish cow. After all I've done for you.'

Grace's eyes widened. 'What?'

'I was only nine when Mum died. I was only a kid myself, but I had to grow up overnight because that was what you needed. There were no tears for me, Gracie. No crying for Mum. You did all of that. All I ever did was comfort.'

'Don't...'

'Why not? You never would have survived at Dad's on your own. You never would have survived the bullies at the home either. Where do you think you'd be today if I hadn't been around when you were growing up? Because you certainly wouldn't be talking to doctors about the baby you're having with your smug, rich husband. No way, Gracie. You'd probably be a basket case in some institution.'

Grace's eyes began to flash. 'Well, we'll never know, will we? I never had the chance to find out because you never gave it to me.'

'You were lucky I was there to protect you.'

'Lucky? You didn't protect me. You suffocated me! I couldn't

move without your permission. I couldn't draw breath without checking it was OK with you first. You didn't want a sister, Meg. You just wanted a shadow. Someone to trail after you like a puppy and tell you how strong and wonderful you were.'

'I never wanted that!'

'Yes, you did. You still want it now. You can't bear the fact that I've gone out and made a life for myself that doesn't revolve around you.'

'So, you don't want me around anymore. Is that it? God, Pete's got you well trained, hasn't he? You think I was controlling but I'm nothing compared to him.'

'He doesn't control me. He loves me!'

'I love you!'

'No, you don't. I'm just a prop for your ego. I remember when we were kids how you used to bleat on about how Mum's death was your fault. About how you could have stopped it, like you were God or something.'

'You leave Mum out of this!'

'Why? She has everything to do with this. When she died a part of you died too. You stopped being a real person and became this...robot!'

Meg slapped her face.

Grace gasped, covering her cheek with her hand. A couple of passers-by stopped to look. Meg ignored them. She was too angry to care.

'Well if that's what you think of me then go to hell because as of this moment I am done with you!'

Grace pushed past her, hurrying away. She remained where she was, breathing deeply and her heart pounding so fast it threatened to burst.

And heard the screeching of brakes.

Followed by a thud.

For a moment she was frozen to the spot. It was only when someone pushed past her that she regained the ability to move.

A taxi had stopped in the middle of the street. The driver was climbing out; his face white with shock as he hurried towards the body of a young woman that lay in the middle of the road.

As Meg ran towards it she heard a voice screaming the same words over and over again. It was only later she realised that the voice was hers.

'I didn't mean it! I didn't mean it! Oh God, I didn't mean it...'

'And you didn't,' said Dan softly. 'It was just a row. You were angry. So was she. We all say things we don't mean; especially when the person we're rowing with is someone we love.'

'Do you know what the worst part is?' she asked him.

'What?'

'I couldn't cry. Not even at her funeral. I wanted to, but it was like I'd forgotten how. Everyone else did; even my father. Everyone was in tears but me.'

'Your father came to the funeral?'

'Yes. I didn't tell him about it. One of our old neighbours did. The funeral was in Wickenham, you see. Grace was buried next to Mum. When it was over Dad told me that he was sorry for what had happened when we were children, but I wouldn't listen. I still hated him too much. That's what I told myself anyway. The truth is that it was easier to hate him than hate myself.'

'You shouldn't hate yourself. Hate him all you want. He deserves it. But you don't. Grace wouldn't want you to.'

She gave a hollow laugh.

'It's true.'

'Shortly before I agreed to this sabbatical my brother in law, Pete came to see me. He had some papers relating to Grace's estate that he needed me to sign. While I was doing so I told him how much I missed her; how much I was hurting, and he just laughed. He told me I wasn't capable of love. That something had died inside me when I was a child and that I wasn't capable of real emotion. He also told me that Grace hated me. The two of them were planning to move away apparently. Grace didn't want me near her baby. She didn't want to risk me messing up her child's life the way I'd messed up hers. And I *did* mess it up. From the moment we arrived at the children's home I wouldn't let her out of my sight. I didn't want her to make friends. I didn't trust anyone else and I didn't want her to either. The only person I wanted her to trust was me. I suffocated her; just like she said. It was because she was trying to get away from me that she was hit by that taxi and…' He saw her swallow. 'And that's why this is so important.'

'What is?'

'Saving Ellen. Kat needs her far more than Grace ever needed me. Their uncle wanted to put Kat in an Asylum. Once Ellen was dead that's probably just what he did. Ellen was the one who kept her safe and I have to make sure that she can keep on doing so. I can't communicate with her yet but I'm going to find a way. I have to.'

She was staring straight ahead at the empty fireplace. Gently he reached out, took her chin in his hand and turned her face towards his.

'Do you remember that conversation you had with your Headmistress where she said you were a good person?'

'Yes.'

'Well she was right. And she was right about something else too. Your mother is still a part of you. A *huge* part. And right now, you are doing her proud.'

She gave a weak smile. 'I wish.'

'I *know*. I know because I'm proud of you too. You're a special person, Meg Parker, and I am proud to call you my friend.'

She started to cry. He held her, saying nothing, letting her release her pain just as once, twenty years earlier, a compassionate teacher had sat in a classroom, allowing a frightened child to do the same.

Chapter 9

Lunchtime. Meg sat in a Truro pub with a copy of 'Crimes of Cornwall' in her hand.

The pub was packed with a mixture of locals and tourists. It was early April and the weather was starting to improve. Already she was noticing more and more walkers passing through Saltran. On the next table an Australian family poured over guide books while complaining about slow service. As she watched them she noticed a pair of local men doing the same. One of them met her gaze and rolled his eyes. Clearly, he thought she was local too. The realisation pleased her.

She turned to the chapter on Ellen's case. It was only five pages long but still more than twice the length of anything else she had found. And just maybe it would contain the clue that she needed.

Crossing her fingers, she began to read.

The murder of Samuel Roberts by Ellen Foley took place in Easton Street, Bamber, on the night of 9th April 1881 in the house of local merchant John Goderidge.

At least they had the right street name. That was something. Sipping her mineral water, she pressed on.

At the time of the murder Ellen Foley was eighteen. She had spent most of her life in the coastal town of Saltran. She had a twin called Kate who was mentally handicapped from birth. The sisters lost both their parents in early childhood; their mother to consumption and their father to a mining accident. As orphans they were taken in by their uncle, John Goderidge, husband of their mother's sister, Clara. There is little information on Ellen's life with the Goderidges but no one who knew her in Saltran recalls her speaking badly of either of them.

'That's because she was afraid to, you bloody idiot!' she said aloud, as if scolding the author. Her voice carried and the Australians turned to stare. Vowing to keep her opinions to herself she read on.

'John Goderidge was a comparatively wealthy man with interests in many local businesses. He had a reputation for being hard-nosed in business matter and was not well liked in the community. His wife was a devout woman closely involved in the activities of the local Church. She was also kind hearted; actively involved in raising money to help families suffering due to the decline of the local mining industry.

The family moved to Bamber in 1879 when Ellen was sixteen. Their departure from Saltran appears to have been prompted by a local scandal. One Sunday, during the Church service, Ellen collapsed in her pew and suffered a miscarriage. The identity of the unborn child's father was never established, though John Goderidge told a neighbour he had often had to reprimand his niece for flirting with local boys. He moved the family to Bamber soon afterwards, presumably with the intention of protecting Ellen from gossip.

She couldn't contain herself. 'Protecting yourself more like, you hypocritical shit!'

Again, the Australians stared at her. 'Sounds like a good book,' observed one of them with a smile. 'Can I borrow it when I finish my Tom Clancy?'

The family settled in Easton Street in the prosperous part of Bamber. A few months after their arrival Ellen was again taken ill very suddenly, prompting a doctor to be summoned in the middle of the night. There is no indication of the nature of her illness, but it is possible that another miscarriage was the cause. At around the same time her uncle again complained to neighbours of her flirtatious behaviour. Those same neighbours remembered Ellen as a pretty but solitary girl whose greatest pleasure was going for walks by the harbour and spending hours at a time sitting on its wall watching the ships at sea.

She pictured an excited child on the cliff. Back then a ship had been a symbol of hope. In Bamber it had probably symbolised escape.

Samuel Roberts was an architect, hired by John Goderidge to design a new house on the outskirts of the town. When he arrived in Bamber in November 1880 he was 25. His parents were dead and his elder brother, Francis, also an architect, had recently emigrated to America. Those that knew Samuel recalled a serious but likeable young man who was passionate about his work and talked often of his plans to join his brother in America and go into partnership with him.

Within weeks of his arrival Samuel had become close to both John Goderidge and his wife. Clara Goderidge told friends that she believed he considered them substitute parents while for her own part she was starting to think of him as a son. Though he was staying in lodgings in the town he was soon taking most of his meals with the family.

No one knows when Samuel's relationship with Ellen began. Clara and John only discovered its existence after the murder. Though Samuel was friendly with some of the young men who shared his lodgings none of them were aware of it either. The only fact that can be established with certainty is that it existed by early February of 1881 when Samuel wrote to his brother in America, telling him that he and Ellen were in love. In another letter to his brother, written only four days before the murder, Samuel again spoke of his love for Ellen and his desire to make her his wife. Neither his fellow lodgers, nor the Goderidges, noticed any change in his mood in subsequent days which only goes to make the events that followed all the more baffling.

At shortly before midnight on April 9th^{h}, William Purdon and his wife Maria were preparing for bed when they heard a series of appalling screams coming from the house of their next-door neighbours; the Goderidges. Mr Purdon went to knock on their door to see if he could be of any assistance but received no answer. Concerned, he went to rouse the local Police Constable; Sergeant Hooper. By the time Sergeant Hooper knocked on the door a small crowd had gathered to watch. Again, there was no answer, but when, *after nearly ten minutes of knocking, Sergeant Hooper cried out that he would break the door down it was opened by an ashen faced John Goderidge.*

'You had best come in,' Mr Goderidge told him. 'There has been a murder.'

Sergeant Hooper, Mr Purdon and two other local men entered the house. John Goderidge led them to an upstairs room where Samuel's body lay. He had been stabbed dozens of times; his eyes cut out, his trousers partly removed, and his genitalia hacked off and thrust into his open mouth. Sergeant Hooper testified in Court that it was the most ghastly crime he had ever seen and that one of the men with him vomited at the sight of it.

There were three people in the room with the body: Clara Goderidge, Ellen Foley and her sister Kate. It transpired that they and John Goderidge were the only occupants of the house that night. Though the Goderidges employed a live-in maid called Molly Bedowes, she was away; visiting her family in Truro.

Clara and Kate were hysterical. Ellen was completely calm. Her dress was covered in blood and the knife was in her hand. 'I did it,' she told the men, 'and I'm glad of it.' She then handed the knife to Sergeant Hooper. When he asked her why she had done it she gave no answer.

A quick inspection of the body revealed a note in Ellen's hand asking Samuel to visit her at that hour. Sergeant Hooper asked why she had wanted to see him. Again, she gave no answer. When he told her she was under arrest, her sister began to howl while Clara, who was growing calmer, tried to comfort her. Before leaving the room Ellen walked over to her sister and kissed her on the cheek. When she was led out into the street the crowd, who had by now heard of what had happened, screamed curses at her. She remained as calm as she had in the room, showing no emotion at all.

She was taken to Bodmin Jail. On her arrival she was questioned as to her reasons for committing the crime; it being suggested that they might help the Judge show leniency at her trial. 'What do my reasons matter?' she is reported to have asked. 'I know they will hang me and I would rather that than prison. What is life but imprisonment? Death at least provides release.' After that she would say no more.

Briefly Meg closed the book; her mind full of questions. Why had Ellen given no reason? Did she even have one? Had she become such a monster by this point in her life that no reason was needed?

Her silence continued during her brief trial. Throughout its course her composure faltered only once when she saw her family sitting at the back of the Court. She became agitated, demanding their removal, which the Judge ordered so the proceedings might continue. Even when the sentence of death was pronounced she remained calm. The only emotion she is known to have shown was on the night before her execution. Warders heard her calling out to her dead mother, cursing her for not helping her child in her hour of need. Some of them asked her again as to her motivation for the murder but she would reveal nothing and took her secret to the grave.

John Goderidge, who had visited his niece in jail, was touched by the kindness a particular warder named Agnes Murray, had shown her. After the trial, to show his gratitude, he gave Agnes and her husband funds to start up a business of their own.

The Goderidge family never recovered from the events of that terrible April night. Ellen's sister, Kate, began to walk in her sleep. Six months after the execution she lost her footing one night, fell down a flight of stairs and broke her neck. Clara Goderidge appears to have suffered some sort of nervous breakdown. She became a recluse who rarely left the house. John Goderidge devoted himself to caring for her; his business interests dwindling as a result and his fortune with it. After the death of his wife in 1886 he sold his house in Bamber, moved to another part of the country and his ultimate fate remains unknown.

She closed the book; her head still full of questions. Had the miscarriages affected Ellen's mind? Had they damaged her so much as to render her capable of killing with such savagery and so little remorse? Was it the years of abuse that had done it, or had she simply fallen from a tree house one summer afternoon like Dan's friend, Alan?

All the explanations were plausible; perfectly so.

But one question plagued her:

If she was a monster how could Samuel have loved her?

Perhaps he hadn't. Perhaps he had just been using her. Then, as now, small towns were a breeding ground for gossip. People would have known of her pregnancies and her reputation for being flirtatious. Perhaps she had been considered 'easy'. Perhaps Samuel had just been a selfish young man with low morals and a high libido looking for a purely physical release.

Yes, it was possible.

Except that if that was the case then why had he written to his brother only four days before his death saying that he loved Ellen and wanted to make her his wife?

Had something happened in those final days that had changed his mind? Had he seen another side of Ellen? Perhaps that was it. Perhaps he had visited the Goderidge house that night with the intention of breaking their engagement.

Yes, that made sense. It really did.

But if that was the case then why had Ellen written, asking him to come? Wouldn't he have been the one writing to arrange a meeting? And why had no one noticed any change in his mood? The ending of a love affair was always painful. Surely someone would have seen some sign of his suffering.

And why had the meeting taken place at so late an hour?

It was like an intricate Chinese puzzle. She could see the pieces before her yet try as she might she could not form them into a coherent shape.

Her mobile buzzed with a text from Dan. He was spending the day in Penzance, helping on another building project. '*Where are you?*' his text read, '*and is there any news?*'

As she typed out a reply saying she was no further forward a new course of action occurred to her.

A barmaid came to clear her table and ask if she wanted anything else.

'Yes,' she replied. 'Do you know a place nearby that sells maps?'

An hour later she arrived in Bamber. It was a small town on the Lizard peninsula, built around a bay with a small harbour. The outskirts were a muddle of ugly, modern developments but as she drove into the town centre they were replaced with cobbled streets full of handsome Victorian stone houses. Signs directed her to a car park on the waterfront. Leaving her car and with the town map in her hand she set out in search of Easton Street.

It was not difficult to find. Running directly up from the harbour it had a handsome looking pub on the corner called 'The Sailor's Rest.' As she passed it she wondered if it had existed back in the 1880s, and if John Goderidge and Samuel Roberts had ever ended a working day sitting at one its tables drinking beer together.

She walked up the street, staring at the houses; many of which were now shops or small hotels. She looked for a plaque marking the site of the crime but found none. A youth with a tray of fudge offered her a free sample. 'It's the best in Cornwall,' he told her. It was indeed good, and she followed him into the shop to buy some.

'There goes the diet,' she joked as he wrapped it for her.

'You don't need to diet,' he replied.

She smiled, grateful for the compliment but surprised at how little she needed it. The Meg Parker of one month ago would have spent an hour at the gym for every piece consumed but that person now seemed very far away.

'Do you know which the Goderidge house is?' she asked.

'Is that a hotel?'

'No. It was the site of the Samuel Roberts murder. It's a very famous case that happened in this street.'

'Did it? I wouldn't know. I'm down here from Reading for the surfing. There's a tourist information office in Wheeler Street though. I'm sure they could help you out.'

The woman at the tourist information was just as friendly and just as unhelpful. 'Wasn't Samuel Roberts a smuggler?'

'No. He was an architect.'

'Oh.' The woman looked surprised. 'I thought he might have been a member of the Killgallan gang.'

'Who were they?'

'A gang of ship wreckers who used to meet in The Sailor's Rest pub after every successful job and split the loot. One night in 1822 the authorities cornered them there. You see one of the gang was having an affair with the wife of the local squire and when he ended it she sold them all out. Most of the gang were killed but the woman's lover escaped. A few days later he broke into her house, strangled her in front of her husband and then escaped. He was never caught. They made a TV movie about it a few years ago. It was lousy but the actor playing the wife's lover was the most gorgeous man I've ever seen. Apparently, he's just landed a regular role in some new Sci-Fi series so when it starts I'll be in groupie heaven!'

'So, you don't know anything about the Samuel Roberts case?'

'No. It's the Killgallan gang who are the tourist draw here. Why not try The Sailor's Rest? The landlord is about seventy and has lived here all his life. If anyone would know about your case it would be him.'

Roger, the landlord, did seem to know what she was talking about. 'Wasn't he murdered by his lover?'

'Yes, that's right.'

'She was crazy, wasn't she?'

Meg found herself feeling protective. 'Perhaps she had her reasons.'

'I'm sure she did. Perhaps she'd got a new hairdo and he forgot to compliment her on it. I know my wife would slaughter me if I made a mistake like that!'

'Do you know which the house was?'

Roger thought for a minute. 'Half way up the street there's a hotel called The Sea Breeze. I think that's it.' His face broke into a smile. 'In fact, I'm sure of it.'

The Sea Breeze was a bigger building than she had expected with steps leading up to the entrance and flower boxes beneath the windows. She stood at the foot of the steps thinking that this was where the lives of both Ellen and Samuel had effectively ended. It was tragic really. She tried to feel sad, but the feeling refused to come.

Climbing the stairs, she entered the hotel's lobby. The receptionist, who was talking to a middle-aged couple, gestured that she would soon be free. As she waited, Meg looked about her, taking in the elegant décor. Though it had a modern feel much of the building's Victorian charm had been maintained. No doubt back in Ellen's day this had been the entrance hall. Where had Ellen's bedroom been? Where had the murder taken place?

And why did she still feel nothing?

The middle-aged couple left. The receptionist beckoned to her. As she made her way over she suddenly realised why.

Roger was wrong. This is not the house. If it was I would feel it and I don't.

The receptionist asked if she wished to book a room. For the sake of politeness, she took a brochure and said she would be in touch. Then, feeling frustrated she left.

Twenty minutes later she walked along the wall of Bamber harbour.

The tide was out, and a dozen small boats and dinghies lay stranded in the mud with seagulls perched on their masts. The sun was shining and for the first time since her arrival in Cornwall the air felt warm. Summer was still some months distant, but it was definitely on its way.

She reached the end of the wall. The bay stretched out in front of her. A lone wind surfer danced across the surface of the water; his movements as graceful as a pirouette. Turning, she stared back at the town. She could see the corner of Easton Street forming a junction with another road. There were no cliffs and the countryside rolled down easily towards the coast. It was a gentler landscape than that of Saltran and prettier too, but she didn't like it as much.

She wondered if Ellen had felt the same.

Her frustration increased. She sat down on the wall and stared out to sea. The waves barely reached the wall but in time they would grow higher as the tide returned. She wondered if Ellen had sat and watched them just as she was doing now; finding in their simple beauty a solace for the ugliness of her day to day life.

Her stomach rumbled. She had eaten nothing all day. Reliving her experiences at her father's house had killed her appetite. As she thought back to her conversation with Dan she realised that he was the only person she had ever told what had happened there. But that was the difference between her and Ellen. When it came to the details of the murder, Ellen had never told anyone.

Was it because you didn't care? Were you really that much of a monster?

She tried to picture Ellen in her cell, refusing to answer the questions put to her. Instead she saw herself sitting in a police station, being questioned about the death of her stepmother. 'Why did you do it?' a policeman was asking. 'What made you commit such a terrible crime?'

'It wasn't terrible,' she answered. 'It was good. She deserved to die and I'm glad I did it.'

It could so easily have been like that. What if her father hadn't come back when he had? What if he hadn't been there to stop her? Would Alison have been able to stop her? Would she have been able to stop herself?

Or would the police have arrived to find a pregnant woman butchered by a blood drenched ten-year-old girl who felt not an ounce of remorse. A girl they would have considered a monster; just as a voracious press and public would have done. Would she have ended up the like one of the ten-year-old boys who killed Jamie Bulger; spending her adolescence in a secure facility before being released to the world with a new identity and the ever-present dread that one day her old one would be discovered.

Is that the only real difference between us? I was stopped and you weren't?

Am I really just as big a monster as you?

Or were you never a monster at all?

There was movement in the distance. A ship sailed into the bay; the wind catching at its sails as it glided on its way. How many ships had Ellen sat and watched? How many times had the sight of one made her dream in vain of escape?

As she watched the ship she heard Jennifer's voice in her head.

With a gift like yours it's not about being analytical. It's about allowing yourself to feel.

The words hadn't made sense then. Now, at last, they did.

It wasn't enough to feel for Ellen.

She had to feel like her.

So, she began to try.

I hate it here. I want to be on that ship. I want to take Kat, swim out to it and have them take us with them. It doesn't matter where they're going. All that matters is that it's so far away that no one will ever find us.

A light breeze blew against the back of her neck. It felt like human breath.

It feels like Uncle John when he comes to me at night, wanting me to make him happy. Will he come tonight? Oh, God, please don't let him come tonight.

The ship was almost across the bay. Soon it would be gone from sight. As she watched it she felt her heart ache.

Time is running out. They'll be waiting for me. They'll be angry if I'm late. I want to stay here but I can't. I have to go home.

Home...

She turned. Her eyes went straight to the corner of Easton Street, following the road that neighboured it as far as it went while in her head she saw a wooden door shaped like an arch with a knocker shaped like a dragon's head at its centre.

Rising to her feet she began to walk.

The road was called Hepton Street. The house with the arch shaped door was on the right-hand side. The door was no longer made of wood and there was no dragon shaped knocker. But it was the house. She knew it with every fibre of her being.

Unable to contain herself she gave a triumphant cry.

A woman with a shopping basket stopped to stare. 'Looking for a place to let?'

'Sorry?'

'Are you planning on taking a let?'

In her excitement she had failed to notice the sign that hung on a rail beneath one of the windows, giving the name of an estate agent and a telephone number.

'Um...yes.'

'Well, I hope it's what you're looking for.'

'Thank you. It most certainly is.'

The woman walked away. Meg remained where she was, studying the house. It was tall and thin; three stories of grey stone with large, rectangular windows. It was as grand as any house she had seen in Saltran; exactly the sort of place where a well to do businessman might choose to make his home.

An alleyway ran down its left side. She walked down it; following it as it twisted around the house which seemed to grow narrower at the rear. There was another door at the back and beyond it she could see a small, well maintained garden. From the outside it looked an elegant place but what was it like inside?

And how quickly could she find out?

Returning to the front of the house she took out her mobile and dialled the number for the estate agency. A recorded message told her that the office was closed that day for staff training. She left a message, describing herself as a prospective tenant and asking them to call her back to schedule a viewing.

The call made she switched off the phone. The sense of triumph persisted.

As Meg explored Bamber, Jennifer sat by the window in her Oxfordshire home, writing a letter to her brother who lived in Canada.

Her hand was aching; the first twinges of the rheumatism that had afflicted her mother and grandmother before her. As she stretched out her fingers she started to yawn. Soon she would have a nap. Once the idea of an afternoon rest would have struck her as ridiculous, but she was older now and the boundless energy that she had once taken for granted was no longer hers to command.

The letter was nearly finished. She imagined her brother's amusement as he read it. For years he had been on at her to buy a computer so that they could e-mail each other but after sitting in blank incomprehension through a week long 'teach yourself computing' course run by the local adult education college she had resolved to stick with pen and paper.

Her garden ran down towards the river. The afternoon was dry and mild, and a collection of boats made their way up and down the water. One in particular caught her eye; a narrow boat with rainbows painted on its sides. A man stood at the helm while two little girls sat on the roof, throwing pieces of bread to the swans that followed in their wake. They were pretty girls of about five who resembled each other so closely that she assumed they were twins.

As she watched them, Jennifer remembered Meg's story about the twin girls waving to ships from a cliff. On a sudden whim she shut her eyes and pictured the troubled young woman she had met in a service station. Keeping the image in her head she allowed her mind to wander; as if stretching out invisible fingers to see what thoughts, if any, she could reach.

At first there was nothing. The distance was just too great. Then there was the faintest hiss; like static on an old radio unable to pick up a distant signal.

And then it came; suddenly and without warning. A crisp, clear cry of triumph.

Her heart lifted. 'That's my girl,' she whispered to the image in her head.

Only for it to vanish; replaced by one of a church.

It flashed before her eyes and then was gone; like the fragment of a dream dispersing in the cold light of day.

Where was it? What did it mean? And what part in Ellen's story did it play?

But she didn't need to know. Meg did, and that was all that mattered.

Smiling to herself, she picked up her pen and continued to write.

Chapter 10

By the time she arrived back in Saltran Meg was ravenous. She made her way to the supermarket to buy some food.

Brian from The Corsair stood outside his pub smoking a cigarette. He gave her a sheepish grin as she passed. 'Bloody smoking ban! Now I have to brave the elements every time I want a puff.'

She laughed. 'Your lungs will thank you for it.'

'Bugger them. When I've got the craving not even a force ten gale can stop me.' He laughed too. 'We've got a quiz tonight. First prize is £50 and second prize is a bottle of bubbly. Are you and Dan coming?'

'Only if Dan's on someone else's team. Unless all the questions are on classic rock and local beer he'll be as much use as a budgie with a chain saw.'

Again, he laughed. His wife appeared to tell him that a barrel needed changing. After taking a final drag he vanished inside. Meg continued on her way, smiling to herself. A couple of weeks ago she had resented people assuming she and Dan were a couple. Now she didn't. They were a team, and she was glad of it.

The supermarket was nearly empty. The only other customers were Lorna and her friend, Aishling. As usual, the two of them were looking at magazines. Both gave her a friendly wave. Aishling's expression was cheerful, but Lorna looked downcast.

'Is something the matter?' Meg asked.

'She's got man trouble,' Aishling explained. 'There's this boy at school called Mark and Lorna wants him to ask her out. He's asked for her number, but he's had it for three days now and still hasn't called.'

'Do you think I should call him?' Lorna asked Meg.

'Do you want to call?'

'Yes…um…' Lorna hesitated. 'I'm not sure.'

'She doesn't want to look keen,' Aishling explained.

'He'll probably say no, anyway,' said Lorna wistfully. 'He's gorgeous.'

'And what's he going to do when he leaves school?' Meg

asked.

'I don't know. I don't think he does either.'

'Well, you do. You're going to be a hotshot lawyer. You've got brains and ambition and you're gorgeous too. He's probably intimidated by you. Most of the boys I knew at your age would have been.'

Lorna's face lit up. 'Do you think so?'

'Yes. Call him if you want. He'll probably be delighted. But if he's not then just remember it's not the end of the world. You're going to meet loads of great guys and trust me a couple of years from now you probably won't even remember his name.'

Lorna gave her a grateful smile. Aishling began to ask questions about where she bought her clothes. As she answered them she noticed Jed standing at the counter, reading a paper as he waited for people to serve. Normally he looked animated and happy but this time he seemed tired and rather sad. The sight worried her. She hoped there was nothing wrong.

And then she noticed something else.

There was a light around him. It was soft and warm and enveloped him like a delicate cloud. Only it wasn't really a cloud. It was more like an aura.

Her senses were heightening. In her head she heard a faint hum like a whisper. The realisation made her feel like an eavesdropper. Quickly she turned away, and when she looked back Jed stood alone, turning the pages of his paper.

Five minutes later the girls had left the shop. After selecting her purchases she went to pay. Jed packed them for her. He really did look tired. He was well into his seventies. Was he finding his job a strain? Why did he still do it? Did he need the money or just the company? Again, she felt worried.

While sensing she was not the only one to feel that way.

Eight o'clock that evening. She sat with Dan at a table outside The Corsair, devouring a plate of fish and chips.

'I can't believe you ate it all,' Dan remarked as she swallowed her final mouthful.

'I told you I was hungry.'

'So was I.'

'Yes, but that's hardly news, is it?'

Chuckling, he lit a cigarette. She shook her head disapprovingly.

'Don't start,' he told her.

'I went out with a smoker once. It was like snogging an ashtray.'

'Does that mean you're not going to snog me?'

'No, but you'd need to shave, visit an oral hygienist and have a dozen tetanus shots.'

He blew smoke at her. Reaching into her pocket she produced the bag of fudge. 'Dessert is served. It's the best in Cornwall, apparently.'

He swallowed three pieces. 'Damn right.'

'Well leave some for me.' She ate a piece too. He watched her with a wry look on his face.

'What?' she asked him.

'It's good to see you eating. You've put on weight, you know.'

'Tell me about it. My jeans feel like they're about to burst.'

'It suits you. You were too thin before. Now you look healthy.'

'Is healthy a euphemism for fat?'

'No! So, tell me about your day. I want to hear everything.'

She did, while he continued to devour the fudge. 'I couldn't believe no one knew where the house was, but now I think about it, it makes sense. The chapter in the book is only a few pages long and doesn't have much that's new in it. Clearly it wasn't that big a case. A girl kills her lover and is hanged for it. Not much competition for shoot outs with gangs of smugglers, is it?'

'And you're sure it *is* the house?'

'Absolutely. Now all I have to do is see inside.'

Again, he gave her the wry look. 'You're really fired up about this, aren't you?'

'Yes. I'm beginning to think that I've been looking at it from the wrong angle. I've assumed Ellen became a monster and that was what I had to change. What if I'm wrong? What if she was just a decent girl who found herself in an impossible situation?'

'Isn't murder a rather extreme reaction for a decent girl to have?'

'Is it? What if my father hadn't stopped me attacking my stepmother? I could have killed her, maybe just as savagely, and I certainly wouldn't have felt any remorse afterwards. I'm no better than her. I'm just luckier, that's all.'

Shuddering, he shook his head.

'But it's true, Dan. Don't you see...'

'It's not that. I'm just thinking about what might have happened if your father hadn't been there. I still think he was a spineless weakling but for your sake I'm glad he was.'

'Me too,' she said quietly.

'Thanks for telling me about it. I know it can't have been easy. I'll never tell anyone. You can be sure of that.'

'I am. That's why I felt I could tell you in the first place.'

Silence. She stared out across the square. Once Ellen had lived in one of its houses. Briefly she wondered which before realising it didn't matter. The story had shifted to Bamber, just as her feelings about it had shifted too.

Two men stood outside The Kings Arms, smoking and sharing a joke. Jed appeared from the supermarket, locking the door behind him at the end of his working day. He saw them at their table and waved. They waved back.

'What do you know about him?' she asked Dan.

'Not very much. He was widowed a few years ago. His wife was called Lily. They were a devoted couple apparently.'

'Did they have any children?'

'No. Just each other.'

She watched Jed vanish from sight. Dan nudged her arm. 'There's one piece of fudge left.'

'You have it. If I eat anything else I'll burst.'

He wolfed it down. As she watched him she remembered a tv

commercial asking the viewer whether they loved someone enough to give them their last Rolo. Only it wasn't a Rolo. It was just fudge.

Brian's wife, Barbara, came to clear their plates. 'Are you two doing the quiz?' she asked. 'It's about to start and the Harrisons are looking for team mates?'

'Is that Viv Harrison from the art gallery?' Meg asked.

'Yes.'

'Then it's a yes from us, too. We'll be there in a minute.'

Barbara left. 'Are you sure?' Dan asked.

'Of course. How many of your paintings has Viv exhibited?'

'A couple.'

'Then it's time to network. Just leave the negotiations to me.'

He gave her a look of faux indignation. 'What if I want to do them myself?'

'Oh, please. You couldn't negotiate your way out of a paper bag. This is what I'm trained for, Dan. Just sit back and watch the master go to work.'

He gave his trademark chuckle. Together they entered the pub.

Later, as she lay in bed waiting for sleep she realised that she was no longer afraid. Instead she felt excited. Every dream brought her closer to understanding what it was that she had to do.

'Show me how to reach you,' she whispered into the darkness. 'Show me how to stop you destroying two lives the way my father stopped me.'

And it was true. He had. As she thought of him she experienced an emotion of which she would never have believed herself capable.

Gratitude.

Her eyes were growing heavy. She lay perfectly still, waiting for whatever revelations the night would bring…

It was dusk. She was in an alleyway by the side of a house; the same one she had stood in that very afternoon.

And she was not alone.

A man and woman stood nearby. They were whispering to each other; their faces so close they were almost touching. The man was about twenty-five; smartly dressed, with light brown hair and a warm smile. The woman was really still a girl; about eighteen with long blonde hair, delicate features and a nose that turned up very slightly at the end.

It's Ellen. It's the Ellen I've seen in my dreams.

Only it wasn't. The face had a shine she had never seen before; transfused with the unmistakable glow of love.

Footsteps echoed in the distance. Meg saw Ellen flinch.

'Don't be afraid,' the man said softly. 'We're safe. No one can see us here.' His face had the same glow Ellen's did. Like Dan his features were too irregular to be called handsome but were made attractive by the character they contained. 'I wrote to my brother today,' he continued, 'and told him we're to be married.' His words confirmed Meg's suspicion that this was Samuel.

Ellen looked anxious. 'What do you think he'll say?'

'I hope he'll be happy for me.'

'But what if he's not?'

'It doesn't matter. He'll love you as soon as he sees you, just as I did.'

He drew Ellen even closer, kissing her cheek. She pulled away slightly. 'Do you really believe that? What if he discovers the truth about my past?'

'He never will. It's a past that was forced upon on you and one that we're going to leave far behind. Once we're in America we'll have a new life, and no one will be able to judge you for it. They'll judge you for who you really are and they'll love you too.'

She stroked his face. He took her hand in his and kissed it. As Meg watched them she felt a warm feeling in her stomach. Then it was gone, replaced by a chilling realisation.

He wrote that letter to his brother only four days before the murder.

The two of them were gazing at each other. They looked so

in love; both of them. She watched them, trying to make sense of what she knew about their fates. How could Ellen do it and then feel no remorse? The girl before her seemed no more capable of murder than she was of sprouting wings and taking flight.

She's no monster, that's for sure. That's the last thing in the world she is.

'I wish we were in America now,' Ellen told Samuel. 'I can't stand it here. What if someone finds out? What if...'

He covered her mouth with his hand. 'No one will. Why would they? You just have to be patient a little longer. It's only a week until the tradesman's banquet in Penzance. Your aunt and uncle will be away all night and by the time they return we'll be long gone.'

'All three of us?'

'Yes. All three of us.'

'I can't leave her here. You understand that, don't you?'

'Of course, I do. She's more than a sister. She's the other half of you. You could never be happy without her. I know that.'

'I could never be happy without you either.'

'And your happiness is all that matters to me.' His eyes became thoughtful. 'Have you told her yet?'

'No. I can't risk it. She might tell my aunt. She won't mean to, but it will just come out. She trusts her.'

'Do you?'

'Yes. I...' Ellen hesitated. 'I want to. But I can't. She'll tell my uncle. She'd be too afraid not to. If she didn't he'd blame her for it and you know what he's capable of.' She began to shake. 'For years he's been telling me that as long as there's breath in my body I'll belong to him. Oh God, if he found out...'

'Hush, now. He won't. How could he? His ego is so bloated he's blind to everything except his own needs.'

'I remember when you first came here. He treated you like a slave. Now he treats you like a son. They both do. You must be a magician to have such an effect on them.'

'It isn't magic. With your uncle, all it takes is a willingness to listen to him boast of his achievements. With your aunt it's even easier. All one has to do is remember to notice she exists.' He shook his head. 'The only magician here is you.'

'Why do you say that?'

'Because you've cast a spell on me.'

They kissed; softly and tenderly; both so entirely focused on each other that Meg began to feel like an unwanted intruder. She knew it was silly. Neither could see her. But still the feeling remained. She turned away, as if to give them privacy.

And noticed something.

The door at the back of the house was opening; just a crack. Someone peered through it. Meg could not make out their face. It was obscured by a lock of long blonde hair of exactly the same shade as Ellen's.

'So, you're not going to tell Kate anything?' Samuel asked.

'No. Not a word. This is our secret. Yours and mine.'

'It'll be worth it. You'll see.'

'It will be alright, won't it? Tell me it will.'

'It will. I promise. Before you know it, we'll be in America. My brother will help me find work and with all the money I make I'm going to build us a house. It'll be the most beautiful one you've ever seen. A hundred times more beautiful than the one I'm building for your uncle. My brother says the countryside outside New York is magnificent. We'll have a parlour lined with oak with a huge fireplace and views as far as the eye can see. No more of these crowded, dirty streets. Our children will grow up with enough space to breathe.'

Sighing, Ellen stared down at the ground.

'Sweetheart…' Samuel began.

'What if there can be no children?'

'We don't know that for sure.'

'Don't we?'

'No. Pray God that we can have children. But even if we can't it doesn't change how I feel about you. Nothing could ever do that. As long we're together I'll go to my grave believing I'm the luckiest man in the land.'

'Do you really mean that?'

'Do you really need to ask?'

'I love you.'

'I love you too. Now I must go. Be brave, my darling. Only a few days and you'll be free.'

They gave each other a final kiss. Meg noticed the back-door closing.

It was Kate. She heard them.

Samuel walked away up the alley. Ellen made for the back door. 'She's seen you!' Meg screamed at her. 'She knows what you're planning.' Oblivious, Ellen continued on her way. As she reached for the door handle, panic overwhelmed Meg who reached out to take her arm, only for her hand to pass through it like mist.

Ellen stopped and turned back; a puzzled look on her face.

'It's me! Why can't you hear me? How do I reach you? For God's sake tell me what I have to do!'

For a moment the look of puzzlement remained. Ellen took a step towards her. Again, Meg screamed out a warning. Then the look was gone. Ellen went through the door. It happened so quickly Meg had no time to squeeze through after.

Perhaps I don't need to. Perhaps I can just walk through it.

She reached out her hand again, only to feel a solid surface against her fingers.

A scream of frustration burst out of her.

Just as her vision began to blur…

When she opened her eyes, her room was no longer dark. A faint light crept in through a crack in the curtains. Her throat was dry. There was a glass of water on her bedside table. She swallowed a mouthful. It tasted stale, but she didn't care. Her head was too full of all she had seen.

Ellen had never been a monster. That much was now clear. And Samuel had truly loved her. That was clear too. He had known about her past and not condemned her for it. He would never have abandoned her; not when there was breath in his body.

So why did she do it?

Kate had seen Ellen and Samuel together. She would have known of their plans. Did she tell Clara? Did Clara tell John? And if so, then what had he done about it?

How must he have felt to know that another man was trying to steal Ellen away? Especially a younger man whom he had befriended and treated like a son? His ego would never have been able to stand it. He would have been capable of anything.

Even murder?

Was it possible? Could he have forced Ellen to write the note, asking Samuel to visit that night? Could he have punished Samuel's betrayal by taking his life?

And could he have punished Ellen's by forcing her to take the blame?

But why would she? She had loved Samuel. If she were not his murderer, then why would she allow the culprit to get away scot free?

She sipped her water, thoughts whirring about her head like angry wasps while outside the dawn continued to break.

Chapter 11

It was three pm. After a morning spent helping to install a new bathroom Dan sat in his studio, rummaging through piles of papers, trying to find his most recent receipts. His annual accounts were due. It seemed like a pointless exercise as his earnings were so minimal but his accountant, who had been pestering him for the relevant figures for months, had started to talk about fines for late submission which was something he really couldn't afford.

His search through the current pile proved fruitless. The next one proved no more successful, though he did at least unearth his most recent bank statements. Had Meg been there she would have scolded him for his lack of organisation. Every girlfriend he had ever had had scolded him too. Of course, as girlfriends, they had been entitled to do so, which Meg wasn't. Yet somehow the prospect of her concerned disapproval seemed far more appealing.

His mobile lay on his desk. The two of them had been texting and calling each other throughout the day. Meg was spending it in Truro, searching through library archives of old newspapers for further information on the case. So far, the hunt had yielded only two new details: the murder had taken place in an upstairs parlour where Clara Goderidge and her nieces often spent their afternoons, and in the build up to the trial Clara had started a petition calling for Ellen to be spared the death penalty, but such was the local anger over the crime that barely a dozen had signed. As neither fact was much use, Meg had sounded rather despondent in their last call. But perhaps she had had better luck since then. He hoped so.

Picking up his phone he began to type a text:

'How are you getting on? Better than me I hope. Still can't find the bloody receipts. If I fake them do you think my accountant will shop me to HMRC?'

Once it was finished he pressed send, smiling to himself as he did so.

And heard a scratching sound.

Startled, he looked around him, trying to identify its source. Was it mice? Surely not. Even he wasn't that unhygienic.

The sound was very faint. At first he thought it was coming from beneath his desk. He peered under it, his eyes roaming over yet more piles of papers, searching for squatters of the four-legged variety but seeing none. The scratching stopped. He rose to his feet, backing away from his desk towards the far wall so that he could properly scan the room.

Then it started up again.

It was coming from right behind him; from the wall he shared with Meg.

Were there bugs in it? Were both houses infested?

He pressed his ear to the surface, expecting to detect the signs of dozens of tiny creatures scurrying in random directions.

But he didn't. The sound was slower and far more rhythmic. And its source was further away.

As if fingernails were scratching on the other side of the wall.

For a moment he thought it was a joke. Meg must have returned and decided to play a trick on him. Only it didn't seem like the sort of thing she would do. And besides, if she had returned he would have heard her car.

Could he have missed it? Had he been too involved in his paper hunt? He went to look out of the window. His van was the only vehicle in the close.

While behind him the scratching continued.

And then his phone beeped.

The sound made him jump. Crossing the room he picked it up. A text from Meg had arrived.

'Still in Truro. No further joy as yet. See you later and if you fake your receipts I will shop you myself!'

He checked the message details. She had only just sent it. So, if she wasn't in her house then who was? Or what was? Again, he put his ear to the wall; realising as he did so that his heart was racing. Again, the scratching stopped. Only this time it was replaced by a new sound: a delicate hiss like a voice whispering in a tone too low to be heard.

His first instinct was to call Meg. Quickly he dismissed it. She had her own work to do and he was big and ugly enough to investigate on his own. Even if the prospect did make his stomach turn over.

The whispering continued. It had a rhythmic sound; like a chant. Or a taunt. As if by way of confirmation, he heard what sounded like laughter. Instinctively he backed away. Silence. He stood perfectly still for one minute, two, then three, just waiting. Then slowly returned to his previous position.

But still there was silence.

Until something slammed into the wall at the very spot where his ear was pressed; as if a fist was trying to punch straight through. He gave a yell. And heard another ripple of laughter.

His heart was now pounding like a drum. A bead of sweat slid into his eye. Angrily he wiped it away. He was a grown man and would not allow himself to be afraid. The spare keys to Meg's flat were in his desk drawer. He grabbed them and one minute later was walking through her front door.

He stood in the hallway; straining his ears to detect sound but hearing nothing. The house was as still and silent as the grave.

And yet...

Something didn't feel right. There was a sense of displacement; as if the heavy air around him had recently been moved. After taking a deep breath he started up the stairs.

Meg's study was on the left. The door stood open a crack. Steeling himself for whatever lay waiting he pushed it fully open and walked in.

The study was empty; just a desk, a chair, a set of book shelves and all of Meg's papers laid out in perfect order.

While a wasp buzzed over them, darting to and fro, knocking against his adjoining wall and the book shelf that hung against it; the books all sloping at an angle while the book end that had held them in place lay on the floor below.

As he watched it, the wasp finally found freedom through the tiny top window that had been left open. Relief swept over him. Acoustics in old houses could sometimes be deceptive; amplifying sighs into screams. He had heard the wasp and his imagination had gone into overdrive. Clearly this whole Ellen business was getting to him far more than he had realised. He started to relax.

So how could a wasp dislodge a book end? How would it have the strength to do that?

Perhaps it had been loose to start with and had only needed the faintest of taps. Besides, there was no one here. Of that he was certain.

There was a framed photograph on the desk. Curious, he went and picked it up. A dark haired young woman was standing on a beach with her arms around two young girls who were pointing proudly to a sandcastle decorated with sea shells. He recognised the older as Meg. She was wearing a smile so big it threatened to crack her face in two. He guessed she was about nine. How soon afterwards had her mother died? He had no way of knowing but the thought of it made his heart ache.

Her mother had been a beautiful woman. The Meg he knew looked just like her. He thought of all the guilt she carried inside and wished he could magic it all away.

But he couldn't. The realisation made him sigh.

And as he did so he felt an infinitesimal displacement of air.

Together with the realisation that someone was standing right behind him.

They were so close; less than an arm's length away. Yet if he were to reach out his hand he would feel nothing but air. Whomever it was had no substance; yet still he could feel their presence; a writing mass of cold, cruel energy pulsing against his neck.

His bladder weakened. For a moment he thought he might soil himself. As he struggled to retain his self-control his eyes remained locked on the photograph and the smiling child that Meg had once been and realised that what he was experiencing was just a taste of what she had been dealing with all her life.

But how could she smile? How could she ever be happy with a gift like this?

Because this is no gift; in spite of what her mother and Jennifer told her.

This is a curse.

For a moment the presence remained. Then it was gone; as if

sucked from the room like a vacuum. Putting down the picture he ran down the stairs and out of the house.

Back in his own home he made for the kitchen, grabbed a bottle of scotch and poured himself a stiff drink. His hand was shaking as he did so. It made him feel weak. Again, he thought of Meg. For him this was new but as a child this had been her life. How many times had she felt afraid? How many times had she wanted to turn and run only for the dead to run faster? How much strength had it taken to shut herself off from her so-called gift only it for the dead to track her down again when she was grieving and at her most vulnerable?

Suddenly his fear was gone, replaced by anger.

Who did I sense? Was it Ellen? Was it someone else?

And why won't you leave her alone?

Fight your own fights. Right your own wrongs. But don't include her in them.

He made his way back upstairs to his studio; the bottle of scotch still clasped in his hand. Everything was as he had left it; papers scattered everywhere and the whole place looking like a bomb site. The newly discovered bank statements lay at the centre of his cluttered desk. As his gaze came to rest upon them again he felt the faintest displacement of air.

And saw what was written on the top page in a jagged script that was not his own.

Two Days.

He dropped the bottle while from somewhere far away he heard laughter.

That evening Meg sat in Dan's living room, sipping wine and listening to him describe the events of the afternoon.

'You must have been terrified,' she told him.

He shook his head.

'I would have been.'

'No, I…' She saw him hesitate. 'Well alright, yes. I nearly shat myself.'

'I'm sorry.'

'Excuse the pun but I don't give a shit about that.' He gestured to the defaced bank statement. 'What I care about is this. What does it mean? What happens in two days?'

'It's a warning. He's trying to warn us.'

'Who is?'

'John Goderidge; Ellen's stepfather. He knows I'm getting close. He wants me to stop.'

'Close?'

'He killed Samuel. I'm sure of it. Think of the way Samuel's body was mutilated. It screams sexual jealousy.'

'So why did Ellen confess?'

'Perhaps because she was protecting Kate. I've been thinking about it all day. John kept threatening to send Kate to an asylum. Maybe that was the deal. Ellen agreed to take the blame and in return, John promised to keep Kate safe.'

'But what would his promise be worth? Once Ellen was dead he could have done what he wanted with Kate. Ellen wasn't a fool. She would have known that.'

'You're right. But Ellen didn't do it. Of that I'm certain. Not the Ellen I've come to know.'

'But you *don't* know her. Not really.' His tone became angry. 'All you've seen is glimpses of her life. What if your father *hadn't* been there when you attacked your stepmother? What if you'd killed her? Do you not think people would have been shocked? Do you not think there would have been people like your old Headmistress who would never have believed you were capable of such violence?'

'Why are you getting wound up?'

'Because I think you should leave this alone. That's why.'

She couldn't believe her ears. 'How can you say that? You were the one who said I had to save Samuel. When I wanted to drop this you were the one who guilt tripped me into sticking with it. Now you want me to just walk away. Where is this coming from?'

'Where do you bloody think? Two days, Meg. What the hell is going to happen in two days?'

She didn't answer. For a moment she felt afraid. Quickly she pushed the feeling aside. She didn't have time for fear. All she had time for was saving Ellen.

'What I don't understand,' she said, 'is why John would try and contact you.'

'Because he knows we're in this together. Assuming it even was him.'

'Who else could it have been?'

'Ellen.'

She stared at him. 'You can't be serious.'

'Why not? She scared the crap out of you at the start. She had you running for the bloody hills.'

'But then I stopped. You made me stop. And I'm glad I did because I know that she needs my help.'

'But how can you trust her? You only know what she's shown you. What if she's playing tricks on you. What if the things she's showing you didn't really happen? What if this is all some sort of trap?'

'Are you crazy? There's no way she's trying to trick me.'

'How do you know?'

'I just do.'

'Like you knew that the vision you had about you and your sister going to stay with your father had nothing to do with your mother dying? Then I take it back, Meg. Your instincts are always infallible.'

She felt as if she had been slapped.

For a moment his face was full of anger. Then the emotion was gone, replaced by shame. 'I'm sorry. That was below the belt.'

'Well below.'

'I'm sorry,' he said again.

'I don't want to hear it.'

'Well you need to! I'm scared, Meg. I'm scared for you.'

She exhaled. 'Scared for yourself, more like.'

'That's not fair.'

'Isn't it? You have your first ever supernatural experience and it turns you into a nervous wreck. Can you imagine what it was like for me as a kid? Can you imagine what it's like now? Do you think this has ever been easy for me? Because I can assure you that it hasn't.'

'That's my point. This isn't fair on you. It never was. I didn't see it before today, but I do now. Yes, I've been telling you to try and help Ellen but now I see that I was wrong. All of this is wrong. You did the right thing twenty years ago by closing yourself off from this part of your life and you need to do it again, because if you don't something bad is going to happen. Something *really* bad. And it's going to happen in two days unless you stop right now.'

'So, what are you suggesting? That I just tune Ellen out?'

'Yes.'

'But I don't *want* to turn her out! She's Ellen. I care about her.'

'And I care about you. You're my friend. Or doesn't that matter?'

'Of course, it does.'

'Bullshit!' His eyes began to flash. 'I'm here, Meg. I'm flesh and blood. My feelings shouldn't be taking second place to those of some fucking ghost who made a complete mess of her life and is now hounding a stranger to try and put things right.'

Her own anger was mounting. 'Don't talk about her like that! You don't know anything about her. You don't know anything!'

'But one thing I do know is that she's not your mother or your sister.'

'You leave them out of this!'

'Why? That's what this is all about. You feel guilty because of what happened to them and you think that saving Ellen will make the guilt go away. Well, I've got news for you, Meg. It doesn't work like that. Saving Ellen will not bring them back. They're dead too, and unlike Ellen they have the decency to stay that way!'

'I'm not listening to anymore of this.' She rose to her feet.

He rose too. 'That's right. Just run away like you always do. Your whole life is one big act of escape from having to feel anything that's real. No wonder the dead seek you out. They know you'll give them the time and the emotion you're too much of a coward to risk giving to the living!'

She threw the remains of her wine in his face.

'You're right,' she told him. 'I'll always put Ellen before you.

At least she's *worth* my time and my emotions. Not like you; a failed artist and odd job man, still acting like a teenager in his mid-thirties. You're the coward, Dan, not me, and because of that you'll never be worth anything to anyone.'

He opened his mouth to protest. Turning, she walked out of his house, slamming the door behind her.

He wiped the wine from his face. Her footsteps echoed in the distance. For a moment he wanted to run after her and apologise; to say that he hadn't mean to be so harsh. That he understood the motivations that drove her and could sympathise and even applaud them.

And he did. He really did.

But the feeling of dread remained.

Slowly he sat down again. The chair sagged beneath his weight. Once it had stood in his parent's living room in Bodmin. When he was a child he had often jumped all over it as he tried to circumnavigate the room without touching the floor. He had only ever managed it once. His sense of balance had always been lousy. It was his friend Alan who had been the agile one. On countless afternoons the two of them had clambered all over the furniture, playing explorers, pirates or acrobats, while his mother had repeatedly put her head around the door, shouting that she would skin them alive if they dared break anything.

He still missed Alan. After all these years the feeling of loss had never completely gone away.

And he didn't want to miss Meg. No matter that her stubbornness drove him mad. No matter that he could sometimes throttle her because of it. He would willingly put up with all the aggravation she could throw at him, rather than have to miss her.

Time passed. He remained in the chair, feeling its broken springs beneath him and remembering all the happy afternoons that had helped put them there.

Meg closed her front door and stood in the hallway, shaking.

How could he say that to me? Why now, when more than ever I need his support?

Maybe it was because he really was the coward she had told him he was. Only she didn't believe it. There was not a cowardly bone in his body. And though she was still angry, a part of her felt ashamed.

What if I am in danger? What if I'm too close to all of this to see it?

She tried to envision the possibility, but in her head all she could see was Ellen's face; the face of a girl who was totally in love and whose only goal was to protect her sister and make a better life for them both. She knew that girl. She knew her because she had been her, and still was inside.

'I won't fail you,' she whispered to the air. 'Even if there *is* danger I am not afraid. I am going to make things right. Just show me how to reach you. If you can do that I swear I'll take care of all the rest.'

Her words hung in the air. She waited for the tingling that told her she was no longer alone, only it never came.

But it was still early. When tiredness came the feeling would too.

For the next two hours she sat in front of the television, half watching a crime drama and waiting for the inevitable sense of fatigue.

In time it did come.

But the feeling stayed away.

That night she dreamed she was back in the engine house, sheltering from the storm that raged around her. Again, she heard the wind drop and heard a cry. Again, she went in search of its source. This time it didn't stop. It kept on and on. But whenever she drew close the wind grew stronger and the rain hammered against her face, driving her back, threatening to push her over the cliff and into the sea, as if the elements themselves were conspiring to keep the two of them apart.

Chapter 12

Dawn. In her bed in Oxfordshire Jennifer stretched out her arms under the sheets, trying to shrug off the musty cobwebs of sleep.

Her head felt heavy. Her sleep had been fitful; caused by anxiety at a doctor's appointment scheduled for early that morning. Recently she had been experiencing pains in her chest and though instinct told her it was nothing but the inevitable aches of old age there was still a part of her that felt afraid.

She sat up in bed, remembering the dream she had left behind. In it she had been back at the service station with Meg; only this time Meg had been a girl who had become separated from her mother and was frightened of never finding her again. As Jennifer tried to offer comfort she had seen two policemen approach, both wearing the anxious expressions of those about to break bad news. Leaving Meg at the table she had gone to talk to them; persuading them that it would be better if their news came from her.

But when she turned back both Meg and the restaurant were gone. Instead she saw an aura shaped like a child; something made of light and energy that darted through the air towards the same church she had seen in her head two days ago.

It was just a dream; a collage of her experiences and memories meshed together to make nothing of any substance.

Yet, for reasons she didn't understand, she felt uneasy.

But that was probably just down to her impending appointment.

Sighing and feeling every bit her age, she climbed from her bed.

Noon. Meg was back in Bamber, standing outside the house in Hepton Street. As she waited for the estate agent she pondered the events of the previous night. Why had Ellen not come to her, and why could she not sense her now?

Is something stopping her? Is that what it is?

And what can I do about it?

A plump man in a tight-fitting suit approached. 'Miss Parker?'

'Are you Mr O'Reilly?'

'Please call me Tim. I hope I haven't kept you waiting.'

'Not at all, and please call me Meg.'

He unlocked the front door and gestured for her to enter. She found herself in a dark hallway with a wooden floor and a staircase at its end. Tim opened the surrounding doors, letting the light in. 'I'm sorry it looks a bit gloomy,' he said as he did so, 'but this should brighten it up.'

It did. She stared about her. The walls were bare and the rooms empty. 'The house comes unfurnished,' Tim told her. 'Did I mention that on the phone?'

She couldn't remember but nodded anyway.

He led her through a door at the rear of the hall and into a large kitchen with views of a garden at the back. 'It's big, isn't it?' he observed.

'Isn't it? Perhaps they could use it for the next series of MasterChef.'

He laughed. She looked about her, wondering how many times Ellen had sat at the table here. There had to have been a table. What kitchen was complete without one?

He gestured to the garden. 'There's a gardener who comes once a week. He's a local man; very good apparently and cheap.'

She nodded. He led her into another room with a sloping roof and a triangular window. 'We're under the stairs, now,' he explained. 'I think this is a store room, though of course you could use it for whatever you want.'

They returned to the hall and explored the other downstairs rooms. Tim tapped one of the walls. 'Rock solid,' he pronounced. 'They don't build them like this anymore.'

'How old is the house?'

'I believe it was built in the 1850s.'

'It must have an interesting history. Old houses usually do.' She watched his face, searching for a reaction but seeing none.

'I'm sure it does,' he said politely.

'Where are the current owners?'

'In Canada. The husband is on a two-year work secondment. They left a week ago, so the house has only just come onto our books.'

'That explains why there are no details on your website.'

He looked sheepish. 'They're being added as we speak.'

'It's alright. I wasn't complaining.'

'Do you have a large family?'

'Actually, I'm looking at properties for my brother. He's being posted here and wants something old and near the sea. Fresh air and space for the children, you know.'

'So, you're not married yourself?'

'No.'

He looked pleased. Feeling self-conscious she focused on her surroundings. All the rooms were large. She moved between them, waiting in vain to sense something.

Come on, Ellen. I need your help. Give me something to work with.

They entered a room at the front with a large window looking out onto the street. 'I believe the family used this as a living room,' Tim told her.

Her ears pricked up. 'Do you mean as a parlour?'

He smiled. 'We don't hear that word very often.'

She smiled too and then remembered that the parlour she was searching for had been upstairs.

'If you look out of the window,' Tim continued, 'you can just about see the sea.'

There was a window seat. She sat on it, peering through the glass but only seeing the street. A young couple rode by on a scooter, tooting their horn and receiving dirty looks from an elderly couple walking a dog. Ellen must have sat here, watching for Samuel; feeling her heart lift at the sight of him while doing everything in her power to keep her emotions hidden.

Clearing her mind of all other thoughts she tried to feel those emotions herself.

I can't let them see I'm excited. If they do they'll know, and all hell will break loose.

She sensed Tim's eyes upon her and imagined he was her uncle; the person she feared most in the world and from whom she longed to escape.

Do something so he won't suspect. Yawn. Act bored. Turn away and look at something else as if you're simply trying to pass the time.

She turned. In her head she saw a room full of heavy furniture with a painting of a stag being attacked by hunting dogs hanging on the far wall. The image remained for the briefest of moments and then vanished, as if an unseen hand had reached into her mind and snatched it away.

It's you, isn't it? You're trying to reach me but something is blocking you.

Masking her frustration, she asked to see the rest of the house.

They climbed the staircase. It was on two levels. Tim led her to the top floor. 'There are three bedrooms,' he told her, 'and three bathrooms. There's also a study but you could use that as another bedroom should you wish. How many children does your brother have?'

'Four.'

He looked surprised. 'Are you sure the house will be big enough?'

Quickly she corrected her mistake. 'That includes a set of twins. They share a room. Four bedrooms will be plenty.'

'Twins. How lovely! Boys or girls?'

'Um…one of each.'

'Do they get on well?'

'No. They fight like cat and dog.' She rolled her eyes. 'Teenagers, eh?'

He raised an eyebrow. 'And they still share a room?'

She kicked herself. If ever she had to do this again she would plan her cover story better. 'Sorry. I'm thinking of their elder brother and sister. The twins are only seven.' She gave a quick laugh. 'That's the problem with having so many nephews and nieces. I lose track of who's who.'

His face relaxed. 'I have the same problem. My family is Irish Catholic. I could fill this whole street with my nephews and nieces.'

'Which room is the study?'

'At the end on the right.'

It was a small, cosy looking room with a low ceiling and a view of the street. Through the window she actually could see the sea. If it wasn't a bedroom now, then perhaps it never had been.

Is this it? Is this the room where it happened?

Again, she waited in vain to sense something.

Tim showed her the rest of the floor. She feigned interest while feeling nothing.

'Well, that's about everything,' he said eventually.

'Didn't you say there were three bathrooms?'

'Oh, yes. The third one is down there.' He gestured to a solitary door on the first landing she had failed to notice on their ascent and began to look sheepish. 'The owners didn't use it much. It's rather small.'

There was a buzzing sound. He pulled out his mobile and checked the display. 'I need to take this. I should only be a minute. Do you mind?'

'No. Please take your time. I'll go and look at the bathroom.'

He gave her a smile that looked more like a grimace then began to talk into the phone. She walked down the stairs and entered the bathroom. Instantly she saw why he had been reluctant to show it to her. Unlike the rest of the house it was dilapidated and in need of renovation. One of the walls was completely bare. She stood with her back against its cold surface, staring out of the window. The garden was pretty. Pretty but useless. Everything was useless without Ellen's help.

A minute passed. Outside she could hear Tim prattling on. The wall didn't seem so cold anymore. Instead it felt pleasantly warm; almost like a radiator.

Just as the wall in Bodmin Jail had done.

But this wasn't a jail. It was simply a bathroom.

Only it wasn't. Not any longer. The bath and toilet were gone, replaced by a sofa and two easy chairs. The tiles on the other walls were gone too. Expensive wallpaper hung in their place while the window was now covered with thick, blue curtains and a fire burned in place of the sink.

No, it was no longer a bathroom. It was a parlour.

And she was not its only occupant.

Someone was sitting in one of the chairs. It was a woman. She had her back to Meg who could see nothing but fair hair that was starting to grey pulled back into a bun.

It's Ellen's aunt. It's Clara.

And she was crying: raw, anguished sobs that sounded as if they were being ripped out of her. The effect was both heart-wrenching and disturbing; making Meg feel an uneasy mixture of pity and voyeuristic guilt.

Why is she crying? When is this? Has the murder already happened?

Is Ellen already dead?

She couldn't know for sure, yet in her heart she was certain. She remembered what she had read about Clara starting a petition to save Ellen's life. Clearly, in spite of her failure to stop the abuse, she had loved her niece. Ellen had wanted to trust Clara with her plans to elope but had been too afraid that she would feel compelled to tell her husband rather than risk his wrath.

Because that's what happened, isn't it? Kate told you and you told him and now Samuel is dead.

Samuel…the young man you treated like a son.

Oh God, how guilty must you feel now?

Clara continued to sob. Meg continued to listen. In spite of knowing that Clara's actions had led to two deaths her sense of pity remained.

And then she heard something else.

Heavy footsteps coming up the stairs.

There was a door to her right. As she turned towards it she saw it open. She recognised John Goderidge straight away, yet the man who entered the room bore little resemblance to the one she had had to watch molest a young girl. That man had projected a menacing confidence, but this one seemed like a shadow; his formerly fleshy features were gaunt, and his shoulders sagged as if he was carrying the weight of the world upon them.

Clara didn't seem to register his presence. He stood and watched her; his expression a mixture of concern and disgust.

'You have to stop this,' he said eventually. 'Clara, for the sake of both of us you must. What's done is done and we can't change it.'

There was no reply. The sobbing persisted; the sound filling the room like the roar of a storm. John continued to watch his wife. Meg studied his face; searching for shame but seeing only resentment and contempt.

But then why would he feel shame? A man who could do what he had done to a child? A man like that could no more feel shame than he could fly in the air.

And she hated him for it. She hated him, and she was going to make him pay.

He turned away from his wife. Suddenly he appeared to be looking straight at her. And his face was full of hate too.

It was you, wasn't it? The one who left the warning for Dan? Because that's what it was. You're trying to scare me, but you won't succeed. There is nothing you could do that would ever make me stop.

He took a step towards her…

And someone touched her arm.

She screamed, while instantly the parlour and its occupants faded, and she was back in a shabby bathroom with a worried looking Tim staring at her.

'I know it's a mess,' he said, 'but surely it's not that horrifying.'

She struggled to regain her composure. 'No. You just took me by surprise. I'm a lawyer. I was thinking about a deal I'm working on. I was completely lost in thought.'

He led her back onto the landing. 'I'm really sorry,' she continued. 'But you know how it is. You get so wrapped up in work it takes over your life.'

'I do indeed, and with some of the clients we deal with I often find myself wanting to scream.'

'Oh dear. I hope I don't fall into that category.'

'No! Not at all. Showing you around has been an absolute pleasure.'

She stared at him. He blushed. An idea came to her.

'Are you going back to the office now?' she asked.

'Sadly, yes. I have a mound of paperwork.'

'It's just that I have some time to kill. Is there anywhere local you'd recommend for lunch?'

'There's…'

'In fact, I was wondering if you'd like to join me. My brother wants me to find out as much as I can about this area and you seem like the perfect person to ask.'

His face lit up, just as she had hoped.

'Well,' he said, 'perhaps the paperwork can wait…'

Half past two. Jennifer stood in the living room, talking to a friend on the phone.

'No. It's nothing to worry about. I've just been told to rest more and drink less coffee.'

'Well, that *is* good news,' said her friend.

And it was. All her worrying had been for nothing. She should have been feeling euphoric; full of vim and vigour, but instead she felt exhausted. The need for sleep was overwhelming. It had come over her so suddenly that it was almost as if it had a will of its own; as if it had been decided by another and there was nothing she could do about it except submit. After ending the conversation she sat down on the sofa and allowed her eyes to close.

And instantly began to dream.

Again, she was in the service station. Again, Meg was a frightened child who then became a mischievous shadow dancing towards a church that looked old and in need of repair.

Only this time, the dream continued.

Quarter to three. Tim O'Reilly stood in his office, trying to pacify his scowling boss.

'They're here somewhere,' he said. 'I'm sure of it.'

'They'd better be. That's the only set we've got! If you've lost them and we have to change the locks then the cost is coming out of your wages…'

'I haven't. I know they're here. Just give me a minute and…'

'Are you looking for these?'

He turned. Meg Parker stood in the doorway, holding a set of keys. Drowning in relief he nodded.

Meg handed them to him. 'I'm so sorry. I must have picked them up by accident. It was only when I stopped for petrol that I realised my mistake.'

'Please don't apologise. There's no harm done. Thank you for coming back so quickly.'

'It's my pleasure. Is this your boss?'

'Yes. This is Mr Topping.'

Meg gave Mr Topping a dazzling smile. 'You're lucky to have an employee like Tim. He's the most knowledgeable estate agent I've ever met. Some friends of mine are considering this area for holiday lets and I'll definitely be telling them to direct their enquiries to this agency.'

Mr Topping's scowl vanished. 'Well, we'd be delighted to help, Miss….'

'Parker. Thank you. And once again I'm sorry if I've inconvenienced you.' Meg touched Tim's arm. 'And thank *you* again for your help. I'll pass all the local information on to my brother. I know he'll be delighted with it.'

Meg left the office. 'Phwor!' exclaimed Mr Topping. 'I wouldn't kick her out of bed.'

'You're married,' the female receptionist reminded him.

'I can still dream.'

Dream all you want, thought Tim smugly. I'm the one who's got her number.

He put the keys safely back in their drawer, never suspecting that a duplicate set now nestled just as safely in Meg's pocket.

As she drove out of Bamber, Meg pondered her next move. She was too fired up to return to Saltran. After what she had seen in the bathroom her head was full of unanswered questions. Why had Ellen written to Samuel on the night of the murder, and why had she so willingly taken the blame for a crime of which she was innocent? And how was she supposed to stop that crime if she couldn't even communicate with the participants, let alone understand the events behind it?

Ellen couldn't help her. Not anymore. John Goderidge had seen to that. In death, as in life, he still had the power to terrorise his niece.

She needed to get back inside the house. With enough time she was sure she could find all the answers she needed. Tim had told her he was showing it to two more prospective tenants that afternoon. For all she knew other appointments were now being made. To be safe, the earliest she could return was late evening; ideally after the pubs had closed when the streets would be empty and there was little risk of being seen. But that was hours away.

Her sense of frustration was so great that she thought she would burst. She wanted to be back in the house now. All its secrets were stored in its walls, just waiting for her touch to set them free.

In the walls...

Unbidden, a memory came to her.

And with it the knowledge of what she had to do.

She began to look for signs for Bodmin.

Dan sat in his study, staring out of the window, watching for Meg's car. He wanted to apologise for the previous night. He had considered phoning but then decided against. It needed to be done face to face. That way she could see the contrition in his face and would know that in spite of what had happened he was still behind her one hundred percent. And he was. He really was.

Even though he was still afraid.

But she was afraid too. Deep down he knew she was. She just masked it better than he did. She was far braver than him, but he would show her that he could be brave too.

He heard the sound of an engine. His spirits soared but the car that pulled into the close was not hers. The number plate was foreign. He assumed the drivers were tourists who were trying, unsuccessfully, to find their way about the town. As if by way of confirmation the driver began a series of complicated manoeuvres to guide the car back out into the square. He watched with a mixture of amusement and concern that his van not be dented in the process.

And felt the tiniest shift in the air.

His stomach turned over. Instinctively, as if seeking sanctuary in darkness, he shut his eyes.

There was warmth at the back of his neck; as if someone were breathing on him. Despising his cowardice but unable to control it, he felt his body start to shake.

For a moment nothing happened. The warmth seemed to fade. He tried to tell himself it was over but still his eyes remained shut while his heart was pounding, and the breath burst out of him in short, ragged bursts.

And then, so softly he could barely hear it, a single word was whispered in his ear.

Tomorrow

A finger brushed his skin. The touch was as delicate as a butterfly's wing yet still it went right through him, as if death itself was reaching into his body to give his heart a playful squeeze.

Then, as before, the presence was gone; sucked from the room as if by a vacuum.

Slowly he opened his eyes. His face was almost against the window. The warmth of his breath had turned to condensation on the glass.

In which was drawn a single cross.

Again, his stomach turned over. He hurried into his bathroom and was sick.

When she arrived at the Jail Meg went straight to the bar.

There was no sign of the local historian. Fortunately, the barmaid remembered her and Dan from their previous visit and gave her his number. When he answered her call she apologised for bothering him. 'There's no need,' he told her. 'I remember Dan. He's a lovely man. Now how can I help you?'

She asked her questions. Once she had the answers she needed she made her way towards what had once been the women's block. As she approached its entrance she saw the gap in the wall and the view that had frightened her so much on her first visit. This time she could look at it without fear. It was just a view, after all, and if she had her way it was one that Ellen would never have to see.

She entered the cell block. This time there was no claustrophobia or panic attacks. Her sense of purpose helped keep her completely calm.

The condemned cell was at the end. It was just an empty shell with a low ceiling and a dirt floor. How many days and nights had Ellen spent it in before being led out to die? It was here that she had cursed her mother; here she would have felt anger, terror and every other emotion in between. And the walls would have absorbed them all; soaking them up like sponges, holding them in readiness for her touch to set them free.

She stood with her back to the far wall, pressing her palms against its cold, damp surface. Facing her was the space that had once held a door. Through it she could hear the birds singing. Once their song had sounded like a warning. Now she found it soothing. Closing her eyes, she allowed her mind to go blank.

For a moment nothing happened. She breathed slowly and deeply, focusing on the beating of her heart.

Her palms began to tingle as if a mild electric current was being discharged into them while the surface of the wall seemed to grow just a little warmer.

She couldn't hear the birds anymore. Instead there were footsteps; crisp and clear as if someone was walking on tiles. From somewhere far away a door slammed shut while overhead someone laughed hysterically, ignoring stern calls for silence. Now there were voices in the cell too; one male, one female and both familiar.

She opened her eyes. The cell was no longer a ruin. On one side was a single bed and on the other a table where Ellen and her uncle sat facing each other. They were talking so softly she could not make out what was being said.

Keeping her hands pressed against the wall she moved around the room until she was standing right beside them.

'This isn't my fault,' John was saying.

'Isn't it?'

'You can't blame me. You caused it; you and Samuel. If you hadn't...'

'What? Fallen in love?' Ellen gave a soft laugh. 'Yes, I can see why you'd condemn me for that. Love is the one thing you know nothing about.'

He stared down at his hands while Ellen's eyes remained fixed on him.

'Why are you doing this?' he asked eventually. 'Do you really value your life so little that you're willing to throw it away?'

'You know why. For the same reason you did what you did. We're both protecting the person who matters most to us. For me it's Kat. For you it's yourself.'

'I didn't force you. You had a choice.'

'No, I didn't. How could I allow Kat to go through this? You were the one who had the choice. You could have done the right thing and told the truth.'

Again, he stared at his hands. 'I did what I had to,' he told her.

'That's right. Keep telling yourself that. Perhaps the day will finally come when you actually believe it.'

'You didn't have to protect Kat. You could have let her take the blame.'

'As I said, you really do know nothing about love.'

'I loved you.'

'And look what it did to me? Your love is a curse. It infects whomever it touches. My love for Samuel caused his death. I couldn't let it destroy Kat too.'

Another silence. Someone knocked on the door and called out

'one minute.'

'I'll keep my promise,' said John quickly. 'I will take care of her. I owe you that much.'

Ellen didn't answer.

'Did you hear what I said?'

'Yes. I was just thinking. I've done a lot of that recently. When I first came here my head was a mess. All that mattered was that Samuel was gone. Now I see things more clearly. I think about that night. I think about it constantly.'

'And?'

'Sometimes I wonder if I made a mistake. Sometimes I wonder if people might just have believed me after all.'

John swallowed. 'No, they wouldn't. You know they wouldn't.'

'Do I?'

'It's too late anyway. You've confessed. You've been found guilty. Nothing can change that.'

'I know. This time tomorrow I'll be dead and what happens to Kat then, if you decide you don't want to keep your promise?'

'But I've given you my word.'

'Like you gave your word to protect us both when our father died? I know what your word is worth, Uncle John.' Ellen exhaled. 'And that's why I've taken steps to make sure that this time I can trust it.'

His eyes nearly popped out of his head. 'Jesus Christ, girl, what have you done?'

'Take care of Kat. Keep her out of the asylum and you'll never have to find out.'

The door opened. A woman warder entered. 'It's time to go, Mr Goderidge.'

'What the hell have you done?' John hissed at Ellen.

'Goodbye, Uncle John. Don't feel sad for me. I'm not afraid. If death means never having to see your face again then I welcome it.'

'Mr Goderidge,' said the warder.

He made no move. 'Ellen, please…'

She turned her head away, staring at the wall by the bed; her back as straight as a ramrod. A sick looking John rose to his feet and left the room, the warder following him out and locking the door behind him. It was only then that Ellen's shoulders sagged.

She seemed to collapse into herself. Suddenly she looked much younger, and terribly afraid. As she watched her Meg felt her heart break.

'I want to help you,' she cried out. 'But you have to show me how. I can't do this alone. I want to, but I can't.'

Ellen turned, staring straight at her.

'You can see me?'

Ellen's eyes shifted, focusing on a point just over Meg's shoulder. 'You're here, aren't you?'

'Yes! I'm here!'

'What sort of mother are you?'

Shock rendered Meg mute.

Ellen rose to her feet. 'I sense you. I sense you all the time. Before you died you told me you'd always protect Kat and me, but you haven't! You don't do anything! All you ever do is watch.'

She thinks I'm her mother. Oh, Jesus Christ, that's what she thinks.

'All my life I've done what you said *you'd* do. I've tried to protect her. I've done everything I can to keep her safe and look where it's got me!' Tears came into Ellen's eyes. 'Why didn't you help me? Why did you leave me to do it all alone?'

By now Meg was also in tears. In her distress she began to rub her hands against the wall. The left one caught on something. She felt a sharp pain; followed by a liquid sensation and realised she was bleeding.

'I hate you!' Ellen screamed. 'You're no mother. You're not worthy of the name. I wish you'd died when I was born. I wish you'd stayed away. I wish…'

She stopped; her eyes widening as she stared down at the ground. Meg followed her gaze and saw a drop of her own blood lying on the floor. Ellen crouched down, reaching out towards it.

She found her voice again. 'You can see it! Tell me you can see it!'

Ellen touched it then stared at her hand. Meg saw one of the fingers streaked with red.

'It's my blood! You can see my blood. You can see…'

'Are you alright? What's the matter with you?'

Someone grabbed her arm, pulling her away from the wall. Instantly she was back in a ruin with an anxious looking couple staring at her.

'We heard you shouting,' the woman told her. 'We were worried.'

'Why did you disturb me? This has nothing to do with you!'

'Excuse me,' said the man indignantly, 'but we have just as much right to be here as you.'

'Eric,' said the woman reprovingly. 'You can see she's upset.'

'Damn right, I'm upset,' Meg snarled.

'And you've cut yourself.'

'I know! And if you hadn't then maybe I could have saved her…'

The woman's eyes widened. 'Save who?'

She didn't answer. Her mind was whirring.

But I couldn't save her. Not here. Not now. Here it's too late. Here the murder has already happened. Here she's been condemned.

I have to go back further.

I have to go back to…

In her head she saw Dan. He was sitting in his living room, his eyes wide with fear, telling her a story about an unknown visitor and a message that had sounded like a warning.

Two days.

Two days.

The woman was talking to her. 'What's the date today,' Meg demanded.

'It's April 8th.'

'So yesterday was the 7th, and tomorrow will be the 9th. The 9th of April.'

'Well, of course…'

'That's the date it happened. The 9th of April 1881. It wasn't a warning. Dan just thought it was because he was scared. It wasn't a warning. It was a clue.'

The man and woman both looked baffled. 'What clue?'

'That's the day when I reach her. That's the date when I save her!'

The woman was now looking alarmed. 'I think you should sit down for a minute. Perhaps we could get you a glass of water.'

She burst out laughing. 'I don't need water. I don't need anything. At last I know how to reach her and everything is glorious!'

The couple stared at her in bafflement. Reaching out she embraced them both. Then she hurried from the cell.

Ten minutes later she walked through Bodmin towards the car park. Her mind was still whirring. Things she had read in 'Crimes in Cornwall,' now had a completely new significance. Like John Goderidge befriending the warder, Agnes Murray. Had Ellen told Agnes what had really happened? Had she written it down and given it to Agnes to keep? Had John guessed what had happened and paid Agnes and her husband to give it to him?

Yes, that was it. She was sure of it.

Oh, Ellen. You shouldn't have hinted at it. In trying to protect Kate you gave yourself away.

Had she even signed her own sister's death warrant?

After the trial Kate had started to sleep walk, fallen down a flight of stairs and broken her neck. But had she fallen or was she pushed? If John had Ellen's written account, then there was no one else to tell the truth but Clara and Kate. Had John invented stories of Kate's sleepwalking as a cover to protect himself from a murder charge?

After Clara's breakdown John had devoted himself to caring for her. Was he really just making sure that she spoke to no one? And when the burden of enforced proximity became too great had he killed her too?

She remembered the broken woman she had seen in the parlour; the woman who knew what her husband had done but was too afraid to speak the truth and instead had sat by and allowed her niece to take the blame. The book had said that unlike her husband, Clara was well liked in the community. With her backing his story, who would believe Kate and Ellen when one was viewed as a simpleton and the other as no better than a whore?

Yes, it made sense now. All of it.

Well, almost.

There were still unanswered questions. Why had Ellen written to Samuel that night, asking him to visit? Why had she not tried to stop her uncle? Had she even been there when the murder took place and if not then where was she?

But it didn't matter. At last she knew how to communicate with Ellen. Soon she would work out all the rest. Unable to contain herself she gave a triumphant whoop.

Her mobile began to ring. Jennifer's name was on the display. Pressing the answer button she cried out, 'I know how to reach her!'

'You're in danger.'

The words were like a blow. Her joyous mood evaporated. 'I don't need this, Jennifer. Not now I'm so close.'

'Meg, listen to me! You're in *real* danger.'

'But I've made contact.'

'It doesn't matter. Forget about Ellen.' Jennifer sounded ever more agitated. 'It's too late for her and if you stay it will also be too late for you.'

'But I can't!'

'You have to!'

'How can you say that to me? I care about Ellen. I *really* care. You were the one who told me this wasn't about being analytical but allowing myself to feel. Well I *do* feel, far more intensely than you can imagine!'

'Do you remember your life in Wickenham?'

The question stopped her in her tracks. 'How do you know about Wickenham? I never told you I lived there?'

'I know because I've been there. I was there this afternoon in my dreams.'

She ran a hand through her hair. 'Look, I don't have time for this. I need to focus. Tomorrow is the day when I save her.'

'The 9th of April?'

'Yes! That was the date of the murder. The 9th of April 1881.'

'No. It's the 9th of April 2017. That's when the murder takes place.'

'What are you talking about? Whose murder?'

'Yours.'

A chill ran through her.

'They bury you at St Alfred's Church in Wickenham. Your mother's full name was Rebecca Frances Parker. She died on 24th October 1995. *Beloved mother at rest with God and all his angels*. Your sister's full name was Grace Rebecca Barrington. She died on 12th November 2016. *Beloved wife of Peter and sister of Meghan. With God in the joy and beauty of youth*. I've seen their graves, Meg. They bury you next to them.'

She swallowed. Suddenly she was nine years old again, standing in the rain watching her mother's coffin being lowered into the earth and wishing that she could climb in and be buried beside her.

A lump came into her throat. She struggled to swallow it down.

'I was there, Meg. I saw it all. If you carry on with this then you will die, and that is why you have to stop.'

'How can you say that to me? You sound like Dan. He wants me to stop too…'

'*Dan* told you that?' Jennifer gave a hollow laugh.

'What's so funny?'

Jennifer didn't answer.

'Tell me!'

'Can't you guess?'

'What?'

'Dan is the one who kills you.'

For a moment she was too shocked to speak.

'Did you hear what I said?'

'Yes.'

'So…'

'You've got it wrong. You must have done.'

'He strangles you. He does it with his bare hands. The police have him in custody. They're trying to get him to confess. Not that they need a confession. They have enough forensic evidence to charge him without one.'

'Dan would never hurt me.'

'How do you know?'

'Because I know him! There isn't a bad bone in his body.'

Meg, please…'

'No! I won't listen to you anymore. You listen to me. Ellen didn't kill Samuel. Her uncle did. Ellen took the blame to protect her sister whom her uncle intended to frame. I used to think I was better than her but I'm not. She died to protect her sister while I caused the death of mine. She's worth a hundred of me. I am *honoured* that she's chosen me to help her put things right and I am not going to let her down.'

'Even if it means sacrificing your own life?'

'Yes.'

The answer burst from her throat. For a split second she considered retracting it. Then she realised that it was simply the truth.

'What is my life worth anyway? The only two people who ever gave it meaning are dead. I'm not afraid of dying. The only thing I'm afraid of is failing Ellen. Thank you for your concern. I'm grateful to have had your friendship, but please don't contact me again.'

'Meg…'

She disconnected the call. The cut on her palm was aching. As she touched it she remembered Jennifer's words when they had met in the service station.

Open yourself up to her. Give of yourself. That's what she wants.

What gift was more precious than blood? Blood symbolised life.

And she was going to save Ellen's. It was as simple as that.

Switching off her phone she continued on towards the car park. Until something stopped her in her tracks.

She was in a small square. People bustled around her;

carrying bags of shopping, gossiping with each other or relaxing on benches, and all oblivious to the young boy who stood waiting in its centre.

He was about nine years old with thick red hair that was as unruly as a bird's nest, just as it had been in the café in Wickenham when she was five years old, and in the playground on the day when her mother died.

For a moment the two of them just stared at each other. She was struck by how small he looked. On their first meeting he had been bigger than her and in their second at least as tall. Now he looked as frail and vulnerable as a china doll and even though she knew that nothing in this world could ever hurt him an overwhelming feeling of protectiveness swept over her.

He opened his mouth to speak.

'You don't need to tell me,' she said. 'I know already. It was different last time. Then you wanted to warn me about my mother. I wish I could have understood what it was that you were telling me, but I'll always be grateful to you for trying.'

'Then listen now,' he told her.

'I can't. I won't. I'm sorry. I'm glad I was able to help you when I was a child. I'm glad I could give your sister the peace that you weren't able to. But I know what I have to do and nothing in this world is going to stop me.'

'You don't know all of it,' he said.

And then, to her surprise, his face broke into a smile.

She found herself smiling back; while noticing passers by giving her wary glances. Perhaps they thought she was mad; talking to someone who didn't exist in plain view of everyone. When she was a child people had looked at her that way too. For nearly twenty years she had denied who she truly was in order to stop anyone ever looking at her like that again. But now they were she didn't care. The whole world could look at her like that and she would feel nothing but pride. Just as her mother had told her that she would. Her gift *was* special. She already knew it could change lives. Now it was going to save them too.

'Is your sister with you now?' she asked him.

'Yes. I'm glad she is. I missed her when we were apart. I used to play the same games we played but it was never any fun without her.'

'Are you still Doug? Is she still Pearl?'

'Yes.' His smile became so wide it threatened to split his face in two. 'We're Doug and Pearl for ever now.'

She tasted salt on her lips. As she wiped them with her hand she realised she was crying.

'Don't be sad,' he told her.

'I'm not. I'm happy. Your sister was the one who was sad for so many years. I'm glad she's not sad anymore.'

'I wish you could play with us.'

'I wish I could too.'

'Maybe, one day you will. I'd like that. We both would.'

Then, still smiling, he turned to go.

'What was it?' she called after him. 'What was it you were going to tell me?'

He turned back. 'It doesn't matter. You'll find out. Thank you, Meg.'

'Thank you for what?'

'For being the best friend I've ever had.'

He blew her a kiss. She returned the gesture. He caught hers in his fist; giving a cry of triumph as he did so. She caught his in just the same way. They both started to laugh, just as once, twenty-five years earlier, they had laughed together in a café in Suffolk as each realised that they had found a new friend.

And then he was gone.

It was after eight by the time she arrived home. An accident on the outskirts of Penzance had added a good hour to her journey. As she drove into the close she saw Dan locking his van. Her heart sank. She was tired and didn't feel up to another fight; especially not with him.

He stood waiting as she climbed out of her car. 'Look, Dan,' she began. 'About last night…'

'I'm sorry,' he told her. 'I didn't mean what I said.'

'I didn't either. I'm sorry too. I really am.'

'I've been feeling lousy ever since.'

'So have I.'

'You shouldn't have done. I deserved it.'

'No, you didn't. I've never met a man who's less of a coward than you.'

'You wouldn't have said that if you'd seen me this afternoon.'

'Why? What happened?'

He told her. Again, in her head, she saw her mother's coffin being lowered into the ground. According to Jennifer she would soon be lying in the next plot and it would be Dan who put her there, but when she looked into his face she knew, as she always had, just how impossible that was.

'You have no need to be afraid, Dan. I'm the one who's in danger.'

'Then why aren't *you* afraid?'

'Because I know you.'

He looked confused.

'Why don't you come in?' she asked him. 'I'll make us both a coffee and explain everything.'

He pointed to the handkerchief tied around her hand. 'What's that?'

'It's nothing. Just a cut. Why don't you put the kettle on while I get a plaster?'

They entered the house. He headed towards the kitchen. She walked upstairs to the bathroom. There was a box of plasters in the cupboard over the sink. She stuck one over the cut. It wasn't bad; just deep enough to bleed.

As she crossed the landing she saw that her study door was ajar. She was sure she had shut it when she had left the house that morning, but perhaps she was mistaken. She reached out her hand towards the handle.

And felt a faint tingling in her fingers.

She waited for it to pass through her body, but it never did. It was like an echo; a faint vibration left by someone who had already been and gone. For a moment she felt euphoric. Ellen was back! Then, as she pushed open the door and saw the devastation inside she realised that her visitor had not been Ellen at all.

All the desk drawers were open. Papers lay strewn about the room. Her laptop was still on the desk; its screen smashed and almost torn away from the hard drive. Beside it was an empty frame that had once held a treasured photograph of Grace and herself with their mother on a beach, the pieces of which now covered the floor like confetti.

She knew she should be afraid, but all she could feel was fury. Walking into the room she closed the door behind her.

'Is this the best you can do?' she asked.

She waited, as if for a response but heard nothing but a mocking silence. 'Is this the best you can do?' Her voice rose to a scream. 'Do you think you can scare me with this? Well I've got news for you. Whatever you do will never be enough.'

There were footsteps on the stairs. Dan burst into the room; his eyes widening at the sight that greeted him. 'Jesus Christ…'

'He's trying to stop me. John Goderidge. He knows I've found out the truth and he's scared. He thinks this will stop me, but it won't. There is *nothing* he can do that will make me stop. Nothing!'

Dan grabbed her arm, pulling her from the room. 'Are you crazy?'

'No. He's the one who…'

'Will you shut up and listen to me!'

'No! You listen! You don't understand…'

'I understand perfectly. If you carry on with this something bad is going to happen to you and that is why you're going to stop right now.'

'Not a chance.'

He slapped his head in frustration. 'You don't get it, do you? This is not a request, Meg. I am *telling* you this is going to stop.'

Her fury intensified. '*You're* telling me? Who do the hell do you think you are? What gives you the right to tell me anything?'

'What do you think? I love you, you stupid cow! That gives me every right.'

'No, it doesn't! I love you too but if you think feeling like that is going to turn me into some passive little mouse then you've got another think coming!'

He opened his mouth to continue his demands. She opened hers to tell him she didn't want to hear them.

And realised what he'd said.

Her heart turned over. As she stared at his face she saw him realising it too and his heart reacting in exactly the same way.

The anger vanished. A wave of new emotions swept over her; vulnerability, fear, excitement and most powerful of all; joy.

'I love you too,' she said again.

He didn't answer; just reached out, pulled her towards him and kissed her. His stubble felt rough against her skin. His breath tasted of tobacco. He felt scruffy and unkempt and everything she hated in a man and she kissed him back with every ounce of feeling she possessed.

They remained like that for some time. Eventually she realised his cheeks were damp. Pulling back, she saw he was crying. Gently she wiped the tears away.

'Why?' she whispered.

'Don't you get it? I love you, Meg, more than I ever thought I could love anyone and now I do I'm sure I'm going to lose you.'

'You won't. That's a promise.'

'How can you promise that?'

'Because it's true. You think I'm doing this to hurt you but I'm not. You're the last person in the world I'd ever want to hurt. Ellen isn't real. Not in the way you are. I can imagine my life without her, but I cannot imagine it without you.'

His stared at her reproachfully. 'But still you want to help her.'

'I have to. Don't you see that? I messed up with my mother and I messed up with Grace and I cannot mess up with Ellen. If I did I could never live with myself again, and if I can't live with myself then how can I ever hope to make a life with you?'

'If you love me you'll stop.'

'If you love me you won't ask me to.'

He sighed.

'Dan…' she began.

'Then I won't ask it.'

She swallowed. 'Thank you.'

'Just do one thing for me.'

She stroked his cheek. 'Anything.'

'Forget about her tonight. For tonight at least I want you to be mine.'

'I am yours. No matter what happens, Dan, from this moment on I will always be yours.'

Again, they kissed, wrapping themselves around each other like two halves forming a single whole.

Chapter 13

Early morning. They lay in her bed, staring at each other. Neither had slept. Though there had been passion, most of the night had been spent just cuddling and talking about the past. He had not wanted to discuss the future. She knew he was still frightened and it made her sad. There was no need for fear. Everything would be alright. She would make sure of it.

'Are you tired?' he asked.

'Do I look it?'

'No. You look beautiful.'

'So do you.'

They kissed. She stroked his stubble. 'Don't worry,' he said. 'I'll be clean shaven from now on.'

'Don't you dare!'

He smiled. 'Still the ball breaker, I see.'

'Sorry. What I meant to say is I wouldn't change you for anything.'

'It's OK. Break my balls as much as you want. I wouldn't change you either.' He began to look hesitant. 'Can I ask you something?'

'What?'

'Now that we've been intimate…well, I was just wondering…'

'No. I'm not going to turn lesbian.'

He laughed. She did too.

'I know what you're thinking,' he told her. 'You're thinking that Ellen should have had all this with Samuel. You're trying to work out a way to make sure that she still does.'

'No, I wasn't thinking that…'

'I'm not judging you.' He ran his fingers through her hair. 'I just wish I could reach inside your head and pull out all the guilt. You have nothing to feel guilty about. I can see it so clearly. I wish you could too.'

'I don't feel guilty when I'm with you.'

'So how do you feel?'

'Blessed. Euphoric. More alive than ever before.' She paused; unable to resist it. 'And maybe just a little bit Sapphic.'

'I love you, Meg Parker.'

'I love you, Dan Penaluna.'

'Thank you.'

'You don't need to thank me.'

'Yes, I do. I'm thanking you for last night. At least if anything happens…'

'Nothing will, Dan. I won't let it. Before last night I was alone. Now I have you and even if I have to fight Hell itself I'll win because I know you'll be waiting for me.'

He didn't answer; just held her as if his life depended on it.

Later, while he was in the shower, she went downstairs to make breakfast. The post lay on the doormat. Amongst a pile of circulars was a hand-written envelope. The script was familiar. At first she thought it belonged to her secretary, Debbie. Then, as she saw the postmark, she realised it was from her brother in law, Pete.

Tearing it open, she read the letter it contained:

Dear Meg,

I should have written this letter a long time ago. I hope that when you've read it you can find it in your heart to forgive the delay.

During our last meeting I said things that I know hurt you deeply. You wrote to me afterwards and said you didn't blame me because you knew I had only been speaking the truth. Well, you were wrong. I was angry and grieving and in my pain I lashed out and told you a pack of lies.

Grace never hated you. She never wanted us to move away or to prevent you from having any involvement in the life of our child. That was the last thing she wanted. From the moment your mother died you were the one person she knew she could always count on; the one person who would always stand by her and protect her no matter what. She often used to talk about what happened with your stepmother and at the children's home and how she never would have survived if you hadn't been by her side. I remember her saying once that though God had played a cruel trick on her by taking your mother away he had more than made up for it by blessing her with a sister like you.

You admitted in your letter that you had always been jealous of me and my role in Grace's life. Now it's time for me to admit that I was jealous of you too. The truth is that Grace loved you even more than she loved me. Of course, there were times when you drove her mad but isn't that always the way with the people we love the most? From her early childhood you were mother, father, sister and best friend all rolled into one and that creates a bond that not even a husband can ever totally eclipse. For what it's worth I'm not jealous anymore. Now that time has given me perspective I can even be grateful because if you hadn't been there to watch over her she might never have grown up to become the wonderful woman I fell in love with.

Your firm tell me that you're living in Cornwall. I hope you've found some peace there and know that Grace would too. You spent so much of your life trying to make hers a happy one. What better way to honour her memory than to now find some happiness for yourself.

Take care. Please try not to hate me too much.

Love,
Pete

She stood very still, just staring at the words on the page.

Dan appeared beside her. She handed him the letter. He read it slowly, his arm around her, then handed it back. 'You see,' he whispered. 'You have nothing to feel guilty about or to atone for. There's only one emotion you should feel when you look back on your life and that is pride.'

She burst into tears.

'Hey, there…' he began.

'I'm sorry.' She wiped her eyes. 'It's just…'

'You don't have to explain. I understand. I love you,

remember. You never have to explain anything to me.'

'I'm happy he wrote that. I really am. I just…'

'Miss her. I know you do but it *will* get better. Pain is always easier when you have someone to share it with and you've got me. I'll get you through it. I'll do whatever it takes. All your life you've been taking care of others. Isn't it time to let someone take care of you?'

He was staring at her; his eyes full of love and concern. As she gazed into them she knew that she could never bear to see him unhappy, and no matter how terrible a sacrifice that entailed it was one she would always be willing to make.

'Alright,' she said softly. 'I'll stop trying to save Ellen. I don't want you to be afraid. If I continue I'll only be hurting you and what sort of love is that?'

His face lit up. 'Do you promise?'

'Yes.'

Lunchtime. The house was quiet. Dan was away on his building job. She had spent the morning tidying the study and now sat at her desk writing a letter to Pete; expressing her gratitude for what he had told her and her hopes that he was finding some happiness himself.

As her pen flowed across the page she kept glancing at the photograph of her mother, Grace and herself that was now back in its frame. She had managed to stick the pieces together with tape and though it would never look as good as it had, the only thing that mattered was that it was still there.

It had been taken on the beach at Southwold the summer before her mother died. Now she was only two years younger than her mother had been on that long-ago afternoon. She wondered what their relationship would have been like if her mother had lived. Would they still be as close? Would her mother have been proud of her career successes? Would she even have the same career? Just how different a path might her life have taken had her mother been there to help shape it?

She stopped writing; just doodling on the side of the page as the questions continued to run through her mind.

What would you think if you could see me now? Would you like the person I've become? What advice would you give me? Would you know how much I still miss you? Did you suffer when you died? Do you know how bad I felt that I couldn't save you? Do you know how bad I still feel today?

Do you know how sorry I am?

She looked over at the window. It was open, letting the breeze drift in. She inhaled, tasting the fragments of earth and salt it contained.

And smelled roses.

Suddenly the scent filled the room; just as it had once filled their house in Suffolk. For a moment she felt as if she was back there; a child again full of hope and excitement and no fear of what the future might bring.

The wind changed direction; sucking the air back out of the window and the scent with it.

As her attention returned to the page in front of her she saw the new lines her hand had written.

There was never anything to forgive.

I love you and am prouder of you than I can say.

Always do what you think is right, my darling, and never be afraid.

Putting her pen to one side she leaned over and rested her head on the page.

Time passed. Her head remained on the paper while the breeze returned, caressing her scalp like an adult ruffling the hair of a much-loved child.

That afternoon she went walking on the cliffs. The sky was clear. Rays of sunlight danced on the surface of the sea, making it sparkle. She spent half an hour sitting on a boulder at her favourite beach watching the seagulls glide in on the wind. A couple of them cawed at her as they did so. Perhaps they had missed her. It had been some time since she had been there, and she had certainly missed them.

Afterwards she walked on towards the outcrop of rock and the engine house. A man stood at its edge with a small boy on his shoulders while a woman knelt, reading the inscription on the memorial plaque. The woman smiled at her as she approached. She smiled back.

'Are you on holiday?' she asked.

The woman nodded. 'Are you?'

'No. I live here.'

'So, you must know this place well.' The woman gestured to the plaque. 'It doesn't seem right that somewhere so beautiful could be the site of such a tragedy.'

'You're right. It doesn't.'

The little boy called to the woman: his voice shrill with excitement. 'He's very noisy,' said the woman apologetically.

'I don't mind. It's lovely to see him enjoy himself. What's his name?'

'Jack.'

'How old is he?'

'Four. He starts school in September. I can't believe it. It only seems like yesterday that he was born.'

'They grow up so quickly, don't they?'

'Yes.' The woman sighed. 'Though sometimes it doesn't feel fast enough.'

'What do you mean?'

The woman gestured towards the plaque. 'It's seeing that. It's a reminder of how fragile life can be.'

'Jack looks a very healthy boy.'

'He is. It's not that. It's…' The woman hesitated.

'Go on,' Meg told her.

'Two weeks ago, my husband and I left Jack with a babysitter and went out for dinner. On the way back, we were involved in an accident. It wasn't our fault, and no one was hurt, thank God, but for a moment I was convinced I was going to die and all I could think about was Jack. He's so young. What would happen to him if his father and I weren't there to protect him? I love the fact that he needs me. I know it will hurt when he stops doing so, but sometimes I wish he was grown up so that if anything did happen…' Suddenly the woman stopped, looking embarrassed. 'I'm sorry. I don't know why I'm telling you this.'

'I do.'

The woman stared at her. 'Why?'

'I lost my mother when I was nine. It was hard but I survived and now my life is good. I'm sure you'll always be there for Jack but even if you're not you'll still be a part of him and that should get him through. That's why I got through; because my mother was still a part of me.'

'I'm sorry you lost her.'

'That's my point. I never did. Not completely.'

She turned to watch Jack and his father. The two of them were waving to something on the horizon. As she looked more closely she saw it was a ship. In her head she saw an excited nine-year-old girl doing the same. That girl had had all of her father's energy and spirit. It should have been enough to get her through. It should have been more than enough.

The woman was watching her son; her eyes full of tenderness. Had the mother of Dan's friend Alan looked at her own son like that when he survived his fall? Would she ever have believed it possible that there would come a day when she might wish he had never survived at all?

She searched for some logic to it all but could find none. No fairness either. It was just the way of the world. There were no guarantees in life. Nothing was so safe that it could not be lost in a second and all you could do was pray that there were people around you who cared enough to help you through the pain and out the other side.

Because if you truly cared for someone then that was what you did. It was an instinct as old as time itself. You did it because you couldn't not do it.

You did it because it was right.

She turned and walked away.

Six o'clock. Jed stood at the counter of the Saltran supermarket, staring out at the aisles. He was tired, just as he always seemed to be these days. The owners of the supermarket were starting to express concern that the job was becoming too much for him. They were probably right but he didn't want to give it up. It gave his life a purpose and helped him forget, if only briefly, that his wife was no longer there.

There were only a handful of customers; an elderly couple debating which micro wave meal to buy and Meg Parker who stood at the back of the shop, holding a basket and staring in his direction. He smiled at her. Her expression remained serious. She seemed to be concentrating very hard. He wondered what she was thinking about.

The elderly couple made their purchase and left. Meg approached the counter. Her basket was empty.

'Is there nothing we can tempt you with tonight?' Jed asked.

'Do you remember that night I bumped into Tom Mercer and his dog? I'd been walking on the cliffs and got caught in the rain.'

'Yes, I remember.'

'You seemed to guess what I was running from. You seemed to realise, as you put it, how good my eye sight was.'

He nodded.

'Lily's worried about you, Jed.'

His legs felt weak beneath him. 'Lily?'

'She wishes you wouldn't work so hard. She knows you only do it to avoid feeling alone. She wishes you could realise that you're not alone. That she still loves you. That she's still there.'

He swallowed. 'But I do feel alone.'

'That's because you believe she's gone. You think that it's all over. But it's not. Death isn't the end, Jed. It never will be. Not for you and her. That's what she wants me to tell you. That's what she needs you to believe.'

He couldn't stop himself. He started to cry.

She reached out, gently stroking his arm. 'I'm sorry. I'm not telling you this to upset you. I'm telling you because however hard she tries she can't tell you herself.'

He wiped his eyes, struggling to bring himself under control.

'Do you want me to leave?' she asked.

'Yes.'

She walked away. He watched her go. When she reached the door, he called out her name and she turned back.

'Thank you, Meg. Thank you from both of us.'

'You don't need to thank me.'

'Yes,' he said softly. 'I do.'

She left the shop. He remained at the counter, staring out at the shop. Normally the sight of all the empty aisles made him feel sad. This time it didn't.

He waited patiently for his next customer.

Half past seven. Meg finished writing a note to Dan. She had spoken to him on the phone earlier; keeping her tone light and breezy so as to give no indication of her plans. In the note she apologised for what she was going to do, attempted to explain her reasons and asked him to try and understand.

Her left arm was sore. There was a bandage around the wrist. On the table beside her was a perfume bottle half full with a thick, crimson liquid. She wasn't sure what message she could give Ellen. She wasn't sure she would even manage to reach her at all. All she knew was that this was the best chance she would ever have and that she would never be able to live with herself if she didn't take it.

She put the note in an envelope and left it on the kitchen table. Once she was in Bamber she would send him a text telling him where to find it. Putting the perfume bottle in her pocket, she headed outside.

As she started her car she heard the roar of an engine. To her horror Dan's van burst into view. He swerved across the entrance to the close, blocking her escape route then marched towards her. Feeling trapped she climbed out of the car.

'And where do you think you're going?' he demanded.

'Um...'

'I knew it! I could tell when we spoke on the phone that you'd changed your mind. Do yourself a favour and never work in espionage. You'd be completely shit at it!'

'I'm not doing this to hurt you.'

'You shouldn't be doing it at all! You promised me. You bloody promised!'

'I know I did…'

'Then why?'

'Because I don't have a choice.'

'Bullshit!'

'Is it? Imagine if you were the one who was in trouble. You've got your parents and your brother and your friends and most of all you've got me. You've got a whole army of people ready to fight for you. Well it's not like that for Ellen. I'm all she's got and I cannot let her down. I've tried, Dan. I swear to God I have but I just can't.'

'But she's not your sister!'

'It's not about Grace! It's not about my mother either. Not anymore. It's about *her*. It's about a girl I've come to care about more than I would have ever dreamed possible whose life is about to be destroyed through no fault of her own.'

His eyes were flashing. 'But it's not your fault either. It's not your fault and it's not your problem.'

'And would you be saying that if it were your friend Alan?'

He shook his head. 'That's not fair.'

'Of course, it's fair!' Her own temper was rising. 'Imagine if you had the chance to go back in time and save him from falling? Imagine if you had that chance and I told you not to take it. Do you think you'd listen to me? Do you really think you'd be able to turn your back on him like you're asking me to turn mine on her?'

He didn't answer.

'Well?' she demanded.

'So, I can't talk you out of this?'

'No.'

He sighed. 'I didn't think so. I just needed to be sure.'

'I love you, Dan. I hope you can forgive me but if you can't…'

'I'll drive.'

She was taken aback. 'Drive?'

'You don't think I'm letting you go on your own, do you? I've told you before, Meg, we're a team. If you go, then so do I.'

For a moment she felt overjoyed. Then she remembered what Jennifer had told her. It was crazy. It made no sense at all. But still she felt afraid.

'No,' she told him. 'You have to stay here.'

'Screw that!'

'You have to, Dan.'

'Why?'

'Because you'll be in danger if you come.'

'But you said you were the one who was in danger.'

'And that danger comes from you.'

He looked baffled. As she told him what Jennifer had said the expression faded, replaced by one of disbelief. 'That's insane.'

'Maybe so, but I don't know what tonight is going to bring and I don't want to…'

'What? Take any chances? Meg, are you listening to yourself? Of all the billions of people on this planet no one is less likely to hurt you than me.'

'I know, but…'

'So, I'm coming with you. End of discussion.'

'Dan…'

'You don't have a choice. I'm not moving my car and if you try and get to Bamber any other way I'll call the police, tell them you're going to burgle the house and you'll never get through the front door. We do this together, Meg. I'm grateful for your warning but it doesn't change a thing. I would never hurt you. My job is to keep you safe and I swear on everything I hold sacred that I will not let you down.'

His face was shining. She could feel the love coming off him in waves.

And knew he was right.

'Very well,' she told him. 'We'll do it together.'

'Good.'

They climbed into his van. He started the engine and steered them out of the close.

Chapter 14

Quarter to eleven. She walked with Dan along Hepton Street. It was empty, just as she had hoped. Lights were on in a few windows, but all had drawn curtains. She kept searching for prying eyes but saw none.

She was feeling light headed. They had spent the last couple of hours in 'The Sailor's Rest' where she had drunk two large glasses of wine. Alcohol always made her drowsy and soon she would need to sleep. Whether she would dream was another matter, but she had to try.

They reached the house. While Dan kept watch she let herself in. After taking a final look around he followed her inside and she closed the door behind them. The hallway was completely dark. All the doors leading off it were closed. Dan began to search for a light switch.

'Don't!' she hissed.

'But we can't see a bloody thing.'

'We can't risk someone seeing a light either.' Quickly she opened a couple of doors, letting in a faint glow from the street.

'Well that makes all the difference,' he muttered.

'It's good enough. Anyway, I know my way about.'

He continued to mutter. Ignoring him she tried to clear her mind in the hope of sensing something.

'Can you feel her?' he asked, as if reading her thoughts.

'No.'

'So how do you know we have to be here?'

'Because this is where it happened, and this is the anniversary of that night. Someone, probably John, is blocking her but she's trying to get through. If there's anywhere she'll be able to reach me then it's here.'

There were voices on the street outside. They both fell silent, waiting for the sound to fade.

'Do you know where she was when it happened?' he whispered.

'No. But I know where it happened. That's my best chance.'

She started towards the stairs. He grabbed her arm. 'That sounds dangerous.'

'This whole thing is dangerous.'

'What if she doesn't come?'

'She has to.'

'But what if she doesn't? What if it's someone else?'

'Then I'll deal with it.'

'How? By throwing your perfume bottle at them? You saw what they did to your study. Do you really think a bottle of Chanel No 5 is going to keep them at bay?'

'Actually, it's Givenchy.'

'Then I take it back. You'll be as safe as houses.'

'Look, Dan, I don't have all the answers. All I know is that time is running out and I have to do something. Now are you in or out?'

'What do you think?'

'Then follow me.'

She led him up the stairs. When they reached the door on the landing she tried the handle. It was locked. Clearly Tim the estate agent was taking precautions against prospective tenants looking inside.

'I need some light now,' she told Dan.

He produced a tiny torch. She studied the key ring under its thin beam, trying to identify the right key. None had labels and with the exception of the one that opened the front door all were about the same size. She tried a couple with no success. On the third attempt the fit was perfect. Feeling relieved she began to turn it.

And felt it snap.

She pulled out a broken stub. The remainder of the key was now wedged firmly in the lock.

'Damn it!' Crouching down she tried to prise it free.

'Let me,' said Dan. 'Just hold the torch.'

As she watched him peer at the lock she heard the soft thud of music playing nearby.

Dan heard it too. 'Where's that coming from?'

'The house on the right. The people who live there must still be up.'

'No shit.'

'Can you reach it?'

'No, and even if I could it wouldn't make any difference. The key's broken. It's never going to work again.'

'Damn it!' she said again.

He rose to his feet. 'So, what do you want to do now?'

'Can you force it open?'

He pushed against the door, testing it out. 'This thing is rock solid, and the lock is strong too. It's not a question of just using my shoulder. I'll have to kick it in.'

The music was now accompanied by laughter. It sounded like a party. She remembered Tim telling her that the neighbours were close friends with the family who had lived in the house. 'I know them quite well, actually,' he had said. 'When they found out I was handling the property they asked me to keep them informed of progress and not to rent to anyone unpleasant.' He had given her a smarmy smile. 'Though I'm sure there's nothing unpleasant about your brother and his family.'

'I could do it,' Dan told her. 'But it'll make a hell of a din.'

For a moment she was tempted to chance it. But if she did the neighbours might hear. They would know the house was still vacant and almost certainly call the police, and that was the one thing she just couldn't risk. Detection would mean ejection and what good would she be to Ellen then?

'Shall I?' Dan asked.

'No.'

'So, what do we do?'

She didn't answer; hoping against hope to sense something.

Ellen, where are you? Tell me where to go and what do to.

Still nothing. She checked her watch. It was eleven o'clock. The murder had happened just before midnight. She needed to be asleep long before then. But *where* should she sleep? Where would Ellen have the best chance of reaching her?

Dan was staring expectantly at her. In the dim light from the torch his eyes looked feral. It reminded her of the eyes of a pack of hunting dogs attacking a stag that she had once seen in a painting.

Just for a second; before the image had been snatched from her head.

She hurried back down the stairs towards the room with the window seat. 'We do it in here,' she told him. 'She reached me here before. She can do it again.'

He peered through the half open door. 'This is too exposed. The window looks out onto the street and there aren't any curtains we can draw.'

'It doesn't matter. The lights are off in the house opposite and as long as we're sitting down no passer-by will spot us.' Crouching down she crawled into the room. Muttering yet again he did the same.

She passed the window, checking as she did so that all the lights were still off across the street. When she reached the far corner, she stopped. 'No one will see us here.'

'So, what do you want me to do?'

'Watch over me while I sleep.'

'And wake you up if you're in trouble.'

'Yes. I mean, no.' She thought for a minute. 'Only if I tell you to.'

'And how are you going to do that? You'll be comatose.'

'I'll think of something.'

'Fuck that! The first sign of trouble and you can kiss dreamland goodbye.'

'But you can't! You'll ruin everything.'

'And how are you going to stop me?'

'Christ, I'm really starting to wish you hadn't come.'

'That makes two of us.'

'So why don't you leave?'

'Only if you come too.'

'No chance.'

'Then you're stuck with me so deal with it.'

As she opened her mouth to protest she heard footsteps pass by the window and stop outside the neighbouring house. A door opened and closed.

'You know what I think?' he whispered.

'What?'

'That after tonight we should give this house breaking lark a rest, as all it does it make us argue.'

He was grinning at her. In spite of her anxiety she found herself grinning back. She was glad he was there. She really was.

'Do you trust me?' he asked.

'With my life.'

'Then trust me to do what's right, OK?'

'OK.'

He tapped the floor with his hand. 'We should have brought a pillow.'

'I'll be fine.'

He removed his jumper and handed it to her. 'Here. Rest your head on this. It will be more comfortable.'

She was touched. 'Won't you be chilly? There's no heating in here.'

'Don't worry about me. Just worry about yourself. Do you think you'll be able to sleep?'

'I have to.'

'You mustn't look at it like that. You're only putting yourself under pressure. What you need to do is relax. I'll help you. Go on, lie down.'

She did as she was told, resting her head on his jumper. The wood floor felt cold beneath her body. The perfume bottle was in her left hand. As she squeezed it she saw the enormity of the task ahead and felt afraid. What if Ellen couldn't reach her? What if she couldn't change anything? What if she couldn't sleep at all?

What if? What if? What if?

Dan began to stroke her hair; his fingers massaging her scalp. 'Just shut your eyes,' he said softly. 'Forget everything except that I'm here, I love you and I'm going to keep you safe. Believe you can do it and you will, and when it's over I'll be waiting for you and nothing will ever separate us.'

'Nothing will,' she told him. 'I won't let it. I promise you that.'

'Hush.' Bending down he kissed her on the forehead. 'Go to sleep, sweetheart. Just go to sleep.'

He continued to stroke her hair. It felt lovely; so relaxing that her head felt as if it could detach from her body and float away. As the sensation continued her fears began to melt away. She could do it. She could do anything. All she had to do was believe.

Her eyelids were growing heavy. She forced them open and stared up at him. His eyes no longer looked feral. Now they were two warm pools in which she could happily drown. Ellen must have felt like that when she looked at Samuel. When he had died a part of her would have died too; her execution merely finishing a job that had started in this very house over a hundred years ago.

And now she was going to change all that.

But how could she when she felt so lazy? She could barely keep her eyes open. All she could do was lie there, feeling her head drifting off into space.

The music was still playing. Its pulse was like one of the lullabies her mother had once sung to her. No matter how awake she had felt they had always sent her sliding down into sleep. It didn't hurt to think about her mother anymore. Not now she was forgiven.

Not now she was doing what was right.

Her eyes closed again. Dan was whispering something. She tried to listen, but his voice faded away into nothing. Soon she could not hear him at all or feel his touch. It was like he wasn't even there anymore; as if she was alone with only her thoughts for company.

But she wasn't alone. Someone was with her. She could sense them; just barely. But it was enough.

She opened her eyes. Ellen stood in the doorway; looking just as she had on that terrifying first night. Now that terror was a distant memory and all she felt was joy.

Ellen began to walk towards her. She was like a shadow; something made of air and light. As she moved she flickered like an image projected from a worn-out film that threatened to snap with every extra frame that was run.

'You can do it,' Meg told her. 'I know you can.'

Ellen turned, looking back towards the half open door. Her

image grew even fainter. In a matter of seconds it would be gone altogether. Meg tried to rise but her body felt like lead. All she could do was raise her right arm and hold it extended.

'Don't be afraid! You're not alone. You've got me. I will fight for you and I will win. All you have to do is reach me. If you do that I swear I will do the rest.'

Ellen turned back. She didn't seem quite so faint anymore. And she was smiling.

'That's it,' Meg whispered. 'Just a bit further. Just a bit.'

Ellen stretched out her own hand. Meg tried to grasp it but couldn't. A weight was pressing on her, forcing her arm back down to the ground. She thought of John Goderidge. She thought of her own father and stepmother. She thought of all the people who had wronged the two of them.

You will not win. Not now. Not ever! You don't frighten me and you will not frighten her. You're the ones who should be afraid.

Anger flooded her veins like fire. It gave her energy. It made her feel strong again. It made her feel that she really could win.

Ellen's hand remained suspended in air. Again, she reached out towards it…

Dan continued to stroke Meg's hair, humming softly and listening to the gentle hiss of her breathing.

She began to speak. For a moment he thought was talking to him. Then, as he listened to her words of encouragement, he realised they were not meant for him at all. Her right arm rose into the air then hung there as if suspended by an invisible thread. Then it dropped, just as her body stiffened; growing so rigid that it was as if he were holding a plank of wood, while about him the air seemed to shift as if blown by a fan.

He whispered her name. She didn't answer; now lost in a world inhabited only by the dead.

She was in a room with a sloping ceiling. It was dimly lit; the only illumination coming from a gas lamp that someone was holding. As she looked about her, struggling to find some bearings, she saw a triangular window.

It's the store room. The store room under the stairs.

As her eyes adjusted to the light she saw there were three people there. An anxious looking Kate hovered in the doorway, watching Clara who was standing over Ellen, who was sitting in a chair. There was no sign of John. Was he already upstairs, waiting in the parlour for Samuel to arrive?

'Go!' Clara told Kate. 'You know what to do.'

Kate gazed at Ellen who threw her a beseeching look. 'Kat, please…'

'Don't listen to her,' Clara snapped. 'You know you can't trust her. Just go.'

Kate left the room. Ellen opened her mouth to call out to her. Before she could do so Clara slapped her across the face.

'There's no point,' she hissed. 'She doesn't trust you anymore. She'll never trust you again.'

'He won't come. He'll know the note isn't from me. He'll know something is wrong.'

Clara started to laugh; the sound shrill and manic. Her hair hung loose around her head and her eyes were shining. She bore no relation to the broken creature Meg had seen in the upstairs parlour the previous day. There was nothing broken about this Clara. This one radiated energy and purpose.

So much so that a new and dreadful possibility crept into Meg's head.

'But it *is* from you,' Clara told Ellen. 'I was the one who taught you your lessons. I taught you how to write properly. I formed your hand and I can copy it too. Perfectly.'

Ellen swallowed. 'He still won't come. Not at this hour. You know he won't.'

'Do I? He knows your uncle is spending the night at the Dawsons. As far as he knows I'm there too. He'll think it's just you and Kate. Of course, he'll come, you fool. Like a dog chasing a rabbit he won't be able to stop himself.'

So, John isn't even here! But he was here when the crime was discovered. When did he come back? Before or after the deed was done?

Ellen opened her mouth as if to scream. Again, Clara slapped her across the face. The blow made Meg flinch. Why wasn't Ellen fighting back?

Then, as she looked more closely she saw Ellen was tied to the chair.

It was cold in the room. Gently releasing Meg's head, Dan wrapped his arms around himself in an attempt to keep warm. The noise from next door was growing louder. Clearly the party was in full swing. He wondered what the revellers would do if they knew what was taking place only feet away from their festivities.

Meg's breathing grew fainter. Suddenly he couldn't hear it at all. Alarmed he crawled around her and lent over until his ear was only millimetres from her mouth. It was slightly open. To his relief he felt a faint trickle of air against his skin. Softly he kissed her cheek. 'I love you, Meg,' he whispered. 'Come back to me. Do what you have to do and then please, please come back to me.'

He resumed his position; keeping watch like a sentry.

Something brushed her cheek. Was it a moth? How could she feel it? She had no substance here. In this room she was the one who was made of shadow and air.

Ellen struggled in the chair. 'Why are you doing this?' she asked Clara.

'You know why.'

'I've never hurt you.'

'Haven't you?'

'You know I haven't. Neither has Samuel. He's your friend.'

'*Friend?*' Clara almost spat the word back at her. 'He was much more than that. He loved me!'

'No, he didn't. How can you say that?'

Meg shook her head, wondering exactly the same thing.

And remembered the answer Samuel had given in the alley when Ellen had asked him how he had made John and Clara view him as a son:

'With your uncle, all it takes is a willingness to listen to him boast of his achievements. With your aunt it's even easier. All one has to do is remember to notice she exists.'

She thought of the woman she had seen listening at the door while her husband raped her niece; a woman with tears of shame and fear rolling down her cheeks. But was that the case? Had they in fact been tears of jealousy, shed by a woman who just wanted her husband to notice she existed?

The way Samuel had.

Had she believed he could give her the love and fulfilment her husband never could, only to discover that he was simply using her to be close to the same niece for whose bed her husband constantly deserted her own?

Again, Clara slapped Ellen. Again, Meg flinched.

Do something! Make it stop!

But how? What could she do?

'I can say it because it's true!' Clara shouted. 'I know he loved me. The way he looked at me. The way he smiled at me. Everything he did told me it was true. He'd still love me now if it wasn't for you.'

Ellen shook her head. She was shaking. She looked terrified. Clara leaned towards her so their faces were almost touching. Meg could see the resemblance between them. They could have been mother and daughter rather than aunt and niece. Both had the same delicate features and wide spaced eyes yet in Clara the combination somehow fell short of beauty. It was as if they were two flowers from the same batch of seeds; one of which had failed to bloom.

'All my life you and yours have taken from me,' Clara hissed at Ellen. 'I loved your father, but your mother stole him, just like she stole everything since we were children. All our lives together she was the sun and I was her shadow. What chance did your father have against her? How could he even notice me when she never allowed me to exist?'

'She didn't mean to hurt you. She loved you! You were her sister. She talked about you all the time. She used to worry about the life you were leading with Uncle John. She knew you weren't happy and that was what she wanted. She used to say that she could never be truly happy if you weren't.'

'She was a liar! A liar and a whore. When she died I told everyone I was heartbroken but inside I was rejoicing! I didn't know then that I'd never be free of her. That she'd left me you to poison the rest of my life. As far as John was concerned the moment you entered our house I ceased to exist. You were all he wanted. You were all he loved.'

'*Loved?*' Suddenly the terror vanished from Ellen's face. 'He never loved me! All he ever did was hurt me! You *know* he did. I used to hear your footsteps in the corridor outside my room when he was forcing himself on me. I know you listened. I know you heard. How can you possibly describe that as love?'

'Because it was more than I had! I could have died in my sleep and it would have taken him a week to even notice. Do you know what it feels like to be a ghost in your own home? Can you even imagine? You say he hurt you, but he didn't. You enjoyed it. You loved every second of it! All that mattered to you was that you were stealing from me, just as it was all that mattered to your whore of a mother!'

Meg couldn't contain herself. 'You sick bitch!'

'My mother was no whore!' Ellen shouted back. 'She was a good woman. She was…'

Suddenly her head turned in Meg's direction; her eyes widening as they scanned the room.

She senses me! She knows I'm here!

'Your mother was nothing!' taunted Clara. 'She never even wanted you! That's what she told me. If it wasn't for your father, she would have happily drowned you and your sister at birth.'

'That's a lie!'

'No, it's not!'

'So, if she never wanted me then why is she here with us now?'

'What are you talking about?'

'She's here! I can feel her. She's watching us!'

Again, Clara laughed. 'You're as crazy as your sister.'

'I'm not! She's here. She can see what you're doing, just as she's seen all you *didn't* do when Uncle John was hurting me. She may have loved you when you were alive but believe me, all she feels for you now is contempt!'

Clara raised her hand to strike Ellen again.

And at that moment Meg knew what to do.

Throw the bottle against the wall! They'll see the blood. Clara will think her sister really is here and she'll be so afraid that she'll stop.

Triumph surged through her. She clenched her left fist.

Only to find her hand was empty.

The room grew ever colder. Dan began to shiver. He stared down at Meg. Her body was still rigid. Where was she now? What was she doing? Was she safe? And how would he know if she wasn't?

He couldn't handle the uncertainty. He decided to wake her. She would be furious, but he could live with her anger. He reached out a hand then pulled it back, unable, in spite of his fears, to go through with it. He knew how much this meant to her. If she failed, she would never be able to live with herself. And he couldn't do that to her. He loved her too much.

The door of the room was half open. In the poor light he could see the hall. From somewhere far away a floorboard creaked; the weary sigh of an old house. Did houses sleep too? Did they dream? Did they see their history played out over and over like a film on a loop? Did they want to change it? Did it give them nightmares?

Or was it like a comfort blanket they would kill to protect?

He didn't know. He didn't know anything except that he was terribly afraid.

Oh God, keep her safe. Please keep her safe.

She stared at her empty hand, not believing what she was seeing.

It has to be here! It has to be!

She stared down at the floor. Had she dropped it? Was it lying under her feet? The light was so poor she had to sink to her knees and feel about her, but however far she reached she could not find it while above her head she heard Clara's hand strike Ellen's face.

Oh Christ, where is it? I need it. I need it now!

'She's not here!' Clara cried. 'She won't help you. No one can help you.'

Meg looked up in time to see Ellen swallow. 'What are you going to do?'

'I'm going to talk to Samuel. I'm going to tell him what you really are. I'm going to make him hate you as much as I do.'

'You won't succeed. He loves me. You can't make him hate me. You can't!'

'Oh, he will. What he feels for you isn't real. He's just been blinded by you, like your uncle was. I'll tell him I'll go to America with him. I'll tell him I'll go to Hell itself if that's what he wants. I'll make him remember I'm the one he really loves.'

'And what if you can't?'

Clara reached into the pocket of her dress and pulled out a kitchen knife.

'Then I'll show him that I'm not a ghost. I'll teach him that I really exist.'

'But you'll never get away with it. They'll catch you and they'll hang you!'

'No. Not me. Your sister is the one they're going to catch. I'll tell them that she did it and your uncle will back me up. He'll have to, because otherwise I'll tell the world everything that he's done to you. And they'll believe me, just as they'll believe me when I tell them your sister is a murderer. I'm a saint, remember. I'm the one member of this family that the whole community respects. I'm not a bully like your uncle, I'm not a simpleton like your sister and I'm not a whore like you!'

Ellen opened her mouth to scream. As quick as a flash Clara

produced a piece of cloth and wrapped it around Ellen's face like a gag before tying it tight behind.

'And now I must go and meet the man I love.' Suddenly Clara's voice was like that of a young girl. 'Wish me luck. Not that I'll need it. I'll make him love me again. I know I will.'

She turned to leave. Meg's brain was racing. She had to do something to show she was there. But if she couldn't use the blood then what did she have?

Yourself

She saw herself standing on the cliff in her first dream. She saw an old man called Stan walk straight through her before turning and saying that someone had stepped on his grave. He had known she was there even though he couldn't articulate it. Now it was time for Clara to know it too.

Ellen strained in the chair, trying in vain to make a sound. Clara picked up the lamp and turned towards the door. Meg blocked her path, bracing herself as Clara drew nearer.

Feel me. Sense me. Know that I'm here and be afraid.

Clara passed through her. She was like a damp cloud made of snakes. The sensation was unbearable. It was like touching the shape of madness. She gave a gasp of revulsion while Clara continued on her way, too wrapped up in her own twisted desires to even notice.

There were more people on the street. Dan could hear them laughing. He envied them their peace of mind. His own mind was full of fears far darker than the room in which he sat.

He looked down at Meg. Her body was still rigid. Again, he raised a silent prayer for her safety.

And as he did so he noticed something.

The bottle was no longer in her hand. He must have knocked it out when he crouched down to check her breathing. He placed it back in her palm; doing so as gently as possible so as not to wake her.

Clara left the room, closing the door behind her. Now they were in virtual darkness; the only light coming from the triangular window that caught the dim gleam of the moon.

Ellen continued to struggle in her chair. Meg watched her, feeling dizzy. The shock of her contact with Clara was still raw. She took a deep breath, struggling for composure.

What are you going to do? You have to do something. You have to!

She turned towards the door. Could she open it? Once before in a dream she had tried but failed. This time she had to succeed.

She touched its surface; feeling nothing but a barrier. She reached for the handle, only for it to dissolve on her touch.

Just as the bottle of perfume reappeared in her hand.

Dan checked his watch. The murder had happened just before midnight. It was now twenty to. As soon as the hour was passed he was waking Meg and they were leaving and never coming back.

Another floorboard creaked. Then another. The sound was no longer like a sigh. Now it had purpose and rhythm.

As if someone was pacing.

A chill went through him.

The sound grew faster and faster. Again, he reached out to shake Meg awake. Again, he pulled his hand back. He still couldn't do it.

But he had to do something.

So, he went to investigate.

Rising to his feet he crossed the room. It didn't matter that someone might see him. All that mattered was determining the cause of the sound.

On reaching the hall he stopped and looked about him. The thump of the music was louder, as was the accompanying laughter. He struggled to blank them out and focus on the only noise that concerned him. His ears caught its frequency and followed it to its source; up the stairs to the room where the murder had happened.

Again, he felt a chill; even greater than before.

The creaking stopped.

He turned, staring back at Meg. She looked as helpless as a child. What was happening to her? Was she now in that upstairs room too? Was she feeling calm and in control? Or was she screaming in vain for him to wake her?

It didn't matter anymore. All that mattered was getting her out of there.

The creaking resumed.

It no longer came from the room. Now it was on the stairs; as if someone was walking down them towards him.

His mind screamed for action but just as in Meg's study fear froze him to the spot. He strained his eyes but could see nothing but shadows and specks of dust dancing in the air.

The creaking reached the bottom of the stairs. Again, it stopped. Next door the party continued. The music seemed to grow louder. The laughter did too. One laugh in particular seemed to seep through the walls and into the hall. It was female; soft but very shrill. Hysterical almost.

Like that of a lunatic.

Someone stroked the back of his neck.

Shock shook him out of his paralysis. He swung round to see an empty space.

While hearing the door of the room in which Meg lay slam shut.

Meg stared at the bottle in her hand.

She gave a scream of frustration. What good was it now? How could she use it when there was only a helpless Ellen left to see?

Ellen stopped struggling in the chair. Once again, her head turned in Meg's direction.

She knows I'm still here. She's waiting for me to help her. She believes in me. She's counting on me and I can't fail her.

She reached out, trying to make contact, only for her hand to pass through Ellen's body like mist, while in the distance she heard someone knocking on the front door.

It's Samuel! He's come and Clara's waiting for him with a

head full of fantasies and a knife.

Unable to bear it, she hurled the bottle to the floor.

Dan tried to force the door open, but it refused to move.

His terror was now at boiling point. He hammered against the wood, screaming Meg's name.

And heard a bottle break.

Ellen heard knocking on the front door of the house. She knew it was Samuel and felt her stomach turn over. She redoubled her efforts to free herself but remained chained to the chair.

Sweat was starting to pour down her face. A drop rolled into her eye. She tried to blink it away.

And as she did so a cold, sticky liquid splashed the bare skin of her leg.

As she stared down at the broken bottle Meg burst into tears.

'I'm sorry,' she said to Ellen. 'I did my best. You have to believe that. If I could stop her myself I would but I can't leave this room and I…'

The words died in her throat. She could feel hands around it; the fingers digging into the skin. For one terrible moment she thought they belonged to Dan; that Jennifer's crazy prophecy was coming true. But she knew his touch and did not feel it now. These hands were smaller and the fingers thinner.

Like those of a woman.

She gasped for air but could find none. Her windpipe was being crushed. She tried to pull the hands away but touched nothing but her own skin, while from far away she heard a door open and close.

Her lungs were emptying. Pressure was building up in her head. It made her dizzy and her legs collapsed beneath her. She reached out her hand in a vain attempt to break her fall and felt a bolt of electricity surge through her.

Together with the realisation that she was gripping flesh.

Someone seized her leg just above the ankle.

She felt fingers sliding through the liquid that covered her skin. For a moment she thought terror was driving her mad. She tried in vain to shake herself free of her bonds, inadvertently banging her cheek against the back of the chair. A bolt of pain shot through her.

And with it came clarity and the sudden joy of understanding.

Tim O'Reilly was not enjoying the party.

He had been looking forward to it all week, but the reality was proving a sad disappointment. From the moment he had arrived all his hosts had done was quiz him about the prospective tenants for their neighbour's house. 'We don't want anyone too young,' Keith Hopkins kept insisting. 'They'll only make a noise.'

Kettle, pot, black, thought Tim to himself.

'But we don't anyone too old either,' his wife Wendy chipped in. 'They'll only want us to run errands for them. Old people always do.'

'That's true,' Keith agreed. 'No old fogies, OK?'

Tim nodded politely while thinking that like doctors, estate agents were never completely off duty. Wanting to escape he told them he was going to the garden for a smoke.

'Good idea,' Keith told him. 'I'll join you.'

'Actually, I need to make a call. I'll go out the front. I'll join you later, OK?'

'Don't be long. I want to ask you about the covenants the tenants will have in their lease…'

As Tim headed for the front door he saw a woman of about his own age smiling at him. She was attractive but not in Meg Parker's league. He wished he had invited Meg to the party. He had planned to call her but had lost his nerve. He stood in the street, searching for his cigarettes. In the distance someone was shouting and banging. What was going on? Had a fight broken out? Was Keith pestering someone else and driving them to violence?

Then he realised the noise was coming from the house next door…

The pressure in Meg's head kept building. She made another attempt to breathe but could swallow nothing. The air in her lungs was almost gone while the grip around her neck grew ever tighter. Unless it stopped soon she was going to pass out.

But before she did there was something she had to do.

She slid her hand up Ellen's leg.

The fingers moved over her body; sliding from her skin to the fabric of her dress. She shut her eyes and willed them to move faster. Instead she felt them stop.

Don't fail me! If you love your daughter, then don't fail her now.

The fingers started to slide down again.

While overhead she could hear Samuel's footsteps as he began to climb the stairs.

Meg realised she was blacking out. The pressure in her head was now so great she could barely think. It would be the easiest thing in the world to just stop and let the world go black.

But she couldn't. She had made a vow and she was going to keep it.

Reaching up with her free hand she punched herself in the mouth. The pain was minimal. Her need for oxygen acted as an anaesthetic to anything else.

But it was enough.

The fingers began to move upwards again. They moved fast, racing over her chest and neck and coming to rest on her face.

She felt them start to slide under the gag. Her heart was racing so fast she thought it would burst while overhead the footsteps kept ascending.

She couldn't go on. The blackness was claiming her. She tried to pull at the gag but found she had no more strength. It was all over.

Then teeth bit down on the tip of her finger. Again, she felt a faint ripple of pain.

And with it found a final bolt of energy.

Grabbing the gag, she pulled as hard as she could.

Her body was still tied but suddenly her voice was free. It was the only weapon she had but it would be enough. It had to be!

Throwing her head back she opened her mouth to scream...

She had no strength at all now. All she had was an all-consuming need for air.

And then the blackness engulfed her.

The door suddenly opened. Dan fell through it, landing in a heap on the floor.

Meg was still lying in the corner of the room. He dashed towards her, calling her name. She didn't respond. Was she still asleep? Was she dead? Had she succeeded in her mission and had he failed in his?

Pain shot through his knee. He realised he was kneeling on broken glass. Letting out a moan he brushed it away and found his hand covered in drying blood.

He stared down at her. In the dim light from the street he could see bruising around her throat. She didn't seem to be breathing.

Bending down he put his ear to her mouth but could hear nothing. Tenderly he began to massage her neck while preparing to breathe air into her half open mouth.

Just as the overhead light went on and people burst into the room.

The pressure in her head was gone. She felt as if she was floating. All around her was white.

What's happening to me? Am I crossing over? Am I dying?

The white began to fade. She saw sunlight streaming through a window so huge it covered a whole wall, revealing a view of fields and trees as far as the eye could see.

The room she stood in was lined with oak and had a fireplace. It was beautiful, as was the view. Everything about it was perfect.

Just as Samuel had promised Ellen it would be.

To her right was a grand piano. A framed photograph stood upon it. Ellen stood outside a church wearing a wedding dress, arm in arm with Samuel. To Samuel's right stood an older man who looked just like him and was presumably his brother. To Ellen's left, a smiling Kate held a bouquet of flowers.

I did it. We did it. Together we bloody well did it!

'What are you doing?' shouted a male voice.

Dan turned. About half a dozen people stood in the doorway. At their head was a plump looking man of about thirty whose eyes widened as he saw Meg's body on the floor. 'That's Meg Parker! What the hell have you done to her?'

'She's not breathing. You've got to help me…'

'There's blood on the floor!' screamed a woman. 'He's killed her!'

'No, I haven't! She'll be alright. She has to be!'

The man who knew Meg by name drew closer, his eyes widening as he saw the marks around her neck. 'He's bloody strangled her!'

'Why aren't you listening to me? She's not breathing. We have to get her breathing again.' Again, he tried to blow air into her mouth.

Only to be grabbed from behind and dragged away.

As she stared at the photograph she realised the room was changing. The oak panelling was replaced by wallpaper; electric lights took the place of gas ones and the wooden floor was covered by a succession of different coloured carpets. It was like watching a nature film where years of growth were condensed into mere seconds.

The photograph on the piano was gone. In its place came a stream of others, chronicling the passing of time. Ellen sat on a swing with a small boy on her lap. Ellen and Kate stood helping a group of children feed a horse. A middle-aged Ellen sat on a sofa with Samuel, surrounded by half a dozen teenagers and young adults, all of whom bore a strong resemblance to one or other of them. A very old Ellen and Kate sat at a table, both laughing as they blew out the candles on a huge cake that spelled out the number 80.

She thought of two young girls standing on a cliff watching a ship at sea. One had been destined to hang; the other to break her neck after falling down a flight of stairs.

But not anymore. Not anymore!

'We need to call an ambulance!' cried a woman.

'That'll be too late!' Dan screamed at her. 'We have to help her now!'

'You're not going near her,' shouted the plump man who knew Meg by name. 'The only place you're going is jail!'

The view from the window was changing. New buildings began to dot the landscape. The room continued to change too. Briefly she saw an anti Vietnam poster on the wall. Then it was replaced by one commemorating the collapse of the Berlin Wall which in turn was replaced by one celebrating the new millennium.

By now the photographs all showed the same person; a small boy moving through puberty and on into early manhood. He was tall and slim with dark hair and features that were too irregular to be called handsome but, like Samuel's, were made attractive by the character they contained. What relation was he to Ellen? How many generations had passed in the blink of an eye?

She saw him in graduation robes; then wearing a ruck sack as if about to go travelling. He was smiling; his face alive with excitement and anticipation.

And he was moving.

The frame could not contain him. He stepped out of it.

While very faintly she heard someone call her name.

One of the women was bending over Meg. 'She's not breathing!'

'I've told you that!' shouted Dan while struggling against the arms that held him. 'Why are you just kneeling there? Pump her chest! Do something!'

Another woman was talking on a mobile, asking for an ambulance. The plump man was doing the same but talking to the police. 'It's murder,' he was saying. 'This lunatic's strangled her.'

'I'm not a lunatic!' Dan cried. 'I love her!'

'Then why were your hands around her throat?' hissed one of the men holding him. 'Just shut up. No one wants to hear it.'

Meg was still lying on the floor. Her face was deathly pale. He could see the last sparks of life slowly draining away.

And he wasn't going to let that happen.

He let his body go limp. Briefly the hold on him relaxed; just giving him enough freedom to move his arm. Clenching his fist, he slammed it into a pair of balls…

The room was gone. She stood in Saltran Square. The young man was taking pictures of the church and talking to a middle-aged couple in hiking clothes. 'My great great grandmother grew up in this town,' he told them. 'She used to tell my grandfather stories about it and he told them to me. I've always wanted to come here. Now at last I've made it!'

The couple smiled at him. Meg did the same.

And again, heard someone call her name.

It was a woman's voice; low, soft and very sweet. The sound was as comforting as the sight of home to a frightened child who had been lost and alone.

She realised it was her mother.

You're calling me home. I've done what you told me. I've done what was right and it's led me back to you.

For a moment she experienced something akin to bliss.

And then she thought of Dan; of how she was leaving him alone in that dark, empty house with her body lying cold and still on the floor.

They'll think it was him! They'll think he was the one who killed me.

Just like Jennifer warned me they would.

Her mother kept calling; her voice growing louder.

No! I can't come to you. Not yet. I have to go back and save him.

She tried to will herself back to her body but remained locked in her dream. The young man was now telling the couple that his trip was nearly over. As she watched him she saw the landscape shift and suddenly he was walking down what looked like a London street.

Her vision was blurring while her mother's call grew louder still.

Stop! Let me go! I'm not finished yet. I still have to do what is right.

In the distance two women were arguing. One turned away, stepping out onto the road and into the path of an oncoming taxi.

Her mother's voice was now deafening. Her vision was all but gone.

But before it vanished completely she saw the young man drop his ruck sack and start to run…

The hold on him relaxed. Dan pushed the woman beside Meg to one side and took her place.

'Come on, Meg,' he shouted. 'Just hold on another second for me…'

Then, bending down, he put his mouth to hers…

Meg opened her eyes.

Her lungs were empty. She gasped, sucking down as much air as she could hold.

'Are you alright?' said a voice.

She looked about her, expecting to find herself lying on a wooden floor with Dan by her side. Instead she was sitting on a chair in a room with posters on the wall and four complete strangers staring curiously at her.

'Where's Dan?'

'Is that the doctor?' asked a man.

'*Doctor?* What are you talking about?' Again, she looked about her. One of the posters advertised a quit smoking programme. 'Where am I?'

'In a hospital,' the man explained. 'You've been asleep. You must have been dreaming. That's why you're confused.'

'Dreaming? No, I wasn't. I…'

Anxiety was accelerating her breathing. Suddenly her senses were overwhelmed by the smell of polish and antiseptic. It was a combination she remembered well; one that took her straight back to that terrible moment when she had learned her mother was gone.

Am I back there? Am I a child again? Am I dead? Is this my version of hell?

There was a mirror in the corner of the room. She hurried towards it, expecting to see a nine-year-old child staring back at her. Instead she saw her adult self; only it was a self she barely recognised. She was dressed in an expensive suit; her hair was immaculate, and her face so lean the cheekbones stood out like razors.

'I don't understand,' she said aloud. 'What's going on?'

'The man said you were to wait here,' a woman told her. 'That he'd come and get you when it was over.'

'What man?'

'The man who met you when you arrived.'

'*What man?* Who was he? What did he look like?'

The woman looked startled. There was a clock on the wall above her head. As she stared at it Meg saw the time shift from 23.59 to 00.00, while simultaneously the date changed from April 9th to April 10th.

'It's now,' she whispered. 'It's today.'

'That's right,' said the woman brightly.

'But where's Dan? I want to see him. I want to tell him that I did it. I want to tell him that everything is alright now.'

'He knows that already,' the woman said soothingly. 'In fact, when you arrived you were far more nervous than he was.'

'Why was I nervous? What am I even doing here? I don't understand...'

A door opened behind her. 'Here he is,' the woman told her.

She turned, expecting to see Dan.

And saw her brother in law, Pete.

His cheeks were wet. He had been crying. Perhaps she really was in hell and it was Grace's death that she would have to relive.

But it couldn't be. The date was all wrong.

And he was smiling; his face aglow with happiness.

'Come with me,' he told her.

Too bewildered to speak she followed him out of the room.

He led her down a corridor. The light was dim and all the doors were shut. All but one. A nurse stood outside it. She was smiling too. 'Now don't be too long,' she told Meg. 'There will be plenty of time on your next visit.'

She walked into the room to see an exhausted looking Grace sitting up in bed with a new born baby clasped in her arms.

'Come on in,' said Grace softly. 'Your niece wants to meet you.'

She tried to move but couldn't. Pete gave her a nudge. 'Go on,' he said encouragingly. 'She's only a little thing. She won't bite.'

'This is a dream,' she said weakly. 'I'm still dreaming.'

'*Dreaming?*' Grace started to laugh. 'Of course, you're not, silly. I know she's a week ahead of schedule but believe me, she's no dream.'

'I'll give you two a moment,' said Pete. 'I need to phone my family.' He gave Meg a grin. 'Make the most of this time with your niece. Once my mother arrives you'll never get near her again!'

'It doesn't matter,' she murmured. 'None of that matters anymore.'

Giving her a puzzled look, he left the room. Moving slowly, convinced that she would wake at any moment, Meg approached the bed. Grace was smiling at her. She stared into her sister's face. It was the face she loved best in the world. The face she had never thought to see again.

And she just couldn't take it. Collapsing into a chair she began to weep.

Grace reached out and stroked her arm. 'Meg? What's the matter? What is it?'

'I'm sorry.' She wiped her eyes. 'It's just…' She shook her head; too choked to speak.

'Isn't she beautiful? Isn't she the most beautiful thing you've ever seen? The labour was just as bad as everyone said it would be. The nurse told me she'd never heard anyone scream so loud! But now she's here, oh God was it worth it.'

Meg stared at her niece; now sleeping peacefully in her mother's arms. 'Yes, it was. It was all worth it. All of it.'

Grace was now looking as puzzled as Pete had done. 'Is something the matter? You don't seem yourself. You don't…'

'You died. You were dead. I lost you.'

'What are you talking about?'

She opened her mouth then closed it again. She could never tell the truth. Not here. Not now.

Not ever.

But she had to tell something.

'I was asleep in the waiting room. I was asleep, and I was dreaming. I was dreaming about that day last November when we'd been to see the doctor. We were arguing, and I slapped your face and you walked out into the road…'

Grace nodded. 'And that tourist grabbed me and pulled me back.' She gave Meg a wry smile. 'I thought you were angry with me before, but it was *nothing* compared to what you were like after. How could I have been so careless? I could have been killed. Sometimes you needed eyes in the back of your head when you were around me. And if that wasn't bad enough I had the taxi driver screaming at me too, while that poor tourist was just standing there…'

'In my dream the tourist wasn't there. I dreamed that you died. I dreamed I saw your body lying there in the road. I dreamed I went to your funeral and then had to go on living without you. I dreamed that I'd lost you for ever.'

'Oh, sweetheart…'

'I'm sorry. I shouldn't be crying. Not now.' She swallowed. 'It's just that I never thought I'd see you again and now here you are, and…'

Grace opened her mouth to speak. Meg covered it with her hand.

'And now that you are there's something I need to tell you.'

Grace nodded.

'I need to tell you that I'm sorry for the way I treated you when we were growing up. I know I smothered you. I know I made you feel like a prisoner. I can see it all now; all the mistakes I made. How I made you pay for my own fears and how I kept on doing so even after you were married. And I want you to know that if I ever made you unhappy then I regret it with all my heart. That if you no longer want me to be a part of your life then I'll understand. The only thing that matters to me is that you and your baby are alive and well.'

'The baby does have a name,' Grace told her.

'Does she?'

'It's Rebecca. I'm naming her after Mum. Rebecca Elizabeth Barrington. That's her name. Do you like it?'

'Yes.'

'I thought about making her middle name Meghan. Then I decided against. In the circumstances I'd prefer to name her after

Pete's Mum.'

She nodded. Once she would have been hurt. Now it didn't matter. Nothing mattered except that Grace was still alive.

'After all, you are going to be godmother. If I named her after you too, then Pete's Mum would have a fit!'

Her tears returned. This time they came with a smile.

'You have nothing to apologise for,' Grace continued. 'You're my sister. All you've ever done is look out for me. I remember when we had that row on the street. You said I would never have survived at Dad's and in the home if you hadn't been there. Well, you were right. I wouldn't be here now if it wasn't for you.' She gestured to baby Rebecca. 'And, more importantly, neither would she.'

'I love you, Gracie.'

'I love you too. Now do you want to hold your niece?'

'More than anything in the world.'

Together they sat cooing over the sleeping baby.

Half an hour later she stood in the corridor talking to Pete.

'Thanks for letting me come here tonight,' she said. 'You'll never know how much it means to me.'

'I'm glad you're here.'

'I won't intrude while your family is here. Why don't you just call me if Grace wants to see me or if she needs me to get her anything?'

He looked surprised. 'I thought you'd be camping out in the waiting room.'

'No. This time is for the three of you. You're a real family now. Congratulations, Dad.'

He smiled. 'She's beautiful, isn't she?'

'Yes. They both are.'

His eyes darted towards the room.

'Go on,' she told him. 'Your daughter has a little finger she's waiting to wrap you around.'

His smile grew even wider. 'She's done that already.'

'Good.'

He turned to go. Then he looked back. 'Will you be OK?'

'I'll be more than OK. You'd better believe it.'

She walked through the hospital towards the entrance. Once she was outside she searched through her pockets and found her mobile. As she switched it on she felt as if she was going to explode. She couldn't wait to tell Dan. He would be just as excited as she was. She couldn't wait for him to meet Grace either. She knew Grace would love him almost as much as she did.

The display appeared. She flicked through the contacts list under D.

But his name wasn't there.

And as she searched in vain she felt a pressure in her head.

A wave of images flashed before her eyes. She saw herself shouting at Grace after an American student called Brett Roberts had saved her life. She saw herself sitting in her office, watching Debbie enter carrying a crate of champagne from grateful clients. She saw herself going on a skiing holiday over New Year and meeting a stock broker called Harry. She saw herself doing interviews with the Legal Press after winning an award for the best young lawyer in her field. She saw herself having dinner with Harry and telling him that their relationship just wasn't working.

Only they were more than images.

They were new memories.

She had gone to Cornwall to deal with her grief. In this new reality there had been no grief to overcome.

In this new reality she and Dan had never met.

Nurse Paula Evans stood outside the hospital entrance, taking a final drag on her cigarette before preparing to start her shift. A woman was standing nearby, staring at a mobile phone display and talking to herself. She was saying the same words over and over again.

'We never met. We never met. We never met.'

Concerned, Paula walked over. 'Is everything alright?'

The woman turned towards her. For a split second her face

was a mask of heartbreak. Then it was gone, replaced by transcendent joy.

'We never met,' she said again.

'I'm sorry.'

'I'm not. It was worth it.' The woman gestured towards the hospital. 'My sister and her new baby are in there. They're alive. They're well, and it was more worth than you can possibly imagine.'

Then she turned and walked away into the night.

Chapter 15

Early April. Twelve months later.

'I love it!' cried Grace.

Meg sighed with relief.

'Becky, look what Aunty Meg has bought you.' Grace held up the bright red top with the words 'World's Greatest Niece' emblazoned on it for her daughter to see. Becky stopped chewing on her teething ring and gave a contented gurgle.

'She doesn't have to wear it,' Meg told Grace. 'I just couldn't resist it, that's all. Her main present is a high tech mobile with lights and music that you can hang above her cot. It's ships with waves beneath them.'

'She'll love that! And she can wear the top on Saturday for her birthday party.'

'Just be careful when you wash it. The woman in the shop said the colour runs like crazy so don't put it in with Pete's work shirts. You'll turn them all pink!'

'Well, if it does I'll just tell him it's his way of supporting gay pride.'

They both laughed. It was lunchtime and they sat together in a crowded coffee bar in the West End. Becky dropped her teething ring. Meg picked it up, wiped it with a napkin and returned it to her outstretched hand.

'The party starts at two,' Grace told her.

'Are you sure you want me there? I know how territorial Pete's mother can be.'

'Tell me about it. If that woman gives me another lecture on child rearing I'll swing for her! But of course I want you there. Neither Becky or I will enjoy the party half as much if you're not.'

As if by way of agreement, Becky gave another gurgle. Meg stroked her niece's cheek, feeling the familiar rush of protective love sweep over her.

'Some of Pete's friends are coming too,' continued Grace. 'One of them is called Oliver. He's 34, works for a merchant bank, and...'

'He just happens to be single.'

'Well, what if he is? You haven't dated anyone for at least a year. Oliver's really nice. I'm sure you'll like him, and I *know* he'll like you.'

'Look, Gracie, I really appreciate the concern but I'm fine as I am.'

'No, you're not. It's a waste you being single. Everyone thinks so. Even Pete's mother said as much when she was having a break from quoting books on child care! I know your career is time consuming, but wouldn't you like someone to come home to when the working day is over?'

She didn't answer. In her head she saw a grinning Dan teasing her about her devotion to work. Though she tried to push the image from her mind it stuck like glue.

She wondered what he was doing. Was he still painting? Was he achieving some much-deserved success? She had lost count of the number of times she had googled him, but her search had never yet led to a result. Was he still living in Saltran? Was he married? Had he finally found a girl who didn't want to change him? Was he happy?

And did he ever think about her?

But how could he? If they met on a street he would pass on by without giving her a second look. She and Ellen had seen to that. By rewriting one history they had totally erased another.

Grace continued to sing Oliver's praises. Meg noticed Becky staring intently at her. She gave her niece a conspiratorial wink and was rewarded with a massive smile.

Dan's was not the only name she had googled. Another search had revealed that in 1881 a girl called Ellen Foley had been involved in a murder. The case had not been widely reported but she had found a useful summary in a book called 'Crimes of Cornwall' that she purchased from the online website of a bookseller in Truro. Even that account had been a mere four pages and by now she had read it so many times she knew all the key passages by heart.

At shortly before midnight on April 9th, William Purdon and his wife Maria were preparing for bed when they heard a series of appalling screams coming from the house of their next-door neighbours; John and Clara Goderidge. Mr Purdon went to knock on their door to see if he could be of any assistance but received no answer. Concerned, he went to rouse the local Police Constable; Sergeant Hooper. By the time Sergeant Hooper knocked on the door a small crowd had gathered to watch. In spite of repeated knocking the door still remained shut.

Eventually, following encouragement from the watching crowd, Sergeant Hooper forced the door open. John Goderidge's body lay in the hallway. He had been stabbed dozens of times; his eyes had been gauged out, his trousers partly removed, and his genitalia hacked off and thrust into his open mouth. Sergeant Hooper testified in Court that it was the most ghastly crime he had ever seen and that one of the men with him vomited at the sight of it.

The house itself was in virtual darkness. The only light came from a parlour at the top of the stairs. When Sergeant Hooper entered he found a hysterical Clara Goderidge cowering behind a chair, her dress covered in blood. A further search of the house revealed three people hiding in a room under the stairs; the Goderidge's niece, Ellen Foley, her mentally handicapped twin sister Kate, and a young man named Samuel Roberts. As Ellen was comforting a distressed Kate it was from Samuel that Sergeant Hooper learned of the events leading up to the murder.

Samuel Roberts was an architect, hired by John Goderidge to design a new house on the outskirts of the town. Within weeks of his arrival in Bamber he and Ellen had fallen in love. Samuel described John Goderidge as a tyrant who had used the threat of having her sister, Kate, committed to an asylum to keep Ellen under his control. Samuel and Ellen planned to elope to America, taking Kate with them so they could care for her together.

In order to allay the suspicions of John and Clara Goderidge, Samuel went out of his way to befriend them. His attempts succeeded and soon both were treating him as a son. However, unknown to him, Clara Goderidge quickly developed romantic feelings for him and became convinced that they were reciprocated.

At some point Clara discovered the relationship between Ellen and Samuel. In her rage she decided to take revenge. After convincing Kate that her sister was going to abandon her she waited until a night when John Goderidge was staying with friends and then forged a note in Ellen's handwriting, asking Samuel to come to the house. She then lured Ellen down to the room under the stairs, tied her to a chair and gagged her while showing her a knife and saying that if Samuel did not renounce their relationship then she would make him sorry for it.

When Samuel arrived at the house he was admitted by Kate. He noticed she seemed frightened but when questioned by him she would give him no reason for her agitation and simply told him that he should make his way to the parlour. As he reached the top of the stairs he heard Ellen, who had managed to loosen the gag around her mouth, cry out that Clara had a knife and that he should take Kate and flee the house. Instead Samuel dragged Kate to the room where Ellen was still tied to the chair. In fear for their lives the three of them then shut themselves in. Clara, who was now in a state approaching mania, tried to gain entrance but without success.

At that moment John Goderidge returned home. He had argued with the friends with whom he was supposed to be spending the night and had left their house in anger. When he saw his wife he demanded to know what she was doing. She told him that she and Samuel were in love, but that Ellen was trying to separate them. According to Samuel, John began to laugh, taunting his wife that no man in his right mind would ever love her and throwing the most vicious insults at her. It was this that drove Clara to murder her husband in the manner already described.

Clara was taken to Bodmin Jail. While there, her fits of hysteria became so extreme that she had to be kept in restraints. She was examined by doctors who confirmed that she had suffered a permanent mental collapse. Judged unfit to face trial she was instead committed to an insane asylum where she died two years later.

Within days of the murder, Samuel, Ellen and Kate all left Bamber. It is believed they took passage to America, though what fate awaited them there is unknown.

Whenever she read the last paragraph she would think of the room with the view and smile. She was glad that to the world at least their fate remained a mystery. All three had more than earned the right to live out the rest of their lives in privacy.

'What do you think?' Grace was asking. 'Will you give Oliver a chance?'

'Yes. If that's what you want.' She tried to change the subject. 'So, do you really like Becky's new top?'

'Of course, I do. Where did you get it?'

'A shop in Piccadilly. My secretary, Debbie told me about it.'

'And how is *her* love life? Her boyfriend's called Kyle. He's American, isn't he?'

She grimaced. 'He's her ex-boyfriend now.'

'Why?'

'You know he's started up his own restaurant? Well it's taking him for ever to earn a living from it. He told Debbie he was going to jack it in and take a regular job so they could be together, but she didn't want him to give up his life's ambition for her sake so she broke it off. She's really cut about it, poor thing. She did overtime for me last week and we ended up talking about it for hours. I tried to persuade her to reconsider but her mind is made up. I just hope she doesn't live to regret it.'

Grace didn't say anything; just gave a wry smile.

'What?' Meg asked.

'Once upon a time you would never have dreamed of spending precious work time talking about romance.'

'Well, times change.'

'And people do too.' Suddenly Grace looked hesitant. 'In fact, there's something I need to tell you. I had a letter last week.'

'From whom?'

'Dad.'

'Oh.' She thought for a moment. 'Wow.'

'Alison's dead. She had cancer. She died last year.'

'I see.' Meg gave a sigh. 'I'm not going to say I'm sorry she's dead, but I am sorry she had to die like that. I wouldn't wish cancer on anyone. Not even her.'

'Dad's retired now. He lives in Harrow. He told me about our half brother and sister. Susan's a film maker. She lives in New York and is engaged to a screen writer. Richard is about to graduate from Bristol Uni. He's been doing a law degree actually. Anyway, hearing from Dad has got me thinking…'

'That you'd like to see him again.'

'I haven't replied yet. I wanted to talk to you first. I *would* like to see him, but only if you're OK with it. I know how you feel about him and I understand why. Most of the time I feel the same but sometimes, in spite of it…I just…'

Meg reached across the table and covered Grace's hand with her own.

'Gracie, listen to me. It doesn't matter how I feel. All that matters is that he's your father. I remember how he was with you when we lived with him. I could see he cared about you. He probably would have cared about me too if I'd let him. I know he did a terrible thing to us and a part of me will never be able to forgive him, but one thing I do know is that he didn't do it because he was a monster. Alison was the monster. He was simply weak. Just promise me that if you do see him you'll take it slowly and not expect too much. If you do that then you have my complete blessing.'

'Thanks. That means a lot to me.'

'Don't mention it. You never know. Maybe, one day I'll want to see him too.'

'He knew what you were doing. He said Richard told him all about your award. He said he was proud and that Richard was too. He said that Richard often talks about you and hopes that one day he can emulate your success.'

She gave a hollow laugh.

'But you *are* successful. They're making you a senior partner next year. You'll be the youngest your firm has ever had.'

'No, they're not.'

Grace's eyes widened. 'But I thought…'

'I'm not pulling in the work like I used to. I'm not as driven as I was and they can sense it. That's why they're giving the appointment to someone else.'

'But they have to give it to you! You deserve it.'

'No, they don't, and no I don't either. What's more, I don't care. It's just a title. All it means is even more money than the obscene amount I'm already earning and a slightly bigger office. Don't feel bad about it, Gracie. I don't.'

'Honestly?'

She smiled. 'Cross my heart and hope to die.'

'You look like Mum. She used to smile just like that.'

'I should be so lucky.'

'It's true. I never used to see the resemblance between you but now I see it all the time. Do you know the first time I did? It was the night Becky was born. It's funny. People say that nothing changes you like becoming a parent. What they don't say is that nothing changes you like becoming an aunt. Because that's what happened to you. From the night Becky was born you've been a different person.'

She didn't answer; her gaze drawn to a man of about her own age who was standing at the counter, waiting to be served. He was staring intently at her. There was something familiar about him though what it was she couldn't say.

'Except that's not actually true,' Grace continued. 'You're not a different person. Not deep down.'

She turned back to her sister. 'What do you mean?'

'You think I don't remember our life in Suffolk, but I do. I remember the person you were back then. You changed after Mum died. Suddenly everything about you was serious. You were always strong and in charge and you never let anything touch you. It was as if you felt that life was a constant battle and you could never let down your guard. Now all of that's changed. Now, when I look at you I see the sister I remember from all those years ago and for what it's worth, I'm happy because I've really missed her.'

'I'm glad you feel that like. But now I'd better get back to the office before they fire me!'

The bill lay on the table between them. Grace tried to take it, but Meg got there first.

'It's my turn to pay,' Grace told her.

'No, it's not.'

'Yes, it is.'

'Don't argue with me, missy. I'm older, remember, and I'm always right.'

'Then I take it back. You haven't changed. You're still the bossy cow you've always been!'

They both laughed. After hugging Grace and Becky goodbye, Meg went to the counter. As she waited for her change, she saw that the man who had been staring at her was now making his way over.

'We know each other,' he told her.

She tried to place him. He was tall, blond and handsome and wearing a smart suit. Was he a client? Had they been at University together? Where did she know him from?

'We were in the same class at school,' he continued, answering her question for her.

The waitress handed over her change. After leaving a large tip she turned back to the man. 'You went to Belton Comprehensive?'

'No. Wickenham Primary school in Suffolk. You're Meghan Parker, aren't you? You had a sister called Grace. The woman you were with was your sister, wasn't she?'

'Yes. Um…'

'I'm Peter Price. I'm the boy whose grandmother died.'

She gasped.

'So, you remember me?'

'Yes.'

'When I was fifteen my Dad got cancer. It was terminal. I had to watch him die and the only thing that made it bearable was having the chance to tell him just how much I loved him. And Christ, I needed to.' Peter gave a sad smile. 'You probably remember me as a total jerk but believe me, I was even worse as a teenager. I made my parents' life hell. When I told my Dad I loved him and apologised for being such a prick he told me that it didn't matter and that he loved me too. And when he did that I remembered what you told me about my grandmother. I was a prick to her too and though I'd never missed her the way I was going to miss Dad there was a part of me that felt guilty about her. When I remembered what you said I realised that I didn't need to feel guilty any more. That in a funny way I *had* made my peace with her, just as I'd made it with Dad.' He stopped for a moment, clearly struggling for the right words. 'Only I wasn't the one who did it. You were. And I just wanted to thank you for it.'

A memory came to her; of sitting in an empty classroom, listening to an old woman telling her that one day, in spite of his current hostility, her grandson would be grateful. She felt a warm sensation in her stomach.

'You don't need to thank me,' she told him.

'Yes, I do. And I need to apologise too. I was vile to you when we were at school.'

'You were just a kid, Pete. We both were.'

'Even so…' He sighed. 'You had so much shit to deal with. Far more than any kid should. The last thing you needed was me trying to make your life a misery.'

She smiled. 'You didn't make it that much of a misery.'

He lowered his eyes. 'You don't have to say that.'

'I know. I'm saying it because it's true. I'm sorry you lost your father the way you did. I really am.'

'You lost your mother too. I remember that.'

'Do you still miss him?'

'Yes.' He looked up again. 'Do you…?'

'Yes. It never goes away, does it? It gets better, but it never totally goes away.'

Silence. She stared into his face, searching for traces of the boy she had once known but seeing none. Now, just like his grandmother, that boy seemed like a ghost.

'Do you remember Stuart Scott?' he asked eventually.

'Yes! We were friends. Are you still in contact with him?'

'I should be. He's my business partner.'

'No way!'

'It's hard to believe, isn't it? I was a jerk to him too. You used to stick up for him against me and everyone else. Now we run a computer graphics company together and I'm godfather to his second child.'

'Wow! When did you two become friends?'

'At Sixth Form College. We were both doing maths 'A' level and were light years behind the rest of our class. Out mutual mediocrity drew us together and then we discovered a shared love of death metal, real ale and Doctor Who.'

She burst out laughing. 'So, how is he?'

'Just as you remember, except that now he's fat, bald and married with three kids; the middle one of whom lives his life like he's in a remake of The Omen.'

'Well, what can you expect with a godfather like you?'

By now he was laughing too. 'I thought you said I wasn't that bad.'

'No. You were probably worse.'

'And you're nothing like Stuart.'

'That's true. I'm still quite slim and I'm certainly not bald.'

'I meant that unlike him, you've aged very well.'

Her laughter increased. 'I'll take that as a compliment.'

'I mean you look terrific. Your husband is a lucky man.'

'I'm not married.'

'Well, your fiancé, then.' A pause. 'Or your boyfriend.'

'Are you hitting on me?'

He blushed. 'Well it makes a change from us hitting each other.'

'It certainly does. God bless puberty, maths and Doctor Who. And no, in answer to your question, there isn't a man in my life.'

'Great.'

'I'm actually a lesbian.'

His jaw dropped. She remembered Dan's doing the same when she had told him that every girlfriend she had ever had had known she was faking it. It still seemed like yesterday. It still seemed so real, when the reality was that it had never happened at all.

'I'm joking,' she told him.

'Thank God for that.' Reaching into his pocket he pulled out a card. 'These are my details. I'm in town for the rest of the week. Perhaps we could meet for a drink? It would be great to have a proper catch up.'

'Yes, it would.' She looked at her watch. 'I have to get back to the office now.'

'Of course. I need to go too. I…um…' He hesitated. 'Look, Meg, I really hope you call me, but even if you don't, I want you to know that I'm so happy I saw you. You made a huge difference in my life and I'll always be grateful.'

'It was my pleasure,' she told him.

He offered her his hand. Impulsively she kissed his cheek. He smelled of aftershave and soap. He smelled nice. Better than Dan had ever done. Much better.

She left the coffee bar; the card safely stored in her pocket.

Five o'clock. She sat in one of her firm's conference rooms, attending the corporate partners monthly progress meeting.

Geoff Brooker; Deputy Head of Department, mediocre lawyer and walking erection, was talking about a prospective new client. 'Claire and I are going to present to them next week. They have subsidiaries in North America and the Far East and with our combined experience in those regions we're bound to impress.' Claire Maddox; now a partner and clearly loving every second of it, gave a smug smile.

One of the male partners frowned. 'Shouldn't you take Meg? Her experience with Far Eastern clients is second to none.'

Claire's smile faded. 'Geoff and I can handle it. We don't need Meg too.'

'Actually,' said the male partner, 'I was thinking of Meg instead of you.'

'*Instead* of me?' Claire's eyes narrowed. 'Absolutely not. Geoff agrees.'

Geoff looked hesitant. 'Well, perhaps…'

'*Don't* you?'

'Um…yes. Of course.'

'What do you think, Meg?' asked Head of Department, Henry Flynn.

'I think Geoff and Claire will be fine,' she told him.

'Well, I don't,' said the male partner.

'And what would you know about it?' Claire demanded. 'All

your clients are based in Europe. I've got much more Far East experience than you.'

'But nowhere near as much as Meg. All your Far East clients were originally brought in by her. You only handle them because she's too busy.'

'I've brought in clients too!'

'None to my knowledge.'

'Well that just shows how little you know!'

As the argument grew more heated, Meg stared at the paintings on the wall. They were huge, abstract works that had cost a fortune but seemed to represent nothing. Dan's work had far more character but would sell for infinitely less. It didn't seem fair. But then he had never really cared about the financial rewards. For him true satisfaction lay in the work itself. He could spend weeks on a single painting and then give it away to someone who would truly value it. Once, in a different life, she had viewed that as weakness. Now she saw it as strength.

She thought of the painting he had given her. Where was it now? Had he given it to someone else and did they treasure it the way she had?

Where are you now? Are you alright? Are you happy?

'I brought in Matalga Inc,' Claire was saying.

'No, you didn't. Meg did all the groundwork early last year. You just jumped in at the end and took all the credit.'

'Why are you making her out to be the firm's golden girl? If she were she'd be getting senior equity, and she's not and everyone knows it's because she's not bringing clients in anymore.'

If I knew you were happy it would be enough. It really would.

'That's a bit out of order,' said Henry quickly.

'No, it's not. It's true.'

'Even so…'

Or at least I want it to be.

'You're being very quiet, Meg,' said the male partner. 'Surely you have something to say?'

All eyes were now upon her. She stared at them but did not see them; too busy following her train of thought to its inevitable conclusion.

But I'm lying. I've been lying to myself for the last twelve months. It's not enough that you're happy. I want to be a part of that happiness.

Because without you I will always be incomplete.

'Meg? What do you have to say?'

'Nothing.'

'*Nothing?* Why nothing?'

She rose to her feet. 'Because I'm leaving.'

A gasp went around the room. 'I knew something was up,' said a woman partner. 'She's been poached by another firm. That's why she's lost her focus.'

'No one's poached me. I just don't want this life anymore.'

'Rubbish,' said Claire. 'You just can't handle the competition.'

She couldn't help it. She burst out laughing.

'It's true,' said Claire spitefully. 'You don't fool me.'

'And that's the difference between us. I don't fool you. You don't fool anyone.'

'I don't need to fool anyone, thank you very much.'

'But you did need to sleep with Geoff to get partnership. The thing I don't understand is why you're still sleeping with him now.'

Claire's colour rose. 'Now hang on a minute…' Geoff began.

'You meet at the Lauter Hotel near Liverpool Street on Tuesday and Thursday evenings. The guy on front desk is the cousin of the Head of our Technology Department.'

'Well, what if we do?' said Claire defiantly. 'Geoff and I are in love. He's leaving his wife, so we can be together.'

'Is that what he told you? How delightful. Did he also tell you that last month he kindly offered to get my senior equity decision reversed if I let him shag me? I don't like you, Claire. I think you're a nasty little bitch and also, frankly, an atrocious lawyer. But believe me you can still do a lot better than that priapic jerk.'

Geoff began to bluster about slander. Ignoring him, she left the room and made her way back to her Department, gesturing for Debbie to follow her into her office. Once they were both inside she shut the door.

'I'm leaving,' she announced. 'And so are you.' Reaching for her cheque book she began to write. Debbie's eyes nearly popped out of her head when she saw the amount on the cheque she was handed.

'Meg, I can't accept this.'

'Yes, you can. Kyle was willing to give up his dreams for you. Now you can make both your dreams come true.'

'But…'

'When he visited here last summer I could see you were made for each other. Don't break up with him, Debbie. If you do you'll regret it for the rest of your life.'

'But it's so much money.'

'But that's *all* it is. Besides, I don't need it. I've got more than enough for what I need to do.'

Debbie swallowed. 'I don't know what to say.'

'You don't have to say anything. Just go and draft your resignation letter. And keep in touch, OK? You've got my number. If I don't get regular progress reports I'm making that money a high interest loan!'

They hugged. As Debbie left the room, Henry Flynn appeared to take her place.

'It's World War Two back in that Conference room,' he told her. 'They're all fighting over who's going to take over your client list. Thank God there are no knives down there. It would be carnage.'

'I'm sorry to have sprung this on you, Henry. I know I should have told you what I was going to do but the truth is that I didn't even know myself until it happened.'

'And I'm sorry to be losing you, but in a funny way I'm also glad. You're the best lawyer I've ever worked with, Meg. But from the moment you joined us I've always had the sense that you were meant for something else. Over the last year I've watched you come to realise it too.'

She remembered him paying her the same compliment on a bleak January afternoon before asking her to take a sabbatical. At the time she had resented his interference; never imagining that it would totally transform her life. As far as he was concerned that conversation had never happened, but it was one that she would never forget.

'I want to thank you, Henry. You've had more effect on my life than you realise, and I am more grateful than you will ever know.'

'Will you keep in touch?'

'Of course, I will.'

'And can I have a hug too?'

As she rested her head on his shoulder she gazed out at the corridor. People rushed about, spreading the news of her departure while an oblivious Debbie sat talking to Kyle on the telephone, telling him news of her own.

A week later she was back in Saltran.

It was a beautiful, clear, April morning. As she drove into the square it felt as if she had never been away. Once she had parked she stood staring up at the sky, feeling the wind against her face, tasting the salt in the air and experiencing a strange combination of exhilaration and dread.

She had booked a room in The Kings Arms. The woman at reception had a familiar face. In another life the two of them had often nodded to each other in passing or in the Supermarket. Now she was greeted with a polite but blank smile. After leaving her bag in her room she walked into the close. There was no sign of life from the house that had once been her home. She wondered who lived there now, and whether they loved the place as much as she had.

A van stood outside Dan's house. It was new but still managed to look shabby. Had he sold his old one? Was he at home now? Did he even live there at all?

As if by way of answer the front door opened. A pretty blonde woman in her late twenties appeared, carrying a baby boy in her arms. He couldn't have been more than three months old but already had a few dark curls.

'Hurry up!' the woman called to someone in the house. 'We're going to be late.' She smiled at the baby. 'Your daddy's a terrible slow coach, isn't he?'

The baby gave a gurgle. He had large brown eyes that already had a mischievous gleam. Meg felt her heart sink.

The woman saw her standing there. 'Hello. You look lost.'

'I'm not. I…um…' She gestured to her former home. 'I know the people who own this place. They rent it out. I was curious to see what it was like.'

'The current tenants are away at the moment. I think they're back on Monday but I'm not sure.'

'What is your son's name?'

'Luke.' The woman laughed. 'I call him my little Lucifer as he's a right devil.'

Luke. It was the name of Dan's grandfather; the one from whom he had inherited his sense of humour. He had told her once that if he ever had a son he would like to call him Luke.

Footsteps came down the stairs. 'Here's my husband,' the woman told her. 'He'll know when the tenants are back.'

She felt herself tense while putting on her best smile.

Only for a clean-shaven giant of a man to emerge.

'John,' said the woman. 'When are the Owens' back?'

He shrugged. 'I didn't even know they were away.'

'Well, you're a great help.'

'It doesn't matter,' Meg told them, struggling to keep the relief out of her voice. 'I'm sure I can find out from the owners.' She hesitated. 'They told me that last year there was an artist living in this close.'

'He lived in our house, actually. We never knew him. There were tenants here before us. His name was Dan, I think.'

'Do you know what happened to him?'

The woman looked at her husband who shook his head. 'Aren't we supposed to be in a hurry?' he asked grumpily.

'I'm sorry,' said Meg quickly. 'I shouldn't keep you.' She waved to the baby. 'Goodbye, Luke.'

Then, battling an urge to skip, she walked away.

Two hours later the relief was gone, replaced by frustration.

By now she had her cover story straight. Some friends had seen Dan's work and told her it was exactly the sort of art they liked to collect. It made asking questions about his whereabouts much easier but the answers she received were as contradictory as they were unhelpful. Someone thought he was living in Truro; another in Penzance and yet another that he had left the country altogether. Brian from The Corsair would probably have known, but he and his wife were away on holiday, while Viv Harrison who had owned the art gallery had now sold it to a German couple who were friendly but had no knowledge of Dan, his work or his current location.

She had found an unfamiliar face behind the counter of the supermarket. Wanting to know what had become of Jed she made small talk with the young man who had taken his place. 'Friends of mine own a house in the close,' she told him. 'They said there used to be a lovely old chap who worked here.'

'That was Jed. He had a stroke, poor guy.'

Shock made her gasp. 'That's terrible. Is he recovering?'

'No. He's in Allerbys. It's a nursing home just outside Penzance. Some people I know went to visit him last week. Apparently, he's fading fast.'

She thought of the sweet man who had always had a smile and a kind word for everyone and a lump came into her throat. It hurt to think of him as helpless, especially as there was no one close enough to really care.

'Are you visiting Saltran?' the man asked.

'Yes. I've come down from London.'

'And how do you like it?'

'It's nice.'

He looked amused. 'I think that's what they call damning with faint praise.'

'No. It's beautiful. It really is. It's just…'

…not the place that I left and still miss.

'I understand,' he told her. 'I love it here, but it must seem quiet if you're from the big smoke.'

'Yes,' she said quietly. 'That's what it is.'

After leaving the shop she wandered aimlessly around the square; ending up outside the Art Gallery, staring at the paintings on display in the window. They were modern pieces; stark and abstract, just like the pieces her firm usually bought and a world away from the sort of work Dan had done.

Where are you? How do I find you?

And why would you even care if I did?

She was so wrapped up in thought that it took her a while to realise she was no longer alone. Two teenage girls stood beside her; one of whom in particular she remembered well.

Lorna was staring at the display on her mobile phone. She looked older now; fast making the transition from girl to young woman. Aishling did too; only she wasn't the one Meg was interested in.

'Who's the text from?' Aishling was asking.

'Mark,' Lorna told her.

Mark! The boy you liked! When I knew you, you would have been ecstatic to hear from him but now you look totally unimpressed.

'What does he say?' asked Aishling.

'The usual. Why do I have to go to Uni? Why don't I just scrap it and stay here. It's so stupid. I'm not going for six months and we'll probably have broken up long before then.'

Lorna began to text a reply; dismissing Aishling's flow of suggestions as to what she should say. Meg watched her; remembering their conversations in the supermarket and the guidance she had tried to give. Now she could see that in a way it had been like trying to help Grace.

Only she didn't need to anymore. Not now Grace was safe.

But the desire remained.

Unable to stop herself she asked, 'Which University are you going to?'

Both girls looked surprised at her interruption. 'Oxford,' said Lorna eventually.

So, you did it after all! I wish I could tell you how proud I am.

Managing to keep her tone neutral she asked, 'What are you

going to study?'

'Law.'

'That's a coincidence. I studied Law there too.'

Lorna's eyes lit up. 'Seriously?'

'Yes.'

'Which College?'

They began to talk about Oxford while a clearly bored Aishling kept looking at her watch. When a bus pulled into the Square she tugged Lorna's sleeve. 'Come on. We're going into town.'

'Wait!' Reaching into her bag, Meg found an old business card and held it out to Lorna. 'I don't work at that firm any more,' she explained, 'but my mobile number hasn't changed. If you have any questions about Uni then feel free to call me. I mean it. Anytime.'

'You're not a lesbian, are you?' Aishling demanded.

Unable to control herself, Meg burst out laughing.

'Ash!' exclaimed Lorna, looking mortified.

'It's alright,' Meg told her. 'I'm not offended, and in answer to your friend's question, I'm not a lesbian either. I'm just trying to be helpful but if you'd rather not…'

By way of answer, Lorna reached out and took the card.

'My name's Meg, by the way.'

'I'm Lorna.'

'And we have to go!' Aishling exclaimed.

'Goodbye,' said Meg. 'It was nice to meet you both.'

'Yeah. Bye.' Aishling pulled Lorna away while muttering something under her breath that sounded like 'bloody tourists.'

As they waited to board the bus, Meg saw Lorna study the card. She turned, gazing intently at Meg. For the briefest of moments there was a look of puzzlement on her face.

Then it was gone; replaced by a smile. She gave Meg a wave.

Smiling herself, Meg waved back.

That afternoon she went walking on the cliffs.

The sky was clouding over. She sensed a storm coming and wondered if it would be as fierce as the one that had forced her to take shelter in the engine house over a year ago. She spent half an hour sitting on her favourite beach; listening to the sea gulls call to each other and watching the waves break against the rocks. As always, the place was full of noise but still utterly restful and as familiar and comfortable as an old shoe. It was strange to think that in this new reality she had never actually been here before.

Later she went to the engine house. The plaque commemorating the accident was still buried in the undergrowth. She uprooted branches of bracken, exposing it properly to sight. It needed to be seen and the men who had died remembered. She stared at the names of Ellen's father and uncle and wished she could have saved them too.

But if I did then Ellen would never have met Samuel

And their great great grandson would never have saved Grace.

Her feelings confused her. She walked to the edge of the chasm and stared down at the sea as it boiled and churned. Once, in another life, she had sat on a rock staring down at it while willing the wind to tear her from her perch and down to her destruction. Now she had reclaimed what she had lost while losing something else in the process. It hurt, but she had no right to complain. For every action there was a reaction. She had made her bargain and she had paid her price.

And in spite of it all she still felt blessed.

There was no point staying. It was time to return to London and plan her next move. She had no idea what that would be, but it didn't matter. Nothing mattered except that she had her sister and niece in her life.

There was a ship on the water. The sight reminded her of Ellen. The two of them had never had the chance to say goodbye. It was something she had always regretted.

But there was one goodbye that she could still say.

Early evening. She sat in a room in Allerbys nursing home, talking to Jed.

He was very frail; a shadow of the man she remembered. His eyes kept wandering. As she spoke to him about his wife she wondered if he was hearing her, but when she finished he squeezed her hand and she knew that he had.

By the time she made her way outside the storm had finally arrived. Rain came down in sheets while bolts of lightning illuminated the sky. As she stood on the porch, searching for her umbrella, she saw that a car had parked right in front of her own.

But it wasn't a car. It was a van. One she had often cursed at as she struggled to manoeuvre around it.

'Am I blocking you in?'

She turned and saw Dan.

He looked just as he had on that last night in Bamber. He was unshaven; his hair was a mess and his clothes were scruffy.

He looked perfect.

Unable to speak she just nodded.

The trademark grin flashed across his face. 'I'm sorry. We're doing building work here.'

Again, she nodded.

'I'm just dropping off some supplies,' he continued.

She found her voice. 'You don't need to rush.'

'It's OK. I've finished anyway.' He adopted an exaggerated Cornish accent. 'You're not from round these 'ere parts.'

'No. I'm from London.'

'So, you're a long way from home.'

'Yes.'

They stared at each other. A puzzled look flashed across his face. 'Were you visiting someone here?' he asked.

'Yes.'

'Who?'

As she had no plausible reason for knowing Jed she said, 'Just someone.'

'Is that a polite way of telling me to mind my own business?'

'No. I just don't think you'd know them.'

Again, they stared at each other. Again, she saw the puzzled look. It was just like the look Lorna had given her, only much more intense.

'I'll move my van,' he told her.

As she tried in vain to think of something else to say he turned to go.

And then turned back.

'Do I know you from somewhere?'

'What?'

'You look really familiar. I'm sure I know you from somewhere.'

She felt her heart turn over.

'Do I?' he asked.

'I don't think so. As you said, I'm not from round these 'ere parts.'

The grin returned. 'No offence, but your Cornish accent really sucks.'

'I *am* offended. I've worked really hard on it. It's always been my dream to talk like I've got a mouth full of potatoes.'

He burst out laughing. 'Ouch!'

'Well, you started it. Anyway, I bet you can't do my accent.'

'You don't have an accent.'

'That's because I have breeding.'

'As do I, dear lady.' His tone became aristocratic. 'In fact, when I stay at the Savoy I am regularly mistaken for a distant cousin of the Queen.'

'Trust me; if you ever go the Savoy and talk like that the only thing you'll be mistaken for is an escaped mental patient.'

He continued to laugh. She started to do the same.

'So where are you staying while you're down here?' he asked.

'A place called Saltran.'

His face lit up. 'I used to live there.'

'Where do you live now?'

'Pengallan. It's just outside Penzance. Are you staying at The Kings Arms?'

'Yes.' She hesitated. 'Well, I was. I'm supposed to be driving back to London tonight.'

'You should; otherwise you'll miss your meeting.'

'What meeting?'

'The important meeting you've got tomorrow morning.'

'But I don't have a meeting.'

'Splendid! Then you don't need to drive back tonight and can buy me a drink at The Corsair. That's the other pub in Saltran. Their beer is wonderful, though you're probably too posh to drink anything but champagne.'

'Absolutely, but who says I want to drink it with you?'

'It's OK. I understand. If I had your breeding, I'd rather die than be seen in public with a common oik like me.'

'You're not *that* common.'

'Great! We're still on for that drink then. Don't worry. You'll be quite safe. I'm not a serial killer.'

'Oh, I know that. Aren't they supposed to be charming and attractive?'

'I'll move my van. You can follow me in your car.' He turned to go, then again turned back. 'Look, are you sure I don't know you? I really feel like I do.'

'Well, I did once work at a mental hospital. Maybe it's the one you escaped from.'

Still grinning he charged through the rain towards his van. Feeling as if she were floating she followed him to her car, only for her euphoria to vanish once she was inside.

What if I'm kidding myself? What if it can't be like it was before?

He drove away, hooting his horn as he did so. She watched his tail lights fade through her steamed-up windscreen.

And saw three words written on it in a childlike hand.

Don't be afraid.

She stared at them, experiencing both joy and sadness as she prepared to say her final farewell.

'Goodbye, Ellen. I'll never forget you. Thank you for what you did for me. Thank you for being the best friend I've ever had.'

The air seemed to move. She felt a soft pressure against her cheek; as delicate as a child's kiss.

She wiped the words from the windscreen. She didn't need them. Not anymore. Fear, like her farewells were now in the past.

Starting her engine, she followed Dan into the future.

Acknowledgements
As this book is about the importance of family, I want to start by saying a huge thank you to mine. My thanks go to my mother, Mary, my aunt, Beti and my cousins Mike, Anto, Liz and Jules for all their love, support and encouragement.

Secondly, a massive thank you to my wonderful agent, Lisa Moylett, and also to Zoe Apostolides and all at the cmm.agency for their help in shaping this novel into its current form and for all their hard work on my behalf.

Thirdly, an equally massive thank you to the fabulous Lisa Hall and Liz Barnsley and all at Manatee Books for believing in this novel and helping to bring it to publication.

Finally, a huge thank you to my friends Graham Watts, Mariusz Mierzwinski, Martin Davy and Paula Hardgrave, who all read this novel as a work in progress and provided invaluable suggestions, encouragement and support.

Printed in Great Britain
by Amazon

60044350R00184